THE WATER WITCH

THE WATER WITCH

A NOVEL

Juliet Dark

BALLANTINE BOOKS TRADE PAPERBACKS

New York

Copyright © 2013 by Carol Goodman
Excerpt from the next book by Juliet Dark copyright © 2013
by Carol Goodman

Published in the United States by Ballantine Books, an imprint of The Random House Publishing Group, a division of Random House, Inc., New York.

This book contains an excerpt from a forthcoming book by Juliet Dark. This excerpt has been set for this edition only and may not reflect the final content of the forthcoming edition.

Library of Congress Cataloging-in-Publication Data

Dark, Juliet.
The water witch / Juliet Dark.
pages cm
ISBN 978-0-345-52424-9 (pbk. : alk. paper) — ISBN 978-0-345-54242-7 ebook)
1. Women college teachers—Fiction.   2. Witches—Fiction. 3. Fairies—Fiction.
4. Imaginary wars and battles—Fiction.   5. University towns—Fiction.
I. Title.
PS3607.O566W38 2013
813'.6—dc23   2012041729

Printed in the United States of America on acid-free paper.

www.ballantinebooks.com

2 4 6 8 9 7 5 3 1

First Edition

Book design by Caroline Cunningham

To Wendy, who's read everything from the beginning

ACKNOWLEDGMENTS

I am grateful to have a circle of friends as loyal and unique as the ones Callie finds in Fairwick. Thank you to Gary Feinberg, Juliet Harrison, Lauren Lipton, Wendy Rossi, Cathy Seilhan, Scott Silverman, and Nora Slonimsky for reading this book in its awkward fingerling stages. Thanks to my husband, Lee, and daughters, Maggie and Nora, for their patience and encouragement as I traveled into the world of Faerie. Thanks to my editors on both sides of the pond for their continued support of the world of Fairwick—Linda Marrow and Dana Isaacson at Random House and Gillian Green at Ebury. And thanks to Robin Rue and Beth Miller at Writers House, Loretta Barrett and Nick Mullendore at Loretta Barrett Books, Gina Wachtel, Lisa Barnes, and Junessa Viloria at Random House, Ellie Rankin at Ebury Books, and everyone whose hard work made this book possible.

THE WATER WITCH

PROLOGUE

*T*he dream began as all the others had, with moonlight pouring through an open window, shadow branches stretching across the floor, the scent of honeysuckle on the air.

"You're back," I whispered. "I thought . . ."

"That you had sent me away," he whispered, his teeth gleaming pearly white as his lips parted. "You did. But it's not too late to call me back. I miss you."

"I miss you too," I sighed.

The moonlight cleaved the dark, carving a cheekbone out of shadow, which I longed to reach out and stroke, so achingly familiar was the face taking shape just inches from my own. But I couldn't move. He was still only shadow hovering above me but I could feel the weight of him, pressing down on me.

"I can't," I panted. "It won't work. We can't be together . . ."

"Why not?" he cooed, his honeyed breath lapping against my face. "Because they told you I was no good for you? That I would hurt you? How could I ever harm you? I love you."

I breathed in his words and let out a long sigh. My breath filled his chest, each muscle rippling in the silver light like water running over smooth stones in a stream. I felt those hard muscles slam down against my chest, forcing the air from my lungs. He sipped the air from my lips and the moonlight drew hands from the dark that stroked my face, my throat, my breasts . . .

I gasped and his hips bore down on mine. I was filling him out with my breath. All I had to do was keep breathing and he would become flesh and blood.

But I couldn't breathe.

He was sucking the breath out of me, draining my life.

His legs parted mine and I felt him rigid against me, waiting to enter me . . .

Waiting for what?

He moved away, his body shifted lower. "You have only to call my name to bring me back," he whispered, his breath hot in my ear. "You have only to want me to make me flesh again." His lips sealed each word to my throat, my breasts, my navel . . . "You have only to love me to make me human."

Oh, *that*. If I loved him he would become human. It seemed a small thing. I was close, wasn't I? As close as his lips were to my skin as they brushed along my inner thigh. Tantalizingly close. I had only to call out his name and tell him I loved him for the waiting to be over, for the teasing to end . . .

He was *teasing* me. The little nips on my thighs, the way he moved against me and then retreated. He was holding back, waiting for me to release him from his exile.

"You're trying to bribe me," I said, my voice betraying my desire. His lips froze on the crook below my right kneecap and grew chill. His face appeared above mine, more shadow than moonlight, already fading.

"I wouldn't call it a bribe," he said, his voice sulky. "Just a little taste of what could be."

"But it cannot be," I said, trying not to let him hear the

regret and frustration in my voice or how much I *wanted* to love him. "I don't love you . . . yet . . . and I can't love you when you try to *make* me love you, so you'll suck the life out of me before I *can* love you."

He frowned. He furrowed his eyebrows and looked confused. He looked sweet when he was confused, like the boy he must have been centuries ago before he became . . . *this*. I could have loved that boy, I thought, but then his confusion turned to anger.

"Nonsense," he hissed, "those are just words." His body curled into a coil of black smoke. "If you could feel what it's like . . ."

The coil of smoke whipped against the windowpanes, smashing wood and glass. Moonlight flooded in, only it wasn't moonlight anymore; it was silver water rushing into the room, a wave crashing over my bed, the water shockingly cold after the warm breeze and his hot kisses. I still couldn't move. I was powerless to save myself as the water rose around me. It began pouring from the ceiling, down the walls, into my mouth. As the waters rose his face floated above me, watching without pity as I drowned. This is what I had done to him, his expression seemed to say. I had exiled my incubus lover to the Borderlands and condemned him to an eternity underwater.

I awoke, gasping in the moonlit bedroom, my body chilled despite the hot summer night. I'd never really feel warm again while he was trapped beneath all that cold water. I'd never love anyone if I couldn't love him.

ONE

One of the perks of academia—the part that was supposed to make up for the low salary, living in a hick town a hundred miles from a good shoe store and a decent hair salon, putting up with demanding, entitled eighteen-to-twenty-two-year-olds, and navigating departmental politics—was getting summers off. I had always imagined that once I was established in a tenure track job I would spend my summers abroad. Sure, I'd pin the trip on some worthy research goal—reading the juvenilia of Charlotte Brontë at the British Library or researching the court fairy tales of Marie d'Aulnoy at the Bibliothèque Nationale—but there was no law that when those venerable institutions closed at dusk I couldn't spend my evenings catching a show on the West End or listening to jazz in a Left Bank café.

What I had *not* pictured myself doing during my summer break was swatting through the humid, mosquito-infested woods of upstate New York in knee-high rubber boots.

I had known I was in trouble when I opened my door that morning to find Elizabeth Book, Dean of Fairwick College and my boss; Diana Hart, owner of the Hart Brake Inn; and

Soheila Lilly, Middle Eastern studies professor, on my front porch. The first time these three women had shown up on my doorstep together had been last year, the night before Thanksgiving, when they'd come to banish an incorporeal incubus from my house.

Only then they hadn't been tricked out in knee-high rubber boots and fishing tackle. Fairwick was big on fishing. The town had been plastered with FISHERMEN WELCOME! signs since Memorial Day. There was a "Small Fry Fry-Up" at the Village Diner, an "Angler's Weekend" at the Motel 6 on the highway, and a "Romantic Rainbow Trout Dinner for Two" at DiNapoli's. Out-of-town RVs with airbrushed vistas of rushing streams and leaping trout had been clogging Main Street for the last few weeks. Our part of the Catskills was apparently the fly-fishing capital of the Northeast. Still, fishing seemed like a mundane activity for these three women. The dean, as I'd learned this past year, was a witch; Diana was an ancient deer-fairy; and Soheila was a succubus. A reformed, nonpracticing succubus. But still. A succubus.

"What's up?" I asked guardedly. "Is this an intervention for my plumbing? It *has* been making some strange sounds."

I was only half joking. One of the reasons I had opted to stay home this summer was to get some work done on Honeysuckle House, the lovely—but time consuming—Victorian I'd bought the fall before. Since I'd been forced to banish my boyfriend four months ago I'd thrown myself into an orgy of home repair. I'd been breathing dust and paint fumes for weeks. Today I'd been waiting for the arrival of Brock, my handyman (who also happened to be an ancient Norse divinity), to fix some broken roof tiles, when the doorbell rang.

"No, dear," Diana said, her freckled face breaking into an awkward smile. When the three of them had come to banish the incubus from my house I'd joked that they were there for an intervention, but when four months later Diana and So-heila had come to break it to me that my lover, Liam Doyle, was that same incubus and that he was draining not just me but a dozen students of our life force, the joke hadn't seemed so funny. I think they all felt a little guilty when we found out Liam was innocent of attacking the students. But he'd been an incubus and you couldn't go on living with an incubus. Could you?

"I'm afraid we have a problem that only you can help us with," Liz said.

"You need me to open the door?" I had learned in the past year that I was descended on my father's side from a long line of "doorkeepers"—a type of fairy that could open the door between the two worlds. By a lucky—or perhaps unlucky, de-pending on how you looked at it—coincidence, the last door to Faerie was here in Fairwick, New York. So far my unusual talent had brought me nothing but grief and trouble.

"Yes!" they all three said together.

"What do you want me to let in?" I asked suspiciously. The last creature I'd let in from Faerie had tried to eat me.

"Nothing!" Diana insisted, her freckles standing out on her pale skin the way they did when she wasn't telling the whole truth. "We want you to let something out. A lot of some-things, actually . . ."

Liz sighed, squeezed Diana's hand, and finished for her. "Undines," she said. "About two dozen of them. Unless you can help us get them back to Faerie they're all going to die."

"It's their spawning season," Soheila explained as we tramped through the woods that started at the edge of my backyard. "It only happens once every hundred years. The undine eggs . . ."

"Eggs? Undines come from eggs?" I asked, appalled. The only undine I knew about was the water nymph in the German fairy tale who marries a human husband and then, when he is unfaithful to her, curses him to cease breathing the moment he falls asleep.

"Of course, dear," Diana answered, looking back over her shoulder. The path obliged us to walk in twos and Diana and Liz were up in front. "They have tails at this stage so you couldn't very well expect them to give birth . . ."

"Okay, okay," I interrupted. Although I'd written a book called *The Sex Lives of Demon Lovers* I wasn't sure how much I wanted to know about the sex lives of fish-tailed undines. Thankfully, Diana took the hint and left out the more graphic details of the undines' sex life, concentrating instead on the life cycle of their young.

"The eggs are laid in a pool at the headwaters of the Undine . . ."

"Is that why the stream is called the Undine?" I asked. I'd heard of the stream. The lower branch, south of the village, was popular with fishermen, but the upper branch, which had its headwaters somewhere in these woods, had been declared off limits by the Department of Ecological Conservation.

Liz Book sighed. "The locals started calling it that because of a legend about a young woman who lured fishermen into the depths of the trout pools and then drowned them."

"They probably just fell in after a few too many drinks," Soheila said. "It's true that undines seduce human men—if they get one to marry them, they get a soul—but they don't kill them unless they're betrayed." Soheila pushed back a vine and let it snap behind her, nearly hitting me in the face. Since she was normally the most charming and sophisticated of women, I had the feeling that the subject was sensitive for her. I'd learned this past year that Soheila had become part human when a mortal man fell in love with her, but he had died because her succubus nature had drained the life from him. Since then she'd scrupulously avoided any physical contact with mortal men, even though I suspected she had a crush on our American Studies professor, Frank Delmarco. A suspicion confirmed by how melancholy she'd been since Frank had gone away a few weeks ago to a conference called "The Discourses of Witchcraft" in Salem, Massachusetts.

"Anyway," Diana continued in the strained, cheerful voice of a grade school teacher trying to keep her class on subject, "the eggs hatch into fingerlings that stay in the headwaters until they're mature—we think it takes close to a hundred years—then, when they've matured into smolts, they begin the downstream journey to the sea."

"The sea?" I asked. "But we're hundreds of miles from the sea."

"Not the Atlantic," Liz said. "The Faerie Sea. The upper branch of the Undine flows through an underground passage into Faerie before it joins the lower branch."

"I thought the door in the honeysuckle thicket was the only way into Faerie. You told me it was the last door."

"It *is* the last door," Liz said, "but there's also an underwater passage to Faerie in these woods . . . or at least there used to be. It's been growing narrower over the years, just as all the other passages to Faerie did until they closed. This passage was only big enough for a juvenile undine to slip through the last time they migrated a hundred years ago. We're afraid that it's clogged now, and when a passage to Faerie clogs it's like when an artery to the heart closes—smaller veins open up around it. Unfortunately many of these smaller veins lead to the Borderlands instead of Faerie. If they don't get through to Faerie they'll die, but if they get stuck in the Borderlands . . ."

Her voice trailed off and I shivered, recalling my dream from last night. To be caught in the Borderlands meant death or an eternity of suffering.

"So," Liz continued, "we thought with your doorkeeper powers you might be able to open the passage wide enough for them to go straight through to Faerie without getting lost in the Borderlands."

"But I have no idea how to open an underwater passage," I said. This was true, but I was also thinking of the dream. It had started seductively enough but had ended with my demon lover trying to drown me. He had been angry with me for trapping him in a watery hell. If that were true, I didn't much like the idea of taking a dip into any body of water that might be connected to the Borderlands.

"Would I have to get in the water?" I asked.

"We don't think so, dear . . . Wait . . . Do you hear that?"

Liz tilted her head and held up a manicured finger. At first all I heard was the buzzing of mosquitoes and flies in the heavy humid air. Even the birds were too tired to sing in the midday heat. I wiped a trickle of sweat away from my eyes and was about to tell Liz I didn't hear anything when I became aware of a soft burbling beneath the drone of insects. A breeze stirred the heavy underbrush, bringing with it the delicious chill of running water.

"We're at the headwaters," Soheila said, sniffing the air and lifting her heavy dark hair off the nape of her neck. "The water bubbles up from a deep natural spring—the coldest, clearest water you've ever seen. Not many ever get to see it because it's carefully hidden."

Although I was still disturbed by the idea of going anywhere near a watery passage to Faerie, the sound of the stream was making my parched mouth water and my sweaty feet ache for a cold dip. If I could help the undines without getting into the water I wanted to do it. After all, they were harmless juveniles.

Only when I'd agreed to follow the three women farther into the woods did I remember just how volatile teenagers could be.

We scrambled through tangles of shrub, following the sound of water deeper into the thicket. Pushing the vines aside, we dislodged the bones of small animals and birds. I'd seen remnants like these around the door to Faerie, the remains of creatures who had gotten stuck in the Borderlands and died there. I felt the pressure of the vines on my skin as we passed and heard the creak of fiber and pulp as the thicket contracted around us—like one of those Chinese finger puzzles.

"Are you sure we can make it through this?" I asked, struggling to keep my mounting sense of claustrophobia at bay. It felt like we were in a wicker basket that was shrinking around us.

"Don't worry," Soheila said matter-of-factly. "Liz knows a spell to keep the thicket from closing in on us."

That's when I noticed Liz and Diana were silently mouthing words as they walked through the woods and that the vines were curling away from us as we approached. I felt reassured until I looked back and saw that the vines were also intertwining behind us. Just when I thought I couldn't stand the claustrophobic woods another second we emerged into open air: a glade encircled by ferns. I felt and smelled the coolness of water before I saw the pool, which was the same deep green as the surrounding woods. When my eyes adjusted to the murk, I realized that the burble that had drawn us came from a spring bubbling up from a cleft in a giant boulder and falling into a wide basin hollowed out of gray-green granite. The women formed a circle around the basin and then crouched down beside it to scoop handfuls of water to their mouths. In this age of bottled water and rampant pollution it went against most of my instincts to drink from a hole in the ground, but thirst overcame my reservations. I knelt beside Soheila, cupped my hands beneath the ice-cold trickle, and brought a handful to my lips . . .

A mineral chill filled my mouth, my throat, my belly . . . then spread outward, plumping every desiccated cell in my body. It was like drinking pure oxygen. I took another sip and it was like imbibing the ether of outer space. After a long draft I bathed my face, resisting the urge to plunge headlong into the shallow basin. Instead I sat back on my heels to look around.

From the basin the water spilled from rock to rock: a granite stairway leading down to a green pool scooped out of the stone. Wild irises grew around the pool; water lilies floated on top of it. I made my way down to where Soheila, Liz, and Diana were bent over, gazing into the water. I crouched beside them and stared through crystal clear water down to moss-covered stones. I leaned farther . . . and found myself looking into a pair of moss green eyes, the same color and shape as the stones at the bottom of the pool. I flinched and the eyes blinked—then vanished in a whirlpool that splashed cold water in my face.

"They're quite frisky," Liz said, handing me a bandanna to wipe my face.

"They're ready to migrate," Soheila said, pointing to the far side of the pool. At first all I could see were rapids spilling into a fast-flowing stream, the clear water twisted into skeins of transparent silk where it braided over the rocks, but as we moved closer I saw that those transparent skeins were actually long thin bodies, slender as eels, slipping over the rim of the pool and into the stream.

"Those are *undines*?" I asked, recalling the illustrations of the winsome maiden Arthur Rackham did for the German fairy tale. She had looked far different from these eel-like creatures.

"Immature undines," Soheila replied, slipping her fingers in the water and tickling the underbelly of one of the undines. It flipped over and stared at us with its large mossy eyes. Up close I saw that it did have arms, but they were loosely clamped to its sides by sheer, weblike netting. On some undines the netting had frayed to long streamers, freeing their arms. "Their arms start to separate from their bodies to help with their passage, but their legs won't form until they get to Faerie. That's why it's so important that they get there. If they're stranded here . . ." Soheila shook her head sadly. "They can't survive past the summer here in this form. Poor things. During the last migration we found several dead ones stranded in the woods."

While I knew Soheila was ancient, it still unnerved me when she spoke about events that had taken place a hundred years ago as though they had just happened yesterday.

"Let's hurry," Liz said, striking out down the narrow path beside the stream. "The first wave will be reaching the junction pool by now."

I followed the women, who now walked single file—Liz in the lead, followed by Diana, then Soheila—trying to keep up with their accelerated pace, but I found myself distracted by the activity in the stream. If I hadn't known about the undines I might have thought the water was just running fast, as these mountain streams ran during the spring thaw or after a heavy rain. But it was the end of June and it hadn't rained in a week.

Nor could the water pressure explain the way the stream leapt over its banks, spraying bright arcs into the air, or the way the stream sounded. Beneath the rushing water was the sound of laughter—the raucous, wild twitter and screech of excited teenaged girls.

"Are all the undines female?" I asked, watching a slender shape break from the frothing rapids and pirouette in the air before gracefully diving back into the stream.

Soheila paused and looked back at me. She seemed unsure if she should answer, glancing nervously ahead on the path toward Diana, but then she said in a low voice, "There used to be male undines, but during the last spawning there were only a few. We fear there might not be any this season. We've noticed that many of the indigenous species of Faerie seem to only produce female offspring—and a few only produce males, and others simply can't reproduce anymore. It's a source of great concern in the fey community because it means, of course, that many species will die out unless . . ."

"Unless what, Soheila?"

"Unless they are allowed into this world to find a mate. Every hundred years, when the juvenile undines run downstream into Faerie, there are mature undines on the other side waiting to come through the door to find a human mate. It's their only chance to reproduce."

"So these undines . . ." I pointed to the roiling mass of bodies in the stream. . . . "are the offspring of an undine and a human?"

Soheila tilted her head and gave me a curious look. Instantly I was ashamed of the surprise—and the little bit of horror—in my voice. Soheila, after all, was an otherworldly being who had fallen in love with a human, the folklorist Angus Fraser. Perhaps she had hoped for children from the union. I myself had made love to an incubus many—*many*—

times. Could I have gotten pregnant with Liam's child? I felt myself go hot with the thought. A splash of cold water brought me back to the moment—and my body temperature back down to normal.

Soheila finally answered: "We believe they're the children of an undine who came through the door in the summer of 1910 and a fisherman by the name of Sullivan Trask. Sul, as he was known. In fact, the pool we're heading for is known as Sul's Eddy." Soheila had resumed the cool, dispassionate tone of a lecturer. If I'd offended her, she wasn't letting on. "The spot is famous in local angling lore. Come, I'll show you the sign."

She turned to go, but I stopped her by laying my hand on her arm. I was startled by how cold her skin felt. While I knew that Soheila was always cold in the winter, since she had forsworn feeding off the life force of humans, it was shocking to discover that she was still frigid to the touch on a broiling summer day. "Soheila, was there something else you were going to tell me?"

Soheila sighed—a sound like wind rippling through the pines, reminding me that in the centuries before she became flesh Soheila had been a wind spirit. "Hmm. Well, we were going to tell you later, after we saved the undines. There's a meeting on Monday, the day of the summer solstice, of IMP and the Grove."

IMP was the Institute of Magical Professionals and a much more liberal organization than the Grove, a conservative witch's club that my grandmother belonged to. I had joined the Grove myself a few months before in exchange for learning how to lift a curse from one of my favorite students—a fact of which my friends at Fairwick were unaware.

"I'm surprised that the Grove would meet with an organization that includes fairies and demons." I was also surprised—and not a little put out—that my grandmother hadn't told me about it.

"So were we. They said they want to improve relations with the witches of Fairwick. The governing board of IMP thought it was prudent to take them up on the offer of a meeting. The Grove has been growing more and more powerful." I could tell by Soheila's expression that she certainly wasn't happy about the prospect.

"What do *you* think about the meeting?" I asked.

Soheila sighed again, but this time the sound was more like a gust of wind before a storm.

"I'm afraid that IMP will be helpless to stop the Grove from pushing their own agenda, which is to close the door between this world and Faerie."

"Close the door . . . forever? Can they even do that?"

"We're not sure. We know that over the last hundred years every door but the one here in Fairwick has closed. Some believe that it's a natural process, that as this world grows more crowded and polluted the avenues between the worlds become . . . *clogged*. But we at Fairwick believe that the witches of the Grove have been working spells to close all the doors, and that they intend to close this one. If they do, all of us who came from Faerie will have to decide which world we want to live in . . ." A look of pain flickered across Soheila's soft brown eyes.

"Why?" I asked. "I mean, I thought you already had chosen to live in this world."

Soheila let out an expulsion of breath that shook the branches of the trees and rippled the water in the stream. "Many of us have, but we still need to go back to Faerie every few years to refresh our power. Otherwise we begin to fade.

If the last door closes, those of us who live in this world will have to decide between going back to Faerie or eventually fading and dying in this world."

"What a horrible choice to make," I said.

"Yes," said Soheila, "but at least we have a choice. The ones who would really suffer would be the creatures who need to come to this world to breed—like the undines." She waved her hand toward the vibrant stream teeming with young, boisterous creatures. "Without access to this world, their species will die out."

TWO

$\mathcal{W}$e continued to follow the stream through the woods, its gurgle accompanying us like a fifth companion. I knew when I agreed to join the Grove that my loyalty to my friends at Fairwick might be tested, but I hadn't known that I'd be thrust into a conflict so soon. If the Grove was really coming here to close the door to Faerie, would I be compelled to take a side?

It was true that I'd seen some pretty dangerous creatures come through the door, but I'd also seen harmless ones. Many of my closest friends had originally come from there. Which of them, I wondered now, would choose to leave this world if they knew it was their last chance to go back?

My thoughts were interrupted by a loud splash. An undine had leapt over a boulder, her slim transparent body twisting in the sunlight as she performed a backward flip. Immediately two others copied their sister with their own flips, the second one adding a double somersault and a midair twist.

"Great, now they'll all have to do it," Liz muttered, hands on hips. She clapped her hands briskly and called in a stern

Jean Brodie brogue, "Come along, girrrls, we haven't got all day. No time for showing off."

In response one of the undines performed a triple axel worthy of Sarah Hughes at the 2002 Olympics.

"Very well," Liz said, the ghost of a smile flitting across her face. "Get it out of your systems." And then, noticing me on the path behind her, she added in a low voice, "Poor things. I can't begrudge them their little bit of fun. They have a difficult journey ahead of them . . . and then, this might be the last time I ever see an undine run."

Glancing at Liz, I noticed the smile had faded from her face.

"Soheila told me about the meeting next week," I said. "Do you think the Grove will really try to close the door? Will IMP go along with it?"

Liz turned to me, her face looking suddenly older. The truth was I didn't know how old she was. Witches could augment their life span with magic. If Liz had seen the undines run before that meant she was more than a hundred years old. Normally, she looked like a stylish, well-preserved sixty, but right now her eyes seemed to have seen a century of woes.

"I believe it is what the Grove has been working tirelessly to achieve for over a hundred years. Before I came to Fairwick I taught at a girls' school in the Hudson Valley. There was a door to Faerie nearby. The school was run by the witches of the Grove, who believed that the creatures who came from Faerie were all evil and must be destroyed." She shuddered. "Some of the creatures *were* evil. But some of us came to believe that not all the denizens of Faerie were bad. There was a rift, followed by a battle in which innocent blood was shed . . ." Liz's voice trembled. She bit her lip and looked away until she had mastered her emotions.

"I wasn't the only one to lose loved ones. The witches of the Grove suffered losses they still haven't recovered from. They closed the door to Faerie near the school and since then all the other doors to Faerie have closed, except for the one here in Fairwick."

"Soheila said that some people believe it's a natural process . . ."

Liz shook her head impatiently. "No more than global warming is a *natural* process. The Grove has been closing the doors with their spells. This door would have closed already were it not for the spells we've cast to keep it open, but over time it's become harder and harder to keep the door open. We were afraid that it was closing for good . . . but then you came . . ."

"If the Grove wants to close the door will IMP be able to stop them?"

Liz sighed. "I honestly don't know. There has been a growing conservative trend among the governing members of IMP. They're concerned—and rightfully—about the dangerous nature of some of the creatures that come through the door. Even some of the fey members of the board would like to limit future immigration. I'm afraid that it's possible that IMP would vote with the Grove."

"If the vote went to closing the door, as doorkeeper would I be able to stop them?" I asked.

Liz gave me a long, considering look. As far as I knew her magical powers didn't include mind reading, but I felt that she could tell I had a guilty secret. "I don't know," she said at last. "You've already demonstrated extraordinary power in opening the door, but you haven't yet had to go up against a really powerful witch—and mark my words, the witches of the Grove are *very* powerful. The truth is we don't know the limits of your power. The combination of fey and witch bloodlines makes for a powerful but unstable mix. You should have been trained from early on . . ."

Liz looked embarrassed to have brought up this detail from my past. My parents had died when I was twelve, leaving me to be raised by my grandmother Adelaide. Since Adelaide was a witch she should have, by all rights, trained me herself, but she hadn't. She later claimed that she had seen no sign of magical power in me and assumed that my half-fey ancestry had canceled out my witch's power. It wasn't until I moved to Fairwick that I discovered I had any power at all—or even that such creatures as witches and fairies existed.

". . . and I have been remiss in getting you the proper training," Liz continued. "I promise we'll start this summer . . . as soon as we've got the undines settled. Your magical abilities need nurturing," she said, turning to walk ahead of me on the path. I only heard her next words because they were carried to me on a gust of wind. "Heaven knows we may all be in sore need of them."

I caught up to Soheila, Liz, and Diana at the edge of a waterfall. They were watching the undines tumbling down into a wide pool. Another stream rushed into the pool from the south. In the distance I could make out several fishermen standing knee deep in the water, casting their lines out over the sun-dazzled water of the lower branch of the Undine.

"Won't the undines be in danger of getting caught in those lines?" I asked. "And won't those fishermen be . . . *surprised* to find a teenage girl on their hooks instead of a rainbow trout?"

"The Department of Ecological Conservation has declared Sul's Eddy off limits until the beginning of July," Liz told me.

"*Officially* to prevent overfishing on the Undine, but really because we've got friends in the department who are giving us time to get the undines out," Diana added.

"But we have to act fast," Soheila said, leading the way down the steep, rocky path to the junction pool. "The underground passage to Faerie is on the far side of the pool, but the undines get confused because of the different currents. They could head down into the lower branch of the stream if we don't help direct them."

At the bottom of the falls there was a metal sign erected by the Fairwick Fly-Fishing Club. It seemed out of place here on the edge of Faerie . . . until I read it.

Sul's Eddy is one of the most famous pools in angling lore. Formed by the waters of the Undine and the Beaverkill, it is a pool with strange and mystifying currents and eddies. Legend says that the confusing flows cause migrating trout to linger for days trying to decide which stream to enter. This indecisiveness causes delay which, in itself, is the reason many of the largest trout in the Undine are taken from this pool.

"The same thing happens to the undines," Soheila said. "Look, you can see them swimming in circles. They're confused by the currents."

I looked into the pool. At first I saw nothing but clear water; then I noticed circular ripples spreading out from the center of the pool.

"This is bad," Liz said. "When a few start swimming in circles they create a whirlpool that sucks all of them into it. It's a sort of mass hysteria."

"How do we get them to stop?" I asked, the spinning circles making me dizzy.

"The way you get all teenage girls' attention," Diana said, pulling a swath of gaily colored material out of her rucksack. "By distracting them with something bright and shiny."

. . .

The objects in each rucksack were kites—fancy, elaborate kites purchased at the Enchanted Forest Toy Store in town. Diana had bought different shapes for each of them, but none for me.

"We'll use the kites to lure them to the far side of the pool," Liz explained to me as she took her kite out of its packing. "You wait on the far side and concentrate on opening the passage."

I wasn't sure how that would work, but I went obediently to the far side of the pool, sat on a rock overhanging the water, and watched the women launch their kites. Liz sent hers into the air with an impressive cast that landed the kite well in the middle of the pool. It lay on the water for a moment, then sank. Liz gave the line a gentle tug and the cloth swelled beneath the clear water and took the shape of a curvaceous mermaid with long red hair and a seashell brassiere, clearly modeled on Disney's Little Mermaid. At another tug from Liz, the mermaid wiggled her hips and shimmied through the water. Within seconds several of the undines were following the mermaid through the water, their mossy green eyes as wide with wonder as any nine-year-old at Disney World.

"They're really quite simple at this age," Soheila said as she deftly cast her owl kite into the water. Instead of merely sinking, the kite performed an elaborate parabola above the pool and then dove in the water as if it had spied a tasty fish.

"Show-off," Diana said with a laugh. "Just because you're a wind spirit doesn't mean you have to make the rest of us feel inadequate."

There was nothing inadequate, though, in the way Diana's deer kite bounced merrily over the surface of the pool and then somersaulted into the water with a flick of its white tail.

My companions might not be giddy teenagers, but they hadn't lost the will for friendly rivalry.

Peering down through the water I saw swarms of undines circling the colorful kites. They had formed three separate circles.

"I'm afraid all we've done is make the current even more confusing for them," Liz said. "The underwater passage to Faerie is right below you. Can you see it?"

I leaned farther to look into the water. At first it was difficult to make out anything among the whirling water, colorful kites, and semi-transparent undines, but at last I saw something flash among the rocks at the bottom of the pool. It looked like a bright gold coin, so bright it was hard to look at. But as I stared, it grew larger and shot out rays of gold light into the roiling water.

"See!" Diana crowed triumphantly. "Callie just needed to look at the passage to make it grow bigger. I told you she was a powerful doorkeeper."

Clearly there'd been some dispute about the matter, which might have bothered me if I didn't have my own doubts about my power. I squinted up at the three women who stood between me and the midday sun.

"You've opened the door before," Liz said. "I know you can do it again."

"The first two times I was letting creatures into this world. I have a feeling that's easier."

"Yes," Soheila agreed. "If the creatures want to come through, it would be."

"And the third time was on the solstice, which is when it's supposed to open," I said, recalling the brief glimpse of Faerie I'd had that time: sloping green meadows and distant blue mountains. It looked lush and beautiful and I had felt a sudden yearning to go there . . . but then, recalling my dream last night, I felt a chill. As Liz had pointed out, my power was unstable. I might find myself in the Borderlands if I tried the passage to Faerie.

"But the last time you opened the door to throw Mara through it," Soheila said. "And she certainly didn't want to go."

Mara was a liderc—a life-sucking bird monster—who had masqueraded as my student. She had attacked me and chased me into the woods and nearly succeeded in killing me. "No, she didn't want to go, but she was going to kill me if I didn't get rid of her, so I was pretty motivated. Also, I used an opening spell from my spell book . . ."

"Really?" Liz said. "You combined witchcraft with your fey power? That's . . . unusual. Do you recall the spell?"

I did, but I didn't tell them that. I also didn't tell them that I'd had help ejecting Mara into the Borderlands. I'd opened the door, but I hadn't been strong enough to get her through it. At the last moment before Mara would have eaten me whole, Liam had appeared in shadow-form, torn Mara off me, and thrown her through the door. Liam hadn't been able to follow because the iron manacles on his wrists kept him from entering Faerie. He was forever trapped in the Borderlands.

I was the one who'd clamped the manacles on him.

I hadn't told the three women about Liam coming to help me. I knew they felt bad about convincing me to banish Liam when it was really Mara who had been feeding on the students. They didn't need to know that Liam had saved me even after I'd condemned him to eternal pain.

Or maybe I just didn't like to admit that the man I'd banished—the man I hadn't been able to make human with my love—had saved me.

I blinked and a tear fell into the swirling water. I bent closer to the pool, pretending to study the situation more closely but really trying to hide my tears from the other women.

"Well, then," Liz said briskly, "you should have no problem being motivated now. These undines will die if we don't herd them through that passage."

I nodded my head, still too close to tears to trust my voice, and lowered my face nearly to the surface of the water. The undines had formed into one circle now, moving so fast that it was hard to make out individuals. I wondered if the undines would melt into water if they kept up this frantic pace—or beach themselves on the bank and die tangled in the thickets. I laid my hand just above the surface of the water and felt a thrumming vibration, a nervous energy that traveled through my hand, up my arm, and lodged in my chest. Like heartburn.

I suddenly knew that the undines' hearts were burning up. If I didn't open the door for them, they'd die. I focused on the chink of light at the bottom of the pool and called out the opening spell.

"Ianuam sprengja!"

The only thing that grew was the burning sensation in my chest. And the tingling in my arm. I was too young to have a heart attack. Wasn't I?

And you couldn't get one from having a broken heart. Could you?

As if in response to my unvoiced question a sadness spread throughout my body—a sadness that was a hundred times worse than my grief over losing Liam, but somehow encompassed that grief. A sadness that had a theme song.

Who will we love? it went. *Will we ever find someone to love?*

Of course. They were teenage girls going to their first dance and they wanted to know if there would be boys there. According to Soheila, there wouldn't be. And if the door to Faerie closed forever these undines would be the last of their species. I was sending them to their extinction. And they knew it. I felt their minds probing mine, their frantic thoughts traveling up the fingertips of my outstretched hand.

Don't make us go! Don't make us go!

With their high-pitched screeching searing my brain, I tried to reason with them. "But you'll die here. Your sisters will be waiting for you on the other side."

I might as well have been shouting at a tornado. In fact, the air around me *was* beginning to spin. The watery maelstrom was spreading into the air. It tugged at my clothes and whipped my hair into my face.

"I think I'm just pissing them off," I shouted into the wind. I started to pull back from the water, but before I could, a translucent hand broke the surface and clamped onto my hand. It was cold and gooey as jelly, but with a grip like a lobster claw. I opened my mouth to scream but got only a mouthful of water as it pulled me into the pool.

THREE

The water was ice cold. The shock of it pushed all the air from my lungs and turned my limbs into useless sticks. Unable to resist the undine's grip on my arm as she pulled me into the center of the pool, I sank like a stone before we were both sucked into the whirlpool of revolving undines.

When we were eleven, my friend Annie dared me to ride the Whirl-a-Gig at the Feast of San Gennaro festival in Manhattan's Little Italy. It was a rusty metal drum that looked like a cake tin and it had reduced my insides to batter when it spun. This was ten times worse and the hand I clutched wasn't Annie's: it was the cold, gelatinous fish hand of an alien creature. Still, I held on tightly as the whirlpool whipped me in circles. I tried to look into the creature's eyes to discover why she had dragged me into their mad dance. Her eyes were full of a manic glee that would have chilled me if I hadn't been already frozen to the bone. Up close, their mossy green was variegated with veins of gold and chips of silver mica. They gleamed like marbles of polished agate. Looking into them was like staring into something *elemental*: the night sky or the center of an exploding atom. Cold, indifferent, and beautiful, they sucked me into their depths as surely as the whirlpool pulled me to the bottom.

As I stared into her eyes, my head was full of a high-pitched hum that crowded out every other thought. It was like trying to study with your college roommate blasting heavy metal.

Turn it down! I screamed inside my head.

The sound went up, reached a pitch that sizzled my neurons, and then, just when I thought I was about to have an aneurism, it abruptly ceased. The undine who held my hand smiled. The cacophony inside my head evolved into something like music—a cross between Enya and the Pixies. It was the song I'd heard before, above the water, the "Who will we love?" song, only it had acquired another verse.

We'll go if you go, we'll go if you go, the undines sang.

Go where? I asked.

To Faerie, Faerie, Faerie. We don't want to go alone.

But you've got one another.

At this they returned to their first line:

We'll go if you go, we'll go if you go.

I had a feeling that they could keep up this argument a lot longer than I could—certainly longer than I had breath, which, come to think of it, I should have run out of already. At the frantic thought that I should already have drowned, my undine companion squeezed me close and pressed her cold lips against mine. I was so startled I let her force my lips apart. Her breath tasted like watercress and tunafish . . . and something improbably fruity and sweet—as if she'd applied raspberry lip gloss after lunch.

Razzzberry? A voice inside my head inquired. *Lip gloss?*

An image of a hand holding out a red berry bloomed in my head. A misty blue sky beyond . . . no, not misty . . . I was seeing the hand through a film of water. Then the film shattered and I felt sunlight warm on my cold skin. A nearly unbearable sweetness swelled on my tongue.

Mmmm . . . razzzberry, the voice cooed inside my head. The sweetness was on both our tongues, filling my mouth, my throat, my lungs . . . then her lips, no longer cold, left mine, and I was staring once again into those cold green eyes . . . only now I thought I saw a spark of humanity or individuality among the mica chips and gold veins.

We'll go if you go, she said as clearly as if the words had been spoken instead of sung inside my brain. Her eyes shifted and I followed her gaze to the bottom of the pool, where the chink of gold light lay like sunken treasure. It was the passage to Faerie. I had only to will it open. I had only to *need* it to open. Just looking at the light now was making it grow. I felt myself being pulled toward it. The undines, seeing the growing light, had begun to swim toward it, as if attracted by a shiny bauble. I was pulled in their wake, all the while feeling undiluted desire thrumming through the swarm.

To Faerie, Faerie, Faerie . . .

We'll go if you go.

They urged me on, excited at the prospect of bringing a prize to show their sisters when they arrived.

Oh, what the hell, I thought, *let's go to Faerie. I'd like another glimpse of it . . .* and I could always get back. After all, I was the doorkeeper.

Ianuam sprengja! I shouted as we plunged toward the bottom of the pool where the light was spreading, yielding to the desire in my voice.

Ianuam sprengja! The undines mimicked. *What the hell!*

We shot through a wall of light that fizzled with electricity. I felt like I'd been electrocuted, but the undines liked it. *What the hell! What the hell!* they chanted. *We're going to Faerie!*

But rather than emerging into Faerie we were plunged into utter darkness. The undines went suddenly quiet, like a group of chattering schoolgirls silenced by the entrance of a stern principal. I couldn't see them but I felt their slim shapes slipping ever closer to me. The one who'd dragged me into the pool still held my hand, but now she seemed to be holding on to it for reassurance.

Uh oh, I thought, *we've strayed into the Borderlands.*

The name sent waves of terror skittering through their hive mind. Vestigial images, encoded into their DNA, flitted through the flock, gaining gruesomeness as they passed from one to another. Skeletons and decaying bodies with crawfish and slugs crawling out of hollow eye sockets, black slimy eels that swallowed their prey whole, sharp-fanged zombie beavers . . .

Zombie beavers?

Yes! The undines shrieked back at me as one. *Zombie beavers! Everyone knows that dead beavers come back in the Borderlands as zombies!*

In a flash, a wealth of urban legend was transmitted to me about these mythical (I hoped) creatures. As a folklorist I was fascinated by the mingling of real-life threat (the beavers snacked on the undines when they were only fingerlings) and the universal love of teenagers for zombie stories. As someone currently swimming in the dark, I could only hope that zombie beavers were no more real than that story about the Hook Man.

They have hooks? buzzed the undines in thrilled and horrified voices.

No, no, I assured them. *That's only a story . . . we just have to stay together and find our way out. I see a light ahead.*

Now that my eyes had adjusted I made out a number of lights ahead, although none as bright as the chink of light I'd seen at the bottom of the pool. Where had that light gone? As I led the undines toward a faint green glow, I wondered if that other shimmery light had been a trick to lure us into this netherworld. *Or maybe,* a sly voice inside my head suggested, *you wanted to go here because it's where he is.* Suppressing the thought—and hoping that my companions hadn't heard it—I swam toward the light.

Nearer to the dim glow, I saw what happened to those who had been left in the watery Borderlands. A tangle of bleached white limbs littered the bottom of the pool, so crowded together it was difficult to make out what sort of creatures they had been in life. I made out human limbs and faces, but also fishtails and deer antlers, bird wings and . . . heaven help us . . . beaver claws. No matter what their shape, all their flesh had been bleached white and emitted a pale greenish glow, like some kind of radioactive decay. A fine luminescent mist rose off them that I thought at first was light until I noticed that it was clinging to my hand.

I tried to rub a greenish slime off on my arm—the undine was still gripping my other hand—but it only spread. It crept up my arm. I tried to pull my hand away from the undine so I could get the stuff off me but our hands seemed welded together. Turning to her, I saw that she was also covered in the chalky green silt. Her face was frozen in a silent scream of horror. Only her moss green eyes remained and the silt was seeping over them . . . except that it wasn't silt. In the glow she gave off I saw that the dust was actually composed of tiny creatures knitting together some kind of hard shell. All around us the undines, coated with the nacreous shells, were sinking onto the body heap. I heard the undines' terrified cries in my head as they sank—one hit the bottom and cracked in two, half her face falling away—but even worse, I heard the tiny minds of the shell creatures. Once they sealed my limbs inside a shiny hard carapace that bore my shape, they would feast on my flesh. *Slowly.* They enjoyed a feast of live human flesh . . . *Mmmm, even better than undine* . . . and they intended to make it last.

I heard a silent scream inside my head and knew it was the undine whose hand I held. She was still alive under the chalky carapace, but soon wouldn't be. I felt her consciousness flicker . . .

Raspberry, I said silently to her. *Remember the taste of raspberry.* Then I squeezed her hand and directed my energy toward the hard shell encasing her. If a spell worked for opening doors, maybe it could break other barriers. *Ianuam sprengja!* I commanded.

The shell burst into a million brittle shards.

Swim up! I screamed to her and to the rest of the undines. *Shake it off!*

I tried to swim upward but my limbs were weak. Already the shell creatures were regathering on my skin. I made one last desperate stroke upward . . . and felt something grab my hand. Above was a dark swirl, some other predator, perhaps come to tussle over my bones with the shell creatures. But this creature was at least pulling me toward bright gold that looked like sunlight. Anything was better than spending the next hundred years as the shell creatures' live snack.

I called out the opening spell again to break the shell creatures' grip on the undines and then sent a message to the undine whose hand I held to grab one of her sisters. Their hive mind still worked, even half-encased in shell goo. By the time we reached the surface, I was trailing two dozen undines behind me. They wriggled out of the water, shucking the last shell fragments off like last year's dowdy hand-me-downs—and shucking their tails as well. Somehow in the journey their tails had split into two legs. They jumped up and ran along the grassy bank showing off their slim calves and long, trim thighs with nary a thought for the poor undine who had died in the Borderlands. *Thoughtless.*

Thought-less? I heard one of them think as she turned around to look at me over her shoulder. She had red tangled hair and I recognized her as the one who had shared her breath with me in a kiss. *But she is always in our thoughts. She is part of us forever.* Then she turned back to her sisters and joined them as they ran over a grassy hill, leaving me gasping on the bank, beneath a weeping willow tree, feeling all the more alone for the absence of their buzzing hive mind.

Alone except for the dark creature who had saved me.

It was still in the water—a swirl of oily black on the surface. I struggled to my knees and leaned over for a closer look . . . and the black swirl coalesced into a face.

His face.

Liam.

But not Liam.

In the months he'd spent as a bodiless entity in the Borderlands he'd lost some of the features of Liam Doyle, the shape he'd assumed to seduce me so I'd fall in love with him . . .

You almost did.

I heard his voice in my head. His lips were parted in a rueful smile, an expression I recalled so well that I automatically reached my hand out to the surface of the water where the image of his lips appeared . . . and touched flesh.

"You haven't forgotten me," he said, this time moving his lips as his head cleared the water. As I watched, he took shape.

"Your desire for me is giving me form," he said, his chest—his bare, nicely muscled chest—rising from the water.

I laughed . . . or tried to. The sound came out hoarse and

raspy. I must have swallowed some water. "I don't recall you being quite so . . . buff, Liam . . . or should I call you that? You're not exactly him anymore, are you?"

"I can be him," he said with the Irish lilt and cocky tilt of his chin I recognized as Liam's. "I can be anything and any-one you want, lass." The Irish lilt had roughened to a Scottish brogue (he'd called me lass before, I recalled), but the glint in his dark eyes was pure incubus. He stood hip deep in the pool now, the water lapping teasingly at his groin. I tried to keep my eyes above the waterline . . . but didn't quite succeed.

"Um . . . I didn't order *that*," I said, blushing.

He laughed and took a step toward the bank, and I sat back on my heels, poised to stand and . . . what? Run? What was I afraid of? He wouldn't hurt me. Was I afraid that if he touched me I would give in to my desire for him?

I didn't get to find out. Something tugged him back into the water. He fell to one knee, those sweet lips twisting in pain. Instantly I forgot my fear and moved toward him. His right arm was twisted painfully back behind his shoulder, his wrist dragging in the water. Leaning over the bank, I reached under the water for his hand . . . and touched cold iron.

It was the iron bracelet I had clamped onto his wrist four months ago to banish him. Once the bracelet was on his wrist all I had had to do was turn the key to the right to send him into the Borderlands, but at the last minute I hadn't been able to do it. Touching that cold iron now I remembered how I'd chosen to dissolve into the shadows with him rather than lose him. I had begun to merge with him—a piece of me *had* merged with the shadows—a piece that still felt like it was a part of his dark matter. I looked up into his face and saw that his eyes were on my chest.

Typical guy, I thought, aware suddenly of how my wet

T-shirt clung to me, but then I realized it wasn't my breasts he was looking at; it was the iron key that hung between them.

He looked up. "You still wear it. That means . . ."

"It means nothing," I said, pulling my hand out of the water. But he grabbed it and intertwined his fingers with mine. He pulled me closer, until his face was even with mine, his lips inches from mine.

"No, Callie, it doesn't mean *nothing*. It means you feel . . ." He tilted his head and moved a millimeter closer. His nostrils dilated as if he were inhaling me. ". . . *sorry*."

"I didn't want to hurt you," I cried out, as if he had just hurt me. But he wasn't hurting me. His lips grazed my cheek in the gentlest kiss.

"I know," he whispered, his breath tickling my ear. "You had no choice. You thought I'd preyed on the students."

"I didn't know it was Mara!" His lips were on my throat.

"Of course not. I don't blame you for hating me when you thought I could do *that*. But even then you hesitated. You wanted to come with me."

I closed my eyes and recalled that dark urge as I rested my head on his shoulder. He ran his tongue down the length of my neck, and brushed his cheek against the top of my breast, nudging my wet T-shirt away. His face was rough with a day's worth of bristle, just the way I liked it best. Hmm . . . hadn't he been clean shaven a moment ago? He was changing right in front of me, becoming what I wanted him to become, doing just exactly what I liked . . . He pulled my bra back with his teeth and ran his tongue in a slow circle over my nipple, then sucked. I gasped and fell against his chest. His solid, warm chest. I felt his heart beating. He *was* real. I wrapped my arms around him, wanting to feel him hold me one last time.

But he still held his arms taut at his sides. He lifted his head and gazed at me out of pain-filled eyes. He slid his eyes to his right hand, the one that still held mine, and lifted it a centimeter above the water. I felt the muscles of his forearm straining. Tendons stood out on his biceps. His jaw was locked with the effort, but he wasn't able to lift his hand even an inch above the water line. The iron manacle I'd clamped on him held him to the water.

"This is as far as I can go, lass. The green groves of Faerie are not for me." He nodded his chin towards the grassy meadows where the undines had frolicked. They'd vanished over a hill, but I still heard their laughter. "Follow the sound of their voices and you'll come to the door back to the human world. You'll be able to open it. You've become more powerful since I saw you last."

"But what about you?" I asked, running my hand down his clenched arm. He was straining just to keep the iron from dragging him deeper into the water.

"I'll stay in the Borderlands. I've learned to avoid the more dangerous creatures who lurk here—like the shell-eaters. I've even been able to help a few creatures across." He smiled. "I know it will never save me—the way your love would have—but I like to think I am making some amends for the souls I've drained over the years in my quest to become mortal. I thought for years that it was their fault for not being able to love me, but after you . . . well, I see now that I never loved *them* and that's why they couldn't love me." A tear slid down his face. He tried to shrug his shoulder to wipe it away, but the effort was too much for him.

"Oh, Liam," I said, reaching over to wipe the tear away. "If only you hadn't lied to me. Couldn't you have told me who you were?"

He shook his head and a lock of his dark hair fell over his

eyes. "No. I'm not allowed. Would it have made such a differ-ence?"

I brushed damp hair away from his eyes. It would always be wet now. I'd condemned him to this watery hell. His skin was cold. He would always be cold. I wanted to warm him with my flesh. I stepped into the water and ran my hands down his arms until my fingers grazed the cold iron. "If I let you come back, you'd drain me. I'd let you. Neither of us would be able to help it."

"I know, Callie. I know I can't go back to your world . . . but if you release me from my bonds, at least I could stay here in Faerie."

I looked into his eyes. "Do you promise you would stay here?"

Tears welled in his eyes. "I'd never risk harming you again."

I touched the iron key. It lay cold and heavy on my chest. Why had I kept it on if not to use it to release Liam? The knowledge that he was in eternal pain because of me had haunted my dreams. This was my opportunity to free him—and free myself from those dreams.

I slipped the chain over my neck and brought the key to the manacle on his right wrist. My hands were shaking so much I could barely fit the key into the lock. Was it from cold? Or fear that I was making a terrible mistake?

"You know I would never hurt you," he whispered in my ear as I slid the key in the keyhole and turned it. The click was as loud as a gunshot. Liam sighed and shook free the manacle, which sank into the water. His wrist was cut to the bone.

"I'm so sorry," I said, fumbling with the manacle on his left hand. "I never meant to hurt you."

As soon as the left manacle was free he raised both hands to my face and tipped my chin up. He lowered his lips to mine and kissed me, gently at first but then hard, opening my lips with his and pushing his tongue deep into my mouth. His hands roved over my body like birds freed from a cage, stroking my breasts, my belly, then cupping my behind and pressing my hips against his hips. His erection strained against my belly.

"Liam," I gasped, freeing my mouth from his. "You promised . . ."

"I promised not to follow you into your world, Callie. I didn't say anything about what I would do to you in this one."

He scooped me up in his arms and carried me up the bank, deeper into the shade of the willow. He laid me on a bed of emerald green moss that felt as soft as velvet. He knelt above me, raking my body with his eyes. I couldn't help doing the same to him. He was Liam, but not. His skin was more golden, his limbs longer . . . *everything* was a bit longer.

His eyes—more emerald than black—flashed.

He stroked his hand down my belly and between my legs. "For months I've done nothing but remember the exact contours of your body outside . . ." He slipped his fingers inside me and I let out a moan. ". . . and *in*."

He lowered himself onto me and I felt the head of his penis graze my clit. I arched up to meet him, but he moved a fraction away. "Let's see if I remembered it right," he said, a sly smile playing on his lips.

"Let's find out," I said, wrapping my arms around his back and my legs around his hips, pulling him down into me. This time he met my thrust with his own. I cried out so sharply he pulled out of me.

"Callie? Are you . . ."

"I'm perfect," I moaned, pulling him back inside me again. "Perfect."

FOUR

*I*f Liam hadn't made me leave, I don't know how long I would have stayed on the bank of the pool beneath the willow.

"The danger of Faerie," he told me after the second time we made love, "is that the longer you stay, the harder it becomes to leave."

"Mmmm," I moaned, nestling my cheek on his broad chest. "Would that be so bad?"

He propped himself up on his elbow and looked down at me. The sunlight brought out red highlights in his dark hair and green sparks in his black eyes—neither of which had been there when he'd been Liam. I wondered if this is how he'd looked when he was mortal, when he'd been a human boy whom the Fairy Queen had stolen away to Faerie where he'd lived so long he lost his human self and became an incubus. But of course he didn't look like a young boy. He had the body of Adonis, and his eyes looked as ancient as if he had in fact been that god. Looking into them I saw the centuries he had passed here under the unchanging sky of Faerie, slowly losing his humanity, becoming this creature who must feed on human life to feel anything.

"You would not like what you would become here, Cailleach." He pronounced my full name with an Irish lilt, *Kay-lex*. "Without human contact, the fey are bloodless creatures: beautiful but unfeeling, ageless but with none of the fire of youth."

A trill of laughter interrupted him.

"That sounds pretty youthful to me," I said, punching his arm playfully. "Are you sure you don't want to get rid of me so you can hook up with one of the undines?"

He made a face. "Those poor creatures? One can only pity them. Sure the young ones come back full of the zest and fire they've absorbed in the muck and mire of the human world . . ."

I remembered the taste of raspberry on the young undine's lips and wondered how she was finding her first moments in Faerie.

". . . but after a century here they lose that. Come." He got to his feet and held out his hand to help me up. "I'll show you."

"You're going like that?" I asked, looking his long, lean, naked body up and down. "They'll never be able to keep their . . ." But before I could finish my sentence Liam was clothed in a loose white tunic, slim dark green leggings, and soft leather boots, and I wore a long linen dress that swished as he pulled me to my feet.

"In Faerie you can make yourself into whatever you like," he said, pulling me close to him. "Although I prefer you unclothed," he growled. "Those damned undines are just as likely to jump you as me."

"Maybe we should stay here," I said, pressing against him. I pictured myself wearing a flimsy nightgown and . . . presto!

I felt the silk slide over my skin. I added a pair of kitten heels and a whiff of Diorissimo.

"I could get used to this—an unlimited wardrobe and no dry-cleaning bills!"

Liam gave me an admiring look but turned to walk up the hill, pulling me with him. "There are other bills to pay," he said.

I followed him up the grassy hill over which the undines had run, a bit crestfallen that my seduction hadn't worked. I changed into jeans and T-shirt as we walked, but then, remembering how pretty those undines had looked, switched to a sundress I'd admired in the Anthropologie catalog. As I'd suspected, the halter top was too snug for my breast size, but maybe I could change that . . .

"Don't you dare," Liam growled without turning around.

"Could you always read my mind?" I asked, adding a lacy cardigan to my outfit.

"Not in your world, but in Faerie everything is transparent. It's one of the things that can get a bit . . . tedious here."

I tried to read Liam's thoughts but got only images—mostly of me naked underneath him.

"Sorry," he said. "I want to remember every moment." We'd come to the top of the hill. He turned to me, his eyes wide with sorrow. "Those memories will have to last me a long time."

"Oh, Liam . . ." I began, anguished that I couldn't give him what he wanted from me, but then my voice froze in my throat as I saw what lay below us. Green meadows starred with wildflowers of every imaginable color rolled down into a valley split by a broad river. Mountains rose on the other side of the river, each range a different hue of indigo, violet and blue, shading away to palest pearl and dove gray. The mountains looked as if the sun were setting over them, but there was no sun. The rest of the valley was filled with honey-gold light.

"It reminds me of a painting by one of the Hudson River School artists," I said as we ambled down the sloping hill. On either side were thick woods. I sensed that they were full of creatures watching our progress, but I saw only the flicker of movement and, once, the silhouette of deer antlers against the ridge behind us.

"The Hudson runs along a rift between worlds," Liam said. "Often you are looking into Faerie when you look across the river—as those painters found. Come on. The undines are by the river. Their sisters have come to greet them."

As we walked down the hill the honey-colored light seemed to roll down with us like a golden tide. The entire valley was drenched with it. I could almost *taste* it—a honeysuckle nectar.

"Aelvesgold," Liam said. "The original substance of Faerie, the building block of all magic."

"Elves?" I asked. "Are there elves, too? I don't think I've met any yet . . ."

Liam looked alarmed. "Let's hope it stays that way. The elves were banished long ago when they tried to take over Faerie and enslave humanity. Some say they were destroyed; others, that they changed into monsters."

I was going to ask Liam to elaborate, but the undines had spotted us and several were running up the hill, a long-legged reddish-haired one in the lead, loping like a filly straight for me. Upon reaching us, she flung her arms around me in a bone-crunching hug. I smelled raspberry on her breath.

"You saved me!" she said out loud.

"We saved each other," I said.

She gave me a smile so warm that I wasn't even scared by

her sharp, pointy teeth. Then she twirled around, her long hair fanning out in a brilliant red-gold wave. Her green eyes flashed when she faced me again.

"What's your name?" I asked.

She tilted her head and I could hear her thoughts flickering. Undines didn't have names until they reached Faerie, I realized. Then she grinned, her sharp teeth glittering in the sunlight.

"Raspberry!" she announced, clearly proud of herself.

I laughed. "That's the perfect name for you. I'm Callie. It's a pleasure to meet you."

She giggled and twirled again, then started pulling me toward the crowd on the riverbank. I gave Liam a questioning look, but he was busy fending off the attentions of a pair of giggling undines. Liam might miss me after I was gone, I reflected as Raspberry pulled me toward her companions, but he'd hardly be lonely.

The undines were certainly vivacious. In just the short time they'd been in Faerie—although now that I thought about it, I really had no idea how long we'd all been here—they had changed. Not only did they have legs now, but also their flesh, which had been transparent back in the human world, had turned golden under the Faerie sun. Not that I could say where in the sky the sun was. No. It was more as if the golden light—Aelvesgold—had filled the transparent vessels of the undines. Their hair was now golden with sea green highlights, their eyes had changed from moss green to sparkling citrine. Clearly they were enjoying the change. They'd imagined sparkly green and gold dresses for themselves that showed off their new long legs and brought out the sea green highlights in their hair—except for Raspberry, who had given herself a pink dress and red highlights in her hair. They flipped their gold hair over their shoulders and held out their tawny arms as if admiring fresh manicures. I could feel heat rising off them as they gathered around me and laid their hands on me.

As they almost all did. They plucked at my arms and stroked my hair—which wouldn't lay as smooth as theirs—and wound their arms around my waist. They chattered in a tongue I couldn't understand, but I got their meaning well enough. They were thanking me for bringing them safely through the Borderlands. They were letting me know they were glad they had come.

Recalling their primary concern about coming to Faerie, though, I looked around for male undines. There were a few—smooth-cheeked, lanky lads who were each surrounded by a bevy of young female undines. One young man, tall, with black ringlets and wearing a tartan kilt and a brooding look, stood off to the side. All the males looked alternately bored and terrified. I'd seen the look on many a young college boy. If they'd had on Ray-Bans and black jeans they would have fit right in at Fairwick College. Well, at least there were *some* boys, I observed, even if the female to male ratio looked worse than at a Sarah Lawrence mixer. I hoped they weren't all gay . . .

"Gay?" Raspberry asked. "They don't even seem happy to see us."

"Maybe they're just shy," I answered. "They've only had their sisters' company all these years." I looked around for one of the older undines. At first I couldn't see any difference between the young women on the bank, but then I noticed that some were more subdued and paler. One of these had just arrived on the riverbank. Although she looked hardly older than her teens, she held herself like an old woman and her hair was ashen white. She wore a long-sleeved, high-necked dress that hung loosely on her bony frame. Her eyes were a sickly yellow-green. She was clearly ill. I hadn't thought there *was* sickness in Faerie.

"Not sickness, but wasting." Liam had come up beside me, having freed himself of his admiring throng.

"Wasting?" I recalled that Soheila had said that the fey had to return to Faerie periodically or they would fade, but she hadn't said that the reverse was true, only that some creatures couldn't procreate in Faerie any longer. "Is there anything that can be done for her?"

"Oh yes. Watch."

The sick—or *wasting*—undine approached a group of new undines. They looked a little startled at her appearance, but in their enthusiasm and trustfulness, they welcomed her into their circle, winding their arms around her thin waist and stroking her long white hair. She smiled wanly and touched their hair and skin, as if remembering when she was young like them. I was just about to remark to Liam on how sad the scene was when I noticed that the wasting undine was changing. Her skin was brightening and her hair was turning gold. She stood straighter—she even seemed to gain an inch in height—and her arms looked rounder. To accommodate her new looks she changed her dress to one of the clingy green and gold ones worn by the younger undines. Within minutes she was indistinguishable from the juveniles.

"Did she just . . . *feed* off them?" I asked, appalled.

"Yes. After a few years here in Faerie, the undines become unable to absorb the Aelvesgold. It's kind of like a vitamin deficiency in your world. No one knows exactly why some of the creatures in Faerie have it—undines, sprites, brownies, goblins—and some do not. The newly arrived undines can still absorb the Aelvesgold *and* they can pass it on to the older ones. But the effect won't last long. The older undines have to go back to the human world or they'll die."

"But if they go back now, they might have to leave in just a few days. The Grove wants to close the door forever." As soon as the words were out I knew I shouldn't have said anything. All the happy chatter and laughter stopped. The undines turned their faces to me in a synchronous wave, like a herd of cattle turning to watch an interloper crossing their field, but their eyes had none of the docility of cows. Instead I felt pinned by a hundred sharp green spears.

"What do you mean," one of the undines asked, stepping forward out of the crowd, "close the door forever?"

I recognized that she was one of the older undines. Although her hair and skin were golden there was a waxy pallor just below the surface.

"No final decision has been made," I said quickly. "There's going to be a meeting to decide the matter. Perhaps they'll decide to keep the door open. I don't really know. In fact I'm pretty new to the whole . . . *fairy thing.*"

"But you have fey blood . . ." She stepped closer and sniffed at me as if smelling sour milk. ". . . mixed with human." She took another step closer, but Liam inserted himself between us.

"Feed off your own kind, Lorelei," he snapped.

Lorelei? He knew her?

Lorelei bared sharp, pointy teeth and hissed. "Like you do, incubus? I can smell her on you. Are you protecting her so you can drain her dry yourself?"

"I will see her to the door safely, just as she has brought these undines here safely. You should thank her for bringing them."

"Why? She's only brought them to a barren land where they'll fade away. They'll never have the joy of love or bearing children . . ."

"But there are a few male undines among you," I interjected. "I saw some."

Lorelei snickered meanly. "Did you? Well, let's give you a closer look. Hans!" She snapped her fingers and one of the wan boys lifted his head and tried to melt back into the crowd. But she turned and pinned him with her hard, glittering eyes. Hans skulked forward, head down and shoulders stooped. When he was a few feet away Lorelei caught him by a hank of his hair and pulled him forward.

"Take off your clothes for the nice lady, Hans."

"Please," I said, seeing the look of dread in Hans's eyes. "I think I get your point . . ."

"My *point*?" Lorelei laughed, baring a mouth full of tiny sharp teeth. "But do you get Hans's?" She snapped her fingers and Hans's clothes disappeared. He clutched his hands to his groin, but unfortunately the motion of his hands drew my eyes there and I saw what Lorelei meant by her cruel joke. His groin was as bare as a Ken doll's. I looked away, but not before I glimpsed the pain in his eyes.

"All the males born in the last spawning were eunuchs," Lorelei said.

"Eunuchs?" The juvenile undines echoed. "Does that mean . . ."

"It means no fun for you and no babies," Lorelei hissed. "It means that if we can't go back to the human world and stay for a season there won't be another spawn. It means we'll all fade away. Open the door for us, doorkeeper, or sign our death warrant."

"But the door might close in a few days and then you would have to come back," I said.

"Who will make me?" she said, baring her teeth.

She had a point. But suddenly I didn't like the idea of letting Lorelei loose on my world. She was mean and her teeth were scary . . .

A gust of wind suddenly tore Liam from my side and Lorelei was at my throat, teeth bared. "Mean? Scary? You haven't seen mean or scary yet, doorkeeper. Let me through or I'll rip your throat out." Her teeth grazed my throat and I smelled her rotting fish breath. I could also hear the juvenile undines' fluttering thoughts.

She helped us, don't hurt her.

Then I smelled the scent of raspberry and saw my new friend plucking at Lorelei's arm. "Let go of Callie. She's my friend."

Lorelei swatted Raspberry away as if she were a gnat. I heard Raspberry's cry of pain and felt her anguished surprise that one of her own kind would hurt her. But the years in Faerie had drained Lorelei of any kindness she might have once had. No way was I letting her loose on Fairwick.

"No," I said. "I'm not taking you through the door." I turned to face Raspberry and the other undines. "I will, however, try to keep the door open in the future for undines who promise not to hurt humans."

Lorelei laughed and the wind roared around us. The honey light of Faerie was gone, replaced by dark scudding clouds. The undines were clustered together, clutching one another. Where had Liam gone?

"Not hurt humans?" Lorelei hissed in my ear, her spit spraying against my cheek just as a needle-sharp rain began lashing at my face. "How dare you dictate terms to our breeding! You have no idea what *hurt* humans have done us. Maybe I should just eat you." Her rough tongue flicked against my face. "Maybe I'll gain your doorkeeper's power. These undines heard the spell you used to open the door. Only a very stupid doorkeeper allows her spell to be overheard."

I was pretty sure she was bluffing, but just in case I drove my elbow into her ribs and uttered a spell I'd learned a few months ago. It was to ward off an attack from above and right now the storm Lorelei was raising was coming from above. I was halfway through it when Liam came up from behind me, grabbed me out of Lorelei's grasp, and clamped his hand over my mouth.

"You can't use spells in Faerie," he yelled over the raging storm. "They do the opposite."

"Shit," I swore, looking up into a green funnel cloud. The tornado picked Lorelei up. She spread her arms and caught the wind in her dress. She snapped her teeth at me but she was too far away to reach me. Which wouldn't do me any good if the storm killed me. "How can I stop it?"

"You can't. The only thing to do is get you through the door. The storm will die out after you go. Quick, before Lorelei gets back down. It's still her storm—she'll use it to rip you to pieces."

The undines were running for cover. The wind tore at their new flesh and ripped the skin from their bones. Then I looked at Liam. The wind was gnawing at him, scratching long red streaks down his face.

"I don't know how to open the door from this side," I shouted, "if I can't use the opening spell."

"You have only to need it to open," he said pressing his lips to my ear so I could hear him over the roar of the storm.

I looked around and saw the destruction I'd caused. My first trip to Faerie and I'd pretty much wrecked the place. I closed my eyes and pictured the door as I saw it the first time—an archway in a moonlit, snow-covered grove, Liam by my side telling me he'd brought me there so we could remember how perfect our first week together had been.

The roar of the storm was suddenly muffled. I opened my

eyes and Liam and I stood together in that moonlit grove. Above us the storm raged, but we were in a protected bubble. Like being inside a snow globe.

I took Liam's hand and stepped toward the door. "Come with me," I said, turning to him.

His eyes widened. "Do you love me, then?" he asked.

Did I? I looked into his eyes for the answer. I could practically feel my heart swelling. Surely *that* was love! But then a cold and barbed coil squeezed my heart and the words died in my throat. I could see the look of disappointment in Liam's eyes and then, as if I'd broken the bubble we were in as well as his heart, the snow globe shattered into a million pieces. Lorelei rode the shattered glass, teeth bared, claws aimed at my throat.

"Go!" Liam screamed. He flung himself on Lorelei just before she struck me. I tried to grab on to Liam's shirt but the impact had sent me sprawling backward. The storm picked me up and carried me through the door—along with something else that seemed to be flying beside me—and then I was sucked into the storm's black maw and swallowed whole.

FIVE

I came to on the forest floor, face in the mud, the rush of water in my ears. *Drowned,* I thought. I tried to move, but I couldn't feel anything but the mud against my face. Every bone in my body felt as though it had been ground to dust.

"There she is!" said a familiar female voice.

At least my ears worked. Or was I imagining voices? They came and went on the shrieking wind and amid gusts of rain.

"She's in the ravine," I heard, and then, "She'll drown if we don't get to her right away."

Drown? Hadn't I already? I felt water pooling under my cheek. I could taste it—it tasted like mud and grass and it smelled like rain. It had reached my nose. If I didn't move, I *would* drown.

I tried to turn my head, but something seemed to have happened to my spinal cord. Lorelei. That's what had happened to me. That bitch undine had raised a storm in Faerie that had slammed through the door. The storm followed me into this world. Had anything else followed me? All I remembered was

Liam tackling Lorelei to give me time to escape. Had he been able to restrain her—or had she killed him?

Something hot slid down my nose. Tears mingling with the rain and mud. Liam had sacrificed himself so I could get away. But it had all been for nothing. My neck was broken. I was paralyzed. I might as well drown in this two-inch-deep mud puddle.

"Is she alive? Can you see if she's breathing?"

The voices were closer. I felt the vibrations of footsteps against my cheek—but nowhere else. I *was* paralyzed. That bitch had turned me into a vegetable. Before I died I ought to at least attempt to tell them about Lorelei—warn them that she was trying to come through the door . . .

I opened my eyes, seeing only the tangle of my own wet, mud-caked hair. Then soft, cool hands brushed the hair away.

"Callie? Can you hear me?"

Soheila's warm amber eyes were so close I felt I could fall into them. I'd seen that color before . . . I tried to move my lips, but only swallowed mud.

She cupped her hands and scooped water out of the pool collecting around my face. She used a dampened bandanna to clean the mud from my face.

"Lore . . . lei," I managed when I could work my lips. ". . . Raised storm . . . might have . . . followed."

Soheila muttered something in Farsi that I suspected might have been a worse epithet than the one I'd given Lorelei. "I might have known it was her. All the undines are quite good at weather, and she's one of the most powerful." Out of the corner of my eye, I saw her turn her head. "It *was* Lorelei," she said to someone behind her.

"That nasty bit of baggage," Diana said. "I don't suppose she cares how many poor innocent animals will lose their homes in this storm."

"We have a worse problem than that," Liz said before lowering her voice and whispering something I couldn't catch.

"It's my neck," I said. "It's . . . broken . . . isn't it?"

Soheila paused in scooping water to cup my face with her hand and bend down so I could see her eyes. That color . . . it was Aelvesgold. Her eyes were the color of Faerie light. "I'm afraid so, Callie, but don't give up. There are things we can do." She looked up, but not before I saw a tear fall from her eye.

"I know a knitting spell," Diana said. "Of course we'd have to set the bone in the right position . . ."

"I have some experience with that from the days I drove an ambulance in the war," Liz said. I wondered which war.

"And I can summon a wind to cushion her spine while we manipulate it . . ."

"I'll need needles," Diana said. "And yarn."

Needles? Yarn? Was Diana truly planning to knit me a new spine? From within, laughter unexpectedly began to erupt, but all three women instantly quieted me.

"You mustn't move, Cailleach," Liz said in her sternest schoolmistress voice. "Diana and I will get what we need and be back as soon as we can. Soheila, stay with Callie and keep bailing the water away from her mouth. We won't be long."

I would have liked to turn to say good-bye, but could not. I had a horrible feeling I would never see either woman again.

"Hey," I said to Soheila after the other women had left, "how good is this knitting trick of Diana's?"

"Pretty good. She heals animal bones all the time with it. And you know what a devoted knitter she is."

"Yeah, she made me a sweater last Christmas . . ." With a lumpy-looking deer on the front and one arm shorter than the other, I recalled. "Soheila, promise me something?"

"Yes, Callie?"

"If it looks like I'm going to wind up looking like Igor, could you just snap my neck instead?"

"Don't talk like that, Callie. You won't wind up looking like Igor, but even if you did, wouldn't it be better than dying?"

I sighed. My breath made ripples in the water that Soheila was so valiantly scooping away. My friends were doing their best to save me. This wasn't the time to indulge in self-pity, but I couldn't help wondering who would miss me if I died here in the mud. Liz and Diana had each other and Soheila had lived for centuries watching her human loved ones die before her. What was one more? I didn't have children, and although I knew my students cared about me, I didn't flatter myself that I was essential to their lives. Even Nicky Ballard, whom I'd saved from a family curse a few months ago, was doing so well on her own that she'd gone away to a study abroad program in Scotland. My childhood friend Annie would be heartbroken, but she had her girlfriend, Maxine. My grandmother Adelaide would probably think I had gotten what was coming to me, dying in the mud from a foolish attempt to help Faerotrash—as she and her club members at the Grove derisively referred to the fey.

And Liam?

I'd just made love to him and he'd saved my life today, but when he'd asked, I couldn't tell him I loved him. If I couldn't say it then, would I ever? If I couldn't, we'd never be together. So what would it matter to him if I were dead?

"It's not like there'd be anyone to really miss me," I said.

Soheila lay down beside me in the mud so that her face was level with mine. "My dear, why set your life at such a low value?"

"I don't . . . it's just that . . ." I was going to tell her that I was afraid I'd never love anyone, but I realized in time that it

was a tactless thing to say to Soheila, who had selflessly re-
nounced any chance at love. Still, I wondered if it were true.
When Paul, my boyfriend of the last six years, had broken up
with me last summer he'd said that he'd felt for a long time
that I didn't love him. He was right. I had kept a piece of myself apart. Maybe I'd been keeping that piece of myself separate and protected since the day I had learned that my parents
were dead. And today, just when I thought I might be able to
tell Liam I loved him, I felt an iron band squeezing my heart—
as if even the *possibility* of loving someone was so frightening
my body had revolted. What was wrong with me? Was I ever
going to be able to love someone?

I had no time to ponder that question, though, because Liz
and Diana returned, both of them sopping wet and out of
breath. Diana plopped herself down in the mud puddle, a colorful quilted bag in her lap. Liz moved behind me. I felt her
hands slide on either side of my neck, gentle but firm. For
some reason I recalled the first time I'd shaken Liz's hand, at
my job interview. I'd been surprised at how firm her hand-
shake was and thought to myself that beneath her pink Chanel suit beat the heart of a steel-willed administrator. Little
did I know then that those steel hands would someday be
around my neck. I tried to distract myself from the thought of
what she was about to do by watching Diana. From the
quilted bag, she had taken out two long knitting needles. I
thought they had unusually sharp points. Then she took out a
skein of bright pink wool.

"Sorry," she said. "It was the only color I had enough of."

"What . . . exactly . . . are you going to do . . . with it?"

"Knit your spinal cord together, of course. I have to make
the first stitch at the exact moment Liz realigns the bones. Oh
my, but is it a knit or a purl? I don't remember."

"Knit, I should think," Soheila remarked. She'd gotten up

and knelt behind me. I heard her voice close to my ear, but if she was touching me I couldn't feel it.

"I think so, too. Hold on. I've got to cast on with an objective correlative spell."

"Isn't that a literary term?" I asked. "Are you going to deconstruct my spine next?"

Diana blinked her large Bambi eyes at me and I instantly regretted my sarcasm. "It's the basis for most magic. It's also called sympathetic magic. I'm going to create a correlation between your spinal cord and the yarn so that whatever I do to the yarn creates the same effect on your spinal cord. Are you ready?"

To have my spine turned into yarn? I thought groggily. I supposed it couldn't make it worse. I told her I was.

Diana nodded and, leaning forward, plucked a hair from my head. She laid the copper strand along a length of the pink wool and made a slipknot while reciting the words *"Vice versa, topsy turvy, arsy versy."*

She slipped a needle through the knot. I felt a slight tug at the base of my neck. Diana positioned the second needle tip inside the loop and looked up.

"This may pinch a little," Liz warned.

"Iuncta hals-bein . . ." The three women chanted in unison. I missed hearing the rest of the knitting spell because of the extreme pain and screaming. I did hear a crack that sounded like a gunshot. I lost consciousness. When I came to, I lay flat on the ground staring up at three concerned faces.

"Callie, can you wiggle your toes?"

I wiggled my toes . . . and fingers . . . and then, tentatively, stretched my arms and legs. I felt . . . pretty good. My back felt as if I'd just had it aligned by a chiropractor. Still, I was just a bit . . . *woolly.*

I looked down at the bundle of knitting clutched in Diana's hand. She'd knitted about two inches of a skinny scarf.

"The woozy feeling will go away when I cast off," Diana assured me. "But it will take me a few days to finish it. Don't worry, I'll keep it safe."

The pile of bright pink wool in her hand was sympathetically connected to my spine. I just had to hope she didn't drop any stitches.

"Thank you," I said to Diana, and then, turning to Soheila and Liz, "Thank you all. You saved my life."

"We endangered it in the first place," Liz said, surreptitiously wiping water from her face. It was still raining too hard to tell if it was a tear. "And soon we'll all be in danger of pneumonia if we don't get someplace dry. This storm doesn't look like it's ending anytime soon."

"I must have really ticked off Lorelei," I said as Liz and Diana each took one of my arms to help me walk. I really didn't need any help, but there was no telling them that. Besides, it made it easier to be heard over the sound of the rain and our Wellies squelching in the mud. Soheila walked ahead, clearing wind-fallen branches and whole tree trunks with gusty waves of her hand.

As we made our way through the honeysuckle thicket, I told Liz and Diana everything that had transpired in Faerie—except for the part where I made love to Liam. I did tell them, however, how he'd twice saved my life.

"It does sound rather as if he's trying to make amends," Diana said in her usually generous manner.

"But it might be just a ploy to gain your sympathy, Callie," Liz added in a sterner tone. "Incubi are extremely manipulative," she whispered, presumably so Soheila wouldn't hear. Soheila could probably hear the slightest whisper carried on the wind, but she seemed preoccupied with the mayhem surrounding us. The storm had knocked down dozens of trees. The last time I'd seen this kind of destruction had been when I'd tried to banish the incubus and he'd retaliated by raising a tsunami-sized wind. Liam had been born that night out of my ambivalence and inability to wholeheartedly banish him.

I brushed away a tear and Diana patted my arm. I saw her exchange a concerned look with Liz, and the women lapsed into a silence that felt weighted by the disaster of my love affair with Liam. I wasn't able to muster the will to speak until we were nearly back at my house.

"What are we going to do about the undines? Lorelei might be crazy, but they're not all like her. The young one I helped—the one who called herself Raspberry—was very sweet. If the Grove convinces IMP to close the door, they'll become extinct. Do you think there's any chance at all that we could convince them the door needs to stay open?"

"I'm afraid that this stormy temper tantrum of Lorelei's will just convince IMP that the door should be closed," Liz said. "I'll contact the other members of the governing board and see if I can get a feel for how they'll vote, but I think we should concentrate on figuring out how to keep the door open should the Grove and IMP vote to close it."

"I'm the doorkeeper. I should be able to keep the door open."

I saw Liz and Diana exchange a look over my head.

"Yes, you should . . ." Liz began uneasily. "It's just that your power seems rather . . . unstable . . ." Liz's voice died away as we reached my backyard. I looked up to see what had made her pause. My house's roof, which Brock had been coming to fix, was in even worse shape than before. A dozen more tiles were missing and the gutter had been dragged off. Damn that Lorelei! She'd probably cost me another thousand in home repair and cost Brock a day's work. His ladder lay on the ground . . . which was odd, because Brock took meticulous care of his equipment and tools. As I crossed the yard I tripped over something in the grass. A hammer. Brock's hammer, hand-forged in the fires of Muspelheim and imbued with magical powers. He'd never leave it in the rain to rust . . . unless . . .

Soheila gasped just as I looked up. Around the corner of the house, she knelt beside Brock in the grass, searched for a pulse in his neck, and then shook her head. I wasn't the only victim of Lorelei's fury. Brock Olsen had been thrown from the roof and killed.

SIX

Soheila ran a hand over Brock's broad forehead and short-cropped hair. His face might have been handsome if not for the many scars and craters in his skin. Looking at him, I realized how little I knew about him. He was a Norse demigod, a blacksmith to the gods who had once forged their weapons and crafted jewels for their human conquests. More recently, he and his brother Ike ran a gardening shop, Valhalla, outside of town, and he did odd jobs and handyman work for me. Although he wasn't particularly talkative, I'd found his presence in the house comforting when I was working and had grown to greatly appreciate his quiet, patient manner.

Soheila held her hands above him. "His life spark has left his body, but I feel it flickering not far away. It was torn away by the storm. It might be coaxed back, but it's not something I can do alone. We need to call his brother Ike."

"Shouldn't we call an ambulance?" I asked as Liz got out her cell phone.

"If he's taken to the hospital, he'll be declared dead. They might even . . ." She held up a finger indicating that her call to

Brock's brother had gone through and turned abruptly away from me as she spoke into the phone. Diana murmured something about blankets and ran across the street toward her house. I stood around feeling useless while Liz talked on the phone to someone in a language that sounded like it could be Old Norse. I decided the least I could do for Brock was pick up his tools. He'd want them if . . .

My vision swam as I bent over to pick up his hammer. What if they weren't able to bring back Brock's spirit? Would he truly be dead? It seemed impossible. I wasn't sure how old Brock was, but I knew he'd come to Fairwick in the mid-nineteenth century. He'd been sweet on the romance novelist Dahlia LaMotte when she'd lived in Honeysuckle House in the first half of the twentieth century, but Dahlia's obsession with the incubus had kept them apart. I'd seen him once or twice out with Dory Browne, the Realtor who'd sold me Honeysuckle House, but didn't know if they were dating. Maybe I should call Dory, but I also didn't know what the protocol might be for interspecies dating. Dory was a Welsh brownie and Brock was a Norse demigod. I knew that some of the groups in the Fairwick community were clannish and didn't mix well with others—succubi weren't supposed to date witches, Soheila had told me, and I'd learned recently that gnomes had an age-old feud with satyrs. Vampires pretty much kept to themselves. It was a lot for a newcomer to follow and I didn't want to step on anyone's toes. I'd learned last fall that I was surrounded by supernatural creatures, but I still knew little about them—or about my own powers. I hadn't even known that I wasn't supposed to use a spell in Faerie. The fact was, I kept blundering into situations I knew nothing about and making things worse. That was why Liz and Diana had exchanged that look when I asked if I would be able to keep the door open. They weren't sure I could.

I circled the house and collected a handful of nails, Brock's hammer, and the iPod I'd given him for his birthday last month. The iPod was still playing. I tucked one of the buds into my ear expecting . . . I don't know . . . Viking sea shanties? But instead I heard the reedy voice of Bjork rasping out her rendition of "Pagan Poetry." It sort of made sense, I thought, my eyes filling with tears. I tucked the iPod in my jeans' pocket, thinking I'd give it to Ike.

When I came around the house I saw that Ike and others had arrived along with a woman with long ash-blond hair. She knelt beside Brock, the skirt of her long green dress spread out on the grass. Her hair was draped around her face, and she held her hand to Brock's chest. Ike, flanked by two men who looked like they could have been Ike and Brock's cousins, stood holding an umbrella over her. Liz, Diana, and Soheila gathered on the other side. The scene looked like a Pre-Raphaelite painting depicting an episode out of the Norse eddas—*Death of a Viking* or *A Hero's Journey to Valhalla*. All it needed was a ship and a funeral pyre.

As I approached the group, the blond woman lifted her head and shook her long hair back from her face, revealing strikingly beautiful features. At the sight of her, I heard bells and felt slightly woozy—invariably my reaction when in the presence of Fiona Eldritch, the Fairy Queen.

"I believe he's journeying in Niflheim," Fiona declared.

"The Shadow Land" popped out of my mouth. Fiona looked up and pinned me with two razor-sharp green eyes. She rose to her feet, the folds of her green dress rippling like sea water, and then I was the one looking up. Fiona could make herself seem taller when she wanted to.

"Ah, Cailleach McFay. Are you the one who brought the storm back from Faerie?"

"I asked Callie to herd the undines back, Lady," Liz interjected on my behalf. "And it was an undine who raised the storm."

Fiona's eyes swiveled toward Liz. As glad as I was to have the force of her gaze off me, I could hardly let Liz take the blame for me.

"I'm afraid I made the storm stronger by using a spell," I admitted.

"You fool! You didn't know not to use a spell in Faerie?" Fiona roared, growing even taller as she turned once again on Liz. "Has no one taught this doorkeeper how to use her power?"

My attempt to spare Liz blame for my behavior had backfired. I didn't seem to be able to do anything right today. When Fiona had finished berating Liz, she turned back to me.

"It's unfortunate you've been trained so poorly," she said, managing to encompass both Liz and me in her icy green glare. "But still you should have known better than to attempt a spell when you didn't know its consequences. It's your fault this has happened to Brock."

"Your Majesty," Liz said urgently, "I don't think we should blame Callie . . ."

"No," I interrupted, "Fiona's right. It *is* my fault." I turned to Ike and his two companions. "Tell me what I can do to help him."

Ike shook his head. "I don't hold you accountable, Cailleach McFay," he said formally, "nor do I know if you can bring my brother back from Niflheim. The Norns, who are here on other business, may be able to bring him back . . ." His eyes flicked toward Liz. "For that I believe we need to call a spell circle."

"A spell circle," Diana echoed, her face pale. "We haven't had one for . . ."

"For too long," Liz said grimly. "I've been too lax. It's time we marshaled our powers."

"Can I join the circle?" I asked, desperate to find any way to help Brock.

Fiona snorted. "That would be like lighting a match in a gunpowder factory. You have no control, no—"

"But she does have the essential spark," Liz broke in, surprising all of us, apparently herself most of all, by interrupting the intimidating Fiona. She swallowed and went on. "Callie might be woefully untrained, but she has power. I'm sure of it. I will take it upon myself to train her. We need her—to help Brock and also to keep the Grove from closing the door."

Fiona's green eyes widened at Liz's last words and her skin seemed to stretch tighter over the fine bones of her face. I had never seen Fiona display any emotion but anger so it took me a moment to recognize her expression. *Fear.*

"May the Goddess Danu help us if *she's* our best hope of keeping the door open," she spit out, glaring at me. "But I will leave it to your questionable judgment. I will make preparations for the likely possibility that you fail, in which case I must set my affairs in order and decide in which world to stay forever."

She turned on her heel, the folds of her dress snapping like a sail in the wind. I heard bells chiming again, but now they sounded as if they tolled for a funeral.

"I've always wondered," I said when Fiona had disappeared around the corner of my house, "why she's here at all. I mean, if she's Queen of the Fairies, why isn't she in Faerie?"

"She left because her husband, King Fionn, was unfaithful," Soheila replied. "He betrayed her with a human girl."

"Is that why she hates humans?" I asked.

"Perhaps," Soheila answered. "Although the first thing she did on arrival here was to take a human lover. I believe she has stayed here to taunt Fionn with her own affairs. But now she has to choose between never being able to return and returning forever."

"As will we all," Ike said.

I stared at him, startled. Ike seemed such a fixture of Fairwick. Would he really consider going? And what about all the other supernatural creatures at the college and in the town? Liz had once told me that about 30 percent of the town, and 40 percent of the faculty, were otherworlders. What would the town and college be like without them?

"We must find a way to keep the door open," I said, looking from Ike to Soheila to Diana and finally to Liz. "Did you really mean what you said about me having a spark?"

"Yes," Liz said firmly. "Although your magic is erratic, you possess a great deal of it. In addition to your fey ancestry, you come from a line of powerful witches. We could train you."

"Can I join this spell circle you're calling?" I asked.

Unsure, Liz looked toward Ike.

"I think Brock would want Callie to be there," he said in response. "The Norns are arriving tomorrow. We can hold the circle at our house and they can help."

"We'll work together to bring Brock back," Liz said, "*and* find a way to keep the door open."

Ike held out his hand and Liz took it. Liz's elegant, manicured hand seemed to disappear in Ike's broad calloused palm. Looking at the two of them I understood something about Fairwick I had never before fully appreciated. It had been founded as a place where fey and human could live together, but it was more than a neutral Switzerland between the warring factions of witch versus fey, human versus otherworlder. The conjunction of fey and human was precisely what made Fairwick strong. Without the fey, Fairwick would be a pale shadow of what it was now. As I watched Ike and his two companions lift Brock up and carry him to a red pickup truck with the Valhalla Landscaping logo on its side, I swore to myself that I would find a way to keep the door between the worlds open.

Liz, Soheila, and Diana left soon after the Norsemen did to make arrangements for the spell circle. I asked again if I could help but they all insisted what I needed most was rest. I suspected they wanted to explain the volatility of my magical power to the members of the circle without my presence. I watched them leave the shelter of my front porch, wondering who belonged to the spell circle. Was it just witches? Or witches and fey? Well, I'd find out soon enough. I turned and went inside my house—my big, empty house.

I'd been doing a pretty good job this summer of not feeling too lonely. In the last two months I'd joined a yoga class, a book club, and a gardening circle. There was even a craft circle that Diana had convinced me to join though, as I kept explaining to her, I didn't practice any crafts. I'd also been working to make my house more homey. But right now, with the clatter of rain echoing through it, it felt larger and emptier than ever. I stood in my foyer and listened to the echoes and wondered, not for the first time, what had possessed me to buy this huge, rambling old Victorian.

A flicker of colored light on the floor drew my attention to the stained-glass fanlight above the door. *Oh yeah,* he's *what possessed me.* The face in the fanlight was that of a beautiful young man. The first time I'd glimpsed it I had recognized the face of my fairytale prince, half-remembered from childhood dreams. I'd thought I made him up as a means of coping with my parents' deaths. But I hadn't. He was my incubus.

Huh, I thought, *what if I had never moved here . . . ?*

The thought was interrupted by a plaintive squeak. I looked down and saw a small gray mouse sitting at my feet. I knelt down and held out my hand. He hopped on, his little body trembling.

"Hey, little guy, did the thunder scare you? Or are you worried about Brock?"

Ralph had started life as an iron doorstop forged by Brock with a spark from Muspelheim. He'd come to life during my first attempt to exorcise the incubus. I'd learned over the winter that not only could he understand me, he could also type messages on my laptop. I took him into the library now, explaining as we went the events of the day, ending with what had happened to Brock, thinking he might want to type a message for me on the laptop now. Instead he scurried up onto the bookshelves and disappeared behind them. A moment later a book fell to the floor—*The Mouse and the Motorcycle* by Beverly Cleary. I'd named Ralph for the motorcycle-riding mouse in the book and it had become his favorite since I'd first read it to him a few months ago. Apparently he wanted me to read it to him again. It was, I thought as I settled into the Morris chair by the fireplace and opened the book while Ralph curled up on the hearth, the one thing I could do that wouldn't cause more trouble.

The rain lasted all that day and into the night, flinging sheets of water on the windows and pounding on the roof, a clamorous reminder of Lorelei's rage. It was especially loud in my bedroom, where the ceiling had recently been raised to add a skylight. Brock had thought it would be good to let more light into the room.

"People around here sometimes get depressed in the winter when they don't get enough light," he'd told me.

Instead of light, though, the skylight now afforded me a view of murk-green sky the color of Lorelei's eyes. In spite of how tired I was, I lay awake for a long time, twisting back and forth so often that my newly knit spine felt like a wrung-out dish towel, listening to the rain, hearing in its mournful sough and sigh a thousand recriminations for all my mistakes. I'd led the undines into the Borderlands and nearly gotten them killed, I *had* gotten Brock killed, I'd used a spell in Faerie, I'd had sex with Liam . . .

Twice!

True, women hooked up with their exes all the time, but most ex-boyfriends weren't incubi. What had I been thinking? I'd taken one look at his sad eyes and forgiven him all the lies he'd told me, brushed my face against the rough stubble on his cheek, and shed my panties . . .

As he knew I would.

Each detail of his physical manifestation—the stubble on his cheeks, the way his arm muscles strained against the weight of the manacles I'd clamped on him, even the scars they left—all were calculated to make me feel sorry for him. How could I have forgotten that he was an incorporeal being? Those scars on his wrists weren't real. He'd played on my sympathies just as he'd tweaked certain other attributes to play on my desires.

At the thought of those other attributes I felt a twinge low in my belly and between my legs. I squirmed at the memory of him above me, teasing me, and then . . . finally entering me.

I moaned at the memory and clamped my thighs together, but the pressure of my flesh only made me recall *his* flesh.

For months I've done nothing but remember the exact contours of your body outside and in, he'd said.

How long would I remember the exact contours of *his* body inside me?

Uff!

I punched my pillows and wedged one between my legs. I had to stop thinking about him.

But I couldn't.

When at last I fell asleep, he was waiting for me.

Under the willow tree, he was stretched out on the moss-covered bank, golden in the Faerie sun that was everywhere and nowhere. I lay beside him on my side, facing him. Although we were inches apart, I could feel the heat of his skin pulsing against mine.

"See?" he asked. "I am flesh and blood. Feel for yourself." He nudged closer until we were almost touching. I laid my hand flat on his chest to keep him from coming nearer, but even that small touch of his skin was intoxicating.

"It's a trick," I said, even as I pressed myself against him. "You're making yourself into a shape to please me . . ."

"Is that so wrong, Cailleach?" he asked, turning me onto my back. "Wanting to please you?"

His legs nudged mine apart. I felt him hard against my belly. His face was above me, haloed by amber Faerie light streaming through swaying willow branches. His eyes were the same green as the long willow leaves. Leaf shadow dappled his skin. I ran a hand along his arms, which were tensed to keep his weight off me, and then down his chest, his muscles rippling like water over stones, his sigh when I touched him like water rushing to the sea.

That's what he was made of—leaf shadow and mountain stream, moss and Faerie light. Once he had been flesh and blood, but over the centuries his body had filled with Aelvesgold, the substance of Faerie. I wanted to pull that thick gold light into me, to feel that rush of wild water moving through me. I looked into his leaf green eyes and asked a question I didn't know was on my lips.

"Will I ever see your real face?" He ducked his head down and brushed his lips against my ear, his breath the first breeze of spring, his tongue the lap of rainwater. "When you tell me that you love me," he whispered.

"I want to love you," I cried, the desire to love him merging with the desire to have him inside me. I was filling up with hot gold light and the rush of the first spring thaw. Now he was the stream and I was the stone, now he was the wind and I was the wild grass rippling beneath him. I flung myself into the maelstrom until I felt my own body melt into the same elements he had become, merging with him in the golden light, on the cusp of loving him and making him real.

But instead of being enveloped in the warm gold light, I was suddenly plunged into ice-cold water. The shock woke me. I was in my bed, alone and drenched. Had it been real? He'd come to me once as moonlight. Did he come to me now as water?

Another splash of water hit my face. I turned on the bed-side lamp. The sheets which I'd tangled and tossed every which way in my dream passion were soaked. I looked up . . . and got another drop of water in my eye. I wiped it away, along with flakes of chalky white grit. I turned on my bedside light, stood on my bed for a better look, and found the source of my watery passion. Brock's newly installed sky-light was leaking. Water was bubbling beneath the plaster in long tear-shaped streaks. As I stood looking at it, a drip swelled and fell with a sullen *splat* on my bed. It was echoed by other drips—one in my bathroom, one down the hall . . . all over the house. My lovely Victorian, which Brock had tended with hammer and magic, was leaking like a sinking ship or . . . the metaphor leapt into my head . . . as if weeping for its lost caretaker, my unloved lover, and all the friends I might lose if they went back to Faerie.

SEVEN

*I*t took me until the early hours of the morning to find all the leaks and place receptacles beneath them. Ralph followed me, jumping in and out of the pots and jars I set up as if playing a game. I found the last leaky spot in the extension off the kitchen where Dahlia LaMotte's heir Matilda had lived, and when I placed a Wedgewood cachepot beneath it, the rain abruptly stopped—as if I'd plugged a hole in the clouds with my motley assortment of cooking pots and ceramic crockery. Weak gray light seeped through the windows of Matilda's bedroom. I went into the kitchen, turned on the coffeepot, and sat at the porcelain-topped table I'd bought a few weeks ago at the Antiques Barn. I'd planned to refinish the wood base this summer because I was going to have *plenty* of time to fix up my house. I'd promised myself that I would spend the summer making a real home out of the great big rambling Victorian I'd bought on impulse last fall. I didn't want to be one of those single women who don't commit to their living spaces because they think a man is going to come along and make their lives complete. I wanted to prove that I was content living on my own and that I could take care of this monster of a house on my own. But clearly I couldn't. The house had been cobbled together by Brock's loving ministrations. Without him, it would fall apart . . .

The smell of fresh-brewed coffee jarred me out of this bout of self-pity. How petty to be worrying about home repairs while Brock lay in a deathlike coma, his soul traveling in the fog world, and all because I'd pissed off an undine and hadn't known better than to cast a spell in Faerie. I couldn't afford to wallow in recrimination and self-pity. I picked up the phone and called Dory Browne for proper directions to Brock and Ike's house. She told me that the spell circle was meeting there this morning. I should come as soon as possible.

I hung up with a nervous flutter in my stomach at the thought of meeting the spell circle so soon. But at least I'd finally be getting some real training so I might avoid stupid mistakes. Maybe I could even learn a spell for fixing leaky roofs.

I drove down Elm Street, past neighbors busy clearing their yards of branches that had fallen in the storm. I spotted Evangeline Sprague, eighty if she was a day, dragging an enormous tree limb out to her curb. I was about to pull over and help, but then saw Abby and Russell Goodnough, the town veterinarians and Evangeline's neighbors, heading across their yard toward her. They had it covered. Good neighbors, Dory had called them last year after the ice storm, and they were. Not in the sense that they were fey. As far as I knew, the Goodnoughs and Evangeline were entirely human, and if they suspected the presence of supernatural creatures in their midst, they didn't make too big a deal about it. They were just good people who helped one another out in a fix.

I crossed Main and headed out of town on Trask Road,

Dory's directions on a Post-it note affixed to my dashboard. The storm had passed, leaving a freshly scoured blue sky and polished green leaves. The world looked newly made and invested with an otherworldly radiance, the thick swaths of sunshine lying on the fields and woods like a coating of honey . . .

Like the Aelvesgold I'd seen in Faerie and dreamed of last night. The dream came back to me, how he'd filled me with the hot gold light, how I had felt, making love with him, as if I'd become a part of the stream and the grass, as if we were merging into the elements and into each other. I could almost feel it now as I looked into the dark forest to my left, and the purple and green grasses swaying in the fields to my right—a sense of being connected to the world in a way I'd never before experienced. A delicious melting . . .

A pickup truck honked its horn at me as I strayed over the yellow line into its lane. I startled out of the erotic reverie . . . and realized I had no idea where I was.

I checked Dory's directions. I was supposed to follow Trask Road past Hoot's Hollow Road and the farm stand at Butt's Corners and then turn onto Olsen Road. But I couldn't remember if I'd passed Hoot's Hollow or Butt's Corners. Trask Road looked pretty much the same wherever you were on it: dense forest to the east, farms on the west. Scanning the road for helpful signs I found one offering GOATS FOR SELL, an advertisement for HUGH-NAME-IT HANDYMAN, and another offering to grind my beaver stumps.

Beaver stumps?

The sign featured a cartoon of a toothy beaver-chainsaw hybrid ravishing a tree stump. It brought to mind the undines' fear of beaver zombies. Perhaps this gruesome sign was the source of their fear. The Undine ran not far from Trask Road. Dory had said if I crossed the stream I'd gone too far . . .

Water flashed to my left and I saw a narrow, stone bridge ahead of me with an old wooden sign that said, THE UNDINE—BEST FISHING IN THE CATSKILLS! above a faded painting of a gaitered fisherman pulling a speckled trout out of rushing water. I slowed and looked for a place to turn around. Just before the bridge was a driveway. I turned into it and was momentarily so blinded by the flash of sun off the water that I was forced to stop the car. I put down my sun visor and blinked into the glare. Ahead was an old, green-trimmed, white farmhouse, perched so close to the edge of the stream that it resembled a boat about to set sail—although it didn't look like it would get very far. The old clapboards were nearly stripped of their paint and looked soft and rotten. The green shutters drooped and the porch listed to one side. The entire dilapidated structure was leaning toward the water as though yearning to cast itself into the bright rapids speeding over the rocks below.

An abandoned fisherman's shack, I decided, but then I noticed a thin stream of smoke coming out of the chimney. I took another glance around the property and saw a shaggy patch of tomato plants and a trellis made of string, on which morning glories and sweetpeas climbed up onto the porch, forming a green screen within which hung bits of tin and glass that swayed in the breeze, making a tinny music that threaded in and out of the gurgle of running water. The surface of the house seemed to ripple in the wavery reflections from the water, making it appear even more run-down and insubstantial—as if the whole place might vanish if I blinked—but also lending it a shabby charm. An orange cat napped on a rocking chair with peeling paint. Nearby, a fishing pole leaned against the porch railing.

I sniffed and smelled grilled fish. Whoever lived here had caught his or her lunch and was cooking it up. But eventually they might notice a bright green Honda Fit in their driveway. They no doubt had a gun as well as a fishing pole and probably didn't appreciate strangers staring at their house.

I put the car into reverse and looked over my right shoulder to back up, but a flash from the stream nearly blinded me again. I squinted against it and pulled out into the road, hoping that this stretch was as deserted as it seemed. When I was back on the road, I paused for one more look at the old house. Something about it—its age and seclusion, the way it basked in the river light like a cat in the sun—had drawn me in, but when I looked back where the house should be I couldn't see anything beyond the trees. It was as if I'd imagined it.

I retraced my way down Trask Road and found the turnoff for Olsen Road. There was only one house on it, a large Greek Revival of the same vintage as the riverside house, but as well cared for as the other wasn't. Its white paint gleamed like fresh buttercream icing, against which the black Italianate brackets trimming the line of the roof stood out like black ink. Baskets of red geraniums hung from the eaves. The red barn was as neat and square as the house, the only touch of whimsy a painting of a stylized hammer. Thor's hammer, I realized, recognizing the symbol from a Norse mythology class I'd taken in college.

I parked between a caramel-colored Volvo with a Fairwick College sticker and an ancient multicolored Volkswagen Beetle plastered with bumper stickers proclaiming MY OTHER CAR IS A BROOMSTICK, LIFE IS A WITCH AND THEN YOU FLY, and THE GODDESS LOVES YOU. THE REST OF US THINK YOU'RE A JERK.

Great, I thought, walking up to the bright red front door, *I'm going to be tutored by a bunch of New Age Wiccans.*

I was greeted at the door by a plump woman with white hair pulled back into a bun and a red-and-green apron straining across her round belly. I introduced myself but in response she only smiled and, taking me by the hand, led me into the living room.

"Amma doesn't speak English," Liz Book said, patting an empty chair next to her. It was the only empty seat out of a dozen red ladder chairs arranged in a circle around a coffee table heaped with blue and white mugs and plates, nut-studded strudel, dishes of cookies, heaps of Danishes, and assorted rugelah. The scene would have resembled a suburban coffee klatch if not for Brock's supine form on the couch.

I took a seat and looked around the circle. Diana and Soheila smiled at me. I also recognized Joan Ryan from Fairwick's chemistry department and Dory Browne, Realtor and brownie. Her chin-length blond hair was held back by a pink gingham headband that matched her skirt. She always reminded me of those cheery Mary Engelbreit illustrations. Next to me sat an older white-haired woman who looked familiar.

"I'm Ann Chase," she said in a friendly voice, but not offering to shake my hand. "We met at the Children's House fund-raiser last month. We appreciated your generous donation."

"Oh yes," I said, remembering her now. Children's House was a home for severely handicapped children. Ann Chase, who had run it for many years, had a reputation in town akin to sainthood. Glancing down at her hands, I also recalled that she had severe arthritis, which was why she hadn't offered to shake my hand. If she was a witch, couldn't she have cured her arthritis? Or perhaps she was another kind of creature. I looked around at those in the circle, wondering which camp each one fell into. The large woman wearing a T-shirt that said NEVER PISS OFF A WITCH probably *was* a witch—and the owner of the VW. But I couldn't begin to guess about a lean man with a prominent, beak-shaped nose, wearing a Levon Helm T-shirt and cowboy boots, or the pretty young woman in khakis and white blouse, or the young man with a goatee, Ray-Bans, and undersized porkpie hat.

The three women sitting closest to Brock, though, were almost certainly supernatural. A faint white mist was flowing out of their mouths, rising into the air and forming a wreath around Brock. Cold seemed to be emanating from this mist.

"Norns," Liz whispered in my ear.

"Aren't the Norns the Norse equivalent of the Fates?" I asked.

"Yes, usually they're called in at childbirth to assure a child's good future. The old woman on the left is Urd." I took a surreptitious glance at the old woman sitting near Brock's head. She looked much like Amma, plump, with a round, pink face and white hair, and a pile of thick wool in her lap. A sweet grandmotherly type, except that on a chain at her waist she wore a sickle-shaped silver blade, which didn't look even remotely grandmotherly. Nor did the pointed knitting needles in her lap look benign. They were sharp as skewers. "Urd controls the past. Her sister, Verdandi, looks after the present." Verdandi was a smart-looking blond woman in a tailored suit and hose. She was working on a piece of needlepoint, stabbing a sharp needle into the cloth as if angry with it. She, too, wore a sickle-shaped blade on a long chain from which also hung a pair of reading glasses. "And then there's Skald." The third of the trio was a young woman with obviously dyed black hair teased into a threatening-looking Mohawk; brow, nose, and lip piercings; and a tattoo of Thor's hammer on her muscular bicep. She was dressed in tight leather jeans and a sleeveless white T-shirt. No knitting or needlework for Skald. She was texting on a shiny silver phone. "Skald is our future. May the gods help us."

"What are they doing?" I asked.

"They're weaving the mists of Niflheim around Brock," Liz answered.

I felt the chill of the Norns' mist on my arms. I shivered, wishing I had brought a sweater. "Is that to keep him from . . . um . . . decaying?"

"Yes, but what's equally important, they are keeping his past, present, and future from unraveling."

"No need to be secretive about it," the large woman said. "We might as well start the circle by introducing ourselves to the newcomer." She pronounced *newcomer* with a note of disdain. "I'll start. Born Wanda Moser, but I was reborn Moondance, devotee of Diana the Moon Goddess and Hecatia of the Crossroads. I have been a practicing Wiccan for thirty years and a member of this spell circle for half that. And I want to go on record as objecting to the inclusion of an untrained witch at this critical juncture. There's no telling how her energy will disrupt our *chi*."

"Your objection has been duly noted, Moondance," Ann Chase tartly replied. Then, turning to me, "Professor McFay knows me, as do you all. I've run Children's House since its founding and been a practicing witch for the last forty years. I started when my daughter was in diapers, much like Tara here." She smiled at the young woman in khakis, who introduced herself as Tara Cohen-Miller, "full-time mom and beginning witch."

"I always knew there were witches in our family, but I was too busy working to pursue it. Then when our son was born, I quit my job and my husband, Chas, and I moved up here. I figured it was a good time to explore my Wiccan tendencies.

Callie joining our circle means I'm not the newbie anymore, so I owe her thanks."

Tara gave me a shy smile that I gratefully returned. The rest of the group took turns introducing themselves. The lean, hawk-faced man was Hank Lester, who had been "a roadie, a rowdy, and a ramblin' man" until drifting here from Woodstock sometime in the seventies and discovering his "wizard side." The hipster in Ray-Bans was Leon Botwin, recently graduated from Bennington and working on a novel about witchcraft. His day job was barista at Fair Grounds, the town's coffee place. Joan Ryan recited her full academic credentials and an explanation of how she'd become interested in magic while reading about alchemists in a history of science class.

"Joan is in charge of our potions," Liz said proudly. "It's helpful to have a chemistry person in the circle. As you see, we're a diverse group—half witches, half otherworlders."

Moondance shifted in her chair and muttered something under her breath that sounded like "half too many."

"May I ask a few questions?" I asked.

Moondance muttered something else under her breath about time, but Ann and Liz both said, "Of course," so I went ahead.

"First I want to thank you all for including me in your circle. I feel responsible for what happened to Brock and I want to do whatever I can to help him."

A polite murmur went around the circle acknowledging my thanks. Even Moondance said something about the goddess welcoming gratitude from wherever it came.

I continued. "It's just that seeing you all here—some of you whom I've enjoyed knowing without realizing you were . . . um . . . witches—has made me realize how little I know about witches. Do you inherit your power? Do all children of witches become witches? Are you all . . ."

"Human?" Ann finished for me helpfully. "Yes, those of us here who have identified ourselves as witches are human.

"As to your other questions," Ann continued, "no, not all children of witches become witches. The power appears in some, but not others. Conversely, sometimes a witch will appear in a family with no history of witchcraft. We call such witches *self-made*."

"I'm one of those," Joan Ryan said. "I discovered my powers during my junior year at Mount Holyrood. I met Liz at the boarding school where I had my first teaching job." Liz and Joan exchanged a look that seemed weighted with sadness. "And she recommended me for my job here. I came here in 1915 . . ." She saw the startled look on my face and laughed.

"Are you all older than you look?" I asked.

"Some witches choose to extend their life spans," Liz replied, patting her hair.

"While others don't," Ann Chase added, looking down at her twisted hands.

"There's invariably a price to be paid for any use of magic," Soheila said. "Ann has chosen to expend hers . . . elsewhere." There followed an awkward silence during which I guessed that the members of the circle knew where Ann's power was used but respected her privacy too much to say so.

Moondance interrupted the silence with a snort. "Are we going to natter on all morning about our problems or are we going to do some magic? I thought we came here to help Brock."

"How can you do that?" I asked.

"We're going to form a circle and generate energy within it to draw Brock back from the shadows," Liz answered. "The Norns have agreed to join our circle to strengthen our power.

It is always dangerous, though, to generate this much energy. Is everyone sure they are willing to take the risk?" Liz looked around the circle, studying each face. When she reached me, I felt a disturbance—a slight pressure of air against my face, like the air puff released during an eye exam.

"Good," Liz said briskly. "Everyone is sincerely committed to the circle."

EIGHT

*L*iz asked Tara, as the youngest member, to draw the circle.

The young mother got up and removed a blue Morton's salt box from a canvas bag. She flipped open the metal spout and poured it on the living room floor as she walked in a counterclockwise circle around the group, including Brock. The group began to softly chant, some in Latin, others in languages that might have been Old Norse, Gaelic, or Anglo-Saxon. Dory Browne had explained to me last winter that spells were in the old languages that were spoken when the fey had first started teaching humans magic.

While Tara poured the salt, Moondance removed a candle from her large, misshapen cloth bag, placed it on the coffee table, and lit it. Leon Botwin took a dagger from his pocket and laid it next to the candle. Joan Ryan opened her briefcase and produced a metal bowl, a plastic water bottle, and a small glass vial. She poured the liquid into the bowl and added a pinch of gold dust from the vial. The scent of honeysuckle wafted through the room.

"Is that Aelvesgold?" I whispered to Liz.

She glanced at me, surprised. "How do you know about Aelvesgold?" she asked.

"Liam explained it to me when we were in Faerie."

"Ah, that makes sense. Yes, we have only a little of it. We use it to enhance the power of our circle. It's dangerous to handle, though. You didn't bring any back from Faerie, did you?"

I assured her I hadn't, thinking she'd be relieved, but instead she looked disappointed. "Pity, we're almost out." Then she turned her attention to Joan, who was whispering over the bowl.

Joan struck a match and held it to the liquid in the bowl. Blue flames danced over the surface and then suddenly flared gold. The light from the flames was reflected in the faces around the circle, making each face glow golden. Tara stepped inside the circle and finished pouring the salt. I felt a little *snick* of energy when the circle was completed and a change in the air pressure, as if we were in a sealed plane cabin and had just changed altitude. The flames from the bowl leapt higher into the air. My fingertips tingled and I was suddenly aware of the beating of my heart and the effort it took to swallow. I looked around the circle of faces, telling myself that I had nothing to fear, that I knew half the people here, but in the gold light of the flames not even the faces of my friends looked familiar.

"Join hands," Liz said, reaching for mine. I put my left hand in hers and my right in Ann Chase's, being careful to cradle her arthritic fingers gently. They felt like a bundle of broken sticks. She reached for Tara Cohen-Miller's hand and then Tara took Leon's hand . . . and so on, even the Norns putting down their respective occupations to join the circle. I noticed that Moondance made a little moue of distaste when Skald took her hand. When Urd took Liz's hand, the circle was complete.

Heat pulsed through our hands. I felt Ann's crumpled fingers relax and become supple. She sighed with relief. I briefly wondered what she was saving her energy for that would keep her from using it to relieve her own pain. Then my body was flooded with a wave of blinding gold light that wiped every thought from my head. I opened my eyes and saw that the mist that the Norns had woven hung like a shroud around the circle. The gold light from the burning bowl filled the circle like shimmering, sun-struck water. I felt as if I were inside a cave . . .

An image of a grotto flashed across my eyes, a sea cave filled with glowing blue water reflecting ripples on the limestone walls, flickering over painted images of horned animals. A figure stood waist-deep in the water, arms raised, a long-bladed dagger in her hands . . .

The image changed and I stood in a clearing in the woods, a fire leaping up to the sky, sparks flying into the branches of the surrounding pine trees. Against the light of the flames that same figure lifted her hands to the sky, her dagger reflecting the rays of the moon . . .

I was on a windswept heath standing in a circle of huge monoliths. Above was the moon. I lifted my arms, cold steel grasped in one hand, the even colder steel of the moonlight flowing through the other . . .

I was standing barefoot in the grass, a figure looming over me. The figure was stretching her hands up to the moon, a blade in one hand. Light flashed on silver metal as the blade came arcing down toward me . . .

I gasped and tried to free my hands. Something snapped. I opened my eyes and found myself back at the Olsens' farm, sitting on the hard chair, my arms wrapped protectively over my chest. Liz was hovering over me, her brow furrowed with concern. "Oh, thank the Goddess! I thought we'd lost you, Callie."

"What happened?" I asked.

"You broke the circle," another voice answered. I looked around Liz and saw Moondance crouched over the chair next to me. "And broke poor Ann's hand."

Moondance shifted so I could see Ann Chase cradling her limp hand to her chest. Diana, kneeling next to her, was gently inspecting the hand while whispering something under her breath.

"Oh my God, Ann!" I cried, leaping to my feet. "I'm so sorry. I don't know what happened. I saw . . . things."

"The circle's energy sometimes grants visions," Liz said. "Especially when it's enhanced by Aelvesgold."

"An experienced witch knows how to tell reality from illusion," Moondance chided. "I told you it wasn't a good idea to introduce a neophyte to the circle. I could feel the energy was off . . ."

"The energy wasn't just off," a quiet voice said. "It was short-circuited."

We all looked toward Skald who held up her phone. The screen was full of intricate intersecting lines that resembled runes. In the center of the pattern was a tangled knot. "I was recording the energy waves during the circle and they went haywire . . ." She looked up, directly at me. "*She* has a very unusual energy signature."

"Because she's half fey," Moondance said. "Everyone knows that cancels out a witch's power."

"That's an old wives' tale," Ann said, wincing as Diana wrapped both her hands around Ann's damaged one.

"What are we but old wives?" Urd remarked, looking up

from her knitting. She must have resumed it as soon as the circle broke. When Ann looked in Urd's direction Diana suddenly wrenched her hand between hers. There was a sharp crack and Ann's face turned chalk white, but then she looked down at her hand and smiled. Her fingers were unbent.

"But I don't believe this one's power has been canceled out," Urd continued. "I felt a strong power in the room and then it was extinguished. As if it were being held back by something." The ancient Norn got up and hobbled over to me. Now that she was standing I saw that she had a pronounced widow's hump, and she was so bent over that she had to twist her neck to look up at me. As the old woman's eyes locked on to mine, I felt a tug at the back of my neck as if she had pulled tight a cord strung through my vertebrae.

"Can you be more specific?" Moondance asked impatiently.

Urd wrenched her head around toward Moondance with the speed and agility of a cobra striking and Moondance reared backward. "No!" Urd snapped. "I can't. Whatever happened to Cailleach McFay is shrouded, but she has more power than the lot of you thrown together."

"How do we get to it?" Liz asked.

"How should I know?" Urd grumbled. She hobbled back to her chair and took up her knitting again, muttering about a dropped stitch. From the chain around her waist, she snatched the sickle knife and cut through a piece of yarn. The pressure on my spine relaxed. I suspected that if the old woman wished, she could have yanked that cord and made me dance like a puppet. Skald groaned, her fingers flying over her keyboard. Verdandi started pulling stitches out of her needlepoint. I turned away from the Norns and went over to Ann. Diana was still holding her hand, stroking it gently between hers.

"Ann, I can't tell you how sorry I am."

She smiled weakly. "It's all right, Callie, you didn't know what you were doing. And my hand is fine now." She held it up and wriggled her fingers. Not only was the hand unbroken, but all signs of her arthritis were gone. Her flesh was smooth and faintly glowing. "See, as good as new—even better."

"You should let me tend to your hands regularly," Diana said.

Ann smiled, but shook her head. "You do enough for me, Diana. And now you've used up all your Aelvesgold on me."

"And all the Aelvesgold we had to cast the circle for Brock," Moondance remarked, clucking her tongue.

I looked back at Ann's hand and saw that the glow in her flesh was the same honey gold as I'd seen in Faerie. A residue of gold was also on Diana's palms, but as I watched, it faded. Not only had I broken Ann's hand; the circle had used up their supply of Aelvesgold to heal her and there was none left to help Brock.

"Can we get more?" I asked.

"Our only dependable supply comes from Faerie," Soheila answered. "But sometimes we find traces of it in the Undine, especially after an undine spawning. Diana and I will look for it."

"Can I help?"

"Haven't you done enough?" Moondance snapped.

"There's no need to be hard on Callie," Liz replied. "If she has power that's been untapped, she may be able to help Brock *and* keep the door open. We just have to find someone to train her properly. Unfortunately, I believe it might be outside the abilities of our circle."

A murmur of consent moved through the group—the first thing they'd agreed on since I'd entered the room.

"She needs a special instructor," Joan Ryan said.

"One with experience unlocking blocked energy," Ann added.

"Kind of like Reiki," Tara volunteered, "or a good chiropractor."

"Isn't there a mage out in Sedona who does something with candle wax and auras?" Leon asked, flipping open a laptop. Several others in the group also retrieved electronic devices. Liz was jotting down suggestions on a notepad.

I felt Soheila's hand on my arm. "Don't worry, Callie, we'll find someone to help you. You should go home and rest. Your first circle is always tiring."

"And dehydrating," Diana added, appearing on my other side. "Make sure you drink plenty of water." Both women were gently steering me toward the door, clearly eager to get me away from the rest of the circle while they were distracted. I looked back at the group and saw that they'd drawn closer together, filling in the space I'd briefly inhabited. I felt the same hurt I had as a child when I didn't get picked for a game at recess. Diana and Soheila walked me out of the house to my car, taking turns assuring me that the circle would figure something out. I was halfway to the car when I thought of something.

"The Aelvesgold can heal people?" I asked.

"Yes," Diana said, her eyes flickering toward Soheila. "It's the essential substance of magic. Used correctly, it mends broken bones, cures disease, and prolongs life. It can also lend great magical power."

"But always at a price," Soheila said. "If a human uses too much, it can deplete their life force rather than prolonging it. Witches have died of overdoses."

"Why doesn't Ann Chase use it to cure her arthritis?" I asked. "Or to slow her aging?"

Soheila and Diana looked at each other uneasily. "Ann has

a daughter who has medical problems," Soheila answered at last. "What Aelvesgold she acquires, she uses for her. We all give her what we can, but there's not enough for her and for her daughter."

"And she can handle only so much of it, so she chooses to channel all she gets into her daughter."

"Couldn't someone else channel it for her?" I asked. "Like you just did to fix her hand?"

"That only works once or twice on the same person. We're not sure why. There's a limit to how much a human can absorb."

"Like a vitamin deficiency," I said thinking about what Liam had told me about how the undines could no longer absorb Aelvesgold after they had been in Faerie too long.

Soheila tilted her head, thoughtful. "Exactly."

"We'd better get back in," Diana said, looking impatient. "I don't want the circle overtaxing Liz. She was up all last night talking to members of the governing board of IMP."

"Did she get a feel for how they'll vote?" I asked.

"It wasn't good. One of the three fey members on the board has resigned and the remaining two couldn't be reached. Delbert Winters, a wizard at Harvard who wrote a paper last year on the science of magic that debunked the idea that the fey taught magic to witches, is in favor of closing the door. Then she spent half the night talking to Eleanor Belknap, a witch at Vassar, who's gotten it into her head that the open door to Faerie has contributed to global warming. A ridiculous notion, but Eleanor and Liz have been friends for years and she felt she had to hear her out. It took a lot out of her and she's still recovering from her illness last winter . . ." She blushed and looked away from me, embarrassed at the reminder of yet another problem I had caused. It had been the liderc I let in through the door who had made Liz sick.

"Go on and check on Liz," I said, getting into my car. But then as they turned to go, I thought of something else. "If the door to Faerie closes, does that mean . . . ?"

"No more Aelvesgold," Soheila said, putting her arm around Diana's shoulder, which I could see was trembling. She didn't have to add that if there were no more Aelvesgold in this world, witches who had used it to augment their life span would suddenly age and die.

NINE

Well, I really messed that up, I thought as I pulled out of the Olsens' driveway. How could I have lost myself so completely that I injured Ann? But that's what had happened: that first rush of power had felt like a flame rushing through my veins, burning a path to those strange images of caves and stone circles and that mysterious figure holding the curved knife. That last image had felt somehow . . . *intimate*. And terrifying. I shuddered, tasting fear in my mouth. I forced my mind away from the moment, back to the sunlit country road in front of me, the old stone bridge and the sign announcing the Undine . . .

"Shit!" I swore, turning into the same driveway for the second time today. I had been so busy reliving the circle that I'd gone back the wrong way again.

I wrenched the gear stick into reverse and backed directly into a pothole. I could hear the undercarriage of my less-than-a-year-old Fit grating against gravel. I looked warily toward the house, sure the sound would have aroused the owner, but the house kept still in its enchanted silence. I looked back over my shoulder . . . and was blinded by a flash of gold sunlight just as I'd been last time . . .

Only last time the sun had been on the east side of the house, now it was low over the west side. What, then, was making that flash of light? I tried staring directly into the glare but couldn't see anything. Oddly, I found that I didn't *mind* staring into that blinding light. In fact, the longer I looked into it, the more reluctant I was to drive away. The trill of moving water and the wind chimes beckoned me to stay. I tore my eyes away and looked back at the house. Still quiet. Even the smoke had vanished. Maybe I'd imagined it before, and the cabin really was abandoned.

I put the car in park and turned off the ignition. Without the noise of the engine, the rush of water filled the air—a soothing sound that could lull a person to sleep. And yet I felt wide awake. The light from the water had recharged me, much like the energy of the circle.

I got out of the car, closing the door as quietly as I could, and walked down to the water, following a stone staircase that had been set into the steep bank. The riverside had been shored up by beautiful stone walls. Crystals and round river stones were set between square blocks of granite. Someone had gone to a lot of trouble to make the river accessible from the house, but judging from the layers of moss and wildflowers growing between the rocks, the work had been done a long time ago. Unlike the house, though, which was suffering signs of decay and neglect, the stone walls and stairs were lovingly—if eccentrically—maintained. Pots of fragrant herbs lined the steps and small clay figures and candles sat in niches inside the walls. At the bottom of the steps was a rustic bench made of twisted birch branches. I ran my hand along the wood, which had been polished to the smoothness of bone, until my fingers grazed something carved into the seatback—a pair of initials intertwined in a heart: L & Q. The initials were nearly as smooth as the rest of the wood, worn down by someone's touch.

I looked from the bench toward the stream. The flash of gold was still there, a bright spot under the water refracted a hundred times into gold waves by the moving water. Staring into it, I felt the warmth I had when lying under the willow tree with Liam in Faerie, the release I'd felt when the circle had joined hands and the gold light had moved through us. Both were moments when I'd been exposed to Aelvesgold, and Soheila had said that they sometimes found traces of Aelvesgold in the Undine.

Well, there was only one way to find out. I took off my sandals and waded into the stream. It was cold but, given the heat of the day, not unpleasantly so. The bottom was covered with wide, mossy stones, not, thankfully, gooey mud. I carefully inched forward, exploring the surface of the rocky bottom with my toes, trying not to think about snakes. The current wrapped around my ankles, then my calves, like silk scarves seductively pulling me deeper into the water.

I stood a foot or so from the source of the gold light. It was so strong that I was now sure that it was Aelvesgold. The circle needed Aelvesgold to cure Brock . . . I needed it to gain enough power to keep the door open. And, after all, it was my fault the circle had wasted their last reserve of the stuff.

I took another step forward . . . and noticed the water was warmer. Looking down, I saw that I was standing in a small pool of amber water. I wriggled my toes, which had gone a little numb in the cold water, and felt the warm current moving up my legs, spreading a delicious sensation of well-being throughout my body. It was like getting a foot massage while drinking a champagne cocktail. I squatted down, not caring that the water soaked the hem of my dress, and reached my hand into the core of the gold light. For all I knew I might have been sticking my hand into a bear trap, but I no longer cared. The light was tingling in my veins, fizzing my nerve endings, and massaging the pleasure centers in my brain. This felt almost as good as when I'd made love to Liam under the willow tree in Faerie yesterday. Maybe if I could grab whatever was making this light, I wouldn't miss *that* quite so much.

My fingers wrapped around something round and hard. It was half sunken in the mud, but I pulled it out with a satisfying *plock*. I dimly recalled Liz saying that Aelvesgold could be dangerous to handle, but I couldn't stop myself. Lifting the stone out of the water, I cradled it in the palm of my hand. It fit perfectly, like an egg in a nest. It was, in fact, egg-shaped and golden—like the proverbial golden goose egg—and glowed as if it were on fire. It didn't hurt me.

Because you were meant to have it.

The voice in my head didn't sound entirely like my own. But I agreed completely. I was meant to possess this stone. I started to slip it into my pocket . . . and heard the click of metal behind me.

"That's not yours to take," a low, gravelly voice growled. "Stand up slowly and hand her over."

I stood up as slowly as I could, gripping the stone hard in my fist. I had images of throwing it at my assailant to knock them out and then grabbing the stone back and running. The person behind me was *wrong*. The stone *was* mine to take.

But, as I surmised from the cold metal rod pressing between my shoulder blades, the person behind me had a gun.

I turned around, expecting some hillbilly he-man in hunting camo, but found instead a woman the size of a fourth-grader with a face like a shriveled apple and a rifle more than half her size held in crabbed and trembling hands.

"I was only taking a stone," I said, in the slow, gentle tones I'd use to calm a nervous animal.

"Thief! Trespasser!" she snapped back. "Hand her over, I say." She nudged my right hand—still curled around the stone—with her rifle. She held the rifle in her left hand, balancing it against her hip. Without the right hand to steady it, the rifle shook like a leaf in the wind. In fact, all eighty or so pounds of the frail, elderly woman were shaking like aspen leaves. One good shove . . .

What was I thinking? She was an old woman and she was right. I *was* trespassing and the stone, no matter how much it felt like it belonged to me—didn't.

I held out my arm, the stone heavy in my hand, and started to step toward her so that she wouldn't have to move closer to me. I didn't like the idea of her tripping and shooting me by accident. When I stepped forward my foot landed on a slick surface below the water. My balance wavered, my arms pinwheeled in the air, and then the sky was whirling above me. My last thought was that I really ought to use my arms to brace my fall, but that would mean letting go of the stone, and I wasn't willing to do that.

When I came to, I was lying on damp green moss, looking up into a kaleidoscope of waving lights. Bright flashes darted over my head. Fish, I thought, strangely bright tropical fish for an inland river. I *must* be in Faerie.

But then my vision cleared and I noticed that the bright flashing lights were pieces of tin and glass hanging from strings. The damp green moss was an ancient settee which smelled like cat pee. I tried to sit up and my head began to pound. I touched the back of my head and found a hard knot the size and shape of a goose egg . . .

Or of the Aelvesgold stone.

"It's here," a voice said. "You held on to it when you went down. Damned thing would have gotten you drowned if I hadn't dragged you out of the river. That's what it does to you, the Aelvesgold. You only had it in your hand a minute and you'd have been willing to crack your head open and drown in the river rather than let it go. Here, put this on your fool head."

The woman handed me a piece of flannel wrapped around a chunk of ice. I placed it gingerly against the bump and looked at her. She sat in a rocking chair in front of a wood-stove, limned in murky light that turned her silver hair green-ish gold. In the shadowy light, her face looked younger than it had outside. She was wearing a red wool cardigan appli-quéd with snowmen over a plaid flannel shirt over red long johns and a long wool skirt. A heavy outfit for a summer day, but then old people were often cold. Plastic sheeting was taped over most of the windows to keep out drafts and a fire was roaring in the woodstove. The room itself looked like it was melting. Long strips of wallpaper hung from the walls, revealing multiple layers of floral patterns. Plaster was curling off the ceiling, and the wide plank floorboards were buckled and wavy. There was a scrabbling noise coming from the ceil-ing that I suspected might be mice.

"You dragged me out of the water?" I asked.

"Couldn't let you drown, even if you were trying to steal my Aelvestone."

Aelvestone. I liked the sound of that. I looked around the room for it.

There was no shortage of stones. Piled on every surface were smooth, rounded river stones, along with pieces of pol-ished driftwood and other flotsam and jetsam that I imagined the old woman had salvaged from the river: shards of broken glass that had been worn milky by their tumble over the rocks, bits of rusted metal twisted by the currents, and enough broken china to make a tea service for twelve. But no Aelvestone.

"I have her safe, or safe as can be. The Aelvesgold works its way with folks—different ways with different folks—but never for good. Most regular folk don't see it." She leaned forward in her rocker and squinted at me. Her face *did* look younger than it had before. "But you ain't regular folk, are you?"

"I have a feeling neither are you," I replied, wincing at the sharp pain in my head as I tried to sit up straighter. "My name's Cailleach McFay. I work at the college. And you are . . . ?"

"You mean you don't know?" She laughed, which turned into a hacking cough. She spat into a cloudy-looking mason jar and wiped her mouth on the cuff of her flannel shirt. "You must be new to the town not to have heard the story of Lura Trask."

"Trask?" The name was familiar. I searched my brain until I recalled the story Soheila had told me in the woods about the fisherman who had fallen in love with an undine. "Are you Sullivan Trask's daughter?"

She made a hoarse noise of agreement and spit into the jar again.

"Then your mother . . ." Lura gave me a sharp warning look, but I persevered. "Your mother was an undine."

Lura scowled. "And what if she was? What's it to you?"

"Nothing—it's just that I didn't know that undines could have . . . *human* children."

"How do you know I'm human?" she asked with a wicked grin. Then when I didn't answer, she slapped her knee and guffawed. "I reckon I'm half human, but say . . ." She looked at me suspiciously. "How do *you* know about the undines in the first place?"

"I helped the other undines find the way into Faerie yesterday."

She leaned back in her chair and looked out the only window that wasn't covered with plastic. It gave a glimpse of the river flowing fast and glinting in the late afternoon sunlight. I must have been unconscious for some time.

"I heard them going," she said, staring into the fire. "I knew it was the day . . . and that they had to go . . ."

"They were your sisters," I said, putting together the bloodlines and realizing that if Lura really was the daughter of the undine who had seduced Sullivan Trask then she must be close to a hundred years old. "Of course you'd miss them."

She made a harsh noise. "Miss them? Hardly. They kept me up half the nights with their singing. They'd swim down here and tangle my fishing lines and steal my bait. Silly, mindless creatures. Good riddance, I say."

She got up and grabbed an iron poker. For a moment I was afraid she was going to hit me with it, but she shoved it in the woodstove instead, stirring up a flurry of sparks that flew into the air and singed the drooping wallpaper. It was a wonder that she hadn't already burned down the place.

"Well, you'll be happy to know then that there might not be any more undines coming here. The Grove wants to close the door . . ."

Lura turned on me, the poker raised menacingly. "They can't do that! The undines must return to this river to spawn or they'll die out."

"I thought they were silly, mindless creatures," I pointed out, "and that you were glad to see them gone. Why do you care if there aren't any more, especially . . ."

"Especially as I'm not going to be around much longer?" She lowered the poker and gave the fire one more angry stab. Sitting back down, she looked into the flames and grew silent. The reflection of the firelight gave her skin the momentary flush of youth and I saw that she'd once been pretty. "I'm not afraid to die," she said after a while, "but to think I'm the last of my kind . . . Well, that's not the way I want to leave this world, even if it hasn't always been a world that's been kind to me."

I wondered what the world had done to her that she'd chosen to live alone in this decaying house with only her half-human sisters for company. Looking at her, small and worn down as one of the river stones she collected, I felt the weight of all the years she had spent here alone. This house seemed infected with sadness, as if the wallpaper and plaster were peeling under its burden. A small, mean voice inside me sang, *This is what happens to you when you don't love anyone.*

"Well, I'm going to try to stop them along with a circle of . . . friends."

"Ha! A circle, eh? You must mean them witches and fairies? They don't know what they're doing most days. They come to me sometimes pretending they want my advice when all they really want is my Aelvesgold."

"You mean you have more Aelvesgold than that stone?"

"Why would I tell you?" she asked suspiciously.

"Hey," I said, holding up my hands. "I just learned about the stuff. My friends said the only reliable supply of it came from Faerie."

Lura snorted and spat in the mason jar. "Your friends are ignorant. When an undine lays her eggs, she lays an Aelvestone with 'em to keep 'em safe till they hatch. The one you found must've been with the undines you brought over to Faerie, so it belonged to my sisters. Why should I share it?"

"Because we need the Aelvesgold to give us the power to keep the door open," I said.

Lura screwed up her face, taking away any remnant of the beauty I'd just glimpsed. She reached her hand into her cardigan pocket and pulled out the Aelvestone. I caught my breath at the sight of it and had to restrain myself from leaping up and grabbing it. She leaned forward and held it up between her thumb and forefinger, as if teasing me with it.

"If I give you this, how do I know that you'd use it to keep the door open? How do I know you won't use it to close the door?"

"Because I'm a doorkeeper," I said without thinking. "It's my job to open the door. If the Grove closes it forever . . ." I thought of Soheila and Diana being forced to chose between this world and Faerie. I thought of Liz growing old and dying without the benefit of Aelvesgold. I thought of never seeing Liam again . . . which shouldn't matter because I'd already made my peace with not seeing him again. So why did my whole body feel as if it had been hollowed out? I think it was that hollowness that Lura saw in my eyes, perhaps because it was the same emptiness I'd seen in hers.

She nodded, spat again, tossed the stone up in the air, and caught it. My eyes followed its progress like a dog watching a bone. She tossed the stone to me. I wasn't the best catch in the world (Annie used to call me Butterfingers when we played softball together), but I snatched the stone out of the air as if I were Roger Maris catching a fly ball. As if I had known it was coming. As if it belonged to me.

"See if that don't give you enough power to hold the door open," she said. "See if it don't open up a whole passel of doors for you. Some of those," she added with a wicked grin, "you just might want closed again."

TEN

*B*efore I left, Lura gave me a flannel cloth to wrap around the Aelvestone. "Don't touch it any more than you have to," she warned. "It gives great strength, but at a price." It was exactly what Liz had told me.

I looked closely at Lura as she stood beside my car in the late afternoon sunlight. She was staring at my right rear tire, stuck in a pothole. Her hair, which had seemed momentarily golden inside the house, was dull gray again, her face even more ancient-looking than when I'd first seen her. The Aelvestone had given her youth—and something else.

"That's how you were able to carry me out of the river," I said. "You used the Aelvestone to give yourself strength."

In answer, she bent down and hooked a tiny hand around my rear bumper. She lifted the entire chassis to the left to clear the pothole. She let it down—a little less gently than was likely to be good for my suspension system—and straightened up, arching her back until it cracked.

"Ah," she said, "I haven't used Aelvesgold in more than twenty years. I'd forgotten how it felt . . . It's probably added a few months onto my life, but I'll pay for it. Remember that. Only use as much as you have to."

I told her I would and promised that I'd do my best to stop the Grove from closing the door. I started to thank her for saving my life, but she spat on the ground and waved me away. Maybe half-undines didn't like to be thanked any more than brownies did.

I drove back home slowly, concentrating on the curving backcountry roads in the gathering dusk. I probably shouldn't have driven so soon after the blow to my head, but I didn't have much choice. I certainly was not going to stay in Lura's house—not that she'd asked me.

The sight of my own freshly painted, squared, and trim house—even with its missing roof tiles and twisted gutter—made me sigh with relief. I'd bought it impetuously and had since had cause enough to regret the decision, but right now I was grateful that I had such a welcoming home.

When I opened the front door and knocked over a tin pot full of water, soaking the mail lying on the foyer floor, the relief evaporated. I'd forgotten about the leaks. I had to find someone to fix them before my house started to look like Lura's. Just the thought of those peeling walls and crumbling ceilings made me feel cold and damp—which, as a matter of fact, I still was, *and* my dress smelled suspiciously of cat pee, which Ralph confirmed when he sniffed me. Wrinkling his nose, he disappeared into the hall closet (where he liked to sleep inside my shearling-lined winter boots).

Ugh! I couldn't blame him. I picked up the bucket and the wet mail and carried them both into the kitchen, sticking the bucket in the sink and spreading the damp mail out on the kitchen table to dry—bills and flyers, mostly, which I could deal with later. What I needed now was a hot bath and bed. I'd rest up tonight and then tomorrow I'd call Liz and tell her that I'd found enough Aelvesgold to power the circle. Heck, I thought, unwrapping the stone from Lura's piece of flannel as I climbed the back stairs, this stone could power a dozen spell circles. When I reached my bedroom I stood by the window and held the stone under my desk lamp, feeling a pleasurable tingle in my hand. Instantly, I felt less cold and tired. But Lura had warned me to use it as little as I could. Regretfully, I wrapped it back in the flannel (the same tartan plaid as the shirt she'd worn, I noticed) and slipped it into one of the little pigeonhole drawers in the built-in desk. I kept an assortment of objects in those drawers—shells and stones, a fairy stone my father had given me, a piece of broken willow pattern china that Liam had brought back from one of his rambles . . . I took out the china shard, recalling Liam's habit of bringing little tokens—stones and bird's nests, pinecones and dried flowers—home from his walks. The house had seemed full of his spirit when he'd lived here . . .

Now the house felt empty. By banishing Liam, I'd rid Honeysuckle House of the spirit of the incubus who'd haunted it for more than a century. In the years she'd lived and written here, Dahlia LaMotte had struck a sort of truce with the incubus, periodically allowing him back into the house. By studying her notebooks I'd figured out that she used her interaction with the incubus to fuel her writing. He was her muse. But after he had served her purpose, she would banish him back to the Borderlands.

I opened another drawer—the only one that had been locked when I moved in—and took out the iron key I'd found there. It matched the one that hung around my neck. At some point long ago, Dahlia had locked the key away. She had broken her tie with the incubus. But I still wore my key.

Why? I'd unlocked Liam's manacles when I saw him in Faerie. He was no longer bound by me. I was glad he was no longer in pain but as I took the chain off and put it in the drawer with Dahlia's key, I felt the loss of that connection. The place on my breastbone where the key had lain now felt as empty as my house.

And how much emptier would my life be if the Grove was able to close the door and my friends chose to leave Fairwick?

Feeling rather desolate, I got up from my desk, checked the drawer where I'd put the Aelvestone just to make sure I remembered where it was, I told myself, then went into the bathroom to run a much-needed bath. I put in the plug and turned on the hot water tap all the way. I'd learned that there was just enough hot water in the boiler to fill up the massive claw-foot tub. The water would start to cool when the tub was about half full and then mix with the hot, attaining the perfect temperature by the time the tub was filled. I'd thought of buying a bigger water tank—Brock had said that the one I had was pretty old and eventually would need to be replaced—but it seemed like a needless expense now that the only one using the hot water was me.

While the bath filled, I peeled off my grimy and odiferous dress, dropped it into the sink, and ran water and added scented shampoo to get out the smell. I brushed my hair, working out the tangles—and a few twigs—and rubbed in a little jojoba oil to condition it. I added some to the bathwater as well. Seeing Lura's wrinkled skin—even if she did look damned good for a hundred—had reminded me of the necessity of moisturizing.

When the bath was full I turned off the tap and, with a shivery sense of anticipation, stepped in . . . to ice-cold water. Squealing, I plucked my foot out so quickly I teetered and nearly fell. Another opportunity to crack my skull, I thought, grabbing my robe and wrapping it around me. I studied the taps and turned the one clearly marked hot. More ice-cold water poured into the tub.

Something was wrong with my hot water heater.

I put on flip-flops and stormed down the stairs, rubber heels slapping angrily as if *they* were mad at the house, not me. Why did it have to pick now to malfunction? I knew Brock had kept the old place in pristine condition, but was it really so sensitive that it started falling apart the minute Brock wasn't here?

By the time I reached the basement stairs I'd calmed down a little. It was petty of me to make a fuss about some minor home repair problem when Brock lay in a deathlike coma, his spirit struggling in the icy fogs of Niflheim.

I remained calm, even when the basement light didn't switch on. The bulb had burned out since I'd last gone into the basement—which wasn't all that often. Truth be told, I hated the basement. It had a dirt floor and stone walls—a good solid stone foundation, Brock said—and many, many spiders. The only times I ever went down there were when one of the fuses went out or that one time I'd forgotten to refill the oil tank (who knew you had to order heating oil?) and the man from the oil company had had to "reprime the pump." Whatever that meant.

I grabbed a lightbulb from the pantry and headed down, keeping one hand on the stone wall beside the staircase to keep my balance. I didn't need any more falls. I went slowly down the stairs and stepped into several inches of water.

At least it wasn't cold.

Resisting the urge to sit on the stairs and weep, I screwed the old bulb out of the overhead socket and screwed in the new bulb. The bulb burst into light and revealed the basement in garish detail. I'd hoped somehow that the puddle I was standing in would be the worst of it, but in fact the bit I stood in was high dry ground compared to the rest of the basement. The ground sloped down from where I stood and water covered the entire surface. The furnace and hot water heater were in several feet of water.

Which probably explained why the hot water heater wasn't working. I scanned the water's murky surface as if I might locate a plug I could pull to make it all drain away. Instead I noticed a dead cockroach bobbing on a current heading my way.

Shuddering, I backed up the stairs all the way to the kitchen, afraid that if I turned my back something might rise out of the water to grab me. Then I closed the door on the mess and sat down at my kitchen table and gave in to the urge for a good long cry.

I was alone in an ancient house that was falling apart. Brock was never coming back to fix it and that was my own damned fault. No one was coming to fix it. Certainly not Liam, because I didn't love him. I probably wasn't capable of love. My friends were all going to leave me and go back to Faerie. I was going to grow old all alone while my house decayed and fell apart around me until it looked like Lura's house and I looked as shriveled and dried-up as Lura.

And smelled as bad as her.

I already smelled like cat pee.

I surprised myself by making a weird sound. Something between a burp and a hiccup. It burbled up out of me twice more before I realized that I was laughing.

The cat pee had done it. In our teens I had gone with Annie to visit her nonna in her fifth-floor walk-up on Elizabeth Street. Afterward, Annie had made me promise that if she ever took to keeping multiple cats and smelling like pee I'd put her out of her misery. I'd only promised on the condition she'd do the same for me. I considered calling Annie and telling her I'd gotten there. I might not have a cat, but I did have a pet mouse, who had crept in while I was crying and was rooting around in the wet mail. He nosed a robin's egg blue flyer into my lap. I picked it up. *Handyman Bill!* it read, *For all your household needs—no repair too big or too small. Plumbing, masonry, roof repair—you name it, it fits the Bill!*

I snorted. "Let's hope his handyman skills are better than his punning," I remarked to Ralph, picking up the phone. I got a garbled voicemail message. I left my name and address and told Handyman Bill I had a basement full of water and a leaking roof and would he please get back to me as soon as possible. Then I hung up and tried three plumbers listed in the phone book. None of them picked up. They must all be out draining other people's basements after yesterday's rain.

Disgusted, and sick of my own smell, I boiled some hot water in the electric kettle and brought it upstairs in one of the plastic basins I'd used last night to catch drips. I mixed the hot into the cold water until it was the right temperature. Then I took a sponge bath.

I wasn't rich but I had enough money to hire people to fix the house—just until Brock came back. And he *was* coming back. I'd make sure of that, just as I'd make sure the door remained open so that my friends wouldn't have to go back to Faerie forever. To reassure myself, I checked on the Aelvestone again. I took it out of its flannel covering and held it in my hands for a moment. Surely there could be no harm in that. Its warmth coursed up my arms and spread through my chest. A sense of well-being suffused my body. It was better than a Xanax! With this much Aelvesgold, I'd be able to help Brock *and* keep the Grove from closing the door. With this much Aelvesgold, I was capable of anything! Ann Chase wouldn't have to choose between helping her daughter and curing her arthritis. Liz would never have to grow old and die—*no one* would ever have to grow old and die! The possibilities were endless . . . but for right now I'd better put it away. Both Liz and Lura had said it was dangerous to handle too often.

Reluctantly, I wrapped the stone back in its cloth and put it back in its drawer. I still felt its warmth radiating through my body as I crawled into bed. I hugged the delicious sensation to my bones and fell into a deep sleep . . .

And straight into Faerie, as if there were a trapdoor beneath my bed that led directly to that grassy bank beneath the willow tree where Liam lay waiting for me, his bare flesh awash in the golden light of Aelvesgold.

"Am I really here in Faerie or is this a dream?" I asked.

"Is there a difference?" he replied, drawing me down beside him. I was naked, too, and drenched in the same golden light. We lay side by side, not quite touching, but joined by the same golden light. "It's one of the gifts of Aelvesgold—it links true lovers together, no matter how far apart."

I snorted. "You're making that up."

He laughed, a deep throaty sound that made the willow branches tremble and something deep in my belly tremble, too. He lifted his hand over my breastbone, holding it about an inch above me. I felt golden light caress my skin. He moved his hand, over one breast and then another, the Aelvesgold running like warm syrup over my skin. "Am I making *this* up?" he asked. "Are you telling me you can't feel the connection between us?"

He moved his hand lower, swirling the hot syrup in spirals around my belly. It pooled in my navel and dripped between my legs. When it reached the cleft between my legs, I moaned and arched my back.

"Yes, I feel it," I moaned, rolling over and straddling him.

"Why haven't we done this before?" I asked, riding the gold wave and coming down on him. "Why don't we do this for-ever?" The gold light moved with me, a wave of heat that lifted me up and then down onto him. I guided him inside me and that heat pushed up into my core. I looked down but the light had grown so bright, so dazzling, that I couldn't make out his face.

"Liam?" I cried, as he rocked into me, our bodies moving as if controlled by some external force. "Liam, is it really you?"

In answer, he drew my head down to his. Through the glare I saw his eyes: black with specks of green, as they'd ap-peared when I'd met him in Faerie. "Who else would it be, lass?" he whispered as the gold light began to spread inside me. It filled me up and then it burst, encircling us both in a golden corona of pure pleasure.

"Ah," Liam's voice crooned in my head. "That's why we can't do this forever, love. We would never want to wake up."

I collapsed beside him onto a bed of velvety moss. "What's wrong with that?" I asked, gasping sweet drafts of air. He turned to me and I could just make out his lips smiling at me through the golden haze.

"You'll lose yourself in the Aelvesgold," he told me. "Here." He took my hand in his and pressed something into it. When I opened the hand I saw that I held the Aelvestone.

"How . . . ?"

"You'd better put it someplace safe," he told me. "Lock it up. Or you'll lose it . . . and lose yourself."

I felt its pulse in my hand, like the heart of a trapped animal trying to escape. I closed my hand around it, but that only made it beat harder. It was beating so hard, I heard it pound-ing.

I turned back to Liam, but he was fading, melting into the golden haze of Faerie.

"Don't go!" I cried, but he was vanishing in a blaze of light so bright I had to close my eyes against the glare. When I was at last able to open them, I found myself in my room in Honeysuckle House. Watery green light struggled through the windows. I blinked at it, confused, unable to tell if it was morning or night. I felt as though I'd just gone to sleep. The time I'd spent making love to Liam couldn't have been more than an hour . . .

I heard pounding. I opened my hand, looking for the Aelvestone Liam had given me in my dream, but my hand was empty.

The noise was coming from downstairs. For a moment I had the confused impression that the Aelvestone was knocking at my front door, but then realized that was ridiculous.

I swung my legs over the side of the bed. My limbs felt watery and weak. I stood up . . . and noticed I was naked. Hadn't I worn a nightgown to bed? Yes, there it was, crumpled in a ball on the floor along with a discarded blanket. I walked to my dresser and pulled on shorts and a T-shirt. Then I walked downstairs, half hoping that my visitor would be gone by the time I got to the door. Who would be bothering me so early in the morning?

A glance at the clock in the foyer told me it was twenty after ten.

Oh.

I swung the door open eagerly and suppressed a sigh of disappointment. A man in a navy blue sweatshirt and baseball cap pulled low over his eyes stood with shoulders hunched, holding a clipboard up to shield himself from a funnel of water cascading through the porch roof.

"Yes?" I asked irritably. He was probably collecting signatures for some local political cause or here to read a meter.

"Cal . . . Leach Mac Fay?" he said, butchering my name.

"Yes," I sighed, not bothering to correct his pronunciation. All that navy blue looked vaguely official. Maybe he was collecting for the policeman's annual picnic. "That's me."

"I'm Bill Carey. You called about some work you needed done?" He squinted up at the leak coming from the porch roof. "I guess you might want me to start on the roof."

"Bill Carey? Oh, Handyman Bill! I did call, but I didn't make an appointment. How . . . ?"

"You left your address on my machine, but not your phone number."

I had? "Really? I guess I was . . . distracted."

"Yes, ma'am, you sounded kind of . . ." He shuffled his feet and looked embarrassed. ". . . desperate."

I bristled at the word, but before I could defend myself a big drop of water splatted on my nose. I opened the door wider and said, "That's because I am."

I gave Handyman Bill the tour of my house of horrors, from the many leaks and dissolving plaster to the moldy basement and broken hot water heater. He took notes on his clipboard and made guttural, monosyllabic grunts at each travesty. Not a big talker, Handyman Bill, but when we reached the basement he uttered the sweetest words I'd heard in days.

"I can't start on the roof until the rain stops, but I think I can pump this out and get the boiler going if you'd like some hot water."

I nearly hugged him, but I restrained myself and managed not to sound too desperate when I told him, "Yes, that would be an excellent place to start."

ELEVEN

While Bill pumped out water from the basement, I made coffee. The kitchen was a mess of mud and pots and pans half-full of rainwater, but the minute Bill told me that there was hot water, and that he was leaving in a few minutes to go to the hardware store, I abandoned the mess and hightailed it upstairs. I took a long hot bath with plenty of scented bath salts to get the cat pee smell out of my hair. The hot water was less effective in rinsing away the memory of the dream of making love to Liam in Faerie. I'd freed him from the Borderlands—shouldn't those dreams be over? Would they ever be over?

I would have stayed in the bath longer, but I was disturbed by someone knocking on the door. Was it Handyman Bill back from the hardware store? Should I give him a key? But I didn't even know him. Maybe I should have asked for references, I thought as I toweled off and dressed. Would that seem weird after he'd been nice enough to get my hot water working so quickly? I walked downstairs pondering the etiquette of handyman employment, something I'd never had to worry about when Brock was around, and opened the door to an empty porch. Maybe my visitor had given up. Then I heard voices coming from the edge of the porch. I looked over the railing and saw Liz and Diana crouched in the honeysuckle bushes at the foot of the porch steps. Liz looked up guiltily, a ceramic gnome in her hand.

"Ah, there you are! We got worried when you didn't answer the door and went looking for your key. Only it doesn't seem to be under your gnome."

The ceramic gnome had come with the house. Practically all the houses in Fairwick had one of the twee figurines in their front garden. I'd considered removing the little apple-cheeked man in blue pants, green suspenders, and red cap, but each time I had, he'd seem to glare at me and I'd thought better of it. I had moved my key a few months ago, though, because it seemed like too obvious a hiding place.

"It's here," I said, nudging a flowerpot full of geraniums with my toe.

Liz and Diana exchanged a puzzled look. "Why would you put it *there*? It belongs with your gnome," Diana said, as if it were the most obvious fact in the world. "Everyone hides their key under their gnome."

"Doesn't that defeat the purpose of *hiding* the key if everyone knows where it is?" I asked, feeling as if I were trapped in an *Alice in Wonderland* tea party.

"On the contrary," Liz replied. "These gnomes are threshold guardians. Your gnome protects your key from those wishing you harm, but lets in friends who wish you well. We wanted to make sure that you were all right after what happened at the circle. A power surge like the one you experienced can have unexpected repercussions. Did you sleep all right?"

"I'm fine," I said, blushing as I remembered the erotic dream I'd had last night. "I'm just a little groggy."

"That's to be expected," Diana said briskly as she came up onto the porch, extracted my spare key from beneath the flowerpot, and handed it to Liz to put under the gnome. I thought I detected a faint glow emanating from the ceramic figure when she righted him over the key.

"There," Liz said. "You ought to name him, though, to seal the threshold spell."

"I'd feel . . ." *like an idiot,* I almost said, but looking into Diana's wide doelike eyes, I amended it to "unsure of what sort of name to give him."

"Oh, any old name is fine. Does he remind you of anyone?"

I looked down at the little bearded, red-capped man. "Well, he does look a little like my high school orchestra leader, Mr. Rukowski." As I said the name, the glow around the gnome grew.

"He likes it. Mr. Rukowski it is. May we go inside, Mr. Rukowski?"

For a moment I worried that the ceramic figure might talk—in which case I would have to get rid of him. Ancient threshold guardian or not, a talking ceramic garden gnome was just plain creepy. But no speech issued forth from Mr. Rukowski's mouth, only a warm glow that spread up the porch steps and into my front door, like a welcome mat that had been spread out for my guests.

"Come on in," I said. "Apparently you're welcome."

I tried to seat Liz and Diana in the parlor while I went to put on water for tea, but they followed me into the kitchen and sat down at the table. Liz folded her hands on top of the table and pressed her lips together. Diana rearranged the sugar bowl, salt and pepper shakers, and a mason jar full of wilting wildflowers.

"What is it?" I asked, finally picking up on the women's tension. "Is something wrong? Has the circle banished me? Is Ann okay? Has her hand gotten worse?"

"Ann's fine," Liz assured me. "And the circle . . . Well, there was some disagreement at first." She pressed her lips together and I guessed that Moondance had probably given her a hard time about bringing me into the circle. "But we found a private tutor who we think will be perfect for you. One of our circle can personally vouch for him and I spent the night *calling* his references." Liz placed unusual stress on the word *calling*. It took me another minute in my groggy state to realize why. Last year when Liz had hired Liam Doyle to take over a creative writing class she had relied on his internet profile and emailed references—all of which had been fabricated by my crafty incubus. Liz was trying to assure me that she wasn't making the same mistake.

"Thank you for being so thorough," I said, turning to pour boiling water in the teapot—and also to hide the blood that had risen to my face. I knew I should be grateful to Liz, but instead I felt a sudden wash of grief at the thought that even if Liz wasn't this careful—and no matter what dreams I had of him—I'd never see Liam in the flesh again.

"His name is Duncan Laird," Diana blurted. "He has a DMA from Oxford!"

"A DMA?"

"A Doctorate of Magical Arts," Liz explained. "He's a wizard of the Ninth Order. We're lucky to get him. He happened to be visiting friends in Rhinebeck. He'll be here early this evening, around five."

"Today?" I asked, appalled. "I've got a flooded basement and a leaking roof. Everything's a mess . . ." I looked around the kitchen and noticed for the first time that it was *not* a mess. The pots and pans I'd used to catch drips had been rinsed, dried, and stacked, and put away in the pantry. The mud on the floor had been mopped up. Even the coffee cup I'd given to Bill earlier was rinsed and drying in the draining rack beside the sink. There was a note from Bill under it that read: *I've gotten a tarp over the roof to stop the leaks for now and went for roofing supplies.*

Wow, a man who cleaned up after himself *and* left notes. What better reference did I need for him?

"The house looks spick-and-span," Diane said. "Better than mine, in fact, which reminds me, I should be getting Dr. Laird's room ready and baking some scones for tea. A British wizard will expect a real high tea."

"He'll also expect that you know the basics of magical history," Liz said to me, unloading a stack of books onto my kitchen table. "I've brought you Wheelock's *Spellcraft* and LaFleur's *History of Magic,* volumes one through five. Try to skim through them today, would you? We don't want him to think we American witches have no standards."

"But he knows I'm a beginner, right?" I asked as I followed Liz and Diana to the front door.

Diana and Liz exchanged a guilty look. "Not exactly. We told him you had an unusual energy signature and had short-circuited our circle. He was . . . intrigued."

Great, I thought, Liz had made me sound like an interesting lab rat. But what difference did it make what Duncan Laird thought of me? The important thing was to gain enough power to bring Brock back from Niflheim and keep the door open.

"Have you heard anything more from the governing board of IMP?" I asked on the porch.

Liz sighed. "I spoke last night to Lydia Markham at Mount Holyrood. She's always been a great supporter of the fey, but she was evasive when I asked how she planned to vote. Then I did a little snooping on the web and discovered that an anonymous benefactor has just given a huge bequest to fund a new science lab for Mount Holyrood. I hate to say it, but I'm afraid Lydia's vote might have been bought."

"That's awful," I said. "But there are still two more members of the board who are pro-fey, aren't there?"

"Yes, Talbot Greeley in literature at Bard. He's an Irish cluricaune who did his DMA dissertation on the fey influence on Shakespeare. And Loomis Pagan, a pixy in gender studies at Wesleyan. I think we can count on Talbot, but I'm not sure of Loomis. To tell you the truth, I never understand a word she's saying. Even if she speaks up for the fey her argument is likely to be so incoherent that she'll do our case more harm than good." Liz got into her car, shaking her head. "Our best bet is to make sure that, no matter how the vote goes, you can prevent them from closing the door."

After Liz drove away, I stood on the porch, thinking about what I could do to help. It didn't sound as if we were going to be able to count on support from IMP. If only we knew for sure what the Grove was up to . . . Then I remembered I *did* have a source at the Grove who might be able to help. I went inside and called Jen Davies.

Jen Davies was the freelance reporter who had exposed my roommate Phoenix's memoir as fraudulent last year. I later learned that she belonged to the Grove (and that she felt bad about her treatment of Phoenix). After I was initiated into the Grove, Jen confided to me that she and a group of other young members had formed a splinter group, called Sapling, that questioned the ultraconservative policies of the Grove. If anyone could tell me more about what the Grove was intending to do next week when they came to Fairwick, it would be Jen.

I reached her voicemail and left a message asking her to call me back. Then I stood in my foyer wondering what to do next. Even with Bill's ministrations, the house still needed cleaning *and* I needed to do that reading before my new tutor showed up. I suddenly felt exhausted and unable to choose which I preferred: for Duncan Laird, DMA, to think I was a slob or an idiot? Of course, he was bound to be impressed when I showed him the Aelvestone . . .

The Aelvestone. With a guilty start, I realized I hadn't told Liz or Diana about it. How could I have forgotten? I must have been too distracted by their news about my tutor. I should call and tell them now . . . but first I should check on the stone to make sure it was still okay.

I went upstairs to my bedroom and opened the drawer where I'd put it last night. The drawer was empty.

I've just forgotten which drawer it's in, I told myself, my heart beating faster. I opened all the little drawers. Shells, stones, feathers . . . all the little oddments I kept, but no Aelvestone. There was only one drawer left: the one in which I kept the key to Liam's manacles, but that one was locked. It couldn't be there . . .

I got out the key from my night table and opened the locked drawer. There between the two iron keys—mine and Dahlia's—lay the Aelvestone, the flannel cloth folded neatly beneath it.

How the hell had it gotten there? I wondered, lifting the stone and cradling it in my hand. The only explanation I could imagine was that I'd gotten up some time in the night and moved it. Only I had no memory of doing that. As far as I knew, I'd spent the night making love to Liam in Faerie . . . but at the end of the dream he had handed me the Aelvestone and told me to lock it up. Maybe I *had* gotten up then and moved it. It was disturbing not to remember doing it, but I'd heard of people on certain sleeping pills getting up and doing strange things they couldn't recall later—and last night the Aelvestone had certainly acted like a powerful narcotic.

I looked at the stone in my hand and wrapped my fingers around it experimentally, waiting to see if it made me sleepier. Instead I felt a surge of energy. The fogginess I'd felt since waking vanished. Strange, I thought. Maybe something in the books Liz had given me would explain the effects of Aelvesgold.

I slipped the stone in my pocket and went downstairs to the kitchen, where I'd left the books, and took them into the library to read.

The library had been my favorite room in the house when I'd first moved in. What book lover doesn't dream of having an entire room dedicated to their books? Mine had floor-to-ceiling built-in bookcases crowned with classical molding and brass lamps above each section, and brass nameplates on each shelf which held little cards to identify that shelf's subject (not that I'd gotten around to filling out the cards). It also had a fireplace, a comfortable couch, and a small television. Liam and I had practically lived in here last winter, building fires, watching old movies, making love on the couch . . .

Which was why I hadn't spent much time in here since. The room had acquired a sad, derelict air—dust floating in the air, ashes in the fireplace, the sofa cushions askew and deflated. I sank down on the couch and stroked the nap of the velour, inhaling the scent of scotch and ash and . . . No, I couldn't smell Liam anymore. I reached my hand into my pocket and cradled the Aelvestone. He had said in the dream that Aelvesgold could connect true lovers . . . but I didn't feel connected right now. Maybe that's why I hadn't been able to love him. We weren't *true lovers*. But then why couldn't I stop thinking about him? And why did I *want* to love him so much?

Sighing, I settled down on the couch with the books, opened up LaFleur, and read a hundred pages.

In about ten minutes.

The words seemed to fly into my brain. I'd never believed in speed reading, but this didn't feel like speed reading. I hadn't skimmed. I had a complete and thorough understanding of the history of magic from the Iron Age to the twenty-first century. I could list all the major witches during that time period (Queen Elizabeth I and Eleanor Roosevelt, who knew?) and name the dates of all the major wars, treaties, council rulings, and grimoire editions. And I had a firm grasp of the differences between practical and sympathetic magic.

All in ten minutes. *Wow!* This stuff was better than the Adderal my freshman roommate had given me during finals week.

I picked up Wheelock's *Spellcraft* and committed the first hundred spells to memory.

In five minutes.

But had I really absorbed all that information?

I decided to give myself a little quiz.

"*Flagrante ligfyr,*" I pronounced.

The candles on top of the mantel burst into flame, then sputtered and went out. Ralph, who had been napping behind the Oxford English Dictionary, poked his nose out and wiggled his whiskers at the smoke.

Okay, so my magic was still a bit erratic. What had Liz said—that my energy signature was unusual? *Huh.* Right now my energy signature felt just fine. I tried an air-moving spell.

"*Ventus pyff!*"

A gust swept across the library, stirring the ashes from the unswept fireplace and the dust off the furniture into a small funnel cloud that bounced off the walls and knocked over a lamp. Ralph scurried back behind the OED.

"*Oblittare astyntan!*" I shouted, recalling the spell for canceling spells.

The dust devil collapsed in a heap on top of the couch. *Great,* I thought, as a coughing fit wracked my body, *I've just made things worse in here.*

I looked around the room again. A crystal tumbler with an amber ring at the bottom sat on the coffee table. I lifted it and inhaled the peaty aroma of the scotch Liam favored. On the rim was an impression of his lips. I touched it, recalling the feel of his mouth on mine . . . but instead of shivering with passion I felt anger. Those hadn't been his *true* lips, they'd been an invention to lure me into loving him—and they'd failed.

I marched into the kitchen, picking up a few other stray glasses and dishes along the way, dumped them all in the sink and filled the basin with hot soapy water. I went back into the library and went to work. I picked up the rug, which usually took two people to lift, and hung it over the back porch railing and beat the dust out of it. I shoveled old ashes from the fireplace. I tossed the couch cushions into the hall and vacuumed the couch frame, throwing pebbles, twigs and bird feathers, which must have fallen from Liam's pockets, into the trash. I mopped the floor with Murphy Oil Soap, getting down on my hands and knees. I polished the brass lamps and fireplace tools. I took out every single book to dust it, dislodging a disgruntled Ralph from behind the OED. While I was at it, I thought I might as well organize the books by subject and label the shelves . . .

Only when the shadows lengthened across the floor did I stop. Then I stood back and looked at the library. The floors and brass lamps gleamed. The books stood on the shelves like soldiers arrayed for battle. I'd also rearranged the furniture. The room glowed . . . and it no longer held any trace of Liam.

It was only a matter of time, I assured myself, before I'd be able to say the same for myself.

I reached into my pocket and took out the Aelvestone. "If we are really connected," I whispered to the stone, "show me! *Monstrare leoht!*"

A blinding gold light blazed out of the stone. And then the doorbell rang.

TWELVE

I slipped the stone back in my pocket and fumbled my way to the door, my eyes still dazzled by the light. I opened the door, squinting against the light that formed a corona around the dark figure of a man. My heart beat harder and I thought of Liam in my last dream of him, his face dark against a blaze of Aelvesgold. He *had* come back to me!

But then the man stepped closer and his face came into focus. *Not Liam.* He was good-looking, though, with fair hair that swooped up from a high brow and then fell over one eye like a wing. He wore a wrinkled linen suit and carried a worn leather satchel—the kind British schoolboys used in *Goodbye Mr. Chips*—strapped across his chest. He would have looked like a British schoolboy if his features hadn't been so severe. He had a strong jaw, high cheekbones, and piercing blue eyes that narrowed at me.

"I'm sorry," he said with a sexy Scottish accent. "You look disappointed. Were you expecting someone else? Dean Book told me to come as soon as I arrived in town. You are Cailleach McFay?"

He pronounced my name correctly, so he'd probably heard

it from someone who knew me. Still, I didn't want to leap to any conclusions.

"Who are you?" I asked brusquely, still trying to get over my disappointment that he wasn't Liam.

He took out a card from the inside of his linen jacket and handed it to me. DUNCAN LAIRD, DMA was engraved on the heavy cream cardstock.

"It doesn't say wizard," I said.

He smiled, relieving the severe lines of his face and revealing very white teeth. "Oh, but it does," he said, "if you look at it the right way. Focus your energy on it. You've got enough magic coursing through you right now to light up the Eastern Seaboard."

I stared at the card *harder,* focusing the energy that was fizzing through my veins. A watermark appeared in the paper—a five-pointed star within a circle. A pentacle.

"Cool," I said. "Does the reverse side have a picture of Jesus blessing the masses . . . ?" I flipped the card over while making my, admittedly, lame joke—really, I was just trying to give myself time to recover from my ridiculous idea that I'd summoned Liam to my door—but the smile vanished from my face when the card burst into flame.

"Uh oh," Duncan Laird said. "It only does that when it senses an overload of magical power. The spell circle was right. You *do* have a most unusual energy signature. It's going to take a lot of work to harness your power, but when we do . . ." He gave me a frankly appraising look that made me blush from the tips of my toes to the roots of my hair. ". . . you're going to be magnificent! But," he added, "I can't start your training on the front porch."

He lifted an expectant eyebrow and I realized I was standing with both arms spread across the doorway, hands gripping the frame, effectively barring his entry. "Oh, I'm sorry,"

I said, letting go of the doorframe and stepping to one side. "Please come in."

Duncan Laird smiled and stepped over the lintel, closing the door behind him. The change in air flow puffed the curtains out in the library.

"It's an old house," I said, apologizing for the noise. "Come in . . ."

I was going to lead him into the parlor but, drawn by the breeze from the open windows, he was already heading for the library. "I love old houses," he said, running his long elegant fingers over my books. Thank goodness I'd just dusted. I caught a glimpse of Ralph scurrying behind the backs of the books and hoped Duncan Laird hadn't seen him. "They have their own power. This one feels . . ." He paused and lifted his head, his aquiline nose creasing as he sniffed the air. "*Charged*. Something has been going on in this room."

"I was just doing some spring cleaning," I said. "I hadn't used this room much recently so I dusted . . ."

"You've been banishing more than dust," he said, laying his satchel down on the sideboard and removing from it a device that looked like a pocket watch. When he opened it, though, I saw it was no ordinary pocket watch. Its face had three circles on it, each filled with a different symbol and an arrow inside it. Two of the arrows were spinning in opposite directions; the third was pointing straight up and trembling. "You've been banishing a presence." He looked up from the device, keen blue eyes burning into mine with a force that was strangely compelling. Although the last thing I wanted to do was tell this stranger about my romantic troubles, that's exactly what I ended up doing.

"That would be Liam, my ex." I was trying for a light tone, but the words came out angry and bitter. "He deceived me!" I didn't realize how angry I was until the words left me. The fury rippled from me in a palpable wave. The back door, which I'd left open while cleaning, slammed.

"Ah." His blue eyes widened and swept around the room and then back to me. "Let me guess, an incubus?"

"How did you know?" I asked, appalled but also impressed at his acuity. "Did Liz Book tell you?"

"No one had to tell me, Cailleach. His presence is still here. An incubus leaves a distinctive mark on a house . . ." He tilted his head and regarded me. ". . . and on his victim. It will take more than a little housecleaning to banish his presence."

"I tried using magic and it went haywire," I said defensively, afraid he'd somehow intuit that at the end I'd tried to summon Liam instead of banishing him. "So I resorted to Pledge and Windex."

"And Aelvesgold?" he asked.

"Oh, well . . . yes. I found this stone and I held it for a little bit just to get some energy from it . . ."

"A stone? You have a whole stone's worth of Aelvesgold?"

I removed the Aelvestone from my pocket and held it up for him to see. He took a step back from it, his blue eyes widening, but then reached out for it. I reluctantly put it into his hand.

"Where did you find this?" he asked, his eyes on the stone as he sank down onto the couch. I found it unnerving to see him sitting where Liam had been wont to sit, especially since he said he could feel Liam's presence.

"In the Undine," I said, taking a seat across from the couch. "That's a stream near here."

"Yes, I've heard of it, and I've heard rumors that traces of Aelvesgold could be found in it, but I've never heard of such a large quantity being discovered or . . ." He looked up from the stone to me, his blue eyes burning as if they'd absorbed some of the stone's power. ". . . of any witch who could handle this much of it."

"I'm part fey, on my father's side, and to tell you the truth, I'm not sure I have been handling it very well. I've had strange dreams since I brought it into the house and when I tried to do some spells from Wheelock . . ." I tapped the book lying on the coffee table. "They went kind of . . . awry."

"Show me," he said or, rather, commanded. His tone was so urgent I dismissed the little bit of pique I felt at being ordered.

"Flagrante ligfyr!" I said, matching his tone.

The candles on the mantel flared so high they singed the ceiling, but a moment later they sputtered out.

"Fascinating!" Duncan Laird exclaimed, lit up as if the candles still burned. "Try another one."

I did the wind spell, grateful that there wasn't any more dust to stir up. Instead a miniature tornado seized Duncan Laird's satchel, upended it, and scattered a dozen loose sheets of paper across the room.

"I'm so sorry!" I said, leaping to my feet and chasing after the pages.

"No problem," he replied, clapping his hands and uttering the single word, *"Retrievo."* All the papers flew into his open hand and shuffled themselves into a neat stack.

"Cool. I could use that for collecting homework assignments."

"If you tried it right now, you'd probably break half your students' necks." He tapped the face of his "pocket watch." "See this arrow?" He pointed to an arrow that was spinning clockwise within a circle inscribed with a five pointed star. "It measures terrestrial magic. That's the magic human witches practice using spells, incantations, wards, and hexes. When you used your spell, it spun out of control, indicating your ability for natural magic is through the roof. Usually, we only get readings like that for wizards of the Ninth Order."

"Like yourself."

"Yes," he said, the corners of his mouth twitching. He was flattered but trying not to show it, which was kind of cute. He cleared his throat and went on with his lecture. "But then look at this dial." He pointed to one that was spinning counterclockwise. It was inside a circle crowned by a pair of outspread wings.

"So the wings stand for fairies?" I asked.

"Yes. A rather crude symbology considering most of the fey don't have wings, but then this Thaumascope is rather old. This dial measures fey magic, or what's sometimes referred to as otherworldly magic. It's what the fey practiced before they encountered human beings. No one knows how it works—or at least no human knows and none of the otherworlders I've spoken to are able to explain it, probably because words don't lend themselves to describing something that exists without words . . ." A look of annoyance flashed across his face and he pushed away a lock of hair that had fallen in front of his eyes—as if *that,* and not the fey's inability to describe their own magic, was bothering him.

"Dory Browne once tried to explain it to me," I said. "She said that when the fey first started teaching magic to humans they just *thought* a thing and it happened. They had no words for spells. But to communicate with humans they needed to put things into words, and then they found that the words added an unexpected power to their magic. She said that the fey loved the little extra *zing* that language gave magic and that they taught humans magic in exchange for . . . language." I blushed, recalling that Dory had admitted that the fey had also traded their magic for sexual favors from humans. Fortunately, Duncan was busy looking at the dials on his Thaumascope.

"We may not fully understand what it is, but we can measure it. This dial indicates that your ability to perform fey magic is also off the charts. I've never seen both dials spinning at the same time."

"But then why don't my spells work?" I asked.

"Because of this." He pointed to the third dial, the one whose arrow had stuttered to a trembling stop in one position. I looked at the circle it was in and saw that inside was a drawing of a naked woman, arms and legs extended to touch the rim of the circle, like a female version of Leonardo da Vinci's *Vitruvian Man*. "This dial measures an individual's innate ability to process magic. It's indicating that you don't have *any*, which is strange coupled with your ability shown by the other two dials. It's why your spells misfire. Two types of magic are meeting inside you, like two clashing weather systems creating turbulence."

"You make me sound like a bad day on the Weather Channel. My grandmother always believed that my magical abilities had been canceled out by my fey blood."

"That's an old superstition among witches," Duncan said with a rueful expression. "I think it's likely that the superstition arose to discourage sexual relations with the fey. Around the time of the witch hunts, a sect of witches believed that if they could separate themselves from the influence of the fey—or demons, as the Church called them—they could escape persecution."

"The Great Division," I said, recalling the expression from the reading I'd done in LaFleur earlier.

"Followed by the War of Fluges," Duncan said darkly.

"I read about Fluges in LaFleur. Witches and fey lived in harmony in the French village until the anti-fey witches closed its door to Faerie and . . ." I closed my eyes, trying to recall the exact wording from LaFleur. It appeared in my head in glowing type. "They erased the town entirely." I opened my eyes. An afterimage of the glowing text hung in the air between me and Duncan. "But LaFleur doesn't say exactly what 'erasing it entirely' means."

"No one knows. But think about it: had you ever heard of Fluges before reading about it in LaFleur?"

"No."

"Neither has any other non-witch human. Not only was it wiped off the map, it was erased from human memory. *That's* how violently the anti-fey witches felt about the fey. Is it any wonder that they started a rumor that contact with the fey would destroy a witch's power?"

"Do you think my magical abilities have been canceled out by my fey ancestry?" I asked.

"Quite the opposite. You have tons of magical ability, but there's a blockage."

"A blockage of what kind?"

Duncan shook his head. I felt a sinking sensation. If Duncan Laird with his Oxford DMA, Ninth Order of Wizardry, and clever gadgets couldn't figure out what was wrong with me, who could?

He must have seen the disappointment on my face. He leaned forward and took my hand. I felt a spark as our skin touched, a little electric *zing* that must have been a leftover effect of my internal magical storm.

"But I know what might fix it," he said, squeezing my hand. "Metaphorical magic."

"Metaphorical magic?"

"Precisely. When Aelvesgold enters this world from Faerie, it fills the spaces between atoms, connecting all things. One of the tricks that the fey taught the first witches was sympathetic magic: how to manipulate that connection in order to effect change in objects—and people—at a distance."

"Oh, like a correlative spell," I said, glad I'd crammed. "My friend Diana did one on me to fix my spine. She created a correlation between my broken neck and some yarn and then knitted the yarn to heal me. Wheelock says that the most powerful spells are correlative ones."

"Yes, you can use Aelvesgold to create a bond in order to strengthen a correlative spell. That's why magic became more difficult as the supply of Aelvesgold diminished in this world. But we don't have that problem. You're brimming with the stuff."

He took my hand and held it out in front of my face. For a moment I was too distracted by the strange prickly sensation his touch roused to see what he was showing me, but then I saw it—a thin gold aura around my hand.

"With this much Aelvesgold running through your body you can do practically anything—*become* practically anything. I think we may be able to release your blocked-up energy by using metaphorical magic to change form."

"Change form?" I asked.

"Some witches call it shapeshifting. When you assume the shape of another creature you can sometimes unlock trapped energy. Besides," he added, grinning and looking especially boyish, "it's fun."

THIRTEEN

$\mathcal{W}$e headed outside to my backyard. Duncan said magic was stronger in the open air.

"The woods will offer us more options for transformation. I'm assuming there's not much in the way of wildlife in the house."

"There's Ralph," I said, explaining how Ralph had come into existence. My faithful companion had stayed hidden behind the books while Duncan was in the library.

"It sounds like he's your familiar," Duncan said. "And you should avoid transforming into your familiar's shape. It creates complications. I think you need a form that's more liberating."

We'd come to the edge of the woods. The light from my back porch had lit our way across the yard, but beyond the trees it was dark. Either the moon hadn't risen yet or there was no moon tonight. I supposed that if I was going to be a witch I should start noticing matters of this sort. I suddenly felt very unprepared for whatever it was we were going to do.

"You mean I'm going to turn into an animal?" I asked.

Duncan turned to me but I couldn't make out his face in

the dark. "It's one of the oldest forms of magic," he said. He twirled his hand in the air and all at once the night filled with luminous pictures, revolving around us like a magic lantern show. Herds of painted deer, horses, and horned cattle galloped around us, so lifelike I heard their hooves hammering the night air and smelled their musk. One figure among them reared up taller than the rest: a two-legged creature wearing a horned mask. I recognized the figure as a being from a cave painting in France that was sometimes called the Sorcerer of Trois-Frères. The ancient image was believed to depict a shaman wearing an animal mask, but as it spun around me I sensed that the creature was neither wholly human nor animal, but was instead a creature caught in the moment of transforming from one to the other.

"No one knows whether the fey taught humans how to transform themselves into animals or if it was the other way around," said Duncan. "Some believe it is a magic older than fey or witch—that it's animal magic. By reverting to a primitive form, you may be able to unlock whatever is blocking your magic. But first you must *connect* with that primitive self."

Duncan held up his hand and a breeze stirred the trees, bringing with it the sweet aroma of honeysuckle. Now that my eyes were adjusted to the dark, I could make out white and yellow blooms glowing in the woods like fireflies. Duncan again twirled his hand and warm, fragrant air twined around me like a caressing silk scarf. Another twirl and the scent sharpened. Something musky rode the air along with the honeysuckle. I took a step closer and saw that the glowing orbs in the woods weren't all honeysuckle blossoms. Some were eyes! We were being watched. I startled back but Duncan put his arm around me and gripped my shoulders tightly to keep me from moving away.

"Look," he whispered, his lips close to my ear. *"Really look."*

I stared, opening my eyes as wide as they could go. Slowly, shapes formed out of the dark—graceful, long-legged shapes. Deer. At first, I made out only one—a large, beautiful doe, her long neck stretching toward me, her ears tensed forward, one hoof delicately splayed to the side as if poised for flight. Then another appeared by her side, a buck whose antlers I had taken a moment ago for branches . . . and then another and another. They seemed to be forming out of the dark spaces between the trees—a herd of deer, all still as statues, watching us.

"Are they . . . *regular* deer or magical deer?" I asked.

"What do you think?" Duncan replied.

I looked closer. At their eyes which were large and golden, at the buck's antlers, tipped with gold . . . The deer were full of Aelvesgold, so they must be from Faerie.

"I saw *him* once before," I whispered. "On Christmas night."

"That's the king of the forest, Cernunnos. I imagine he's been keeping a keen eye on you. Look, he wants you to approach."

The buck stepped past the beautiful doe and stamped a hoof on the ground. Summoned, I moved forward. I put my hand out, as I might for a dog or horse. He lowered his head with the grace of a courtier bowing before a lady and touched his velvety muzzle to my hand. He huffed and his warm breath misted the air in a golden cloud that grew between us. I looked up and met those large golden eyes, feeling a spark of recognition.

"Do you see the Aelvesglow?" Duncan said from behind me. He suddenly seemed far away. "Do you see how it connects you to all things?"

Lifting my hand I saw it was surrounded by an aura of gold. My whole body was surrounded by a nimbus of gold.

"You're made of the same substance, all interconnected. When you move . . ." He reached around me and held his hand a few inches above mine. Gold light filled the space between us. When he lifted his hand I felt a tug on mine, as if we were connected by invisible strings. It reminded me of my dream: how Liam had stirred the gold light over my naked body.

"You can do it, too," Laird said.

I lifted my hand above his and saw his hand trail behind mine. I swung my arm in a wide balletic arc. It was like stroking through warm water. The branches of the trees above us swayed in the same arc; a shower of honeysuckle blossoms drifted down and landed on the buck's antlers, forming a flowery wreath. The deer were swaying, too, their golden eyes following the motions of my arms. The drifting flowers danced in the air like tiny ballerinas. I laughed and the golden air rippled in concentric circles that spread outward into the woods. I felt the ripples touch the trees and move through them. I *felt* the trees, their rough bark, the sap that flowed in them, the prickle of leaves sprouting from branch tips . . . I looked down and saw where the gold light limned my fingertips, the shadow of branches.

"The Aelvesgold heightens your connection to the rest of the world," Duncan whispered in my ear. "When you are *like* a thing, you can become that thing. That's the root of metaphorical magic—the *oldest* magic."

I stretched my arms out and felt them sway in the breeze with the branches. I wiggled my toes and felt the stir of roots. I could be a tree if I wanted to . . . or perhaps something more mobile. I concentrated on the doe. Her nose twitched and I sniffed the air. The night was awash with rich scent. Mingled with honeysuckle was the musk of the herd, the tang of pine in the branches, the sap moving through the trees, the bitter taste of bark that we would eat in winter . . . but not now when it was summer and there were fields of fresh grass and tender leaves . . .

My mouth watered. I lifted my nose to the air . . . and felt my neck lengthen. I heard the deer stir and my ears pointed and twitched at the sound. My skin itched to be gone and I felt fur bristle down my legs . . . felt my legs and arms grow long and strong, my fingers and toes hardening into hoofs. I stamped the ground and looked back to Duncan, but where he had stood was another buck, as large and golden as Cernunnos, his antlers branching against the sky. The two bucks huffed at each other, and I felt the air crackle with tension and saw the tawny skin of Aelvesgold stretched taut between them. They both lowered their heads, but before they could charge, the beautiful doe pawed the ground and tossed her graceful head. As if that had been the signal they were waiting for, the herd turned as one, like a flock of birds wheeling in the sky, and sprang away. I felt the tug of their movement and followed without thinking.

A fire leapt up my legs, a delicious spark that traveled from my hooves to the tips of my pointed ears. The other deer had melted into the woods, but I felt them ahead of me and Duncan at my side. We ran together, our hoofbeats keeping time with each other, moving deeper and deeper into the woods until we exploded into a moonlit field. I felt the openness like a dangerous tingling all over my body, but when I lifted my head I saw Cernunnos and the beautiful doe grazing on the hilltop, so I knew it was all right. I looked to Duncan and saw that he was also grazing. I lowered my head and nibbled the silvery moonlit grass. It tasted like *summer*, like life: delicious, but fleeting. I didn't even bother chewing it. It slid down my long throat into my second stomach where I would store it until I had more time. Now I sampled one tuft of tender green shoots and then another, drifting across the field with the others. A young fawn kicked its hind legs and butted its head into its mother; a group of young bucks rubbed their antlers against the back of a fallen log. I rubbed my face against a clump of clover and lifted my nose to sniff the fragrant air. Beside me, Duncan lifted his head and rubbed his neck against mine, spreading clover and musk into my fur. A delicious tingle spread in my legs, and before I even knew I had decided to move, we were running. Just Duncan and me now, across a wide meadow and then back into the woods. I felt Duncan's breath hot on my neck as we ran side by side. Out of the corner of my eye I saw him, his strong neck stretched forward into the run, his fur tipped with gold, his antlers glistening with moonlight. A wild desire spurred me on while at the same time I wanted to knock myself against him, twine my neck with his, feel his rough fur against mine . . . but for now running together was enough. We were linked by the Aelvesgold, bound as surely as if we had been yoked.

I don't know how far or long we ran. The nearly full moon hung low in the western sky when we came to a stop at last beside a rushing stream that reflected the first blush of dawn in its rippled water. Duncan dipped his head to the water first and then, when he lifted his head, water dripping in moonlit pearls from his velvety antlers, I lowered my head and drank. The water was icy and tasted like winter. Of bitter bark and deep snows and hunger. It seemed to fill my veins with an icy sadness, but I would have drunk longer if Duncan hadn't huffed and stamped the ground. I looked up, but whatever danger he sensed was invisible to me. I was losing a bit of my *deerness* as I grew tired, but I was still deer enough that when Duncan leapt across the stream I leapt after him.

Something in the water reached up to stop me, something cold and wet that snagged my hoof and pulled me down to my knees in the fast-moving water. I cried out in a voice that was neither fully deer nor fully human. A face rose out of the water level with my own. I was looking into wide moss-green eyes as cold and dispassionate as river stones . . . and then long cold arms wrapped around my neck and pulled me under the water.

Lorelei. She had followed me through the door and had lain in wait to drown me. I kicked out against her, but my hooves only scrabbled along the creek bottom. Lorelei rode my back, forcing my face under the water. My limbs, so graceful on land, were now clumsy. And I was tired. I had run for miles. Still, I bucked and struggled. As I did, I felt myself changing. I was turning back into my human form.

If only I could change into a fish, I thought. As quick as the thought flitted through my brain I felt myself contracting. My legs and arms hewed to my sides, my skin flaked into scales. I took a breath and drew in oxygen rich water. I was slipping free of Lorelei's grasp . . .

But I'd forgotten what undines lived on. Before I could get away, sharp claws pierced my gills. She'd skewered me like a shrimp on a spit and now she was lifting me into her gaping, needle-toothed mouth. I thrashed to get out of her grip, but her claws only sank deeper into my skin. Her eyes glowed with malice and delight as she squeezed . . . but then they widened with surprise. Something jarred her. I felt the reverberation in my gut. I looked up and saw the shadows of branches spreading over her head—then another jolt. Lorelei screamed and turned to face her attacker, flinging me aside in panic. I hit something hard and dry. I was on land, gasping to breathe like a fish out of water . . . No, that wasn't the image I needed. *Like a drowning person dragged ashore*. I pictured myself—my own human body—and then I was retching up water, my limbs bruised and battered but once more my own. I was on a large flat rock that hung over the stream. Duncan, still in his deer form, stood a few feet from me, his head lowered to ward off Lorelei with his antlers. Her hair was wild and matted, her green eyes flashing, her lips curled over her sharp teeth in an angry snarl. Blood ran down her pearl-slick skin, pooling in crimson swirls around her slim legs. When I sat up, her eyes snapped from Duncan to me.

"I see you didn't waste time finding another male to protect you, Doorkeeper. Is that why you don't want the undines free to come to this world—because you want all the men to yourself?"

"I'm trying to keep the door open!" I cried.

Lorelei laughed. "By running naked in the woods?"

I looked down at myself and saw with horror that she was right: I *was* naked.

"And copulating with that handsome buck?" She gave Duncan an appreciative look.

"I was not . . ." But before I could finish she raised her arms and summoned a thunderclap that drowned out what I was going to say. The boom was followed by a torrent of rain that came down like a curtain on the last act of a bloody and tragic opera. Lorelei dove into the water and disappeared in the current. Duncan lifted his head and turned, becoming a man again. A rather nicely built man, I noticed as he waded through the water toward me. That linen suit had been hiding a muscular chest and strong arms.

"You're hurt," he said, laying his hands on my ribcage. "Lie back and I'll work a binding spell to heal your skin."

"What if she comes back?" I asked as I lay down on the rock, mortified that we were both naked. I hadn't minded running through the fields with Duncan Laird or nuzzling him in deer form, but I was now all too aware that we'd met only hours ago.

"She won't come back," he said. "She's hurt, too. I speared her with my antlers." His lips twitched into a smile at his prowess, but his eyes stayed on the wounds on my ribcage as he moved his hands over them. He was making a motion with his right hand that resembled sewing. Great, I thought. My spine had been knitted and now my ribs were being sewn up with invisible thread. I'd be a Raggedy Ann doll before long. I felt a tug on my skin and looked away, back to his face.

"She was going to kill me," I said, trying to focus on Duncan's face instead of what his hands were doing. It was a nice face. Without the distraction of his messy hair—plastered now to his skull—I could admire his high forehead and the angular line of his cheekbones. "Even though I told her that I was trying to keep the door open."

"You can't expect rational thinking from an undine, especially one in heat—and believe me, that one *was*. You said you wouldn't let her come through the door when you met her in Faerie. That was enough for her to decide you're trying to keep her from breeding. No matter how much you may actually be trying to help the undines, she sees you as an obstacle to her breeding . . . Hold on, this is going to pinch a little . . ." Duncan made one last tug that hurt like hell, then he laid both his hands on top of the wounds, closed his eyes, and uttered a few words in a language I didn't recognize. I felt a warming sensation and my skin went agreeably numb. Opening his eyes, Duncan looked straight into mine. Against the backdrop of gray rain clouds, they were a fiery gold that smoldered with the same warmth I felt in his hands. Which still lay on my bare skin.

"Are you . . . um . . . still healing me?" I asked awkwardly.

He shook his head. "I'm trying to feel if your power has been unblocked. It feels different, but still *tangled*. Perhaps another transformation would work better. Another shape might be more liberating. We have to try something else. Now it's more important than ever that you gain control of your power."

"Why?" I asked.

"To protect yourself. As long as Lorelei believes that you're in the way of her breeding cycle, she'll try to kill you."

Duncan walked me back to my house, supporting me with his arm around my waist. He'd conjured clothes for both of us, but they were soon so wet they didn't do much good keeping us warm.

"There's one thing I don't understand," I said, after we'd been walking through the rain in silence for several minutes.

"Hm . . . just one thing?" he asked.

I laughed. "No, actually there are *many* things, but one uppermost. Aelvesgold comes from Faerie, right?"

"Yes. Creatures from Faerie bring it with them when they come into this world."

"Right, and witches use it to make magic . . ."

"Yes," he said, holding back a sodden branch for me. The path was narrow here. I was conscious of my wet clothes brushing against him as I passed and glad it was too dark for him to see clearly how my clothes clung to me. Which was pretty ridiculous considering that he'd seen me naked not half an hour ago. "But Liz said the circle had a limited amount of it, and yet tonight I saw it all around me," I said, trying to keep my mind on the Aelvesgold.

"Yes, that's because after you handled the Aelvestone you

were filled with the stuff and drew even more of it to you. Think of the Aelvesgold as having a magnetic charge—the more you have inside you, the more you draw it to you."

"Huh. Okay, so couldn't there conceivably be enough Aelvesgold in this world to supply all the witches and fairies even if the door closes?"

Duncan shook his head. "Without replenishment from Faerie, it would run out rather soon. Unless . . ."

"Unless what?"

"Unless there was a creature who produced its own Aelvesgold even outside Faerie."

"You mean the way the undines lay an egg of Aelvesgold to protect their young?"

He made a face, either from pain or from squeamishness at talking about female reproductive cycles. "Not exactly. Undines only make enough Aelvesgold to protect their eggs. Once they lay their eggs they're entirely depleted of Aelvesgold. If they don't go back to Faerie, they'll wither and die. No, I'm talking about a creature that makes its own Aelvesgold in this world and never needs to return to Faerie. If there was a race of creatures like that, they would rule the whole world and we wouldn't have to worry about the door closing. I could do some research into it today and return this evening."

We'd reached my back door. "What about Lorelei?" I asked. "We have to tell Liz and the others that she's here in Fairwick."

"I'll alert your dean to the situation. You should try to get some rest. Transformations take a lot out of you."

Before he left, he lowered his head and touched his cheek to mine, less a kiss than a nuzzle, a brief reminder of how we'd touched last night when we were deer. But instead of leaning into it, as I had when we were deer, I flinched. He stepped back and stared at me.

"I'm sorry," I said. "I'm . . ."

"Exhausted," he finished for me. "Get some sleep." Then he was gone.

I opened the back door, chiding myself for reacting to Duncan's touch like a . . . well, like a *startled deer*. Duncan was a nice man. He was trying to help. If I acted like that with every man who touched me, I was going to be alone for a long time in this big silent house.

Silent.

I listened for a moment until I had confirmed my first impression. The rain pounded on the roof, but there was no ping or patter of falling water within the house. Glorious silence. Bill had managed to seal the leaks—at least temporarily—with his tarps. What a prince! I might end up alone in this big old house, but at least I'd found someone to take care of it.

FOURTEEN

I slept soundly and dreamlessly. In the morning I awoke to sunshine and the sound of hammering. I dressed, noticing that the wounds on my ribcage were almost entirely healed. Duncan Laird was quite a powerful wizard. I shivered a little recalling his hands on me—on my *naked* body. How would I ever face him again? The transformation I'd undergone last night hadn't unlocked my power and now we had another problem—a crazed undine on the loose who had the mistaken impression that I was keeping her from breeding.

I wasn't going to figure out what to do without coffee, though. In fact, I was so foggy that I could swear that I *smelled* coffee. I went downstairs and found Bill, in navy sweatshirt and baseball cap, in the kitchen pouring coffee into my favorite mug.

"I hope you don't mind that I let myself in," he said, handing it to me. "I wanted to get an early start so I used the key under your gnome."

"Oh," I said, taking the mug, "how did you know the key was under the gnome?"

He grinned. "Everyone in this town keeps their key under their gnome. Anyway, I just wanted to check that the tarps kept the water out last night."

"Oh yes," I said taking a sip of the coffee. It was delicious, a perfect combination of the two blends I kept in my freezer. "I didn't hear any leaks at all. You did a great job."

He pulled his cap over his eyes and looked embarrassed at the praise. "It's just a temporary solution," he mumbled. "I'd better get to work on the roof. I think the rain's letting up."

I looked out the window above the sink and saw a line of clearing sky through the woods in back. Lorelei must have gotten tired of making it rain . . . or her wounds had worn her out. *Ha!* I thought. She probably didn't have a talented wizard like Duncan to heal her wounds.

". . . so if you just okay this estimate . . ." Bill was holding the clipboard out to me, head ducked, feet shuffling.

"Oh, of course. You'll need a down payment. How much . . . ?" I looked down at the statement and was pleasantly surprised by the total. "That seems fair," I said. "Can I write you a check for half now and half when you're done?"

Bill grunted assent and I went to get my checkbook out of my desk drawer. When I came down he was in the foyer on his hands and knees. At first I thought he'd slipped on the wet floor and I wondered if the house was deliberately sabotaging anyone who tried to fix it, but then he looked up and I saw he was holding an old rag in his hands.

"Just mopping up a little spill," he said, getting to his feet and tugging his cap over his eyes. "I didn't want you to slip."

"Thank you," I said, handing him the check. "That was very considerate of you."

He folded the check and stuck it into the pocket of his sweatshirt. Then he stuck the rag—a scrap of plaid flannel—

into his back pocket where it hung out like a flag on the back of an oversized load on a truck. Bill wasn't a spiffy dresser, but if he fixed my roof the way he'd fixed my hot water heater I was going to nominate him for Man of the Year.

"Should I give you a key?" I asked.

"I can just use the one under the gnome," he said, shifting awkwardly from foot to foot, "if that's all right?"

I hesitated, wondering how these things were usually done. I'd gotten used to Brock coming and going as he pleased. Was Bill worried I'd accuse him of stealing something later? Or maybe he thought I was naïve for trusting a total stranger with the key to my house. Maybe he was right. But every instinct in my body told me to trust Bill Carey. Then I remembered what Liz and Diana had said, that no one wishing me harm could get to the key under the gnome. If Bill could use it, that proved he was as trustworthy as I thought he was.

"It's perfectly all right," I said. "I trust you."

He lifted his head. For the first time I got a good look at his eyes—warm, golden brown eyes the color of good whiskey. They were shining, almost as if filled with tears. "I promise you I won't give you any reason for ever regretting that," he said in a rush, then he turned abruptly and fled.

"I'll see you later, then," I called as he headed for his pickup truck—a shiny new red Ford. He grunted and waved. What had happened in Bill's life, I wondered as I closed the door, that made a simple expression of trust so moving?

I was heading upstairs to get dressed when my cell phone rang. I almost didn't pick it up, but then I thought it might be Duncan Laird. I answered it without checking the number.

"Callie McFay?" a woman with a gravelly Australian accent asked. "It's Jen Davies. Sorry I took so long getting back to you."

"Not at all, Jen," I said sitting down on the bottom step. "I know you're busy. I saw the piece you did on Sarah Palin's wardrobe stylist. Nice one!"

"Yeah, I felt a bit like I'd found Deep Throat."

We both laughed, but Jen stopped first. "Hey, I appreciate the good review but I don't think you called about that. Have you heard about the meeting in Fairwick?"

"I heard the Grove is coming to discuss with IMP whether the door to Faerie should be permanently closed."

Jen snorted. "That's not the half of what they've got planned. I think we'd better talk. I got into town early . . ."

"You're in Fairwick?" I asked, surprised that Jen would spend any more time in the country than she'd have to.

"Yeah, the muckety-mucks sent me on first to scout out the lay of the land. I'm staying at a motel out on the highway. No offense to your pal Diana, but if I stayed at her inn one more time I'd never fit into my jeans."

"I know what you mean," I said, remembering how Diana had stuffed me full of sweets and baked goods when I stayed at the Hart Brake Inn last year. Jen Davies, as I recalled, looked like she did Jivamukti yoga twelve hours a day and lived on agave protein shakes. She probably hadn't eaten a carb in the last decade. "Where do you want to meet? You could come to my house."

"Could we meet at the diner in town?"

"Sure," I said, glad the meeting would include food. I was suddenly ravenous—probably from running through the woods all night. I hung up, wondering how guilty I'd feel having toast and home fries in front of Jen Davies . . . and decided I was willing to risk it.

I walked into town, enjoying the sunshine. Now that the rain had passed it was a beautiful morning. The trees glistened as

if polished by the rain and the pavement sparkled. I stopped
to inhale the scent of freshly mown wet grass in the Lindis-
farnes' yard and Cherry Lindisfarne came out onto her porch
to ask if it was true that Brock Olsen had fallen from my roof.
I told her it was and that he was recuperating at his family's
farm. Evangeline Sprague came out when she heard us talking
and asked after Brock as well. We all chatted for a few minutes about what a nice family the Olsens were and how their
farm always donated food to Meals on Wheels and the home-
less shelter in Kingston. "Good neighbors," Evangeline said.
"We need more like them, especially when the town is so full
of strangers. Did you hear there was a break-in down at the
motor court?"

I left Evangeline and Cherry talking about the break-in and
walked into town. Main Street was indeed bustling with tourists and fishermen shopping at Trask's Outdoor Outfitters
and filling the outdoor tables at Fair Grounds and the red
vinyl booths at the Village Diner. I might not have gotten a
booth if the waitress, Darla, didn't happen to be the mother
of one of my students.

As she seated me at a booth behind one that was full to
overflowing with three large men in identical plaid flannel
shirts, she whispered, "I always try to make room for a local,
even when we're bursting with out-of-towners. I've never seen
a more popular fishing season!"

"I've never seen the Undine run so full," one of the men in
plaid commented, having overheard Darla's throaty whisper.
"It's like they're trying to get out of town!" His comment was
greeted by guffaws from the two other men in the booth. I
smiled at them, realizing I'd seen them around town before.
All three men had the same beestung lips and full round faces.
In their identical flannel shirts and Orvis baseball caps, they
looked like an illustration of the same man at different stages

of his life: young, middle-aged, and old. Son, father and grandfather, I presumed.

I was studying the menu when Jen Davies walked in. Dressed in tight black leggings and a tank top, her dark hair coiled in a long braid, she turned quite a few heads as she sauntered down the aisle, including all three of the men in plaid. I heard the youngest one whisper to his father, "She must be one of those New York models!"

"You're looking fit," Jen said, leaning over the table to kiss me on both cheeks and then sitting down across from me. Her keen eyes narrowed at me. "*Quite* fit. I wouldn't have pegged you as one of those witches who uses Aelvesgold to make themselves look younger."

"I'm not . . ." I began to object, but was interrupted by Darla coming to take our order.

"What are those three strong men having?" Jen asked, turning her slim neck to look at the men in the next booth. I saw the youngest one blush from where I sat.

"Angler's Special," Darla replied. "Three scrambled eggs, wheat toast, home fries, and sausage. It's exactly the same as the Farmer's Special, which is what the Stewarts here . . ." She winked at the men in the next booth. ". . . have ten months out of the year, them being farmers, but during fishing season they like it if we call it the Angler's Special."

"I'll have that," Jen said. "Minus the toast and home fries." Surprised—I would have pegged Jen for a vegan—I ordered the same thing, but with the carbs.

"I am *not* using Aelvesgold to look younger," I whispered when Darla had finished taking our order. "At least not deliberately. I'm using it to . . . explore my power."

Jen snorted. "Explore, my foot! You're wallowing in the stuff. But hey, I'm not here to criticize. I just thought I'd give you a little heads-up."

"Thanks, Jen. Not to *criticize,* but you could have told me earlier that the Grove was coming here. I learned about it from my dean who doesn't know I'm a member."

"Fair enough," Jen said equably. "I would have, only I didn't know until two days ago. The higher-ups have been secretive lately. A bunch of them, including your grandmother, went off to London last month and when they came back they announced—*announced,* mind you, not proposed—that we were now affiliated with a club there. The Seraphim. There was a bit of a controversy because the Seraphim is an extremely conservative wizards' club that doesn't allow women."

"Why would the Grove—an all-women's club—affiliate with an all-men's club?" I asked.

"That's what I wanted to know. So I started looking into the Seraphim and couldn't find out diddly. Me, who got Sarah Palin's stylist to talk! I couldn't get to square one with this outfit. The only thing I could find out is that the club is older than Methuselah and richer than God—Oh, this is brilliant, love," Jen interrupted herself to exclaim over the huge plates of food that Darla put down in front of us. When Darla had finished serving the food, she continued, her voice low and conspiratorial, "And when those women got back from London they were all hepped up about going to Fairwick to close the door."

"To close the door?" I asked. "Not *discuss* closing the door?"

Jen snorted so hard she got orange juice up her nose. "Grove women don't *discuss.* Besides, they've already gotten half the IMP board on their side . . . Mmm . . . This is fabulous. I bet these eggs are fresh." Jen clearly wasn't going to tell me anything more until she had sated her appetite. I might as well eat. I took a bite . . . and nearly swooned. Had eggs always tasted this good? Why hadn't I had home fries in so long? What was wrong with sausage anyway? I dimly recalled the concept of weight gain, but hey, if I ran twenty miles every night I could afford to eat like this. I'd probably *lose* weight.

When I had polished off my entire breakfast, I looked up to find Jen Davies studying me. "Aelvesgold increases the appetite," she remarked. "But no worries, it also speeds up the metabolism, so you'll never get fat—or old—or, as far as we know, dead."

"Really? It can make you live forever?" I asked, but Jen wasn't listening to me; she was listening to the Stewarts in the next booth.

". . . just plain vanished. They found his van parked at the top of the lower branch and his tackle scattered in the woods."

"Wouldn't be the first fisherman to go missing on the Undine," the oldest Stewart remarked.

The middle-aged man made a rude noise and cried, "Don't be filling the boy's heads with those tales, Dad." Unswayed by his son's objection, the old man asked his grandson if he had heard the one about the mermaid and the old fisherman. The conversation quickly degenerated into dirty guy talk, the kind of hearty bluster that usually covered up real fears. Jen was furiously two-thumb typing on her iPhone. When she finished, she noticed me watching her.

"Force of habit," she said.

"Are you thinking of writing a story on fishing in the Catskills?" I asked.

Jen's eyes slid to one side and she fiddled with the lid of the tin creamer. "The Grove sent me up to see if there was any unusual activity going on in town—or in the woods. They're afraid that when word gets out that the door's going to be closed there will be a mass exodus from Faerie. They want to know if there's been any increased traffic through the door.

That fisherman . . ." She looked over her shoulder at the next booth, where the Stewarts were getting up to go. ". . . isn't the only one who's gone missing. And where there are missing fishermen, there's likely to be an undine. Would you happen to know anything about that?"

I almost started to tell Jen about the undine run and seeing Lorelei last night, but stopped. "I might," I said cautiously. "But I have a few questions of my own first."

Jen tilted her head and smiled. "Well, look at you, Cailleach McFay. Proposing a little friendly exchange of information, are we? Fair enough. What do you want to know?"

"First, why does the Grove want to close the door?"

"That's easy. They've hated the fey since the witch hunts of the fifteenth and sixteenth centuries. They believe that it was the association with the fey that got witches persecuted and that they are evil and destructive. To give them credit, they're right about a lot of them. That creepy bird creature that attacked you and Phoenix last fall . . ."

"How did you know about the liderc?"

Jen rolled her eyes. "I have my sources, love, and they've informed me about a whole lot of dangerous creatures roaming at large in Fairwick. That incubus that preyed on you, for instance . . ."

"Let's leave Liam out of this," I snapped. I saw Jen's eyes narrow with interest at my outburst; her fingers drummed on her iPhone as if she'd like to make a note on it. "I get that the Grove hates the fey, but I don't understand what they hope to accomplish by closing the door. A lot of the fey who are already here will stay . . ."

Jen shook her head. "Most won't. When they know the door is closing, they'll go back to Faerie. They have to. If they don't return once in a while, they fade. The Grove has been spreading rumors for weeks in the fey community that the last door is closing for good. Fairies and demons have been flocking here to be ready to leave."

"Flocking? I don't think so. I think I would have noticed a sudden influx . . ." Halfway through my objection a Winnebago rumbled past the diner, its silver surface winking in the sun. "The fishermen?" I whispered.

Jen nodded. "What better camouflage than a pair of giant waders and a booney hat?"

I looked around the diner at the innocuous-looking clientele. Among a number of locals I recognized—one of Dory's cousins having breakfast with a young couple who looked like city people house-hunting in the country, Tara Cohen-Miller cutting the crusts off a grilled cheese sandwich for her little boy, Abby Goodnough picking up a to-go order—were a dozen or so strangers outfitted in fishing garb: T-shirts emblazoned with leaping trout, khaki shorts with multiple pockets, and wide-brimmed hats (the booney hats Jen had referred to) decorated with colorful fishing flies. Were they really fairies and demons in disguise?

"Okay," I said, "but tell me this. Don't the witches of the Grove need Aelvesgold for their magic and to stay young? Isn't it . . ." I recalled Duncan's phrase. ". . . the basis of all magic?"

"You *are* learning," Jen said approvingly.

"So where will the witches of the Grove get Aelvesgold if they close the door?" I asked, determined not to be swayed by Jen's admiration.

Jen leaned across the table and whispered. "They have another source. Don't ask me where. It's one of the most closely guarded secrets of the Grove. Not even I can get close to it. Now if you're done with your questions . . ."

"Not quite," I said, holding up one finger. "I've got one more. *How* are they planning to close the door?"

Jen shook her head. "I don't know. But I did overhear Adelaide talking to one of the other women and your name came up. She said 'as long as we have a doorkeeper we'll be able to close it.' "

"So they need me," I said, not sure if this was good news or bad.

"Apparently. Are you thinking of *refusing*?" Her eyes glittered hungrily at the idea.

"Is that what you wanted to ask me?" I said, picking up the check that Darla had slapped down on our table.

"Not so fast, McFay. You haven't told me about the undine yet. Is it true you let one through the door?"

"How . . . ?" I began, but then realizing it was useless to question Jen about her sources—and probably useless to deny what she already knew—I answered honestly. "Yes. It was an accident. But that doesn't mean the undine has anything to do with the missing fishermen."

"Let's hope so, for your sake," Jen said, grabbing the bill out of my hand. "All those IMP members are bleeding-heart liberals until they feel threatened. Nothing is likely to sway the vote more than an undine attack . . . unless of course," she added slyly, "it's an incubus invasion."

FIFTEEN

I walked back home thinking about all I'd learned from Jen Davies . . . and all I hadn't. It wasn't encouraging. And what had Jen meant by that crack about an incubus invasion? She'd refused to say anything more about it, but I suspected she'd said it for a reason. Did she think that my incubus was back? Did she know something I didn't?

I got out my cell phone to call Liz, but realized I had a problem before hitting her number. How did I tell Liz what I'd learned from a member of the Grove without telling her that I was also a member?

As I was trying to decide what to do, I saw Ann Chase on the opposite side of the street. She was with a young woman, coming out of a trim, pretty bungalow, its front path lined with thick clusters of zinnias and daisies. They were carrying piles of brightly colored flyers. Ann saw me and waved. I put my phone away and crossed the street, glad of a diversion from making a hard decision.

"I hope you haven't lost a pet," I said as I approached, thinking that the most likely reason for putting up flyers. The woman with Ann raised a stricken face. I saw that she wasn't as young as I'd thought—and that she had Down syndrome. "Not ours! Silver is safe at home. We're not going to let her out until it's safe."

"That's right, Jessica," Ann said, patting her daughter on the arm. "Nothing's going to happen to Silver. That's our cat," Ann added to me with a patient smile. "We're keeping her in while there are so many . . . *strangers* in town."

"I'm not supposed to talk to strangers," Jessica said, shuffling the stack of flyers in her hands. They had been Xeroxed in multiple DayGlo colors. I looked at the one that they'd just stapled to the telephone pole and saw that it featured the face of a young man above the words MISSING: TOBIAS GRANGER, AGE 26, LAST SEEN FISHING ON THE LOWER UNDINE, JUNE 16.

"He's been gone for two days?" I asked.

"He works at the animal shelter and he's my friend," Jessica said.

"I'm sure he'll come home soon," I told Jessica, hoping it was true.

"Thank you," Ann said, a pained look on her face as she looked away from me to Jessica. "Jessica wanted to do something to help."

"I'm sure that these flyers will help," I said. "And they're in such bright colors. Everybody will notice them."

"I picked out the colors," Jessica said proudly, and then, turning to Ann, "We need to go. There are a lot more to put up."

Ann smiled apologetically at me as she continued down Elm with her daughter—and I continued up the hill in a somber mood. Soheila had told me that Ann used what Aelvesgold she could find for her daughter. I knew that a number of physical ailments and a shortened life expectancy often accompanied Down syndrome. It was painful to think what might happen to Jessica if the supply of Aelvesgold was cut off.

As it was bound to be if we didn't stop the Grove from closing the door. Wasn't it cowardly to worry about keeping my affiliation with the Grove secret when so much was at stake? What I needed, I decided, as I walked up my front path, was a sign . . .

Something heavy fell at my feet.

I bent down to look at it. It was a hammer. What the hell kind of sign was that?

"Are you okay?"

The voice came from above. Was that my message? I stepped back and looked up at my roof, shading my eyes against the sun. A dark figure limned by white light stood above me. It reminded me of the dark lover in my dream, the way he'd been haloed by light . . .

"I'm so sorry," the figure on my roof said, "It slipped."

No, not a guardian angel or my dream lover; it was Handyman Bill. I'd forgotten all about him.

"It's okay," I said, handing him his hammer, "no harm done. But maybe it's a sign . . ." I smiled to myself at the wording I'd chosen. ". . . that we both need a break."

I made a pitcher of lemonade and a turkey sandwich and ordered Bill off the roof. It was clear he'd been working all morning. His T-shirt was drenched and clinging to his chest—a rather nice chest, I couldn't help noticing—and sweat was beading his forehead below the rim of his baseball cap, which he kept on while draining the lemonade.

"How's it going?" I asked, refilling his glass and handing him the sandwich. I tried to steer him to the table on the porch, but he remained standing.

"Good. I've replaced about half the missing tiles. Did all these tiles come off in the last rain?"

"No, some were damaged in that storm last fall. You must remember it—that big ice storm the day before Thanksgiving?" Of course I remembered it only too well. The storm had been a result of my first attempt to banish the incubus. He had become enraged and lashed back with hundred-mile-an-hour winds that snapped trees like twigs, took down power lines, and incapacitated the town for a week.

"Oh, *that* storm. I was . . . out of town for that."

"Lucky you," I said, determined not to pry into my handyman's private life. "It did a lot of damage. The town's still recovering . . . Of course, I guess that's good for you. There's plenty of work."

"I'm grateful for the work, but I don't like to think it comes at the expense of other people's bad fortune," Bill said gravely. "I'm just glad I can fix some of it."

"Oh well, I guess there's not much you can do about bad weather . . ." I faltered and looked away, recalling that I'd been the unwitting cause of the last two storms and all the damage they'd caused—including the human damage. I looked back at Bill and saw him staring at me. He probably thought I was nuts. "Anyway, I'm glad you're here to fix the roof now."

"Me too," he said, handing me his empty glass and plate. "I'd better get back to it . . . unless the noise is bothering your . . . writing . . . or researching . . . uh . . . or other college professor stuff."

I laughed. I could only imagine what my work might seem like to a handyman. For a moment I envied him. It would be nice if all my problems could be fixed with a hammer and a handful of nails . . . then I realized how foolish that was. The problem I had right now could be solved with a couple of words. "No, I need to go by my dean's office. And you'd better get back to work." I looked up at the clear blue sky. "Who knows how long it will stay like this?"

I walked across campus to Liz's office determined in my resolve to confess my membership in the Grove and tell her everything I'd learned from Jen Davies. It felt good finally knowing what to do about at least one thing . . . as good as it felt to be walking in the sunshine after last night's rain. All the storms on the horizon were still rumbling but I felt a power of my own growing. Maybe it was anger at the Grove for conspiring to hurt my town, or maybe last night's transformation *had* released some power. Just thinking about running through the woods with Duncan made my fingers prickle with energy and my skin itch to change again.

By the time I walked up the two flights of stairs to Liz's office I was setting off sparks. When I touched her doorknob gold cinders sizzled in the air. Some protection spell? I wondered. But if it was, it wasn't strong enough to withstand my new power. I walked in without knocking.

And was immediately sorry I had. Liz Book was on the couch in a close embrace with a woman. I was embarrassed enough when I thought it was Diana, but when the two women sprung apart I saw that the second woman was Soheila—and that Liz's face was wet with tears.

"What's wrong?" I asked, alarmed at the sight of the usually composed Elizabeth Book crying. "Has something happened?"

"Liz was upset over some bad news in my family . . ." Soheila began, but Liz put a hand on her arm and shook her head.

"There's no reason not to tell Callie—she'll find out soon

enough. I'm upset because Diana has told me that if the door is closing forever she will go back to Faerie." Liz's voice wobbled at the end and Soheila handed her a tissue. I sank down into a chair.

"Diana would go back to Faerie *forever*? But why? If it's because she's afraid of living without Aelvesgold, we might have a solution for that." I was going to tell her what Duncan Laird had said about some creatures producing their own Aelvesgold but Liz was shaking her head.

"It's not *just* that. Diana has a responsibility to her people, the fairy deer. She is their guardian. She has guarded them in this world against the growing dangers here—hunting, pollution, the clearing of the forests—but the deer folk have decided that if the door is closing they will go back to Faerie. Diana feels it's her responsibility to go with them . . ." Her voice trailed off as she was overcome with emotion. I patted her arm and exchanged a look with Soheila.

"I'm so sorry, Liz. But maybe she won't have to make that choice."

"Have you found a way to keep the door open?" she asked eagerly, drying her eyes and sitting up straighter. "Duncan Laird was here earlier. He said you have great promise. If you can keep the door open, Diana won't have to choose between this world and Faerie."

The hopeful smile on Liz's face was heartbreaking—and reminded me of what I'd come to do.

"I'll try my best, Liz, but there's something else I have to tell you."

I took a deep breath and looked straight at Liz, who was regarding me with an expectant half smile. "I've been hiding something from you . . . A few months ago, I went to the Grove to ask my grandmother for a way to break the Ballard curse. I'd found out that one of our ancestors had cursed them. She told me that I was the only one who could remove the curse, but only if I joined the Grove. So I did. I joined them and promised to inform them of any situations at Fairwick that posed a threat to humans. Adelaide promised me that no harm would come to anyone as a result of the information I gave them . . . but I see now that it was probably foolhardy to believe her."

The smile on Liz's face had slowly faded as I spoke, replaced by a stony expression—the one that students dreaded when they had committed an infraction. "And have you reported anything to them since you became a member?"

"No," I told her honestly. "I haven't seen anything that constituted a threat to humans. I guess Lorelei would have been the first thing . . . Did Duncan Laird tell you that we saw her last night in the woods?"

"Yes," Liz said. "*Are* you going to inform the Grove about her? I would have to say that she poses a threat to humans."

"I'm afraid they'll learn about Lorelei whether I tell them or not. I met with Jen Davies this morning. She was sent by the Grove to monitor activity in the woods. She already suspected there's an undine on the loose, and I couldn't deny it."

Soheila sighed and tucked her hands into the sleeves of her burnt umber cardigan as if she were freezing.

"But I did at least get some information in return." Relieved to move on from my own guilty secret, I told Liz and Soheila that the Grove had apparently made a decision to close the door after forming an alliance with the Seraphim Club in London. The women exchanged an anxious look.

"The Seraphim goes back to the sixteenth century," Soheila said, shivering. "They're powerful wizards and even more anti-fey than the Grove. Their members looted the temples of my country and drove out our old gods. They decorated their club with the spoils of their pillaging."

"They are marauders of the worst kind!" Liz exclaimed, her cheeks flaming pink. "Common thieves and tomb raiders!"

"Perhaps that's how they found an alternative source of Aelvesgold," I said.

All the color drained from Liz's face. "An alternative source of Aelvesgold? That's impossible. The only source of Aelvesgold is Faerie. And this is the last door."

"Duncan told me that there are creatures who can produce their own Aelvesgold," I said.

"There *are* stories about creatures of that sort," Soheila said, turning to Liz. "Do you think . . . ?"

"Those stories have never been proven," Liz replied, her eyes wide.

"What stories?" I demanded. "What are you two talking about?"

"Elves," Soheila replied in a hushed voice, looking anxiously around the room. I recalled Liam's cryptic reference to elves when we were in Faerie.

"Liam told me that they had been destroyed for trying to take over Faerie."

"Some believe that they became monsters in their banishment—creatures who hate the fey and humans alike."

"*Nephilim.*" Liz and Soheila whispered the word together.

"I thought Nephilim were fallen angels," I said.

"My people believed that the legend of the fallen angels came from the expulsion of the elves from Faerie," Soheila said.

"But those are only stories," Liz said nervously. "No one knows if the Nephilim exist. And if they did exist, surely not even the Grove would have anything to do with them."

"Unless they were offered an unlimited supply of Aelvesgold," I said.

Liz and Soheila exchanged a worried look. "That would indeed be a strong inducement. Nephilim and witches working together would make a powerful combination." Liz shuddered. "We must stop them. You must gain enough power to keep the door open. Will you transform again tonight?"

"Yes," I said, shivering with anticipation at the thought. "Duncan said he thought there was another shape that might be more effective. It will also give us a chance to look out for Lorelei. We'll have to do something about her, but we have to find her first."

"I've been thinking about that," Liz said. "It's possible she's sought sanctuary with her daughter."

"Her daughter? Aren't all her children in Faerie . . . ?" But then I realized who she meant. "Lura?"

Liz and Soheila nodded.

"We were all surprised when Lorelei, after laying her eggs, gave birth to a human child," Liz told me. "It may have been because Sullivan Trask was a witch. But witch or no, Sullivan wasn't able to keep Lorelei from going back to Faerie, and then we all felt bad for Lura when Lorelei abandoned her. Lura was an awkward child, clumsy as a fish on dry land. We were happy for her, though, when she got engaged. During the Depression she rented out rooms to fishermen to make ends meet—the house was still presentable then—and one of them that summer was a painter from over in Ulster County named Quincy Morris, here sketching the woods. We were all glad Lura had found someone and thought maybe someone with an artistic temperament might do all right by her. The wedding was planned for the first weekend in September. It was to be held in the old Fairwick Hotel on Main Street. People got to talking that it wasn't in a church, but we figured that was because the Church hasn't always been friendly to undines."

"Or succubi," Soheila added.

Liz nodded and continued her story. "On the day of the wedding, we all arrived at the hotel. It was done up in blues and greens like an underwater paradise. Lura's dress was cut from a moiré silk that shimmered like water and was embroidered with a thousand seed pearls. I was there when the message came from Quincy Morris's best man. He'd seen Quincy heading into the woods at dawn that morning and he hadn't heard from him since. Lura insisted the townspeople search the woods for Quincy, convinced that he'd had an accident, but it was clear to most of us that he'd gotten cold feet and cleared out."

"Poor Lura," Soheila said with a sigh that rippled through the room. "First she was abandoned by her mother, then she was left at the altar. She'd always been a bit moody, but she went crazy after that. Shut herself up in that old house and refused to let anyone in. She doesn't even come into town for food. She grows her own vegetables and fishes in the stream. Cuts her own wood and heats the whole house with a wood-burning stove. The Women's Club volunteers drop off packages of secondhand clothing and other essentials—sugar, coffee, flour—and one of us drives by regularly to make sure the packages get taken inside and there's smoke coming out of the chimney."

"She looked pretty fit when I saw her." I told them about finding the Aelvestone and how Lura dragged me out of the river and then lifted the back of my car.

"That much Aelvesgold would confer a tremendous amount of strength and power!" Liz gave me a curious look but refrained from asking why it had taken me this long to tell her about the stone. "I've heard that undines laid eggs of Aelvesgold with their young but I thought they always were absorbed by the time the young were fingerlings. Now we can have another circle for Brock. Can you bring the Aelvestone tomorrow?"

"Of course," I said. "I'll bring it today if you want. Right now. Why should we wait until tomorrow?"

Liz shook her head. "The circle is still recovering from the surge of power they experienced two days ago. Bring the stone tomorrow. That will impress the group. But remember, keep it carefully wrapped. In the long run, using too much Aelvesgold can deplete your power."

"And what about Lura?" I asked, anxious to deflect the conversation from the use I'd already made of the Aelvestone. "Do you think she's harboring Lorelei?"

Soheila and Liz looked at each other. "It's hard to say," Liz said. "Lorelei never seemed to have much maternal affection for the girl."

"And Lura would have ample reason to resent Lorelei abandoning her," Soheila added. "But still, we should check." The two women looked at each other again. I imagined neither of them relished the idea of approaching surly, inhospitable Lura, but Soheila finally heaved a gusty sigh. "I'll go," she said with a rueful smile. "At least I know what it feels like to be neither fish nor fowl."

SIXTEEN

I left Liz's office, relieved that I'd confessed my membership in the Grove and about the Aelvestone but more uneasy than ever about the threat the Grove posed to Fairwick and the horrible consequences if they were successful in closing the door. I couldn't imagine not having Diana living across the street. If Liz chose to leave with her, what would become of the college? I'd just begun to feel at home in Fairwick, but what kind of home would it be if my friends left? As I left campus, I thought about ways of keeping the door open even if the Grove tried to close it. I mentally flipped through the spells I'd read in Wheelock yesterday. There had been spells to make someone fall in love or fall out of love, spells to make a baby or to keep from having a baby, spells to find something that had been lost or to hide something so no one would ever find it, spells to make money or cause an enemy misfortune. But nothing about keeping a door open. By the time I got home, the energy I had felt earlier had faded. Instead, I was headachy and tired.

When I opened the front door, a slip of paper that had been stuck in the doorframe came loose and drifted to the floor. It was a note from Bill. He'd fixed the missing tiles on the roof and tomorrow was going to start replastering the ceilings that had been damaged by the leaks. He'd noticed that my gutters needed cleaning and had taken care of that. As I looked around the foyer, I saw that he'd picked up the mail and put it neatly on the foyer table. Upstairs, I discovered that he'd swept up the plaster dust that had fallen from the ceilings and mopped the floors in the hall and my bedroom. I turned on the tap for the bathtub and discovered there was plenty of hot water.

While the bath was filling, I sat down at my desk and picked up Wheelock. I looked through the index for door-opening spells, but found only a ward to bar your door from intruders and a whole section on threshold gnomes that was fascinating (apparently their function as guardians went back to a treaty made in Prague in the fourteenth century), but that wasn't helpful in keeping the door to Faerie open. Most of the spells about doors had to do with keeping people from coming through them, not keeping them open.

While I was flipping through the book I came across a section on correlative spells. There was something I'd been trying to remember about them last night when Duncan was explaining how to shapeshift. I reread the section carefully.

The most powerful—and dangerous—form of correlative magic is when a witch creates a bond between herself and the object or person she wishes to control . . . *

The sound of lapping water interrupted my reading. Crap! The bathtub was overflowing. That was all I needed after the water damage the house had already suffered. I rushed into the bathroom, turned off the tap, and unplugged the drain to let out some water. The water felt deliciously hot. I'd finish reading Wheelock later. I undressed and got into the tub, sinking gratefully up to the nape of my neck. I felt all the sore spots from last night's run through the woods untensing. I closed my eyes and leaned my head against the cool porcelain rim of the tub.

There was something in that passage about correlative spells that could be useful . . . but I felt myself drifting, my body weightless in the warm water, a warmth that surrounded me like liquid sunshine . . . or like the fluid Aelvesgold that had wrapped around me when Liam and I had made love in Faerie. Behind my closed eyelids I summoned the image of Liam as he'd appeared to me there, his skin golden and glowing. I pictured him moving above me, the gold light limning his body, but leaving his face in shadow. I couldn't quite bring his face into focus, but I felt his body stirring the liquid Aelvesgold between us and I remembered how the golden light had entered me before he had. Just as the warm water seemed to be moving over me now, caressing my breasts, stirring between my legs . . . I spread my legs to let the water inside me. I arched my hips and felt it move against me in a wave. A wave that had fingers and a mouth. I gasped as the water caressed me and the image of Liam, his face still in shadow, pressed his mouth against mine. My mouth was flooded with the hot, syrupy sweetness of his tongue. I drew it into me just as I drew in the wave of warmth between my legs. He rocked into me so hard, filling me so completely, that I sank beneath him. I would have gasped but his mouth was locked on mine, sucking my tongue, my lips, the very breath out of my lungs.

We were both sinking, our legs wrapped around each other, our mouths locked, our bodies rocking to the rhythm of the ocean's tide. I opened my eyes and saw his hair spread out in a dark corona around his head, his aquamarine eyes staring wide into mine . . .

Liam didn't have blue eyes. Who was this man? A fantasy? Or some creature made out of water and Aelvesgold fucking me into a watery grave? I bit down on his lip and, startled, his head snapped back. Not Liam, but someone else I recognized. Duncan Laird. He smiled at me and opened his mouth . . . and a small crayfish crawled out.

I tried to scream but only sucked in water. I thrashed against Duncan—or the creature that had taken his face—but he only tightened his hold on me and pushed himself deeper inside me. Deeper than any man could go. The thing that was inside me wasn't a man. It had a life of its own, snaking deep into my womb, and to my horror and dismay I was still rocking against it. Even as I struggled to get free, even as I knew I was drowning, I was still arching my hips again and again, meeting each thrust with a thrust of my own and finally, with a last push, I felt my limbs—and his—loosening in an orgasm that released shockwaves through the water . . .

. . . and brought me up into the air, gasping, clutching the rim of my tub, in my bathroom.

"What the hell?" I cried out in the echoing, tiled room. But I was alone. The floor was soaked with water, and the porcelain inside of the tub, when I ran my hand along it, was coated with gold glitter.

The worst thing, I decided after rubbing my skin raw with towels and drinking three cups of hot tea to get warm, was that it had been Duncan's face in my drowning-by-sex dream. Because clearly there were only two possible reasons: either I was sexually attracted to him or he was trying to hurt me. I wasn't sure which suspicion was more disturbing. I knew I should have been more disturbed by the thought that I'd imagined my tutor trying to drown me, but it actually bothered me more to think that I was attracted to him. Sure, he was handsome, but I'd just made love to Liam three days ago. How could I be attracted to someone else so soon? Even if I didn't love Liam, he'd saved my life twice in Faerie. It seemed fickle—if not downright slutty—to be having dreams about Duncan after knowing him for less than twenty-four hours. Besides, I wasn't sure I *was* attracted to him. I'd flinched when he'd touched me last night.

By the time Duncan knocked at my door, I was hopped up on caffeine and my skin was pink from the two extra showers I'd taken (I wouldn't be taking any baths for a while). I was wearing jeans, a black turtleneck and a sweater, and I still felt cold. When I opened the door, though, and saw him—dressed in a body hugging black T-shirt and black jeans, the last evening light glancing off his high cheekbones and turning his blue eyes to aquamarine—I felt a surge of electrical sizzle inside. It must be attraction, I realized with dismay. Seeing someone who had tried to drown me wouldn't make me go all warm and fuzzy.

My face mustn't have looked so good to him.

"What happened?" he asked, his eyes locked on mine (*the way his mouth had locked on mine* . . .). He grasped my arm and pulled me closer. His touch, even through my sweater and turtleneck, stirred that fizzy current inside me. "You look . . ."

"Awful?" I asked weakly.

"No, actually you look amazing, like you're lit up from inside. But you're dressed for subarctic temperatures in June and you're still shivering."

"I am?" I held out my hand and saw that it was indeed trembling. But I didn't feel cold anymore. I felt warm and tingly. I peeled off the sweater and stepped back to let him in. "This old house," I said. "The temperature's always fluctuating. You wouldn't believe my heating bills last winter. Do you want some tea? Or a glass of wine? Or Scotch? I think there's still some scotch from when Liam lived here . . ."

I kept up a steady babble as I led him into the library to the cabinet where Liam had kept his scotch. There was an open bottle on the shelf. Duncan touched my hand as I reached for it and I flinched so hard I knocked over the bottle. He caught it before a drop could spill.

"Sit down," he barked.

Startled by the force of his command, I sank down on the couch.

"Before you hurt yourself," he added more gently. He brought the bottle and two glasses to the couch, placed them on the coffee table, and sat next to me. He poured an inch of the amber liquid into each glass. I watched, mesmerized by the way the liquid caught the light. No wonder Liam had always drunk scotch—it looked like liquid Aelvesgold.

"What's wrong with me?" I asked as Duncan handed me the glass. My hand was shaking so badly I could hardly hold it. He wrapped his hand around mine and guided it to my mouth. I took a long sip. When I lowered the glass, my hand was steadier.

"Sometimes Aelvesgold has this effect on new witches. Tell me what happened."

I told him about the dream, looking down into my glass the whole time, nervously swirling the scotch around the bottom. I told him I couldn't see the man's face.

"But you thought this man was your incubus . . . Liam?" he asked when I was done.

I gave the scotch a clockwise swirl. "Um, yes, at first . . . but then when I saw his face, it wasn't him." I took a sip in mid-swirl and got a mouthful.

"Did you recognize who it was?"

I swooshed the scotch counterclockwise and looked up. Into the same aquamarine eyes I'd seen in my dream. I felt myself gravitating toward those eyes. "It was you," I said.

"Oh," he said. "*Oh*. That's . . ."

"Embarrassing?" I suggested, shaking my glass at him. "Mortifying?"

"I was going to say *flattering*, but I guess that's from my perspective. You do know why you saw my face, don't you?"

I raised my glass for another gulp of scotch, but he touched my hand and made me lower the glass. He covered my hand with his, steadying it. A warm tingling current flowed through my hand, up my arm, and into my chest. I tried to remember if this was how I'd felt when Liam had touched me for the first time.

"It's because I'm your guide. Aelvesgold can grant visions, but often those visions are confusing. That's why it's important to have a mentor. Your subconscious superimposed my face on your dream lover to remind you that you weren't alone in this. You have someone to guide you." He squeezed my hand and the warmth in my chest expanded throughout my body.

"But what was the vision trying to show me?" I asked. "I mean, it seemed to be trying to *drown* me."

"You mean *I* was trying to drown you, don't you?"

I nodded, my throat thickening at the memory.

"That's because I am taking you to places with the Aelvesgold that you're afraid to go. Part of you senses that you'll have to face who you really are, witch or fey. You've got both in you, but which is stronger? Which side will you pledge allegiance to?"

"Do I have to choose?" I asked. "I thought Fairwick was the place where witch and fey lived together in peace."

He laughed. "More like an uneasy alliance. And that alliance will be cracked in two if the Grove closes the door. I think your dream was partly a result of that anxiety."

"I guess I can see that," I admitted. "I have been feeling edgy lately, torn between my promises to my grandmother and the Grove and my loyalties to my friends at Fairwick. But why would the vision try to drown me?"

"Oh, that's because you've got a water witch in your house."

"A . . . ?"

"Look down."

I looked down into my glass. Although I'd stopped swirling the scotch a minute ago and Duncan was holding my hand steady, the liquid was still moving in circles.

"Something's controlling the water in your home. And I'm pretty sure we know who that is."

"Lorelei."

"Yes. Now drink up. Once she's strong enough, she'll come for you. You'd better have all *your* strength by then."

"Are you telling me that Lorelei sent me that dream?" I asked Duncan a half hour later as we walked into the woods. "Because . . . *ew*!"

"Not the content of the dream," he assured me, flashing me a grin. In his dark clothes, all I could see of him were his teeth and eyes, which caught the reflection of the moon. "*That* was the Aelvesgold, I'm fairly sure. But I believe the drowning part was the water witch. The water took on the shape of your dream and tried to drown you."

"I thought a water witch was a forked stick dowsers used to find water."

"Wheelock lists three definitions of 'water witch' in his glossary. One is indeed what you describe, but there's an older kind of water witch, a creature who can control the flow of water, who can summon rain from the sky, make rivers flow backward, or turn the ocean tides." His pale hands moved like moths in the darkness as he waved them in the air between us. "A water witch can move any kind of water—from a glassful to an ocean. Lorelei can't get into your house because it's warded . . ."

"I haven't placed any wards on it!"

"Someone has—probably your handyman Brock. Unfortunately, with him unconscious, the wards aren't as strong. Lorelei is looking for ways in, and the most direct route for her is water. She's reaching into your home—and into your mind—through her most familiar element."

"No wonder everything's been leaking," I said angrily, batting a branch out of the way. "The bitch. When I think of the plumbing bill . . . We have to find her. Liz and Soheila thought she might be hiding out at Lura's house." While I explained that Lura was Lorelei's daughter, Duncan listened, but his voice sounded impatient when he replied.

"Even if Lorelei's hiding there during the day, she won't be there tonight. She'll be hunting. We have to find her before she finds her prey."

I was surprised by the anger in his voice. "And if we do find her," I asked, "what will we do with her?"

Duncan stopped and turned to me. We'd come to a clearing where the moonlight wasn't blocked by the trees.

He tilted his head and stared at me. I was distracted by the way the moonlight sculpted Duncan's cheekbones. He *was* a handsome man. It would be natural for me to feel attracted to him, but I still wasn't sure that's what I felt. Right now I felt chilled.

"I think you know what we must do," he said.

"We can't kill her!" I hissed. "She's—well, she's a nasty

piece of work, but she's only doing what comes naturally to her."

Duncan nodded. "Your compassion is admirable, but misplaced. What do you plan to do—ask her politely to please return to Faerie?" he asked, but then lifted a peremptory hand to silence me. "Listen," he said.

At first I heard only the breeze rustling the leaves in the trees, but then I made out a low throaty trill riding the night air.

Ooooh lu lu lu
Ooooh lu lu oooh

Looking west toward the sound, I saw nothing.

"Turn around," Duncan whispered. "He's thrown his voice to fool you."

I turned and looked east, where a half moon hung in the branches of a white pine. At first I only saw the feathery branches outlined against the moon, but then one of those branches moved and acquired tufted horns and yellow eyes.

"A great horned owl," Duncan said with pride, as if he'd conjured it himself. "I was hoping for one. It's the strongest and smartest of the owls. Look at his eyes. Do you feel the Aelvesgold in your blood pulled by them?"

"Yes." What I didn't say was that they reminded me of Duncan's eyes and the pull they'd had on me in my dream. As I stared at the owl, he bowed to us, hooting a long-drawn-out cry as if releasing the sound through the movement of his body.

Duncan bowed back, sweeping both arms out in a graceful swoop. In the moonlight, his shadow swirled around him like a cape. I imitated the motion. When I swept my arms out I felt the air moving over my skin, raising goosebumps on my flesh. When I lifted my head and met the owl's eyes again, my skin bristled—from the nape of my neck down my spine to my tailbone. The owl called again. *Whoooo are youuuu?* It seemed to ask.

"*Kay-lex,*" I answered, my name becoming a series of clicks in the back of my throat. I bowed again, feeling my arms rise weightlessly on the breeze and my tailbone lengthen. My whole body was weightless. When I lifted my head this time, I saw that the owl's eyes were not the only things glowing in the forest. Each branch and pine needle was tipped with moonlit white gold—another shade of Aelvesgold. Duncan had said the Aelvesgold inside me drew more Aelvesgold to it like a magnet. I was in control. I would find Lorelei and *compel* her to return to Faerie. How could she resist this much magic flowing through me?

I opened my mouth and let out a long, strange call. I heard an answering call beside me. I swiveled my head—how wonderfully flexible my neck had become! I would never need a chiropractor again!—and met Duncan's azure eyes. Now they were set in the face of a great horned owl. He stretched out his wings and lifted off the ground. I raised my arms—now wings so long and strong I felt I could touch the moon—then swooped them down and felt myself rise on the night air into the trees. I would have gone higher, but Duncan's voice in my head called for me to land beside him on a branch. I settled beside him, tucking my wings in and swiveling my head around to check that we were alone. We were. The other owl had flown away.

Listen, Duncan said, *do you hear the water?*

I twisted, bobbed, and dipped my head, twitching my ears toward a faint sound threading through the branches. One of my ears was higher than the other and, by positioning my head just right, I could not only hear the faintest sounds, but could tell exactly how far away they were. Yes, I heard running water. Thirty feet southeast of us.

That's the Undine. We'll follow it south through the woods. I'll take the east side, you take the west. If you see anything, call out.

I hooted a reply. Words seemed superfluous in this sound-rich, moonlit world. Not only could I hear every branch-creak and leaf-sway, I could see through the darkness as though it were day. Duncan hooted back and launched himself off the branch. I couldn't hear him moving as he glided in between the trees. His enormous wings silently rode the wind. Then I couldn't see him either. He had vanished into the thickly intertwined branches.

I had a pang of human fear. I was about to dive into the dark woods. Jen Davies had told me that the fey were flocking to Fairwick to be ready to return to Faerie if the door was closing. From deep inside me, I sensed that there were many otherworldly creatures in the woods, lurking in its shadows. That place inside me seemed to call to them—as if it *knew* them. Lorelei was not the only monster in these woods.

A breeze ruffled my feathers and I heard the sough of wind through the branches. My feathers *itched* to take flight. I stretched out my wings and plunged headlong into the woods.

SEVENTEEN

I followed the silver thread of the Undine south through the woods, the same path I'd followed with Liz, Soheila, and Diana only three days ago. I remembered slogging through the underbrush, pushing thorny vines out of the way, and swatting insects. Now I soared smoothly through the sky, effortlessly threading through low-hanging limbs. Not only could I clearly see where the limbs were, I *felt* them blocking the flow of air. All I had to do was follow the wind. I remembered that Soheila had told me once that the first incarnation she had taken as a wind spirit had been an owl. I understood why now. I was a *master* of the wind! I was faster than the deer that ran beneath me. Faster even than the beautiful doe and the great stag I'd seen last night, who looked up at me with fear when I swooped low over their heads. I was *master* of the forest, too!

I dipped up and down on my great silent wings, my eyes taking in every detail of the forest floor. I saw every twig and leaf, every field mouse in the underbrush and tadpole in the stream. I felt as if my eyes were truly open for the first time in my life. Was this my power unblocked? I felt stronger than I ever had before and . . . *unfettered.* Not just by the bounds of gravity, but also by the qualms of conscience I'd felt moments ago over Lorelei's fate. She had threatened me and hurt me. She was my prey. When I found her, I'd swoop down on my silent wings and dig my talons into her slimy flesh. We'd see who ate whom.

But first I'd have to find her. It made sense that she'd be near the water, but as I sailed through the woods I realized that the Undine wasn't the only water in the forest. My new eyes, which seemed to turn night into day, spotted flashes of water everywhere. Springs bubbled up from beneath rocks, still pools were scattered like silver coins under the trees, swampy marshland stood in the low places. As much water as I saw, though, I could *hear* even more. It was percolating deep below the earth in hollow caverns and running in underground streams. The whole forest was a honeycomb channeling water through a thousand secret passageways.

And the streams were full of plump trout, their gills iridescent with Aelvesgold. My mouth watered at the sight of them. It took all my willpower not to dive down and spear one with my sharp talons and tear into its raw flesh.

It would have been easy. Where springs bubbled up into pools, the trout hovered in the currents, transfixed. Easy prey. At one of these pools I found a fisherman standing knee-deep in the water, casting his line. I landed silently in an oak tree above him and observed. He wore rubber waders and a flannel shirt (big surprise!). His hair was cut short, exposing the meaty nape of his neck. When he drew back his arm to cast, I caught a glimpse of his face. His full lips were pursed with concentration, soft blond down grew over his plump cheeks . . . I recognized him. He was the young man from the diner who'd been chowing down on an Angler's Special with his father and grandfather. The Stewarts, the waitress had called them. Apparently the stories his grandfather had told him about fishing the Undine hadn't deterred him from trying it. I soon saw why.

Within seconds of my landing on the branch, young Stewart was reeling in a huge trout. I clenched the branch with my talons to keep from stealing it out of his hand. He had plenty! His creel was full. I inhaled the smell of fresh fish . . . and something *less* fresh. A smell like spoiled sardines that was oddly familiar . . .

A splash in the water drew my attention away. I swiveled my head and cocked one ear toward the sound. It had come from the far bank of the pool. I trained my eyes on the bank and saw nothing . . . but then I noticed strange ripples in the water: a V-shaped pattern trailing streamers, heading straight toward young Stewart.

Stewart was too intent on his catch to notice the disturbance in the water. He took the hook out of the fish's mouth, then slid it into his creel, trying to find room for it among the other fish, swearing when his new catch slipped from his fingers and landed in the water. He bent over to retrieve it . . . and a slim white hand broke the water's surface and grabbed hold of his wrist. A puzzled look overtook his bland, plump face, and then the hand yanked and he toppled headfirst into the river.

I let out a screech and dove, talons out. I grabbed the collar of the young man's shirt and pulled back, my wings beating the air. It was enough to bring his head and arms out of the water. He thrashed and sputtered, windmilling his arms, very nearly clocking me. I let go to get out of his way. A head rose out of the water beside Stewart, a head with long streaming hair, fish-belly-white skin, and malevolent green-black eyes: *Lorelei*. When Stewart saw her, he screamed and tried to backpedal away, but he tripped and fell backward into the water. Lorelei no longer seemed to care about the fisherman. Her eyes were fastened on me.

"You!" Lorelei screeched. "Interfering again. What's the matter? Can't you find a man of your own?"

In answer, I dove straight at her, talons fully extended. At the last second, she ducked and evaded my attack. My claws grasped a hank of her hair and ripped it out. She screeched and flailed her arms, reaching for my wingtips. I beat the air backward to evade her grasp, and landed on a branch just above her head.

Lorelei snarled and snapped her teeth at me. "So now you've become a hunter, Doorkeeper." Through her defiance, I heard the fear in her voice. It made me hungrier for her blood. I spread my wings out for another attack and her eyes widened. "Keep your prize. I like my meat fresh and this one's nearly dead."

As I dove, she plunged into the pool in a great wave. My claws grasped only water. I could just make out her long, sinuous white body cleaving the black water, and then she vanished in a flash of light. I felt an urge to follow her, but then I recalled what she'd said about young Stewart. I swiveled my neck and saw that he was still lying on the muddy bank. The water level had risen above his head. He'd drown if I didn't do something. I flew over him and snagged his shirt collar in my talons, dragging him backward. It was hard work: he was a big guy, his sopping clothes and rubber waders adding weight. I got him halfway out and then cocked my head to his chest to listen for breathing. Even my acute owl senses couldn't pick up any.

I gave one more screech and then I willed myself back into human form. I tilted back the young fisherman's head to clear his airway and struck his chest, once, twice, three times. Opening his mouth, I winced at the reek of chewing tobacco, but still I blew in. I repeated the procedure until he heaved and spit pond water in my mouth. I spat, wiped my mouth, and sat back on my heels to watch him cough and retch, unsure what else I should do but not feeling right about leaving him. It was too late to try to follow Lorelei anyway. Besides, now that I was in human form, my bloodlust had dissipated.

When he'd finished coughing up water, I patted him on the back and, not sure what else to say, said, "Thataboy. It's okay."

He turned and stared at me, his eyes going round as marbles and then going up and down. *Crap.* I was naked. I started to cross my arms over my breasts, but then thought *Heck, what's the point?* Covering myself at this stage seemed kind of cringing and undignified.

"You!" he gasped. Was he about to faint? Or attack me? He might think I was the one who'd tried to pull him underwater. "You!" he spluttered again, staring at me wide-eyed as he painfully pulled himself into a sitting position. "You are the most beautiful woman I have ever seen in my entire life!"

I snorted pond water out my nose. The guy was . . . what? Nineteen? He lived on a farm with his father and grandfather. How many naked women could he have ever seen?

"Thank you," I said, wiping my nose. "That's nice of you . . ."

"I mean it! You're more beautiful than . . ." He creased his brow, clearly trying to think of beautiful women of his acquaintance. "Angelina Jolie!"

I laughed again. He *was* kind of cute. "Well, I don't know about that, but again, thank you. I'm just glad you didn't drown. You know, you really shouldn't fish here."

His eyes went even wider. "Are you the Lady of the Lake? Did I break a rule so you had to punish me?"

"No! Or . . . er . . . yes!" I straightened my spine and

shook out my hair. "I am the Lady of the Lake," I intoned in a deep, sonorous voice. I used a little bit of what I'd learned as an owl to make my voice echo-ey. "I protect these woods and streams. Tell all your friends that no one should come fishing here. Or else!"

"Or else what?"

"Um . . . or else they'll feel my wrath!"

He furrowed his brow again. "But you saved me," he said.

"Only so you could spread the word. Next time I won't be so lenient."

"You've got feathers in your hair." He leaned closer to me, not at all cowed by my act. "Hey, you're not the Lady of the Lake, are you?"

I slumped, disappointed at myself for not being able to pull it off. Angelina Jolie would have. "Okay, you got me."

"You're an owl princess!" he said, plucking a feather from my hair. "You're one of those animals that turn into beautiful women. My nana told me stories of your kind—selkies and swan maidens."

I sighed. I would get the one fisherman raised on animal-bride tales. "I'm not an owl princess."

"You are! And I've got your feather, which means you gotta come with me and be my wife."

I punched him in the arm. "That's the thanks I get for saving your life?"

"Ow!" he said, rubbing his arm and looking hurt. "You don't want to marry me?"

"Sorry, but no. Not that you're not a perfectly nice young man . . . um . . ."

"MacKenzie Stewart, but my friends call me Mac. I just got my associates degree in ag business from SUNY Cobleskill. I'm a partner in my family's dairy farm. I'm going to turn the whole thing organic. You should like that, being a bird and all . . . Oh, gosh, we do raise chickens, though. We could go free-range if that would make it better . . . and I guess I could become a vegetarian . . ." His brow creased again, no doubt wondering if I was worth giving up Big Macs. ". . . or maybe you don't mind eating meat, you being a carnivorous bird."

I looked at Mac's eager face and sighed. Poor guy. He must not meet many girls who wanted to come live on the family farm. He seemed willing to do about anything for me. "Thank you, Mac. I'm flattered, but I'm sure you'll find a nice human girl . . . as long as you stay out of these woods!" I added in my Lady-of-the-Lake voice.

"Yes, ma'am," he said, cowed at last. *Ma'am?* Would he have called Angelina Jolie *ma'am*? "But I wish there was something I could do to repay you for saving my life. Can I do some . . . heroic deed, or something?"

"Yes," I said, shivering. "You can give me your shirt."

I walked back toward home in Mac Stewarts's flannel shirt, which thankfully came down to my knees and only smelled a little of cheap cologne and man-sweat. I followed the stream back, keeping my eyes and ears open for Duncan, sorry I no longer had the vision and hearing of an owl. The woods felt darker and denser, as if the trees had moved a few inches closer to one another and were readying themselves to pounce on me. I called Duncan's name, my voice frail in comparison to the powerful hoot of the owl. *I* felt frail. As an owl I'd felt as if something had opened up inside of me, but I no longer felt that channel of power. Instead I was depleted, weaker than ever. When I reached my backyard, I didn't need any special powers to find Duncan Laird. He was sprawled out naked across my back steps, the gash on his chest black against his human flesh.

I let out a cry that could have been the hoot of an owl for her wounded mate and ran to him. His eyes were closed, but when I knelt beside him and touched his arm he stirred and moaned. His eyes flicked open, revealing a slit of glittering blue.

"Cal . . ." he managed, his voice sounding like the croak of a frog.

"What happened? What did this to you?" I touched the edge of the gash on his chest and he moaned. There were fainter scratches in his skin, which looked like they had been made with claws.

"An undine . . ." he said. "Not Lorelei . . . another . . . one . . ."

"I knew it couldn't have been Lorelei, because I was with her." A loud moan interrupted this thought. I could tell him what had happened to me later. "Should I take you to the hospital?"

"They wouldn't be able . . . to treat *this*," he muttered, turning slightly to the side. I gasped at the sight of his back. It was scored with slash marks.

"I'll get Diana," I said. "She'll know what to do . . . or Liz . . ."

"No," he said, grabbing my wrist. His grip was surprisingly strong for a wounded man. "You can do it . . . You have the power of the Aelvesgold in you. Just . . ." He looked anxiously toward the edge of the woods. "Just . . . help me inside."

I put his arm around my shoulders and got him to his feet, then realized I should have opened the door first. But Duncan held out his hand and the door flew open. "You still have so much power," I said, ushering him through the door, "even though you're hurt."

He stumbled over the threshold and we both nearly crashed

to the kitchen floor. "Not so . . . much," he croaked with a strangled laugh. "But you . . . you have all the power I need."

I tightened my grip on his waist, noticing in spite of myself how firm his muscles were and how warm his bare skin. In the library I settled him on the couch, pulling an afghan over him to spare his modesty . . . or mine, I supposed. He was probably in too much pain to think about being naked in front of me, but I was going to have to concentrate, and Duncan Laird's naked body was . . . distracting, to say the least. Apparently I wasn't the only one who was distracted. When I knelt beside him on the couch I caught him staring down the opening of my flannel shirt where a button had come loose. "Where did you get this?" he asked, fingering the worn fabric.

"From a fisherman named Mac," I said, rolling my eyes. "Long story. I'll tell you all about it after . . . What *am* I supposed to do, Duncan? Tell me! You're losing blood!"

He smiled weakly and took my hand. A heat flash moved straight from my hand into the core of my body as if he'd touched me . . . somewhere intimate.

"The Aelvesgold in your body is reacting to mine," he said. "You can use it to perform a binding spell on my wounds." He guided my hand over the deepest gash, the one on his chest, holding it barely an inch above his flesh. "Concentrate on the heat between us."

I blushed again. There *was* heat between us, and not just of the Aelvesgold variety, but I tried to concentrate on the Aelvesgold right now. I felt the warmth of his torn flesh radiating just below my palm and the pulse in his wrist above mine. As I focused on the heat, it grew and spread. He moved my hand slightly, in a small circular motion, and the heat moved with it. I *saw* it now: a syrupy red-gold light, like the liquid Aelvesgold Liam had moved across my body when we'd made love in Faerie. Only this light was stained red, perhaps because Duncan was wounded.

Duncan slowly guided my hand along the length of the gash in his chest while the viscous light coated the edges of his wound. He winced once and I stopped, but he grimaced and told me to go on, saying it only hurt because I was binding the skin. I nodded, and focused my energy on directing the Aelvesgold into his flesh. As I did, I felt the Aelvesgold building in me as well. Every inch of my skin prickled with energy. The rough couch upholstery was like sandpaper on my thighs; the flannel shirt rubbing against my breasts made my nipples harden.

Duncan took my other hand and, moving the afghan, guided it to a long gash on his thigh. Gold threads sprung from my fingertips and interlaced across his body between my hands, weaving a criss-cross pattern over his skin.

"This is different from when you bound my wounds," I whispered, looking into his eyes. "It's . . ." I faltered when I saw how he was looking at me. His eyes burned with desire. I felt its pull as I'd felt the pull of the gold threads of Aelvesgold in the woods, connecting me to everything. He reached out to stroke my face. As his hand passed across the table he knocked over the glass of scotch I'd left on the table earlier. Its smoky aroma jarred me with a memory of Liam. I pulled away, breaking the connection between Duncan and me. Sparks flew into the air, cascading over the couch, burning holes in the upholstery. One landed on Duncan's bare skin and he cried out in pain.

"I'm sorry," I said, leaping up to put out the smoking cinders. "I guess I'm not ready . . ."

Duncan seized both my hands in his and gazed deeply into my eyes.

"It's all right, Callie. I didn't mean to rush you. I didn't realize you were still attached to the incubus."

"I'm not!" I objected.

Wordlessly, Duncan turned my hands over and held up my palms. An intricate network of golden spirals was inscribed on my skin. They looked like the Celtic knotwork designs in the margins of the Book of Kells—an ancient script of magic.

"These are wards," Duncan said. "Internal wards to protect you from unwelcome advances. They mean your heart is spoken for."

EIGHTEEN

J think I would know if I were in love," I objected, seating myself on the chair opposite the couch and pulling the flannel shirt over my knees. "The whole problem with Liam was that I *wasn't* in love with him. If I had been, then he would have become fully human."

"I didn't say you loved him," Duncan said, leaning back on the couch and arranging the afghan over his chest like the folds of a Roman toga. "I said your heart *belonged* to him. He must have bound you to him. He doesn't want you to love anyone else."

"No, he wouldn't . . ." I began, but then I recalled what he'd said in my dream about the threads of Aelvesgold linking true lovers. Had that been his way of telling me that we were bound together?

"The bastard," I swore. "He might as well have put a chastity belt on me."

Duncan looked at me curiously. "So you don't want to be bound to him?"

"I most certainly do not! I want to make up my own mind about loving him . . ." Too late I realized what that sounded like. Duncan looked away from me, something flickering darkly in his eyes—disappointment, I guessed, although it looked almost like anger.

"So you're really not sure how you feel about him." He started to get up, remembered he was naked under the afghan, and cast a spell that conjured clothes—tightly fitting jeans, a soft white shirt, and a black leather jacket. The perfect outfit to make me sorry that he was going. He winced as he adjusted his shoulders under the jacket.

"I haven't healed your back," I objected, following him to the door.

"My wounds will heal," he said with a wry smile, "probably faster than your feelings for Liam will change."

"How can I know how I feel when I have these wards on me?" I asked. "Is there some way I can remove them?"

Duncan turned to me in the doorway. The porch light shining through the red pane in the fanlight cast a ruby streak across his face, making him look like a savage in war paint. "Do you really want them gone?" he asked.

"Yes," I said.

He nodded.

"They can be removed the same way as the wards that are blocking your power can be removed. Through transformative magic."

"But that hasn't worked," I objected.

"It *is* working," he said. "You felt the power tonight when you were an owl, didn't you?"

"I did, but then it faded."

"But you were still strong enough to heal me. And the fact that Liam's wards are visible is a sign that you are growing powerful enough to shed them. One more transformation and you'll be strong enough to break through them all."

He leaned toward me. I felt the wards flare up on my skin,

but I clenched my fists and willed them down, long enough for Duncan Laird to place a chaste kiss on my cheek. "See," he said, leaning back, "you're stronger than you think."

I was expecting the dream that night. Liam was there beneath the willow tree, wearing nothing but leaf shadow and honeyed sunlight, but I was dressed in a magnificent gown embroidered with a thousand golden spirals.

"Ah," he said, reaching for my hand. "You've found them!"

I snatched my hand away from him. "You branded me!" I hissed. Coils unwound from my sleeve like long supple snakes and hissed with me.

"It's not a brand," he said, holding up his hand to the rippling coils. "It's the history of our lovemaking written on your skin." The coils approached his hand tentatively, as if sniffing, and then slipped onto his hand and wound themselves around his wrist and forearm, twining themselves into golden patterns on his skin. As they traveled up his arm I felt a corresponding tug on my arm pulling me toward him.

"You bound me to you!" I cried, pulling back, even in a dream determined not to give in to his seduction.

"I am equally bound," he replied, looping his arm in the air and wrapping a long skein of twisted thread around it. The dress made of coils unraveled as I fell to my knees by his side. The threads spread across his chest and I felt a corresponding tug in my own chest, a tightness coiling around my heart and tickling my bare breasts. My dress had vanished. Golden coils writhed on my bare skin. I knelt naked on the mossy bank beside Liam, entwined with him in a shimmering net of desire.

"Our desire," he whispered, crouching beside me, our knees touching. "When we make love, we create friction." He lifted his hand and held it, palm out, an inch above my skin. Gold tendrils quivered in the air between us. My nipples tingled and hardened. He lowered his hand to my navel and twirled his fingers. The spirals coiled back on themselves and formed a knot. There was a tightening in my core, a small knot of tension that felt . . . *good*.

"We can shape that heat and tension . . ." He moved his fingers and the spiral knot began to revolve. The warmth expanded and spread. I moaned. It felt delicious . . . so what if he was binding me to him . . .

"No!" I cried, grabbing his hand. As soon as our hands touched, the golden coils tightened, taut as violin strings. His eyes locked on to mine. He squeezed my hand and the knot inside me exploded. I came, gasping at the suddenness and force of the orgasm. Liam cried out at the same instant, his face suffused with golden light. The spirals around us unwound and snapped in the air, sputtering and sparking like loose electrical cables. As their energy rippled outward the air buckled and cracked with thunder and lightning.

"You are mine!" he cried.

"But you aren't really here," I sobbed, collapsing onto his chest, wanting the contact now as the heat from the coils began to fade.

"Aren't I?" he murmured into my neck. "Listen. Do you hear that?"

I heard thunder in the distance, the last reverberations of our stormy lovemaking. It was fading just as he was fading, vanishing in my arms just as he had when I'd banished him.

"That's me," he whispered, his voice now no more than a faint stir of the honeyed air. "I'm here."

My eyes flicked open. I was in my bed, alone, naked in a tangle of sundrenched sheets. I lifted my hand in front of my face and saw the golden spirals fading from my skin. My heart was pounding as if I'd just run a race . . . or made love all night to my incubus lover. It was so loud I thought I could hear it . . .

I'm here, he had said.

I sat up and listened. The pounding seemed to be coming from everywhere at once. From the air itself. I felt it deep inside, matching the beat of my heart.

I'm here, it said.

Where? I threw the sheets to the floor and stood up. My bare feet felt the pounding in the floorboards. It came from below. From the front door . . .

I nearly ran out of the room naked, but grabbed my damp and twisted nightgown off the floor and wrestled it over my head as I ran down the stairs.

I'm here! I'm here! The pounding was definitely coming from the front door. I stumbled into the foyer and lifted a trembling hand to the doorknob . . . and then hesitated.

If it really was Liam, did I want to let him in?

Yes! every inch of my skin screamed. *Yes!*

I turned the cold iron knob and flung open the door. Duncan Laird stood in the doorway. When he saw me in my thin nightgown, my hair wild, my skin glowing, his blue eyes widened and he smiled a slow, silky smile.

"It's you!" I cried.

"Were you expecting someone else?"

"Um . . . I . . ."

"Should I come back later?" His eyes were amused at my confusion.

"No! I just didn't expect you quite so early."

"I had something to tell you that I didn't think could wait, but . . . I can't really tell you out here."

"Oh!" I said. "Come in. I'm sorry. I was having a dream . . ."

"Was I trying to drown you again?" he asked as he came inside.

"No," I said, blushing. The heat on my skin made me aware of how close to naked I was. I grabbed a sweater from the hall closet and pulled it on over my nightgown. "You weren't in it."

Or had he been? *I'm here,* Liam had said in the dream, and then Duncan had appeared at the door. But Duncan couldn't be my incubus. Liz had carefully vetted him . . .

". . . and I thought you should know."

"Thought I should know what?" I asked, realizing I hadn't heard a thing he said.

"Grove members are arriving today in Fairwick."

"They're here early," I said, "The meeting isn't until Monday. We still have two days."

"I suppose they wanted to make a weekend of it." Duncan smiled wryly at the idea of anyone choosing to spend any more time in Fairwick than they had to. I had felt the same ten months ago, but now I was offended for my town. Perhaps sensing that, Duncan's smile faded. "Or maybe they know you're trying to increase your power and they're worried."

"Good," I said. "They should be worried."

Duncan smiled again, but guardedly. "I just don't want them to force you into a conflict prematurely. I thought I should warn you that they're here."

He touched my arm and I felt the gold spirals tightening inside me. I studied his face. The high cheekbones and strong jaw, the aquamarine eyes, skin the color of honey . . . Yes, he looked like a creature from another world, but was he *my* creature? Shouldn't I be able to look into his eyes and recognize him?

But I didn't. And when he dipped his head to mine and brushed his lips against my cheek, the spirals flared up in the air between us and singed the lock of hair that was always falling over his eyes.

"Damn," I said, "I'm so sorry. I don't know why . . ."

Duncan smiled, his jaw tight. "I think I do," he said. "As long as you're still bound to the incubus, no mortal man will be able to come close to you. It's your decision, Callie. I'll be here when you make it."

He turned and left. I watched him walk down the porch steps and toward the driveway, where I now noticed Bill's truck was parked. Had he just arrived . . . ? But then I spotted the ladder leaning against the side of the house and saw Bill climbing down from it. He reached the ground just as Duncan walked past him. As the two men nodded at each other I thought I saw the air between them sizzle, but it might have been a trick of sunlight. Bill, cap pulled low over his eyes, looked from Duncan to me. I was suddenly aware of what the scene looked like: Duncan leaving my house early in the morning, me standing in my flimsy nightgown and sweater in the doorway. I blushed.

I closed the front door—slammed it, really, in my frustration at myself. The panes of glass in the fanlight trembled with the impact. I looked up—into the stained-glass face that so resembled my incubus lover. His full lips and almond-shaped eyes seemed to mock me. *You are bound to me,* they seemed to say, *You will be mine forever. I will keep you in this house for all time.*

"Like Lura," I muttered as I stomped up the stairs, taking my anger out on the old, worn, and bowed stair treads, which creaked and groaned as if personally offended. Like Lura, who was moldering away in her decaying house because she'd been jilted by her fiancé. I'd live alone in this house while it fell apart around me, bound to a fantasy lover.

At the top of the stairs I turned to go down the hall to my

room, but paused outside of the door to the room that had been Liam's study in the brief time he'd lived here. I'd never cleaned his stuff out of my house. I had thought I'd recovered, but I'd never even gotten up the nerve to go into his room. If I really was over him, I should be able to.

I turned the doorknob, steeling myself for the sight of his desk, where he used to sit looking out the window to the street.

I paused, the door half-open. I recalled my dream from last night—the way Liam had made me come by just grasping my hand—and felt my knees go weak.

I opened the door . . . and froze on the threshold, stunned. The room was empty. The desk and chair Liam and I had bought together at an antiques market in the country were gone. The windowsill, which he'd lined with stones and bird's nests and pieces of wood, was bare. For a moment I suffered the vertiginous sensation that maybe Liam had never existed at all. I'd made him up. An incubus indeed! It sounded like the delusion of a crazy person.

But then another explanation occurred to me. In the weeks I'd raved in the shadows, while my friends sat watching me, someone had decided it would be a good idea to remove all trace of Liam from the house. So they had emptied the study. They probably told themselves that they were sparing poor hapless Callie any further heartache.

I was so overcome with rage that my vision blurred and I thought I might faint. I clenched the doorframe to steady my-self and noticed that my arm was glowing. Spirals and knots moved beneath my skin like a nest of angry snakes. My bonds, but also my protection. They were made out of my own power. I could let them control me or I could control them.

I straightened and stepped back into the hall. I held up both arms and splayed my fingers, willing the energy inside me to go out—all the hurt and anger, the disappointment and fear. Sparks sizzled off my fingertips, gold rays shot out of my hands. The spirals and knots inside me uncoiled. I felt them stretching within the boundaries of the house, from attic to basement. *No one will* ever *take something from my home again,* I swore. I closed my eyes and pulled the spirals back inside. *Or from* me *again.* The wards snapped back through my fingertips like a rubber band and coiled up inside me, hotter and more powerful for their walk on the outside. I felt like I'd swallowed the universe. It felt *good.*

NINETEEN

*T*en minutes later I left my house, dressed in tight black jeans, snug white T-shirt, and motorcycle boots, the Aelvestone tucked into my jeans pocket. I was going to rock that spell circle and bring back Brock. Then I was going to tell the Grove to go to hell. I was the doorkeeper. They weren't going to close *my* door. I was ready to take names and kick ass . . .

"Cal . . . leack?"

The voice from above, calling my name, stopped me short halfway across my lawn. I whirled around, prepared to face an avenging god ready to smite me for my hubris, but it was just Bill sitting on the edge of my roof. Of course, I chided myself; an avenging god would have known how to pronounce my name. I shaded my eyes with my hand to look up at him. He sat with the sun at his back; his face was under the brim of his cap in shadow so I couldn't see his expression, but his voice sounded concerned.

"Yes, Bill, is something wrong?"

"I was going to ask you the same thing. There was a lot of banging coming from inside."

I'd forgotten about Bill up on the roof while I was throwing around my wards. Thank goodness he hadn't been knocked off.

"Sorry about that," I said. "I was just . . . um . . . rearranging some old furniture."

"It sounded like you were throwing around the furniture," he said. "Was it that man who left before who you were angry at? He didn't hurt you, did he?"

I flushed with embarrassment, then anger at being made to feel embarrassed. Then Bill leaned forward and took his cap off, and I could make out deep brown eyes the color of warm chocolate. There wasn't a smidgen of judgment or censure in them, just concern.

"No, it wasn't Duncan. It's just . . . I had a bad breakup a few months ago," I said, not sure why I was confiding in him. "And I haven't been able to . . . move on. So I thought I'd clean house, so to speak."

"Oh," Bill said, his brown eyes looking thoughtful. "So you were angry because of how this ex-boyfriend treated you? Was he that bad?"

"He lied to me," I told Bill, compelled to honesty by the concern—and pain—in his eyes. I was betting that Bill had a bad breakup in his history, too. "And I was idiot enough to believe his lies. It's hard to trust anyone after that—it's hard to even trust myself."

"You weren't an idiot," Bill asserted with surprising conviction. "Your ex-boyfriend was. He'd have to have been to hurt you like that." He ducked his head back into the shadows, looking embarrassed, and put his baseball cap back on.

"It was a bit more complicated than that," I said, smiling up at him. "But thanks for the vote of confidence."

"Any time," he said. "If there's anything else . . ."

"Just be careful up there, Bill. I don't want you to get hurt."

As I turned to go I heard Bill say, "You too. Be careful."

. . .

I drove out of town, my fiery mood tempered by a few kind words from Bill. I'd left Brock's iPod plugged into the sound system so I turned it on. Kate Bush's voice filled the car, singing about something trapped beneath the ice. I'd always found the song haunting, but now it made me think of Brock's spirit struggling through the icy fogs of Niflheim. I hoped that today's circle would finally release him.

As I went up the long drive to the Olsen farm, I noticed how the house sat high on a hill above the surrounding countryside. When I got out of my car, I turned to admire the view. Fields of hay, corn, and fenced grassy pastureland spread out north as far as the outskirts of the village and south to a neighboring, smaller farm. I'd always thought of Brock and Ike as small businessmen, running the Valhalla nursery and doing odd jobs in town for extra money. I hadn't realized that they came from such a prosperous farming family. The Olsen farm must be one of the largest in the valley. It felt, standing here, as if it *commanded* the whole valley—not just its own fields and pastures, but the other small farms dotting the valley, the village to the north, and the dense woods that lay to the east.

I blinked and looked harder at the view. At the golden hay waving in the breeze and the deep emerald pastures. At the neat white fences and bright red barn. All glowing in the summer sunshine. But it wasn't the sun that made them glow. Everything, from each blade of grass in the meadows to the red paint on the barn, was glowing with golden light. And when I looked even harder, I saw rays of light coming from the fields and fences—delicate gold lines that formed an intricate pattern over the Olsen farm like a foil overlay on a book cover. A pattern that extended over all the farms in the valley, crossed Trask Road, and stopped at the edge of the woods.

"We can spin wards of protection across the farms and village, but not into the woods."

I turned around. Ike stood behind me, wearing jeans and the ubiquitous flannel shirt.

"How did you know I wasn't just admiring your farming techniques?"

"You've got so much Aelvesgold in you that you're disrupting the patterns. Look . . ."

I turned back, raising my hand to shield my eyes . . . and saw the net of golden threads ripple over the fields.

"You couldn't have that much Aelvesgold in you and not see the wards," he said.

"Am I hurting your . . . wards?"

"They're pretty resilient. The Norns reinforce them once a year, always the week leading up to the solstice. That's when all magic is at its strongest."

I looked again at the acres of intricate patterns. "It must be a lot of work."

"It is, but it's necessary. If not for the wards, the farms and the village would be open to the woods. Anything could come out of them."

Or get lost in them, I thought, remembering the fishermen who had gone missing in the woods. "How's Brock?" I asked.

A shadow passed over Ike's deeply furrowed brow. "I'm beginning to fear he'll never wake up. It's been four days. I don't know what we'll do if he's still unconscious when—I mean, *if* . . . the door closes."

"What do you mean?" I asked.

"I don't know whether I should bring him to Faerie or not. I don't know his wishes. He's very attached to Fairwick. Since we came here, he's seen himself as the guardian of the town. And I know he won't want to leave you here unprotected. But then, if Dory goes . . ."

"Dory is planning to go?" I asked, shocked and dismayed that she would think of leaving Fairwick. She was such a fixture of the town—a member of the Rotary Club and head of the library board. What would the town do without her? What would *I* do without her and all the other *good* neighbors? I felt a tug at my chest, as if someone had tightened a knot there.

Ike gasped. Looking out at the fields, I saw that the gold patterns were now quivering like live electrical wires.

"What happened?" I asked.

"It's your pain at the thought of your friends leaving." He looked at me strangely. "You're part of the pattern of Fairwick now. You feel the loss of all our good friends."

"Of course I do," I said, laying my hand over my heart. The knot hurt like a cramped muscle, but I had a feeling that it would hurt more if the knot weren't there. Then it would be only an empty place. "That's why we're not going to let them leave."

Ike gave me a hopeful smile and then turned to lead me around the side of the house. "We're outside today," he told me. "The Norns thought that the circle would be more powerful if it was held in the labyrinth."

"The labyrinth?"

"Yes, Brock built it some years ago for our amma so she could use it to meditate. It's always available for the circle, and for anyone who wishes to walk the labyrinth."

We passed through a wooden arbor covered with roses and followed a stone path bordered by hollyhocks, dahlias, and poppies toward a formal garden of neat boxwood hedges and parterres surrounding a circle marked out by sunken bricks. Brock lay on a bench at the center, his honest face looking as serene as if he were sunbathing instead of in a coma. The members of the circle were assembled around the perimeter, some sitting on the grass, a few standing. Moondance, regal in a flowing orange and purple caftan, greeted me by demanding what I had been doing. "The Norns say the wards have been disrupted."

"Sorry, I guess it's this." I took the Aelvestone out of my pocket and unwrapped it from the flannel cloth. Twelve heads leaned in to look at it.

"That's what made me drop a stitch before," Urd hissed.

"And tangled my thread," Verdandi said, holding up a knot of multicolored embroidery thread.

"Yeah, my screen crashed five minutes ago, but I knew it was going to happen so I backed it up." Skald held up a flash drive that was hanging on a chain around her neck along with her silver scythe.

"You might have told us," Verdandi snapped.

"Ladies," Ike interrupted, "were you able to fix the wards? Did we suffer a breach?"

"Of course we fixed the wards." Urd held up her knitting. The bundled afghan in her lap was knitted in the same rune and knot pattern as Verdandi's needlepoint and Skald's computer game. The same pattern, I saw now, that overlaid the fields and buildings of Olsen farm and the surrounding valley. "Do you think we were born in the last millennium? We know how to circumvent a power surge."

"You didn't prevent her from short-circuiting the circle last time," Moondance grumbled, glaring at me as I sat down on a bench between Ann Chase and Tara Cohen-Miller. Ann smiled and patted me on the hand as if to make up for Moondance's hostility.

"We were unprepared," Verdandi said, shooting Skald a reproachful look.

"I can't keep an eye on everything," she retorted, rolling her eyes like any exasperated teenager. "Would you like tomorrow's Dow Jones index or next week's weather in Kuala Lumpur while I'm at it?"

"Really? You know all that?" Hank Lester asked. "Do you know who's going to win in the fifth race at Belmont today?"

Skald smirked at Lester and clicked the smooth gold ball embedded in her tongue against her teeth. "Would you like to know how long you've got to live while I'm at it?" she asked sweetly.

"Stop it, Skald," Verdandi told her sister. And then to Hank she added, "Don't pay her any mind. The future she sees is only one possible future—it's always changing and she's wrong half the time. But she *should* be able to plot out Callie's future for the next hour and tell us if we're going to have a problem in the circle today."

"Yeah, I can do that," Skald said, hunching over her phone. She moved her thumbs on the keypad rapidly, her eyes flicking over the screen.

"Is that my future?" I craned my neck to see Skald's screen, but all I saw on it were enigmatic runes, squiggles, spirals, and, in the center, a huge ugly knot. My future looked like a mess. Skald seemed to think so, too. When she looked up, her customary smug expression was replaced by one of perplexity. It made her look very young. "I can't read you at all," she said. "You're all tangled up inside."

I nearly laughed. That was exactly how I felt—not sure whether I really loved Liam, afraid to move forward with Duncan Laird, torn between the promises I'd made to my grandmother and my loyalty to Fairwick. I felt the knots inside tightening as I looked into Skald's wide-open pale-gray eyes.

"If even Skald can't read her, should we really risk another circle with her?" Moondance asked. "She might be working with the Grove to sabotage us. After all, her grandmother is a member."

Liz cleared her throat. "Callie's already discussed her connections to the Grove with me and I'm confident she's not working with them to undermine us. As a token of her sincerity she's brought the Aelvestone with her. With this much Aelvesgold, we should be able to help Brock find his way home."

"How are we going to release him?" Ann asked, her voice oddly hushed. Glancing at her, I noticed that her eyes were locked on the Aelvestone and that her hands were curled into tight fists. Of all the witches in the circle, she was the last one I'd have predicted to be so affected by the stone, but then I remembered her daughter and realized she was probably thinking about what that much Aelvesgold could do for her.

"We're going to use the spiral labyrinth to send Callie on a vision quest."

"A vision quest?" I asked. "You mean like the Native American rite?"

"Sort of," Liz replied. "Witches use a vision quest to journey along the spiral path to tap into their essential power. I'm hoping that you'll be able to find and bring back Brock."

"A vision quest requires days of fasting and preparation," Moondance said. "How can you possibly think she's ready?"

For once, I agreed with Moondance. I'd read up on vision quests for a paper I'd done in grad school on Native American mythology, and I knew that initiates sometimes prepared for months for the rite.

"I don't think we have a choice," Liz replied. "We don't have time for Callie to fast and pray. The Grove and IMP meet on Monday." She knelt in front of me and clasped both my hands in hers. "The transformative magic you've been doing with Duncan Laird hasn't unlocked your power. I confess I'm disappointed he hasn't been able to help you, but perhaps there's some reason why he hasn't been the right guide for you . . ." She faltered and I wondered if she guessed about the conflicted feelings I had for Duncan and suspected they were why he hadn't been able to help me more. "Be that as it may," she continued, "this might be the only way to save Brock. I wouldn't suggest this if I didn't think it was the right thing for Brock—and for you."

I looked into Liz's eyes. The thought of taking a walk through that tangled mess inside was not appealing; it was terrifying.

"What exactly will I be doing?" I asked.

"You'll walk the spiral path into the shadowland where Brock is lost. If you can find him, you can lead him back."

"If you can find him," Moondance parroted.

"Do you have a better suggestion for getting him back?" I asked, anger spiking my voice though I tried to keep it calm and level.

Moondance's chin jerked back. She shook her head, the soft flesh under her chin wobbling. She looked frightened.

"I think someone should explain to Callie how dangerous the vision quest is," Ann Chase objected, her voice trembling. "Not everyone who walks the spiral path returns. She could get lost in the shadows, as Brock has."

I took my hands out of Liz's grasp, laying one hand over Ann's twisted and shaking hands. "I want to do it. I need to."

What I didn't add was that I suspected I was already half-lost in the shadows and needed to find my way back out.

TWENTY

$\mathcal{L}$iz placed the Aelvestone at the center of the laby-rinth, beneath the bench where Brock lay. Diana placed four candles around Brock and lit them while Tara poured salt around the outside perimeter. We all sat on the ground, spaced out around the circle so that we could just reach one another's hands.

"It's important to be grounded when summoning this kind of power," Liz explained.

Liz looked around the circle, her gaze resting on each face. "Before we join hands, I want to remind everyone that once we send Callie down the spiral path it's essential that the circle remain unbroken so that we can bring her back. Anyone who breaks the connection will be putting her in grave danger—and will answer to me." When her gaze reached mine, Liz said, "Skald will keep a record of the energy so we'll know if anyone breaks the circle."

I wondered why Liz thought it necessary to make such a warning. After all, I was the one who had broken the circle last time. Shouldn't the rest of the witches know it was dangerous? Instead of reassuring me, Liz's warning made me even more nervous. Did she have some reason for thinking that someone in the circle might be planning to sabotage my vision quest and send me spinning out into the void?

"Is that understood?" Liz asked. When everyone had voiced their consent, Liz directed us to join hands. When the circle was complete, I felt the surge of energy as a sizzle at my core. Liz began a wordless chant—kind of like the *om* my yoga teacher used to begin and end class but made up of different sounds. As the others joined in, the sounds merged into one liquid rush—like water flowing or wind blowing—and I found myself joining in, my own voice merging as seamlessly with the rest as a drop of water in a flood or a gust of breeze in a storm, as if I'd been born knowing this wordless music. Just as my voice merged with the voices of the others, so my energy—all that prickly tangle of conflicting urges—spun out into the circle and joined the flow.

I saw the energy racing around in the circle, a gold band of light created by each of us, feeding off the Aelvestone in the center. The Aelvesgold was filling each member of the circle, suffusing their faces with light. Skald no longer wore the ironic scowl of a teenager. Leon had let go of his hipster pretensions. The lines of pain and anxiety had fallen from Ann's face, leaving her looking twenty years younger. Even Moondance's face, drained of her perpetual annoyance and skepticism, was as radiant as the heavenly orb she had taken as her name.

I wondered for a moment what my face looked like, what freight of worry might have fallen from me, but then I was filled with a greater wonder as the band of golden light began to spin up from the circle, spiraling into the air above our heads. The spiral rose into a cone shape, the energy moving faster, the voices growing louder, the light burning brighter, obliterating the faces around me. I heard, among the human voices, the ululations of owls and the howling of wolves, and saw in the light every color of the rainbow—and a few colors that weren't. There was moonlight and sunshine, the tender blush of dawn and the cobalt blue of twilight, and the whirl of stars before they became stars. The spiral contained all time. Just as it reached its peak, a voice—perhaps all our voices—cried out.

Now!

The spiral cone hurdled into space . . . and I went with it.

I was traveling through the darkness, through shadows so deep I could almost taste their darkness on my tongue. I felt that if I breathed the inky blackness, it would rush inside me. I nearly panicked but then felt the coil of the spiral around me and knew I was protected as long as I stayed in the circle. Dimly, in the distance, I heard voices keeping me afloat. As my eyes adjusted to the dark, I caught flashes of images illuminated by the spiral—a sea cave filled with reflected light, a clearing in the woods, a stone circle on a heath—the places I'd glimpsed the last time in the circle. These places were *always* inside the circle, outside of time, layered within the spiral. And always at the center of each circle stood the same figure—the hooded woman wielding the silver knife.

I hadn't known she was a woman the last time.

When I saw her I wanted to retreat, but then a voice spoke in the shadows.

Here.

It was Brock.

I willed myself—and the spiral—to stop. The coils dropped from me like a discarded hoopskirt and I stood inside a six-petaled flower inscribed in black on pale stone—the center of a labyrinth inside a vast cathedral. The outer edge of the circle was lined with lit candles. Outside the circle a man sat on a stone bench.

"Brock!" I called and started walking toward him, but the instant my foot passed over the lines of the labyrinth a jolt of electricity shot through my body. I took another step within the lines and felt nothing but a warm hum. Apparently I had to walk the labyrinth to reach him. As I carefully trod between the lines I recognized where I was—the medieval Cathedral of Our Lady of Chartres. I'd visited it during my junior year abroad. When I reached the exit of the labyrinth Brock smiled at me and patted the spot on the bench beside him.

"Cailleach, I thought you might come," he said as calmly as if we'd run into each other at the Village Diner.

"The circle has been trying to find you since you fell off my roof," I explained as I sat beside him. I wanted to throw my arms around his neck, but aside from how much I knew it would embarrass him I was also unsure if we should touch in this . . . dimension, or whatever it was. Although he looked like the Brock I knew—plaid flannel shirt straining over muscular arms and broad chest, his face pockmarked, his eyes as kind as ever—he had a strange glow.

"I thought they would," he said. "That's why I came here. Dolly told me about it once when she was writing a book about medieval France. She told me that in the story the heroine waited in the labyrinth for her friend to rescue her. I figured you would know the story, too, and that you'd come if I waited long enough."

"*The Unicorn and the Rose,*" I said, recalling the Dahlia LaMotte novel in which the heroine, Rosamond du Montmorency, time travels back to medieval France by walking the labyrinth at Chartres. I was touched that Brock knew I would come looking for him. "Are we really in Chartres?" I asked, looking around the vast cathedral for signs of tourists.

Brock chuckled and shook his head. "Not the Chartres that's in France, but a replica of it inside the spiral. I don't really understand," he admitted sheepishly. "Dolly said that the labyrinth exists outside time, but I'm not sure what that means."

"I'm just relieved to find you," I said. "Everyone will be so happy to see you . . . but how do we get back?" A mist crept across the floor, blurring the lines of the labyrinth.

"We have to walk the labyrinth back to the center," he said, taking my hand in his broad, calloused one. "And I'm afraid you must go first."

"Okay," I said, taking the lead and looking for the entrance, which was barely visible in the fog. I had to crouch down to see the lines of the labyrinth, which made it awkward to hold on to his hand, so he let go, promising to stay close behind me. I slowly moved forward. Whenever my feet touched a line, I felt an electric jolt warning me not to step over the boundary.

"What would happen if we stepped out of the lines?" I asked Brock. When he didn't answer at once I started to turn around, afraid I'd lost him, but he caught me by the shoulders and turned me back away from him.

"You mustn't ever turn backward when walking the spiral!" The fear in his voice and the strength of his grip startled me. Brock was the gentlest of men. He'd have to have good reason to handle me so roughly. "Just keep walking," he said.

I crept on. I could tell by how small the revolutions had become that we were near the center of the circle. A few more turns and we were at the six-petaled flower at the center of the labyrinth. It was filled with a twilight blue mist that seethed and roiled like a storm cloud. Veins and sparks of lightning crackled within it. I was terrified to step inside.

"What's in there?" I asked Brock.

"Something you have to face in order to be free. You have to go alone . . ." His voice faded. I wanted to turn and look for him, but I didn't. I stepped into the roiling eye of the hurricane . . .

. . . where it was a calm and clear summer night. I stood on a grassy lawn beneath a twilight blue sky, surrounded by the flickering light of fireflies. The place tugged at my memory. The smell of smoke and night-blooming flowers riding the warm summer air, the thick blue dark pinpricked by pulsing fireflies, the damp grass beneath my bare feet . . . my bare feet? I looked down and saw my pale feet half-buried in grass, except . . . they looked smaller than my feet. I wriggled my toes. Definitely my feet . . . A noise caught my attention. A humming that blended with the cicadas and tree frogs but wasn't cicadas and tree frogs. I looked up . . . and *up,* as though I had shrunk and the world had grown taller around me. A cloaked figure towered above me, arms raised to the crescent moon. As I stared in amazement, the figure took hold of the moon and drew it down toward her. I gasped and the figure spun around, robes billowing in the warm air, wafting the smell of smoke and something else toward me, something bitter . . . Then there was a flash of silver as a sickle knife arced down toward me . . .

I screamed and turned . . . and felt the coil wound inside me snap. Instantly, I was spun out into the void with the force of an exploding star. I'd broken the spiral by turning and now I was hurtling through space. Far away I heard a distant hum, an echo of that summer night insect hum . . . or of the circle trying to sing me home. But I was out of their reach. Out of anyone's reach. Brock was lost and I was lost, all because I hadn't had the courage to face my past. I had been that little girl standing in the grass watching the tall woman pull down the moon and slash the air with it. That knowledge did me no good now. Without the spiral I had no path home . . .

Then I remembered Liam's voice telling me that Aelvesgold linked true lovers together, no matter how far apart. I imagined Liam's face and saw him, his face above me as we made love, a halo of gold light blazing around him, his eyes looking deep into mine, reaching into my core. Warmth uncoiled in my chest, wrapping around me and unspooling like a loose ball of yarn.

See, he said as the thread came to its end, his voice as clear as a bell in the emptiness of space, *like I said. True lovers.*

The thread snapped back, hurtling me back into space. I reached out my hands and felt a hand grasp mine. I slammed up against something hard.

Damn, I thought. *Love hurts.*

I opened my eyes. I was lying on the ground, surrounded by a circle of concerned faces, but not the one face I wanted to see.

"Brock? Is he . . . ?"

"I'm here, Callie." I saw Brock hovering over me.

"Oh thank God," I said. "I thought I lost you."

He knelt down on the ground beside me as Liz and Ann Chase helped me sit up.

"I turned around and the spiral broke. I thought we were spinning out of control."

"We were, but you pulled us both back."

"It was Liam," I said. "I heard his voice . . ." I stopped as an expression of dismay crossed Brock's face.

"That damned incubus!" he swore with unaccustomed anger. "It's his fault I was trapped in the shadows in the first place. I was on your roof when I saw the storm coming, carrying something with it—a creature from Faerie . . ."

"That was Lorelei," I said.

"No. I saw her descend into the woods, but the storm came on, carrying with it another presence and heading straight toward Honeysuckle House. I realized then that although I'd warded the house—"

"That was you!" I interrupted. "Duncan Laird said some-one had."

"Duncan Laird?"

"My tutor, and a wizard of the Ninth Order. The circle found him to train me."

I noticed Liz exchanging a look with Ann Chase. The rest of the circle were picking themselves up from the ground, brushing grass off their clothes, and stretching cramped limbs. Ike and Amma approached from the house, tears streaming down the old woman's face at the sight of her grandson restored. Brock, though, was focused entirely on me, his face creased with guilt.

"A wizard of the Ninth Order would have no trouble recognizing my humble wards. The problem was that I'd just put in a new section of roof that *wasn't* warded and that meant the creature in the storm could get in. I couldn't leave you unprotected like that so I stayed on the roof until the storm arrived."

"Oh Brock, you shouldn't have! You shouldn't have put yourself at risk to protect the house. It's only a house . . ."

"It's your *home,* Callie. If a creature breached its wards, it would have power over you. Power over your mind and body and even your dreams. That's how the incubus possessed Dolly. First it possessed Honeysuckle House." Brock dropped his head and covered his face with his calloused, work-worn hands. "I'm so sorry, Callie. I let the incubus back into your house."

TWENTY-ONE

Liz insisted on driving me back. "Diana can drive my car back to the inn," she explained as we walked to my car, "and I don't think you should be driving so soon after your . . . journey." She started to say something else but then glanced out at the fields and motioned for me to get inside the car. As soon as we were inside, with the windows rolled up, she didn't waste any more time getting to the point. She turned to me. "Brock's right," she said. "Your incubus is back."

She said it as if I'd had a reccurrence of shingles or bed-bugs.

"Maybe that's not such a bad thing," I said defensively. "I'd still be spinning through space if Liam hadn't pulled me back, and that wouldn't have worked if he weren't my true love."

Liz clucked her tongue and started the car. "According to him, Callie!" she said, keeping her eyes on the road and grasping the steering wheel so tightly that her knuckles turned white. "He's enslaved you. Look at yourself. You've got so much Aelvesgold in your system that you're glowing. He's gotten you addicted to the stuff."

"Oh, so now I'm an addict *and* a sex slave . . . Hey, wait a second, I've been using Aelvesgold under the direction of Duncan Laird, the tutor *you* got for me."

A pained look crossed Liz's face and she took her eyes off the road long enough to give me a doleful stare.

"You don't think . . . ?"

Liz turned her eyes back to the road but not before I saw her lip tremble. "I'm sorry, Callie, but yes, I think Duncan Laird is your incubus."

"No," I said, my stomach roiling. "You said he was recommended by a member of the circle . . ."

"Yes, but I'm afraid it's possible that the circle member who recommended him might not have been acting with your best interests in mind."

"Who . . . ?" I began, thinking of Moondance's obvious hostility and wondering if she had been the one to recommend Duncan, but Liz silenced me with a raised hand.

"I'd rather not say until I've verified my suspicions, but I think we have to consider the possibility that Mr. Laird might have been foisted on us under false pretenses."

"But you checked his references personally."

"Such things can be faked. I'm afraid now that I might not have been careful enough. Believe me when I say that the thought that I may have made the same mistake twice and put you in harm's way again is deeply mortifying to me."

Liz's face, even in profile, was so pained that I had to look away. I looked out the window at the woods that lay to the west of Trask Road, into the deep shadows of the pines. The same woods where I'd roamed as a deer and an owl with Duncan Laird. I had felt an attraction to him—he was undoubtedly a handsome man—but when he'd tried to kiss me, the wards had prevented him.

"Duncan can't be the incubus. My wards pushed him away."

"That might be a trick, Callie."

But it hadn't just been the wards. "*I* pushed him away," I said, turning back to Liz. "I wouldn't let him kiss me."

"Well," Liz said with a tentative smile, "maybe you've finally developed some sense."

I sighed. I'd very much like to agree with Liz that I was developing better judgment in my love life, but I doubted it. I had slept with Liam in Faerie and in my dreams. So why would I have any better judgment if Duncan were my incubus in the flesh?

I pondered in silence until we headed up Elm Street to my house.

"What are we going to do? Duncan Laird is coming over tonight. Should I still go ahead and transform with him? If he's the incubus, it could be a trick."

"It may indeed," she said with a grim set to her lips. "I'm afraid that what Duncan's been doing with you hasn't unlocked your power . . ." She slammed her hand against the steering wheel. "What an idiot I've been! I've compromised your power just when we needed it the most—and Lorelei's still on the loose."

"Soheila didn't find her at Lura's house?" I asked.

"Lura wouldn't let her in."

"I could try talking to Lura," I said. "She let me into her house before."

"I think it's better if you try to rest up. I have another idea of how to trap Lorelei. I'm going to ask the Stewarts to help."

"The Stewarts?" I asked, remembering the plaid-shirted farmers at the diner and the guileless boy I'd met last night in the woods. "Do you mean Mac Stewart's family?"

"Oh, so you've met him . . . a nice boy, although a bit thick. Yes, his father, Angus, and his brothers are part of an ancient order that has protected the woods for generations. I'll coordinate their efforts . . . oh, hellfire!"

"Liz!" I'd never heard her swear before.

"Look!" We'd pulled up in front of my house but Liz was pointing across the street to the Hart Brake Inn, where a large black SUV was hulking like a malevolent water bug in the inn's driveway. Three doors clicked open at the same time; two disgorged men in identical navy blue suits, both so tall and blond and similar in features they might have been twins. Each carried a long furled black umbrella. The third occupant of the car was a silver-haired woman dressed impeccably in a St. John knit suit and carrying an ox-blood Birkin bag.

My heart sank. "I didn't know my grandmother was going to stay at the inn . . . It's not exactly her style."

"I didn't know either. She must have made the reservation under a different name. Diana will be beside herself."

We both watched in horror as my grandmother led the way up the path, glancing disdainfully at the ceramic gnome at the foot of the porch steps. She said something to one of the men and he touched the tip of his umbrella to the offending gnome. The red-capped figure began to vibrate, then rock back and forth on his stubby feet, then, with a high-pitched whine, he exploded.

In the car Liz flinched and cried out, "Oh no, poor Aethelready! He's been with Diana since she moved to Fairwick."

Adelaide brushed powdered plaster off her suit jacket and proceeded up the steps, followed by her gnome-smashing minions.

"I'd better help Diana cope with them," Liz said, flustered. "Don't worry about tonight. I'll organize the plan to trap Lorelei. In the meantime, try to . . . um . . . fend off Duncan Laird, if you know what I mean."

"I had no intention—" A bang from inside the inn made both of us jump.

"I really must be off," Liz said.

I got out of the car and hurried up my front path, swooping up Mr. Rukowski and bringing him into the house.

"There you are," I said putting the statue down in the foyer and locking the door. "You'll be safe here."

But would I? As Liz had pointed out, my threshold had been breached. I might already have let an incubus into my house. Who knew what else might be coming?

I hurried upstairs and into Liam's old study to get a view of the inn. I caught sight of Diana hurrying out onto the porch with a basketful of bric-a-brac. Her face looked pinched and pale. A series of pops, crackles, and loud bangs from the house made her look over her shoulder. A trail of smoke wiggled out of a second-floor window.

Poor Diana. I'd always thought that the inn was too cluttered with bric-a-brac. Only now did it occur to me that the ceramic creatures might have greater significance to her. Why would Adelaide be getting rid of them if they didn't have magical powers? It couldn't be just because she was offended by the twee decor. Perhaps, like the gnome, they were guardians that protected Diana's home and person. I recalled the way Liam brought home little tokens from the forest—round river stones, twisted bits of wood, birds' feathers—and lined the windowsills with them. Had he been weaving a protection spell?

I looked around the empty room, running my hand along the windowsills. I crouched on the floor to check for loose floorboards.

"Are you looking for something?"

My hand jerked at the unexpected voice and I jammed a splinter into my finger. Looking up, I found Bill standing in the doorway gazing down at me, his cap, even indoors, pulled low over his eyes.

"I'm sorry I startled you," he said, crouching in front of me and taking off his cap. "I thought you knew I was up here painting the ceiling. Let me see that splinter. I'm good at getting them out, seeing as I'm always getting them myself."

I laid my hand in his wide cupped palm, where it fit as snugly as a bird in a nest, and felt a swell of warmth that made me dizzy. It must be exhaustion from today's circle or the pain of the splinter, which Bill was now prodding with blunt calloused fingertips—only it wasn't really pain. The current of sensation his touch released felt a lot more like *desire*. The feeling was so overwhelming that I let out a little moan.

"Sorry," he said.

"It's all right! It's my own fault!" I squeaked, trying to mask my reaction to Bill's touch. I must still be under the effects of Aelvesgold. Liz was right. It was making me attracted to my handyman . . . who really was quite handsome, I thought, getting my first good look at him with his cap off. He had beautiful eyes—the color of leaves in autumn or aged brandy flecked with gold . . .

"Why your fault?" Bill asked.

"Oh . . . I was checking the planks for hiding places like I was Nancy Drew or something. My . . . um . . . boyfriend stayed in this room last winter and I thought he might have left something behind."

"You mean like a note?" he asked, his gaze bent down, his fingertips deftly stroking my finger . . . which made me wonder what it would feel like to have those fingertips stroke other parts of my body.

"Yeah, I guess," I said, shaking off the image of Bill's hands on me. "It was a silly idea, though. He had to leave . . . in a hurry. He wouldn't have had time to leave a note."

"Unless he knew he might have to leave suddenly," Bill said. "Then maybe he'd have hidden a note somewhere. I'll keep an eye out if you like . . . There. It's out."

I looked down and saw a half-inch of jagged wood tipped with blood squeezed between Bill's thumb and forefinger. "Wow, I really skewered myself!" I exclaimed, looking into Bill's eyes, eyes full of compassion, and something more. Longing.

"I'm sorry I hurt you," he said, still looking into my eyes.

"It doesn't hurt a bit now . . ." I said, leaning toward him. An inch farther and our lips would touch . . . but then my cell phone, which was in my pocket, chimed, startling us both.

"Oh," I said, feeling as though I'd been woken from a dream. "I suppose I should get that."

"Sure," Bill said, dropping my hand. "Just make sure you put something on that. Those kinds of wounds can fester."

"Uh huh . . . I will . . ." I said, blushing as I retrieved my phone from my pocket. There was a text from Duncan.

The Grove has descended, he had written. *We need one more transformation to free your power. I'll be there before dark.*

TWENTY-TWO

*I*s something wrong?" Bill asked.

He was still crouched beside me, brow furrowed, a look of concern in his kind brown eyes. *What a nice guy,* I thought, immediately followed by *I have to get rid of him.* Liz had said to stay away from Duncan but I had a better idea.

"No, it's just . . . that was my . . . um, advisor. He needs to speak to me about a project."

"Your advisor? Is that the guy who was here before . . . the one with the messy hair? Sort of snooty-looking?"

I laughed at Bill's description of Duncan Laird. "That's him. He's . . . Scottish," I added, as if that explained the snooty look. "But yeah, he said this was important . . . so I'm afraid . . ."

"Oh, I see." Bill got to his feet. "You want me to clear out."

"It's just that I'm afraid we'll be in your way . . ." I stood up, too, and put my hand on Bill's elbow. Then took it off again when I felt another jolt of raw heat and desire. "I really do appreciate how hard you've been working on the house. I can't thank you enough," I said, my embarrassment making the words come out stilted and formal.

"You don't have to thank me at all, Ms. McFay," he said stiffly, picking up on my tone. "It's my job. Shall I come back first thing in the morning . . . or maybe not quite *first* thing?"

I bristled at the implication that I might have company that early. "First thing will be fine, Bill," I replied, matching his formality.

He nodded, put on his baseball cap, and turned to go. I bit my lip to keep from calling him back to apologize for kicking him out. I waited until I heard the front door close and then watched him drive away in his truck. I felt rotten about going all "lady of the manor" on him, but I didn't want an audience for what I had planned.

I'd lay a trap for Duncan and find out for sure if he was the incubus. It bothered me that I couldn't tell. If we were true lovers, as Liam had said in my dream, shouldn't I have swooned in his arms? I certainly shouldn't be falling into my handyman's arms.

I headed for the bath off my bedroom to take a quick shower before Duncan arrived. I needed to look my best. Shucking off jeans and T-shirt in my closet I heard a clink as my jeans hit the floor. The Aelvestone rolled out of my pocket. I knelt down and picked it up. It pulsed in my hand like something alive. I'd already absorbed too much Aelvesgold from the spell circle, but I couldn't resist closing my hand around it.

A wave of warmth swept through my body and buckled my knees. I sank to the closet floor, my back cushioned by a soft quilted suitcase that held winter sweaters and scarves. I let my head sink back onto the bag, the smell of wool and lavender bringing back memories of being little and hiding in my mother's closet.

I was five or six, small enough that I could fit in the space between suitcases. There were lots of suitcases because we were always going places. That's because my mother and father went to faraway places to dig things up—wonderful treasure they sometimes brought back for me, like brightly colored beads and globby coins with smushed-in faces. Sometimes I went with them but sometimes they left me with Grandmother. I didn't like that. Grandmother always looked at me as if I might be about to explode all over her white couch, which made me feel like I might throw up. She never touched me. This was supposed to be one of those times when they left me. The car to take me away was outside waiting, but if they couldn't find me then maybe they would send it away and I could go with them instead. I heard them calling my name, making a game of it like they always did, my daddy calling "Kay" and my mommy calling "Lex," but then they stopped right in the middle of my name and I heard my father say, "I hate her going there as much as she does. One of these times Adelaide is going to notice . . . ?"

"There's nothing to notice. She's been warded."

"That's another thing. That can't be good for her, having all those locks and binds on her spirit. It's like she's been caged up. Sometimes, Katy, I swear she looks at me like she's lost. What if she has gotten lost? What if she's lost now . . ."

I heard my father's voice crack, and I couldn't hide anymore, even if it meant going to my grandmother's.

"Here I am!" I cried. "I'm not lost . . ."

"I'm not lost, I'm not lost . . ." I woke in the closet, murmuring the words to myself. The Aelvestone lay on the floor by my side. How long had I held it? It had taken me into some kind of fugue state. Into some part of my past . . . my mother saying I had been warded. My parents had known about the wards on me!

I picked up the stone. It throbbed against my hand like a trapped animal. *Like she's been caged up . . .* My father had sounded scared. As if I might be in danger. Then why hadn't they removed the wards? I shoved the stone into the suitcase with my winter sweaters.

In the bathroom I looked longingly at my deep claw-foot tub, but I didn't think it was a good idea to surround myself with that much water.

She's been warded . . . I heard my mother's words again as I stepped into the shower. Strange. I had very few memories from my childhood of my parents beyond the stories they read me at bedtime. That had been the time I'd loved best, nestled between them in bed, their voices alternating as they took turns telling stories about fairies, princesses, wizards, and magic . . .

She's been warded . . .

It's like she's been caged up . . . like she's lost . . .

My parents' words seemed to float on the steam that writhed around me. Feeling skittish, I didn't linger. I toweled off and then put on a rose-scented skin lotion that Liam had liked and a slinky blue jersey dress that he had loved. When I put it on—for the first time since he'd left—I could almost feel his hands on me. Catching my eye in the mirror I asked myself what I would do if Duncan were the incubus. Would I really send him back to Faerie?

I looked away and slipped the emerald-and-diamond ring Liam had given me onto my right ring finger. Then I went downstairs and straightened the library, plumping the couch cushions and picking up several books from the floor that Ralph, who had taken to hiding in the bookcases lately, had knocked over. I picked up Fraser's *Demonology*, which had fallen open at a woodcut of a winged creature with nasty claws that made me shudder, and reshelved it. Then I picked up Wheelock's *Spellcraft* from the coffee table and turned to the chapter "Magical Disguises and How to Uncover Them." It was divided into three sections (Wheelock, and all witches, I was discovering, had a thing for threes): a) Disguises for Self-Protection; b) Disguises for Sexual Uses; and c) Wards.

Wards? I hadn't realized they could be used as disguises.

I read on.

It is this author's belief that sometimes it may be necessary to hide one's true identity to survive an attack from an enemy. Therefore the wards of disguise are included here to be used as a means of protection in life-threatening situations only. The author disavows responsibility for any other uses. If these terms are agreeable, please depress the author indemnity icon below.

I flipped the page and saw that the next several pages were blank. Then I flipped back to what Wheelock called the author indemnity icon. It was a tiny picture of a closed book surrounded by a spoked circle. Small print below it explained that by touching the icon I agreed to the terms stipulated above and that I would not hold the author responsible for any mishaps attached to the use of the following wards and spells. There was some even smaller print below that I would have had to get a magnifying glass to read, but I was impatient to find out about these wards of disguise. Pressing the icon was like checking the "Agree to Terms" box on the internet, I figured. Whoever read the full text?

I touched my finger to the icon. The spoked wheel turned; the book shimmered and opened. A stream of text flew out and spilled down the page. Pages flipped so that the text could continue filling up the empty sheets. When the blank section filled, the pages automatically flipped back to the beginning of the section.

Cool, I thought. *Who needs a Kindle?*

Twenty minutes later I understood why Wheelock had protected himself against the retribution of those deceived by these spells. The disguise wards he described could be used to alter a person's face and body so thoroughly that husbands were unable to recognize wives and mothers didn't know their own children. They could be used to impersonate another person—Merlin had given Uther Pendragon such a ward to make him assume the shape of Gorlois, Ygraine's husband, so that he could lie with her and conceive Arthur—and induce emotional states of thralldom. Here Wheelock referred the reader to the section on sex, hinting that disguise wards were often used in sexual role-playing games.

Ew. In my dream Liam had shown me how to use wards to increase sexual pleasure, but the idea of using the wards to assume other shapes—objects of fantasy and desire—struck me as . . . well, *icky.* But I supposed if they were used between consenting adults there was nothing really wrong with it.

Wheelock was clear, though, that cases in which one witch deceived another into having sex while under the influence of disguise wards constituted rape.

Most disturbing, he wrote, *are the cases in which an otherworldly creature uses disguise wards to pretend to be human in order to seduce a human. Such stratagems have been used by Nephilim, succubi, incubi . . .*

If Duncan were the incubus, why would he be using wards to disguise himself? When the incubus had incarnated as Liam, he hadn't needed wards.

Reading farther, I came upon a possible answer:

Wards are often employed in order to fool a practiced witch.

Perhaps the wards were necessary now that I was coming into my power. But how then could I determine if Duncan was the incubus?

There is a way to tell if a witch has been deceived by an incubus. Anytime a witch comes into contact with a warded disguise her own wards will be activated.

I thought of how my wards had flared when Duncan touched me. I continued reading, looking desperately for an explanation for how I felt but finding no resolution of this conflict between desire and repulsion. What was wrong with me?

One of these times Adelaide is going to notice, my father had said. And my mother had replied, *There's nothing to notice. She's been warded.*

Had my parents warded my power in order to hide it from my grandmother?

I opened Wheelock again and went back to the section on disguise wards. I found what I was looking for in a footnote at the bottom of the last page:

Wards have also been used to disguise a witch's power, most often when a witch is young and may not be able to defend herself because her powers are not fully developed. If the wards are not removed at adolescence, the young witch may not even recognize her own power. Such a witch, rendered powerless by wards, is sometimes known as a Water Witch.

I stared at the footnote until the print grew blurry—at first, I thought, because of the tears in my eyes, but then I realized it was because the print was actually fading. Apparently there was a time limit to the magically produced text. As the words vanished I recalled that Duncan had said there were three definitions of a water witch, but he'd only told me two of them. Had he deliberately left out the third because he knew it applied to me—that *I* was a water witch?

I turned to the section on dissolving wards. There was a way that I could both undo the wards that had been placed on me *and* the ones Duncan was using to disguise himself. If I loved him, the minute the wards came off, he would become human.

But if I unmasked my incubus and I did not love him, he would be destroyed.

TWENTY-THREE

As I sat in the library sipping scotch and waiting for Duncan's arrival, watching the sky darken and the rain begin again, I concluded it came down to a choice between illusion and reality.

When I was a teenager living in my grandmother's cold, formal apartment, she chastised me for still reading fairy tales. "You're trying to escape reality," she told me. The therapist I saw said I was trying to regain the world of my childhood—the world in which my parents still lived. She was closer to the truth but not entirely on target. It wasn't the world of my parents I was trying to recapture; it was myself. All those tales about children lost in the woods, princesses forced to live under the dominion of evil stepmothers, mothers watching over their children as trees or animals, princes charmed into beasts or frogs . . . were all stories about seeing through illusion into the truth. Perhaps my parents had told me these stories so I would know how to survive in a world in which they were absent, or the stories were meant to tell me who I really was.

There was one in particular that my father and mother

both loved to tell me. It was called "Tam Lin" and it came, my father always clarified, not from a fairy tale but from an old Scottish ballad. Which was the same as a fairy tale, my mother always added.

A girl named Jennet was forbidden to go to a ruined castle in the woods—Carterhaugh, the haunt of ghosts and boggles and the "good neighbors" who weren't good at all. But despite the warnings Jennet goes to Carterhaugh, because the castle once belonged to her people and she is determined to reclaim it. When she plucks a rose from the ruins, a young man appears, a handsome prince in green velvet and plaid. He tells her he is Tam Lin, the laird of the castle, kidnapped by the fairy queen to live eternally in the Ever-Fair where no one ages or dies. But on All Hallow's Eve, when he rides with the fey, they will sacrifice him as their tithe to hell. The only one who can save him is his own true human love, who must wait by the holy well and pull him from his horse as he rides by. Then she must hold on to him, no matter what shape he takes, until he is human again. This Jennet does, holding on to him while he becomes a snake, a lion, and then a burning brand— all the while keeping faith that what she holds in her arms is her own true love.

"Because," my mother said at the end of the story, "sometimes love requires a leap of faith." She would smile at my father then, and he'd press her hand to his lips, as courteously as any prince in any fairy tale, and I would feel encircled by love.

After my parents died, I imagined that the prince in the story himself would come and tell me the tale—only it wasn't imagined. My prince and the incubus were one and the same. I brought him into the world by a leap of faith, just as Jennet saved her prince.

But I wasn't a child anymore and love meant looking

squarely in your lover's eyes and seeing past illusions. I couldn't shut my eyes and pretend I didn't know what I knew. If Duncan turned into a beast in my arms, I would have to hold on until he was human again.

I went into the kitchen and gathered the supplies I needed for the spell to uncover a warded disguise. I brought them back into the library and found Ralph sitting on top of Wheelock, riffling through the pages. "You have got to cut this out," I told him, taking the book away from him. "Some of these books are old . . ." I stopped when I noticed the page Ralph had turned to in the section on correlative spells. He was tapping his little paw on the sentence I had read last night. *The most powerful—and dangerous—form of correlative magic is when a witch creates a bond between herself and the object or person she wishes to control.**

"Yes, I know Ralph, but I'm not trying to create a bond with Duncan . . ." But then I noticed the footnote. I looked down to the bottom of the page and read the footnote, my eyes widening and my heart pounding as I read the tiny print.

"Ralph!" I cried, patting the mouse on his head. "You're a genius! This might just be the answer." He preened under my praise and I reread the note. It explained how a doorkeeper could keep a door open by creating a bond between herself and the door. At the end of the footnote was a magical icon, shaped like an open doorway, that promised to disclose the spell. Before I could press it the doorbell rang. I quickly bookmarked the page and went to answer it.

Before opening the door I looked up at the fanlight. With no sun shining through it the stained-glass face was dim and opaque, like that of a dead person. As if I'd already killed Liam with my plans.

I opened the door, braced for reproach and recriminations. Instead I got flowers. Duncan stood on the porch, dripping from the rain, holding a bouquet of wildflowers. His gaze slid down the length of my body, practically carving the curve of my hips with his eyes.

"Whoa!" He whistled appreciatively. "That dress!" He bent to kiss me on the cheek. At the touch of his lips, I felt the gold tattoo beneath my skin flare into life, but whether with desire or to ward him off, I couldn't tell. I stepped back and took the bouquet, which looked handpicked. There were wild roses, daisies, black-eyed Susans, and Queen Anne's lace. Fat raindrops clung to their petals. Looking up, I saw that rain clung to Duncan's hair and eyelashes. He'd walked through the rain to pick flowers for me.

I lifted my hand to brush the rain from his hair, determined to see if touching him aroused desire in me, but he caught my hand in his and turned it in the sun so that the emerald ring cast a spray of green sparks across the foyer floor.

"A gift from Liam?" he asked, tilting one eyebrow up. "I have to confess that I'm jealous."

"Oh," I said, looking down at the flowers and wondering why he would be jealous if he was the incubus. "I didn't mean to make you jealous. Liam wasn't really . . . *real*. At least he was almost real. If I'd loved him . . ."

"*Yes!*" Duncan said, stepping closer. "That's what I realized today. You didn't love Liam or he'd have become human. So I don't have any reason to be jealous, do I?"

As he stepped over the threshold I felt the gold coils in my blood flare.

"Let me put these in some water," I said, stepping backward. "You can make yourself a drink in the library. There's some scotch on the sideboard and there's a fire laid if you want to light it."

I turned away and walked through the library to the kitchen, feeling his gaze on my back. In the kitchen I ran cold water over my hands while I filled up a vase and then arranged the flowers with shaking hands.

When I came into the library, flames were crackling in the fireplace and he was pouring himself a glass of scotch from the crystal decanter I had set up on the sideboard.

"More of Liam's stock?" he asked, holding the glass up to me. I hadn't turned on any lights, so I couldn't quite make out his expression in the flickering firelight, but I heard the edge in his voice.

"Sorry," I said, lifting my own glass from the coffee table. "I guess I developed a taste for the stuff. This is the last of it, though. I thought we'd finish it together."

His teeth flashed in the firelight. "Good, I like the idea of finishing it." He held his glass up to me. "Here's to new beginnings."

We clicked glasses. I took a big gulp, but he swirled the gold liquid around in his glass and sniffed it.

"Checking for water witches?" I asked.

"Just savoring the aroma," he replied. He smiled and a dimple appeared on his right cheek. Liam had had one on his left. I almost stopped his hand as he lifted the glass to his lips and took a long drink.

"Ah . . ." he said, "that tastes like a good beginning."

I took another sip of my scotch and sat down on the couch. "That's what I want," I said. "A new beginning. Our transformations haven't released my wards. In fact, they seem more volatile."

"That sometimes happens when wards are breaking down," he said. "Some wards are so ingeniously placed that they contain a fail-safe device. When you try to disarm them, they dig themselves deeper into their host. Taking them out can be like removing a barbed fishhook."

I winced at the image. "All the more reason to get them out

quickly," I said. "I think I've found something that will work more quickly than another transformation."

I got up to get the books I'd left lying on the coffee table. I could easily have reached them without rising, but I needed to put a little distance between us. I sat back down with the open Wheelock on my lap a good foot away from him, but he moved closer to see the page I'd bookmarked.

"Ah, the skeleton key spell," he said, reaching across me to turn the page. "I had thought of that one, but it's not very precise and it needs a vehicle to deliver it."

"I thought I'd ask the rain," I said.

"*Ask* the rain?"

"Yes, I read here . . ." I handed him another book that was already open to the place I wanted. ". . . that a witch should never try to command the elements, but there's an incantation for asking an element to carry a spell. I thought I'd ask the rain to become a skeleton key to unlock my wards. And then I'll ask the wind to blow them away." I didn't add that I planned to use the skeleton key I invoked to unlock his disguise wards.

He leaned closer and narrowed his eyes at me, their blue burning like gas flames. I could smell under the peaty aroma of the scotch his own scent, a mixture of pine and musk that reminded me of how he'd looked as a stag. But his eyes reminded me of the owl's. "Will you ask the earth to move next, Cailleach McFay? You're getting almost too powerful for me to keep up with."

"I doubt that," I replied. "Do you think it will work?"

"I think you don't really need me to tell you that it will work," he said. A burst of light from the fireplace as a log tumbled flashed in his eyes, reflecting glassily as if they were brimming with tears. He looked away and took a long gulp of scotch.

I reached for his hand, steeling myself for the lash of my wards. They *did* feel a bit like fishhooks. "I'd like you to stand by me when I do it."

He looked down at our interlocked hands, the coils beneath our skin lashing at each other like warring snakes. "Of course," he said, draining his glass, "but if you don't mind I'd like to stay out of the rain. I think I'm coming down with a cold."

"Sure," I said. "I thought we'd do it on the back porch. The wind is blowing from the west—away from the back of the house. We'll stay dry."

I got to my feet, keeping his hand in mine, pulling at it to make him get up. As he got to his feet he pulled me to him and brought his head down to kiss me. His mouth tasted of peat and smoke and wild heather. He tasted like Liam, but there was a bitter taste as well. Like ashes . . .

Or maybe that was the taste of our wards burning away.

"Come on," I said, pulling away from him. "We'd better get outside before we set something on fire."

He followed me through the kitchen out onto the back porch. The wind was blowing away from the house so the porch was dry, but Duncan still held back as I moved to the railing. I concentrated on clearing my mind of everything but the invocation I'd memorized, first calling upon the Basque rain goddess I'd read about in Wheelock.

> *Mari, goddess of the rain, I call on you,*
> *you who reward the just and punish the false,*
> *you who wield the rain and the wind,*
> *daughter of earth, wife of thunder.*

Thunder rumbled in the west and the wind lifted up the ends of my hair.

Let the lock that was locked
unlock.
Let the door that was closed
open.
Let the bird that was snared
fly.

As Wheelock had instructed, I pictured each image as I spoke it: a key turning in a lock, a door opening, a bird flying free. At first I felt nothing, but then a gust of wind blew the rain into my face. It felt deliciously cool on my skin. As it dripped down my neck, I felt as if it was seeping deep into my body.

As the rain seeps into the parched earth
come into me,
as the stream finds its way to the sea,
find your way into me,
as the drip cracks stone over time,
crack the bonds that bind me.

Something moved deep inside, like rusty chains unraveling, unoiled hinges creaking, rock cracking. The rain, carrying my spell with it, was seeping down into the core of my being . . . into a hollowed-out cave beneath the sea. Undulating light rippled over painted limestone walls. It was the grotto I'd seen in my vision during the circle. Then, quick as the flash of light, I was in the woods, the windswept heath, the labyrinth at Chartres, and then barefoot in the grass surrounded by fireflies. The robed woman towered above me and pulled down the moon. I gasped and the woman spun around, moonlight flashing on the silver blade in her hand. I started to turn and run—as I had before—but then I didn't.

The labyrinth exists outside time, Brock had said. I felt its spirals coiling around me now. I held my ground and looked up into . . .

My mother's face.

I gasped at the sight of her, not out of fear but because she was so beautiful. I had almost forgotten. Black hair framed a white face and pale blue eyes that softened at the sight of me. She knelt in front of me until her face was level with mine and put a hand on my shoulder.

"Callie, what are you doing here? Did you have a bad dream?"

I remembered this moment. I must have been six or seven. We lived in a house on a college campus somewhere in New England. I'd woken in the night from a nightmare and called for my mother, but no one had come. Lights danced over the wall of my bedroom like a swarm of fireflies. I heard my mother's voice coming from the backyard and had gone outside to find her, but found instead the frightening woman with the silver knife.

"You were warding me, weren't you?"

Her eyes grew wide and her hand flinched away from my shoulder. I smelled the fear on her—my own mother looked at me as if I were a monster. Tears fell down my face, so many tears it was as if I stood in the rain. "Was that why you warded me? Because you were afraid of me?"

"Oh, my sweet baby, no!" she cried out, quicker to reassure me than to wonder what stranger had possessed her little girl, but then I saw the understanding dawn in her face.

"You're Callie grown up, aren't you?" she asked. A tear slid down her face. "You *will* grow up then."

"Yes," I said, "but you . . ."

I couldn't finish. Couldn't tell her that she wouldn't be there to watch me.

She shook her head and placed a finger over my mouth. "It's okay. Don't tell me. As long as you're okay . . ." She looked at the glowing spiral. It had begun to spin. "But you aren't, are you? You're trapped here where I set the wards on you. Oh my darling, I'm so sorry. I only did it to protect you."

"From what?"

"From your grandmother discovering your power. The Grove would have used you . . ." My mother's eyes skittered away from me toward the perimeter of the circle.

"Used me for what?" I cried, my voice high and whiny as any six-year-old crying for her mother's attention.

My mother turned back to me, fear in her eyes. "To close the door. They tried to do it with your father but we found a spell to stop them. We were afraid they would try to do the same with you if they knew you were a doorkeeper."

"How?" I cried.

"It's your blood," she began, but then she looked back at the circle. This time my eyes followed hers. The glowing spiral was spinning faster, its coils contracting, drawing closer to us. I felt its heat on my skin. "I don't have time to explain. The spiral is collapsing," she told me. "You can't stay for long in the past. I wish we had more time, but I'm grateful for *this*, Callie; I can't tell you how much. Just to know that you'll survive. That you'll be all right. You will be all right after this, darling, won't you?"

I thought of how many times I'd wished that I could speak to my mother one more time. Of the questions I had . . . I knew I should use the few moments we had left to ask about the spell I needed to keep the door open, but I had Wheelock for that, so instead I asked something else.

"Mom, there's this guy . . . and I *almost* love him, but something's in the way. Is there something wrong with me?"

"Oh baby, no! There's nothing wrong with you. It's these."

She held her hand to my chest. "It's the wards I put on you to keep you safe. How can you be safe if you love?" She touched my face, brushed my tears away, stroked my hair. "But there are some things better than safe. If you're ready, we can cut the wards away. Your power—and your ability to love—will be released as the wards unwind . . . but they might take some time. They were never meant to be on you so long. They've become intertwined with your fears and doubts. It might hurt as they unravel."

"That's okay," I said. "It couldn't be worse than how I have been feeling."

A look of pain crossed her face and I was sorry I'd told her that, but then she steeled her face and laid the knife to the coils. Sparks flew from them and they lashed out at her.

"I can't do it," she said. "It has to be you."

She handed me the knife. It felt cold and heavy in my hand. She showed me where I needed to cut. I lifted the knife to the coil . . . but then hesitated. I looked her in the eye. If I didn't cut the coil, I'd be trapped in this moment with my mother. I could stay here with her forever, with the one person, along with my father, I was sure I loved, who understood me . . . as she understood me now. She opened her mouth to say something, then closed it. I was old enough to make my own decision. That look decided me. She had been willing to risk her own safety for me. I touched the knife to the coils.

Something inside snapped and I was back on the porch. Duncan was pulling my hand back, tugging me away from the rain. The coils were unwrapping around me, hissing in the rain, turning into white mist. My mother had been right. It hurt, as if someone was pulling a length of barbed wire through my flesh. Duncan tried to pull me out of the rain, but I was doubled over in pain. I got myself together enough to keep hold of his hand, and with my free hand I felt in my pocket for the bag of herbs I'd stashed there. I took a pinch out and held it up to the wind. Through teeth gritted with pain, I recited the last bit of the spell I'd memorized.

> Carry these leaves on your wind.
> Let all whom you touch put away their disguises.
> You who reward the just and punish the false,
> wash away all illusions with your rain.

Duncan tried to lunge at my hand, but he was too late. I let go of the herbs and the night was suddenly full of the scent of clary sage and bluebells. The wind blew the rain straight onto the porch. Duncan tried to step back but I had slipped my hand around his wrist and held on tight, aided by the power of the goddess I had called on. She was in me now. My wards were rising off my skin and dissolving in the mist as I turned around.

Claws slashed across my face, blinding me. I screamed and raised my hands to my eyes and fell to my knees. I heard Duncan's footsteps running down the porch steps, then his cries of pain as he fled into the rain, and then nothing but my own ragged sobs mingling with the falling rain.

TWENTY-FOUR

e'd missed my eye, but the pain from the slashes was unbearable. My mother had said that the wards would hurt as they unraveled, but they didn't hurt as much as Duncan's betrayal. He'd also been in pain, I told myself. He knew that if I saw his face there would be no chance of his being freed from the enchantment, but what kind of monster was he?

The thought made the slashes across my face throb and the barbed coils tighten around my heart. I had to get inside and tend to my wounds . . . find a healing spell . . . or call Diana. I tried to get to my feet, but slipped on the porch's wet floorboards and fell painfully to my knees, my limbs flailing, weak and helpless. Instead of gaining power from cutting the wards, I'd crippled myself. What if they had become so intertwined with who I was that I couldn't live without them? What if my chains had become the strongest part of me?

Clinging to the porch rail, I struggled to my feet, took a tentative step toward the door, and fell flat on my face.

I turned my damaged cheek away from the floorboards. The rain was still blowing onto the porch, soaking my face.

All I could think of was how Duncan had struck me and left me. My tears mingled with the rain, stinging the cuts on my face . . . and then I felt a hand on my back and one on my face.

Then strong warm hands moved down my back, my legs, my arms, their touch gentle but firm, feeling, I thought, for broken bones.

I'm broken inside, I wanted to shout, but I couldn't. Razor wire gripped my throat. Besides, I liked how these hands felt. They were turning me over now, cradling my face, stroking wet hair away from the gashes. A face came blurrily into focus. Not Duncan's.

"Bill?" I managed in a hoarse croak.

He looked up, startled, his brown eyes flaring like hot coals.

"Who did this?" he growled. Anger transformed him from an unassuming handyman to something quite different. For a moment I was frightened, but then he cupped his hand around my face and the fear slipped away—but not his anger. "Was it that blond man?"

"'s complicated," I managed.

"No, it's not," Bill muttered, sliding his hands under me and then scooping me up into his arms. "It's really very simple. No one should hurt you. No one. Not ever." He kept up this monologue—more than he'd said in the two days I'd known him—as he carried me inside and upstairs to my bedroom. I rested my head on his chest and felt his words as a reassuring rumble that made the barbed-wire coils inside me loosen their grip. When he laid me down on my bed, Bill's monologue had turned into a list of rather colorful things he was going to do to Duncan Laird. I must have briefly lost consciousness because when I next came to, Bill was gently swabbing my face with a washcloth and singing. It was the song I'd heard him singing once before. It had sounded familiar then, but the words weren't in English.

"That's pretty," I whispered. "What is it?"

"Just an old song my mother used to sing to me . . . Hey, you're shivering. Are you cold?" he asked, drawing a blanket up over me. "I should have taken off your wet clothes . . ."

"Too much a gentleman, eh?" I quipped through chattering teeth.

"Not anymore," he said, unbuttoning my damp dress. "I promise not to look—" His voice froze, his eyes widening as he stared at my chest.

"Hey! That's *looking*!"

"I'm an idiot," he said, stripping off my dress. "There's poison spreading through your body."

I looked down and saw jagged red lines—like claw marks—spreading across my skin. The red made them look like burns, but they felt like ice daggers ripping open my chest.

"So . . . cold . . ." I bit out between shudders.

Bill gave me a frantic look and then started to chafe my skin with his hands. He started with my legs, working his hands up my calves, then my thighs. He did my arms next. Wherever he touched my skin warmed, and the red marks faded. It felt so good I forgot to be embarrassed that he was rubbing his hands all over my naked body—or to wonder how he knew what to do—but when he came to my chest he looked up at me and I saw that he hadn't forgotten.

"I have to keep your circulation going to get rid of the poison . . . especially around your heart."

"It's okay," I said, taking his hand and placing it over my left breast. The blood rose to his face and his eyes widened and seemed to burn into mine, then he bent his head and carefully, methodically stroked my breasts and my throat. The red marks faded under his hands and warmth poured into my body. When he reached my stomach, the warmth pooled in my navel and cascaded down my legs like a waterfall. I'd felt like this before but at the moment I couldn't remember when. Nothing seemed to exist but Bill's hands touching me . . . caressing me . . .

Then his touch changed: his hands moved slower, lingered, and trembled. *He* was trembling, I saw when I looked at him, shaking as if he'd absorbed the poison into him. His eyes caught mine and I felt something click. The wards that had been loosened inside me began to melt. When he met my eyes, he took his hands off me.

"I'm sorry. I didn't mean to . . ." he began. Bill was always apologizing to me, I realized. And yet he had been unfailingly kind and gentle to me since we'd met—*only two days ago,* a little voice reminded me. But I shushed that voice. Looking into his eyes, I felt I'd known him forever. His hands on me were more right than anything I had experienced since . . . well, since *forever.* I wanted them on me again. *Right now.*

"You have nothing to be sorry for," I murmured as I pulled his head down to mine and found his lips. He moaned as he kissed me, something between a growl and a purr, a deep sound that I felt reverberating in his chest as I slid my hands beneath his shirt. There was tension in his body, as if he was holding himself very tight, afraid he might hurt me. I pressed against him and forced his mouth open with my tongue, wanting to break through.

There are some things better than safe, my mother had said.

He gasped and pulled back, looking into my eyes, a question in his, and then, as if that question had been answered, he slid one arm under my hips, sliding between my legs. I felt him hard, straining against his jeans, pressed against my belly. I struggled with buttons while he stripped off that damned flannel shirt. Beneath it his chest was smooth, his skin golden. I ran my hand over those smooth rippling muscles and heard him gasp as my hand brushed against his erection.

"*Kay-lex!*" My name came out as a growl—when had he learned to say it right? I thought—and then he was inside me and I didn't think at all.

I woke up the next morning reaching for Bill and found myself alone. A terrible emptiness swept over me, then longing, followed by embarrassment—*I slept with a man I barely knew!*—and the fear that it had all been a dream. But then I heard noises from downstairs, a clanking of pans that suggested Bill hadn't fled. Relief flooded me as I reached for a robe and started downstairs . . . but stopped in my bedroom doorway. From here I saw the open door to Liam's study . . . Liam's *empty* study. That's where my last impetuous affair had gotten me, pining for a man who wasn't even entirely human.

I felt the sharp coils of the wards clutch at my heart. So they weren't entirely gone yet. They had unraveled when I cut them in the vision with my mother and eased their grip last night with Bill, but they were still there. Although every nerve in my body yearned to run downstairs and throw myself back into Bill's arms, I made myself go back into the bedroom and change into jeans and a T-shirt and comb my hair. In the mirror, I saw the scratches over my eye. They'd healed remarkably well—no doubt due to Bill's swift ministrations—but they were still clearly visible. If Duncan was the incubus, what did *that* say about my romantic judgment?

I walked downstairs, schooling myself. *Take it slow, give it time, don't rush in . . .* all the admonitions my friend Annie would give me if she were here, but when I walked into the kitchen and saw Bill bending over the oven, his firm behind filling out faded blue jeans, I went weak in the knees. And when he retrieved a pan of fragrant corn bread from the oven and turned, a speckle of flour dusting his hair and loose flannel shirt, other parts of my body went soft. I heard Annie's voice in my head concede, *Okay, with an ass like that* and *cooking skills, maybe you shouldn't be taking it so slow.*

"Hey," I said. "I was afraid you were gone when I woke up."

He frowned. "I wouldn't do that. I just thought you might like breakfast. I hope you don't mind . . ."

"No!" I cried, a bit too vociferously. I stepped toward him, wondering how we'd managed to get off on the wrong foot. He stepped toward me . . . but he still had a hot pan in his hands. He turned to put it on the counter . . . and the front doorbell rang.

The thought that it might be Duncan come to explain what had happened last night flashed through my head. I looked guiltily at Bill.

"Maybe you should get that," he said.

"I could just wait until whoever it is goes away," I said. Vigorous knocking suggested that wasn't going to be a possibility.

"I think you'd better answer it," Bill said. "Do you want me to go?"

"No!" I cried. "I mean . . . not unless you want to. Or have to. You probably have other things to do . . ."

The doorbell rang again.

"Let me just see who that is . . . I'll be right back. Don't go anywhere." I leaned toward him to kiss him, but he placed his hand on my face, his thumb stroking the scratches on my cheekbone. His touch made my entire body tingle. "I'll be right here," he said. "Take your time."

. . .

Despite Bill's directive, I ran to the door, determined to take care of whoever was there and get back to Bill. If it was Duncan I'd tell him to get lost. There was no good explanation for what he'd done last night. As soon as I saw Liz, Soheila, and Ann Chase on the porch, though, I knew I wasn't going to be able to get rid of them easily. They looked grim.

"Let me guess, another intervention? What have I done wrong this time?"

"You haven't done anything wrong," Liz said, twisting her hands nervously. "It's all my fault . . ."

"No, it's mine," Ann said, laying a hand on Liz's arm.

"We need to talk," Soheila said. "Can we come in . . . or . . ." She lifted her head and sniffed. The scent of fresh-baked cornbread had wafted out from the kitchen, but I had an idea that Soheila was scenting the man who had baked it. "Do you have company?"

"No . . . yes . . . I mean, Bill is here . . . He's my handyman . . ." The minute I said it I could have bit my tongue. I heard a door open and close in the back of the house. Had he heard me? "Come in, I'll be right back."

I ran back to the kitchen and found it empty. The pan of corn bread rested on a folded dishcloth next to a pot of tea, all laid out on a tray. There was a note beside it. *It looks like you're busy and I did have some other things to do. I'll be back later to check on your basement. Yours, Bill.*

"Crap, crap, crap," I muttered as I went back into the library carrying the tray.

"I can understand why you're upset," Liz said, taking the tray from me and placing it on the coffee table. "But first let me tell you the one piece of good news. We've located Lorelei. She's at Lura's house. The bad news is that Lura won't let anyone in, but we've placed a guard around the house so at least she won't hurt anyone."

"That *is* good news," I said, "so why do you all look so grim?"

Soheila and Liz looked at Ann.

"Duncan Laird," Ann said, lowering her eyes. "He came to my house the morning after our first circle and told me he wanted me to recommend him as your tutor. Of course I said no, but then he said he had enough Aelvesgold to make Jessica well forever. He told me he didn't want to hurt you. He said he was your incubus and he only needed some time with you . . ." She raised bloodshot, hooded eyes to my face and gasped. "Did he do that to you, dear?" She raised a trembling hand to my face.

"Duncan Laird did this when I used a spell last night to unmask him. Are you really sure that he's the incubus? I didn't know incubi had claws."

Soheila picked up a book from the coffee table, flipped through it, and laid it back down open to a full-color insert. The picture that leered up from among the teacups was Fuseli's *Nightmare*—a pointy-eared imp with long claws leering evilly as he crouched on the breast of a swooning maiden. Was that the face that would have greeted me if Duncan hadn't struck me? Was that why he had lashed out—so I wouldn't see him like that?

Ann craned her neck to look over at the picture and shuddered. "Is that what they look like in their natural state?"

"We have no *natural* state," Soheila answered. "Incubi and succubi feed on human desire. We take the shapes humans imagine for us. We become their dreams . . . or their nightmares. I tried to explain that to Angus when he went up against your incubus to destroy him . . ." Soheila's eyes glistened when she mentioned Angus's name.

"You don't have to talk about it if it's too painful," I told her. It wasn't just Soheila I wanted to spare; I wasn't sure I wanted to know how the creature I'd once slept with had killed the man Soheila loved.

"I think you should know," Soheila said, wrapping her hands around the mug of tea Liz handed to her. "After Angus saw his sister destroyed by the incubus, he spent years studying the lore, but in the end it wasn't the stories about incubi that helped him. It was one of the old Scottish ballads that gave him what he needed."

"A Scottish ballad?" I asked, feeling a strange chill. "Was it 'Tam Lin'?"

"How did you know?" Soheila asked, clearly surprised.

"My parents told me the story when I was little . . ." I stopped, trying to recall something on the edge of my memory. Some other time when I'd heard the ballad recently, but the thin filament of memory had slipped away.

I continued, "I thought about the story last night. How Jennet has to hold on to Tam Lin while he becomes a snake, a lion, and a burning brand, and how that was what I'd have to do . . . Only I didn't. I let go." I heard my voice wobble on the last words. Liz patted my arm and Ann took out a tissue from her purse and handed it to me.

"How could you help but let go when he lashed out at you? That's what Angus discovered. He believed that if he tracked the incubus down to where he had been created and waited for him on Halloween night, as Jennet does, he could turn him into a human being and then kill him. But when he grabbed hold of him he became the one thing that Angus couldn't fight—his sister, Katy."

"Oh," I said, "that must have been awful."

"It was. He was so shocked that he let her go—and then the incubus became a horrible beast with claws that struck him down. Angus lived through the attack and came back to me, but he was already dying from the poison. I tried to save him, but I couldn't." Soheila touched the marks on my face. "But I don't sense any poison in you."

"There was," I said, blushing as I remembered how Bill had rubbed my skin to release the poison. How had he known how to do that? "But it passed out of my system."

"You were lucky," Soheila said. "Angus died within a month and in great pain. But the fact remains that Duncan Laird attacked you."

"*And,*" Liz added in a despairing wail, "all this time that we thought he was helping you gain power, he's probably been draining you. You haven't gotten rid of your wards, have you?"

"Not completely," I admitted, feeling the coils lash inside me at the question. "But they've been loosened. I think they're almost gone. And," I added, remembering the footnote I'd read in Wheelock last night, "I think I've found a way to keep the Grove from closing the door."

"Good," Liz said. "We may need it. The Grove and IMP have announced a schedule change. The meeting is today."

TWENTY-FIVE

*T*oday?" I cried, touching the marks on my face. "But we need more time!" I still had to study the spell in Wheelock and I needed time for the loosened wards inside me to dissolve.

"Well, we don't have it," Liz said briskly, glancing at her watch. "I should be there already. Ann and I will go ahead and let Soheila help you with those scratches. You can't go looking like that."

Liz got to her feet and smoothed her skirt. I noticed now that she was dressed in her best tweed Chanel suit, ready to face her opponents in pearls and vintage couture. "This schedule change is meant to unnerve us. We mustn't let it."

Liz and Ann went on ahead while Soheila stayed behind to help me apply makeup over the marks on my face. She used a touch of Aelvesgold and said a spell that she told me her sisters used to cover wrinkles. "Better than Botox," she assured me.

I dressed carefully in my best interview suit. For luck, I pinned on a brooch my father had given me. It was fashioned out of two interlocking hearts—a Scottish design called a luckenbooth brooch. Downstairs, I tossed Wheelock in my leather briefcase. When Soheila gave me a look, I told her about the footnote.

"If the icon has a door on it, that means only a doorkeeper can read the spell," she said. "Be careful, though. Those correlative spells can be very dangerous."

So everyone kept telling me.

We walked together to Beckwith Hall, where the meeting was being held. It had stopped raining. The day had turned muggy and hot, the air holding a sultry threat of another downpour.

"There's something I don't understand," I said as we walked. "If Duncan is really the incubus, why don't I feel more attracted to him? Whenever he tried to kiss me, I pushed him away."

"Hm." Soheila tilted her head and looked at me, then touched her hand to my arm. "Maybe the wards are keeping him away."

"They didn't the first time," I argued, "with Liam."

Soheila shrugged and hugged her arms around herself. "Maybe you are becoming stronger. A strong human can resist the pull of an incubus."

I told her then about the dreams.

"Oh," she said, "but still, you resisted him in the flesh and . . ." She slanted her eyes toward me and the corner of her mouth tugged into a half smile. "You slept with someone else, didn't you? That fellow Bill?"

I blushed, but there was no point lying to Soheila. "Yes. It sort of just happened. He was there after I was attacked and was so sweet."

"It's good you've moved on to someone else. It means you're breaking the hold the incubus had on you. It's better this way. There's no future in a relationship between a human and one of his kind."

I had a feeling we weren't talking about me anymore. "Frank would miss you if you went, Soheila. We all would, but Frank most of all."

Soheila nodded, her face a mask of pain. "I'd miss him, too," she admitted. "But it's because of him I must go. If I were trapped here without access to Aelvesgold eventually I would be driven to feed on humans. If I ever hurt him . . ." She shivered despite the warmth of the day. "I'd never forgive myself."

She forced a grim smile and squeezed my arm. As she turned to continue walking, I wondered if that's how Duncan had felt after he struck me—and if that's why he ran away.

We found a small gathering outside the lecture hall. The only sign indicating the event read SYMPOSIUM ON THE DIALOGUE OF DISCOURSE DETERMINED BY THE DEBATABLE DEXTERITY OF DYNAMIC DISSENT. No doubt it was boring and intimidating (not to mention alliterative) enough to drive away any laypeople. Caspar Van der Aart from earth sciences was talking to Joan Ryan from chemistry, and also some people from town—Dory Browne and two of her cousins and the guy who ran the Greek restaurant, whom I always suspected might be a satyr. I noticed a number of the witches from the circle—Moondance and Leon Botwin and Tara Cohen-Miller—talking among themselves. When they saw us they stopped talking abruptly, as if they'd been talking about us. Moondance, wearing a T-shirt that read I BELIEVE IN FAIRIES, approached us.

"We heard the meeting had been moved up and wanted to show our support, but they're not letting us in. They say it's private. I say if this meeting is going to determine the fate of our friends and neighbors, we should be allowed to attend."

"I agree completely," I said, glad for once to be on the right side of her belligerence. "Let's see what we can do."

One of Adelaide's blond minions was stationed just inside the door to the lecture hall. Soheila strode toward him, but the second her toe crossed the threshold she shrieked and fell to the floor. I knelt quickly beside her to see what was wrong . . . and recoiled in shock. Her arm was spidered with a pattern like tree branches. As I watched they broke through her skin and wrapped themselves around her slender forearm and wrist, growing thicker and rougher. Bark formed over their surface and leaves sprouted. A tree branch was growing out of Soheila's arm. I reached forward and touched it gingerly. Soheila winced.

"My God, that's horrible. How can we get rid of it?" I looked up at the impassive face of the fair-haired man.

"The branch will recede in a few minutes as long as she doesn't commit any more infractions," he said.

"She only tried to walk through a door—a door on *our* campus! She works here, for heaven's sake! This is outrageous!"

"We sent an email out this morning specifying that no demons would be allowed in the meeting, unless specifically summoned. We can't have them influencing the proceedings."

"And yet the proceedings will decide our fate," a gruff voice called out from the circle of onlookers. Recognizing it, I got up from Soheila's side and eagerly peered through the crowd as it parted to let one large, flannel-shirted man through.

"Brock!" I cried, so glad to see him up and looking well that I threw my arms around him. A red welt appeared on his face, always a sign he was embarrassed. I unwound my arms from him and stepped back. Brock gave me a wistful smile, but when he raised his head to look at the fair-haired guard, an ugly red stain spread across his face and his brows knitted together. "My family has lived in Fairwick for more than a hundred years. You can't force us to leave."

"No one is being forced to do anything."

The soft but precise voice came from behind the blond man. I saw the smooth silver chignon first and then smelled Chanel No. 5, a scent that always sent a chill down my spine.

"Adelaide," I said, greeting my grandmother by her first name, mostly because I knew it would annoy her. "Why can't Brock and Soheila attend the meeting? Brock's family has watched over the woods and protected Fairwick for more than a century. Soheila *teaches* here. It's hardly fair to exclude them from a meeting deciding their fate."

"We've provided a video simulcast," Adelaide said, pointing to two flat-screen TVs mounted on the lobby walls. "You are all welcome to stay out here and listen. But we can't have any demons who are capable of magically influencing the proceedings inside. It's a simple precaution."

"Brock's not a demon!" I said. "He's a Norse divinity! And Dory!" I cried, pointing at my friend, who was wearing a floral skirt, a yellow sweater set, yellow espadrilles, and carrying a quilted handbag. "She's a brownie. What could be more harmless than a brownie?"

Adelaide gave Dory a withering look. "Brownies are one step away from boggarts. Do you know why brownies don't like to be thanked?"

This was something I'd always wondered about. Dory and her cousin brownies were always doing good deeds, but they did hate being thanked for them. "I assume it's because they're modest," I answered.

Adelaide laughed. "Shall I tell her?" she asked Dory, whose pink cheeks had gone pale.

"No, let me," Dory said, turning to me. "Many, many

years ago a brownie did a favor for a human being, but the human didn't thank him. The brownie got so angry that he . . . well, he killed him."

"And ate him," Adelaide added.

"Yes, ate him. The brownies were in danger of being thrown out of this world. In atonement we agreed to do favors and services without benefit of thanks. Every time we're thanked, we lose a step toward that atonement."

"Oh," I said, trying to imagine one of the brownies *eating* someone. "Well, at least they're *trying* to make up for their wrongdoings . . ." I gave Dory a reassuring look. Brock put his arm around her.

"We'll agree to remain peacefully outside if you'll allow Callie to speak for us," Brock said.

He turned to me, his face full of hope and trust. "You're our only chance, Callie."

I looked past Brock and Dory and saw Ike Olsen. He was standing next to the Norns. Skald held up her phone for me to see. The screen was full of the enigmatic lines I'd seen there before when she had consulted my future. They looked more chaotic than ever, but the knot at the center had loosened and was opening like a fern unfurling. Perhaps the lines represented my wards loosening. I felt them letting go with the trust my friends had in me. I felt a few more links dissolve as I turned back to Brock and Dory and told them, "Yes, I will speak for Fairwick."

Beckwith Hall was one of the oldest and most elegant classrooms on the campus. A large, handsome rectangular oak table, which had once been in the refectory of a monastery, sat in the middle of the room. One side of the room was taken up by arched windows alternating with niches that held busts of great philosophers and writers. Today the blinds were drawn over the windows and the busts of Homer, Plato, Sappho, Dante, Shakespeare, Jane Austen, and Charlotte Brontë were invisible in their shadowy niches. A projector shot images onto a screen behind the table and onto the covered windows: images of a sunlit grove surrounded by tall trees accompanied by a soundtrack of rustling leaves, birdsong, and the flutter of wings so close that I had to resist the urge to duck as I crossed the room to sit beside Liz.

She was on the near side of the long table, next to a woman with very short silver hair that stood up in bristly tufts, whom Liz introduced as Loomis Pagan. The pixy gender studies professor from Wesleyan, I recalled. I was introduced in turn to Delbert Winters from Harvard, Eleanor Belknap from Vassar, Lydia Markham from Mount Holyrood, and Talbot Greeley from Bard, who didn't look like a cluricaune, whatever that was. All the IMP board members sat on one side of the table. The other side was empty.

"They wouldn't let Soheila in," I whispered to Liz after I'd been introduced to everyone and had taken my seat. "Or Dory or Brock."

"I know," Liz said, clucking her tongue. "They've made us weaker by excluding the fey. They even tried to ban Talbot and Loomis, but we objected and got them admitted."

"Exclusion is the hobgoblin of little minds," Loomis Pagan began, but then the entrance of the Grove members silenced her.

Six figures filed into the room. For a moment they appeared to be wearing hooded robes and beaked masks, but then that illusion faded and I saw they were all wearing somber dark suits. They filed behind the table and each stood for a moment behind a chair. The slide show resolved into a single image of the tree-encircled glade and the light brightened as if the sun had come to stand directly above the open clearing. I looked down at my hands and saw that they were dappled with leaf shadow . . . and something else. A shadow of wings passed overhead just as the sound of wings on the soundtrack grew louder. I looked around, half-expecting some giant bird to come swooping down from the ceiling, but there was nothing but a stirring that seemed to be coming from the shadowy niches—as if the luminaries enclosed in them were trying to get a better view of the proceedings.

Adelaide's two blond companions stood at either ends of the table. I was surprised that they were actually on the board. I'd thought the Grove was an all women's club and that the men were security guards, but perhaps they were representatives from the London Seraphim Club. My grandmother stood at the center, between an older woman and a young woman with bangs and horn-rimmed glasses. Except for the blond twins, the council was made up of women in sensible, boxy suits and low-heeled pumps. It could have been the board of the local PTA or garden club instead of the governing body of an ancient order of witches.

A bell rang and the six Grove members pulled out their chairs and sat. The audio loop grew quieter and the light grew brighter over the long table. My grandmother clasped her hands, leaned forward, and addressed our side of the table as if we were a large crowd a long way off.

"As Chancellor of the Oak, I call this meeting between the Grove and the Institute of Magical Professionals to order." I thought I saw the two blond minions sneer a bit at the word *professionals*. Adelaide turned to the older woman on her right. "Miss Davis, do you have the report on Fairwick?"

"That's Garnette Davis," Liz whispered. "She's descended from a witch who was executed at Salem."

Garnette Davis opened her briefcase and took out a bound

report that was at least four inches thick. As she handed it to Adelaide the pages rustled. Adelaide put her hand on the cover as if to calm the pages within, then opened to the first page and read aloud, her clear aristocratic voice silencing even the recorded noises in the room.

"In the autumn of 2009, a committee was formed to investigate irregularities at the institution of Fairwick College, the village of Fairwick, and the outlying woods and farmlands. Because the last door to Faerie existed in the woods of Fairwick the area has long been a haven for supernatural creatures—fey, demon, and undesignated."

"Could you please clarify what you mean by the term 'undesignated'?" Loomis Pagan asked archly.

Adelaide gave Loomis a withering look, picked up a separate sheet, and began reading aloud in a bored monotonic voice. "Vampires, werewolves, shapeshifters, half breeds . . ."

Half breeds? I wondered. Wasn't I a sort of half breed? I focused back on Adelaide, who was still listing creatures who came under the undesignated label. ". . . trows, poltergeists, revenants, zombies . . ."

"I think we get the idea," Delbert Winters interrupted, glaring at Loomis Pagan. "Can we get on with this? I'm catching a plane to Iceland tonight."

"I'd be happy to get *on with it,*" Adelaide replied, picking up the report and reading where she had left off. "For many years it had been thought the door was inactive, but when it came to our attention that the door was not only active, but that creatures were passing freely between worlds without any supervision, the Grove decided to investigate the nature of the college and community. We found that at least three hundred fifty-three undocumented aliens were living in the town, among them races known to feed on humans, such as incubi, lidercs, and succubi, and that numerous attacks had been made on humans."

Liz cleared her throat. "Excuse me, Madame Chancellor. May I ask where you are getting your information?"

"Certainly. Because we wanted to be sure that there could be no accusation of bias, we subcontracted a report from an independent third party—the Internal Affairs Division of the Institute of Magical Professionals."

"I was not aware that we were being investigated," Liz trilled in full Jean Brodie mode.

Adelaide lowered her glasses and gave Liz a withering look. I would not have imagined that anyone could intimidate Elizabeth Book, but I saw her stiffen under my grandmother's scrutiny.

"Your awareness of the investigation would have invalidated it. Dr. Greeley can attest that the investigation was conducted under proper IMP guidelines."

Talbot Greeley adjusted the knot of his bow tie and recrossed his legs without looking at Liz. "We'd had complaints, Liz. My hands were tied."

Liz's face had gone very pale and she was clenching her hands so tightly under the table that I saw her knuckles bulging. "I see. May I know what this *agent* discovered?"

"If you have no objection, you can hear it from the agent himself."

"I have no objection," Liz replied, squaring her shoulders and leaning forward in her seat. "I would very much like to see who has been the spy in our midst."

TWENTY-SIX

*W*ithout looking to his left or right, Frank Delmarco entered the room. He walked to the chair set at the end of the table, slouched in his seat and glared at the Grove members. When his eyes met mine, he started to smile, then scowled, straightened his suit jacket, and pulled at the cuffs of his shirt. I'd never seen Frank in a suit jacket before. He looked like he was wearing a medieval torture device.

"Please state your full name," Adelaide said.

"Frances Dante Delmarco," Frank said with a look that dared anyone in the room to crack a smile at his middle name. Which wasn't likely. I could feel Liz's shock as she struggled to absorb the fact that brusque, gruff, but kind and decent Frank Delmarco had been a spy. At least Soheila would be spared seeing the man she secretly loved betray Fairwick—but then I recalled the video monitors. *Damn.*

"And please state your affiliations."

"I'm a full professor of American studies at Fairwick College," Frank said, looking straight at Liz. "I received tenure five years ago."

"I'll be damned if that'll keep me from firing you," Liz muttered under her breath.

"And . . . ?" Adelaide prompted.

"I also work for the Internal Affairs Division of the Institute of Magical Professionals. They—specifically, Dr. Greeley here—asked me to report on any suspicious or unusual supernatural occurrences at the college."

"And have you found *any suspicious or unusual supernatural occurrences* here at Fairwick?"

I held my breath. Last winter when I'd found out that he was an operative for IMPIA he'd gone on a rant about the unorthodox and dangerous activities on campus—ranging from unauthorized tampering with the weather to harassment of civilians by supernatural creatures. And that had been before he'd had to save me from a winged, life-sucking liderc.

Frank sighed. "I compiled my report for IMPIA, not the Grove. I was never told that the information I was gathering would be used in a witch hunt."

Loomis Pagan and Eleanor Belknap gasped.

"We are hardly likely to instigate a witch hunt," Adelaide said, enunciating each word, "since we ourselves are witches, Dr. Delmarco."

"I was using the term figuratively. I'm a witch myself, although I prefer the term wizard. Hunting down creatures because of their supernatural identities is just as intolerant as persecuting witches for their practices."

"So you think it's acceptable for supernatural creatures to prey on human beings?"

"Of course not," Frank snapped.

"But you did document a case in which . . ." Adelaide turned to a bookmarked page of the report. ". . . in which an incubus invaded the home of a Fairwick professor and sexually molested her, did you not?"

Frank's eyes flicked to mine for a brief instant, but long enough, I was sure, for him to have seen the pain in my eyes. I shouldn't have been surprised that he'd reported on my relationship with Liam, but it hurt that he'd expressed it in those terms.

"Yes, but I also reported that the professor in question was able to banish the incubus with help from her colleagues, including some otherworldly colleagues. They got the job done. And I'd say the same about Fairwick College: the people here may not always play by the book, but they get the job done. They're good people, by and large, whether human or otherwise."

Eleanor Belknap grunted assent and Loomis Pagan nodded her head in agreement. A little bit of my anger against Frank was dispelled.

"But then you don't always know which you're dealing with, do you, Dr. Delmarco? Are you acquainted with one Soheila Lilly?"

"Yes, I know Dr. Lilly. She teaches Middle Eastern studies here."

"And what is your relationship with Dr. Lilly?"

"We're colleagues—and friends," Frank answered warily, looking questioningly at me. Frank had told me once that he didn't exactly know what Soheila was. I hadn't volunteered the information that she was a succubus.

"So you've had ample opportunity to observe her. Do you know if she's human?"

"I know that she's a kind, intelligent, generous woman, an excellent teacher, and an outstanding scholar. She's never hurt a soul. That's good enough for me."

"Hm, but if you don't know what she is, how do you know that your judgment of her hasn't been compromised?"

Before Frank could answer—an answer I believe would have included a rich array of expletives—Adelaide raised her voice. "The Grove calls Soheila Lilly."

The door opened and Soheila appeared, escorted by Jen Davies. She and Soheila, arms linked, looked as if they might have been girlfriends out shopping together. She escorted Soheila to the end of the table opposite where Frank sat and, giving Soheila a small apologetic smile, left her. Soheila glanced first at Liz, then at the Grove members—then she saw Frank. A spontaneous smile of surprise and pleasure spread across her face and I realized she must have been sequestered somewhere and couldn't watch the proceedings. She didn't know yet that Frank was an Internal Affairs agent—or that he'd just been asked if he knew what sort of creature she was.

"Please state your full name," Adelaide ordered.

"Soheila Lilly," she replied.

"Is that your *full* name?"

Soheila sighed. The sigh turned into a musical trill of wind that passed through the room, carrying with it the scent of cardamom and cloves and the warmth of a desert night. I saw Frank smile when the breeze reached him—we all smiled, I think, warmed by its touch in this cold, hostile room, even Loomis Pagan, who looked like she hadn't smiled in decades. But then Adelaide lifted a hand and the warm gust turned icy cold.

"You are not allowed to perform magic at this meeting," she roared.

Soheila's eyes widened but she spoke with controlled grace. "I was not performing magic. You asked me my full name and I gave it to you. My name belongs to the wind. I cannot help what effect it has on you."

"It had *no* effect on me," Adelaide snapped, a smug look on her face, "because I am warded against such tricks, but I imagine the effect is most seductive to unwarded humans . . . or to a witch unaware of your nature." Adelaide turned to Frank. "Were you aware, Dr. Delmarco, that your colleague Soheila Lilly is a succubus?"

Frank shook his head, his eyes on Soheila. Her eyes were wide and glassy with pain.

Liz made a strangled noise. I glanced at her and saw that there were tears in her eyes. I looked at the other members of the board and saw that they were looking at Soheila intently.

"We are waiting for your answer, Dr. Delmarco."

"No," Frank said, "I wasn't. But it doesn't matter. It doesn't change *who* she is."

"But it does." Adelaide's voice was almost soft now. "She merely had to say her true name to make you swoon. Who knows what effect her power has had on you, or how it has compromised your judgment?"

"I have never wielded my power over Frank," Soheila cried. "Nor over any other man—not for decades. I have abstained from that sort of contact for more than sixty years." Soheila lifted her chin.

"Ah," Adelaide purred, "but you just said you don't have control over your power. Merely saying your name is a prelude to seduction. It is what you are. The Grove cannot blame you for that, Dr. Lilly, but it can take steps to protect humanity from you."

Beside me Liz made a noise that started as a sob but then turned into a snort of laughter. "Humanity!" she cried, rising to her feet. "This proceeding is a mockery of humanity. I call for a recess . . ."

"We all have to agree to call a recess," Delbert Winters said. "And I, for one, would like to hear what Dr. Lilly has to say."

Liz glared at Winters. "This is my college. I won't stand by and let my teachers be interrogated."

"And yet you stood by and let an incubus prey on one of your teachers. Your judgment has been rendered invalid, Dean Book. As has Dr. Delmarco's. You have both been seduced by those creatures from whom you are pledged to protect humanity. Why, less than one week ago you, Dean Book, let into this world an undine who has been rampaging through the woods, preying on young men."

"That wasn't Dean Book's fault," I said, rising to my feet. "I let in the undine—inadvertently—and Dean Book has done everything in her power to apprehend her. In fact, this rogue undine was apprehended last night. She's being held under guard until tomorrow when she will be escorted to the door and brought back to Faerie. It's that kind of cooperation between witches and fey that makes Fairwick work. If we close the door and force part of our population to leave, the town and college will lose its heart. We'll be diminished."

"A very heartening sentiment, Dr. McFay," Delbert Winters said, his voice thick with disdain, "but since you are not a member of the governing board of IMP, you have no standing in these proceedings."

"She's been called in as an expert witness—" Liz began.

"I hardly think that writing a book about the sex lives of vampires makes her an expert in anything but . . ." Delbert Winters sneered. ". . . *sex*. If anything, her proclivities make her a suspect witness. Didn't she have a relationship with an incubus last year?"

"That was months ago. I banished him—"

"And yet you still wear the marks of your dalliance with him!" Adelaide waved her hand and I felt something rough brush against my cheek. I was reminded of an incident when I was fourteen and Adelaide caught me wearing makeup to school. She'd scrubbed my face with a washcloth. I felt the same shame now, coupled with a tightening of my wards as I realized that Soheila's protective makeup had been wiped from my face, but I held my head up.

"This was no dalliance," I said. "It was an attack from a creature I was attempting to unmask."

"However you acquired the marks, dear, it's clear you are unable to protect yourself, let alone your friends and neighbors." She looked down at the report in front of her. "Since coming to Fairwick, you've let in a liderc who fed on students and faculty. You let in an incubus who fed on *you*. And now you've let in an undine that has been attacking fishermen."

Adelaide snapped her fingers and the slide projection of a bucolic wood changed to a graphic depiction of a body of a young man, his legs twisted at an unnatural angle, his arms splayed out to either side, lying beside a forest stream. His face and chest were covered with blood and gore. Lydia Markham and Talbot Greeley gasped.

"This body was found in the woods near the source of the Undine," Adelaide said into the stunned silence of the room. "As was this one." She snapped her fingers again and another corpse appeared on the screen, this one without a face.

Frank stood up and moved closer to the screen, the red gore spreading over his own face as he scrutinized the picture.

"Do we know for certain that this was done by an undine?" Liz asked.

Adelaide shot her a cool stare. "They were found near where Lorelei was last spotted."

"Still, that doesn't mean she did this to those men," I said.

"This isn't how undines usually behave," Soheila added, staring at the gruesome image. "Something's wrong."

"Yes," Adelaide agreed. "Something is *very* wrong. Those woods have become a breeding ground for creatures from the other world. These aren't cute fairies and brownies—these are monsters. Not only has Fairwick failed to control the traffic of immigration from Faerie, it has created an atmosphere in which such creatures thrive. It has been suggested by some members of this council that the only solution is to shut down the entire town."

"You mean," Liz said, blanching, "like Fluges?"

"It's your own fault for hiring so many otherworlders," Delbert Winters hissed at Liz, his face dyed red from the slide projection. "I've warned you about that before."

"Clearly there should have been stricter monitoring structures in place," Lydia Markham remarked, her face also a mask of blood.

"This is what happens when the avenues of discourse are severed due to self-fulfilling paradigm shifts," Loomis Pagan remarked enigmatically.

" 'Violence is the last resort of the helpless,' " Eleanor Belknap quoted somebody. "These creatures need help."

"Otherworlders who cannot control their urges—as the rest of us have—need to be escorted from this world and never let back in again," Talbot Greeley said, adjusting his now crimson bow tie. "Lest they ruin it for the rest of us."

I turned toward each board member but saw only bloody, scared faces, their voices mingled with the restless rustling sound that seemed to be growing and coming from everywhere. It sounded like a stampede—or a flock of angry birds. Frank was standing with his back to the table, still staring up at the slide. The Grove members were talking among themselves, Garnette Davis leaning toward Adelaide, whispering in her ear. Adelaide shook her head several times, then nodded once and held up her hand. Instantly the room went quiet.

"My esteemed colleague, Garnette Davis, has another suggestion. If we announce that the door is to be closed and the captured undine is escorted under the armed guard of the Stewarts to the door, the majority of otherworldly creatures in the forest will also leave this world. It may take some time to clean up the woods entirely, but we may be able to save the town and the college."

The IMP board members murmured their approval.

"That is, if Dr. McFay is willing to close the door for us," Adelaide added.

"And if I don't?" I asked.

"That would be regrettable," Adelaide said severely, "but I assure you we have our ways of doing it ourselves. You won't be able to stop us."

"What about the otherworlders living in Fairwick?" I asked. "What will happen to them?"

"The creatures who have made their homes here are free to choose which world they will live in," Adelaide replied.

"That seems eminently fair," Talbot Greeley said with a relieved sigh. "Don't you think so, Delbert?"

Delbert Winters snorted. "Too fair by half, but I suppose it will do."

"But if the door is closed forever, many will be forced to choose Faerie," Liz said.

"So they'll have to choose," Lydia Markham said brusquely. "We've all had to make hard choices. Why should fairies be any different?"

"And what of those who have used Aelvesgold to lengthen their life spans?" Liz asked. "Or to control illnesses? Lydia, didn't your mother receive treatment when she was sick last year? And you, Talbot, I know you don't maintain your physique through going to the gym." Neither professor met Liz's gaze.

"Vanities," Eleanor Belknap remarked. "We'll learn to do

without them. Are we ready to take a vote? All those in favor of closing the door forever, raise their hands."

Five of the six board members raised their hands. Liz kept her hands clasped in front of her, fingers knotted together.

"Very well, then," Adelaide said, smiling. "We're agreed. The door will be closed forever."

"When?" Soheila asked, the single word gusting from her mouth with a force that snapped the window blinds and chilled the room.

Adelaide smiled. "Since tomorrow is the solstice, it seems a fitting time. The door will be closed tomorrow morning at dawn."

TWENTY-SEVEN

*R*ising as one, the Grove members began to file out. The IMP board members got up more slowly, but they too left the room, avoiding looking at Liz, who remained in her seat. Soheila got up and started walking toward Liz and me. At the same time, Frank turned around from the slide screen and started toward her, his arms out as though to grab hold of her.

"Soheila, I'm so sorry. I didn't know . . ."

She held up her hands. I think she only meant to ward off Frank's apologies and to keep him from touching her—maybe she was afraid of what effect her touch might have on him in her highly emotional state—but the motion caused a gust of wind that blew him backward. He hit the wall, his arms splayed out to steady himself, in a pose eerily like the twisted limbs of the murdered fisherman. Soheila made a sound like a wounded bird and fled the room. With a pained look on his face, Frank watched her go and then addressed himself to Liz. "I had no idea that the information I was collecting would be used by the Grove. It looks to me like IMP has been compromised by the Grove."

Liz nodded. "We're in agreement there," she said. "I don't understand how they can turn their backs on the fey. Even Loomis Pagan and Talbot Greeley have turned on their own kind."

I filled Frank in on what I'd learned from Jen Davies about the club in London that the Grove had joined forces with.

"The Seraphim Club?" he repeated. "I've heard something about them . . ." His voice drifted off. He was staring at me, his eyes narrowed. "What *did* happen to your face, McFay?"

"Oh," I said, embarrassed. "It's a long story—" Before I could finish he stepped closer and put his hand up against my face, but the wards on my skin sizzled and popped. He kept his hand there, though, even though the wards were beginning to smoke and I smelled singed flesh.

"Frank, don't!" I grabbed his hand and pushed it away. He looked at me, then down at his hand. The coils had been seared into his flesh. He nodded once, as if what he saw confirmed something he'd long suspected. Then he turned and left without another word.

Liz's face sagged. She seemed to have aged a decade in the hour we'd been inside this room. I was afraid she was going to cry, but instead she asked the last question I wanted to hear. "Can you stop them from closing the door?"

"Yes," I said with more confidence than I felt. "I read in Wheelock that there's a way for a doorkeeper to create a bond with the door to keep it open."

"I've read that footnote in Wheelock," Liz said, "but only a doorkeeper can access the spell." Her face looked troubled. "I've also heard that doorkeepers have died in the attempt to prevent a door from closing."

"It won't come to that," I told Liz.

She held my gaze for a moment, then nodded. "Let's hope not."

. . .

I walked quickly across the campus, my anger at the Grove pumping in my veins. They had tricked and manipulated us. Clearly they had gotten to some of the IMP board members and influenced their votes. The others had been swayed by those awful pictures of undine attacks. The Grove was using fear and prejudice to control us. Well, I wouldn't be controlled. I was the doorkeeper. There had to be a way I could keep the door open, despite the Grove's intention to close it—and the answer was in Wheelock.

When I reached my house I opened my briefcase and took out the spellbook. Standing on the porch I opened to the marked section, reread the footnote, and then depressed the magical icon. Instead of pages filling with text as had happened before, I felt a sharp stabbing pain in my right eye, as if a hot cinder had blown into it. I blinked and a red film covered my vision. It took a moment to realize that words were imprinted on the film and that they were scrolling across my vision.

In order for a doorkeeper to gain complete dominion over a door to Faerie and prevent others from closing it she may cast a correlative spell that links her own person to the door. This can be accomplished by spilling a drop of her blood on the threshold of the door. Once the bond is established she only has to repeat the words Quam cor mea aperit, tam ianua aperit *("Just as my heart opens, so the door opens") in order to cancel out any opposing closing spells. The best time to perform this ritual is at dusk on the eve of the summer solstice.*

"Eureka!" I said aloud, blinking my eyes three times. The words *There is one caution* . . . flashed as I blinked but then began to fade. *Shoot!* Blinking three times was probably the way to end the transmission. Never mind, I thought, I knew enough to make the bond. It was nearly dusk now. I had to go to the door right now to establish the bond before tomorrow morning.

Without bothering to change out of my suit and pumps, I took off into the woods, walking as fast as I could in heels to the clearing where the door to Faerie stood. As rushed as I was, I ground to a halt when I reached the edge of the clearing. I'd stood here before in the middle of winter and thought it was magical when glazed with ice and snow, but I'd never seen it before in full summer, on the eve of the summer solstice. The trees were draped with honeysuckle vines in full bloom, their white and yellow blossoms filling the air with sweet honeyed scent. The vines had twisted themselves into an arch directly across from me. Heavy wisteria blooms hung over the arch like a fringed curtain. The air inside the arch shimmered like the skin of a soap bubble. I approached it warily, feeling my resolve waver with the undulating colors. I was going to bond myself to *this,* I thought, a portal to another world? I was already a mess of conflicting desires. What would it do to me to connect myself to an unstable, volatile entity?

Perhaps I should have read that caution in Wheelock.

But I'd left the book behind and I didn't have time to go back. It was dusk. The Grove was closing the door tomorrow. Clearly they thought they could. This might be the only way to stop them.

I moved closer until I was inches from the door. The transparent film pulsed as if sensing my presence. Weren't we already connected? I stretched out my hand and held it up to the surface of the door, palm out. The film swirled, forming a pattern like the one I'd seen on Skald's phone. Yes, this was my fate. Whatever it did to me, I had to forge this bond.

Still holding one hand up to the door I unpinned the luckenbooth brooch from my jacket. Its design of two hearts seemed fitting for a spell that linked my heart to the door. I pricked my finger with the pin, squeezed it until a drop of blood welled up, then turned my hand over to let the drop fall on the threshold of the door.

"*Quam cor mea aperit,*" I said, "*tam ianua aperit.*"

The transparent pattern swirled into a spiral. As it moved, I felt a tugging sensation in my chest. Yes, we *were* connected, for better or for worse. *Like a marriage,* I thought wryly, looking down at my hand. The drop of blood reminded me of Bill drawing out the splinter. I suddenly wished he were here to cradle my hand in his . . .

But that was silly. It wasn't as if I was really injured—just bound to an ephemeral ancient gateway. I turned and walked back to my house. It began to rain again, but the trees were so thick that the raindrops barely touched me. I could hear them, though, rustling through the high branches. When I looked up, I saw a shadow moving through the branches.

A shadow? In the pouring rain?

A branch cracked overhead, the sound loud as gunfire in the rain, and I took off toward my house. Something burst out of the trees above me, but I was too frightened to turn around and look up. I sprinted across my lawn, up the porch steps, and onto the shelter of my porch. My hands were wet and shaking as I dug in my pocket for my keys. I'd just found them when I felt a hand on my back.

I whirled around, the point of the house key gripped between my fingers ready to stab the intruder . . . and looked up into Duncan's blue eyes.

"Callie, it's me. Are you all right? I saw you running from the woods and came to see if you were okay. You looked frightened."

I edged past Duncan to the porch railing and looked up into the sky. A large branch had fallen at the edge of the woods.

"I thought I heard something in the trees," I said warily. "For all I knew it was you, come to finish what you started and claw out my other eye."

Duncan blanched. "Callie, I'm sorry. I can explain . . ."

"Really?" I leaned against the porch railing and crossed my arms over my chest. "I'm waiting."

"That spell you cast summoned a creature—some kind of imp with bat wings and claws. It flew between us so quickly I couldn't stop it, but when it struck you I pulled it away from you and then chased it into the woods."

I snorted. "I don't believe that for a minute. I was holding your hand. When I turned . . ." I faltered. I had turned and the slash of claws had blinded me. I'd assumed it was Duncan—or Duncan turned into a clawed beast—but really I hadn't seen the thing that had attacked me. "If that was true, why didn't you come back?"

"I followed it into the woods. I didn't want it to come back to hurt you. I chased it all night and finally cornered it, but it lashed out at me just as it did at you. This is what I got for my trouble." He took a tentative step closer to me and rolled up his shirtsleeve. Five deep gashes ran from elbow to wrist.

"You could have done that to yourself," I said.

"Really?" he asked, lifting an eyebrow. "Could I have done this?" He turned, ripping off his shirt to expose his back, which was raked with claw marks. I reached out to touch one and he winced.

"You weren't at the meeting today," I said.

"How could I go with these marks on me?" he asked, turning to face me. He was close, his bare chest radiating heat across the few inches that separated us. I felt a tug, like static electricity or centripetal force, pulling me toward him. My heart, newly bound to the door, beat erratically. Were heart palpitations part of the warning I hadn't read?

"Ann Chase told me you asked her to recommend you as my tutor. She thinks you're the incubus."

"Is that who you think I am?" he asked, lifting his hand to my cheek and gently tracing the scratches over my eye with his fingertips. I shivered at his touch, suddenly aware of how cold and wet I was. "Is that who you want me to be?"

"I . . . I don't know," I said, my voice trembling. "I thought I might love him. I thought if I saw him once more . . . as he really is . . . then I'd know."

There was a flicker in Duncan azure eyes, a shadow that swam in and out of my vision as Duncan lowered his head and pressed his mouth against my mouth. The instant his lips were on mine the shadow resolved into the shadow that had moved through the trees and I felt a jolt of fear. I tried to pull away but he wrapped his arms around me and held me tight, his lips locked on mine, his tongue probing my mouth, his bare chest pressing me up against the porch railing. But now instead of warmth rising off him, I felt cold. Pure ice-water cold. I wasn't sure if Duncan was the incubus but I was sure of one thing: he felt *wrong*. I summoned the sizzle of energy I'd felt last night when I released my wards, wriggled my hands between our bodies, and *pushed*.

Duncan flew across the porch and hit the front door so hard the doorbell chimed and the glass fanlight shook in its frame and cracked. A sliver of green glass plummeted straight down onto Duncan's bare chest and lodged there like a miniature dart. Duncan winced and brushed it away, streaking blood across his chest. He wiped the blood on his pants and got to his feet, his eyes locked on mine.

"I'm getting a little tired," he said, biting off each word as he moved toward me, "of these mixed signals."

"I don't think there was anything mixed in that last signal the lady sent you."

The voice, low and ominous, came from behind me. I turned around and found Bill, hands clenched into fists, glaring at Duncan.

"This is between Callie and me," Duncan said. "I don't think we need the handyman to weigh in."

I moved closer to Bill and put my hand on his arm. "Bill's right. I think you should leave."

Duncan narrowed his eyes at Bill, clearly assessing the threat he represented. The muscles in Bill's forearm clenched under my fingers, turning hard as steel. I could practically smell the testosterone in the air. Any second now the two men would fly at each other. I stepped between them and felt the hair on the back of my neck rise. "If the two of you are going to fight over me like two dogs fighting over a bone, I'm going to talk to you like dogs. Go home, Duncan. You stay, Bill."

Duncan lifted one corner of his mouth in a half smile–half snarl and walked past us, getting close enough to brush against Bill's arm. I felt Bill tense, but he remained still. We both turned, though, to watch Duncan walk down the stairs. When he got to the bottom he looked over his shoulder at me. "Remember that this was your choice, Callie." Then he walked across the street to the Hart Brake Inn.

It wasn't until he was halfway across the street that I felt a release of the tension in the air and then I nearly collapsed. If Bill hadn't steadied me with his arm, I'd have slumped to the floor. "Let's get you inside," he said, helping me toward the door.

"Okay," I said, leaning against him and letting him practically carry me over the threshold. I felt weak. It wasn't just the release of tension; it had something to do with the power I'd used pushing Duncan away. "Thank you for coming to my defense."

"You looked like you were doing a pretty good job yourself," he said. "I'd have stepped in sooner, only I wasn't sure you wanted me to."

"You were watching us?"

Bill pointed up. At first I thought he was pointing at the fanlight, which I saw to my dismay was indeed cracked. A splinter had come loose from the stained glass eye of the young man, making it look as if a single tear was falling from his eye. "I was on the porch roof," Bill explained when he saw me staring at the fanlight. "I didn't mean to listen in, but I couldn't help hearing . . . I heard you say you thought you loved someone."

"Oh, that," I said. "I thought Duncan Laird was someone else . . ." I looked up at Bill. "I've been pretty confused lately. I seem to keep making mistakes . . ."

"Do you think last night was a mistake?" he asked, his face pained.

"No! I didn't mean that. Last night was great . . . lovely . . . but . . ."

"But what?" he asked, taking his arm from my shoulder and leaning against the wall. "Do you want to be with that man?"

"Duncan?" I shuddered. "No, I don't. But it's complicated. There's history between us that I can't completely ignore."

"Oh, I see. Complicated. Too complicated for the likes of me, I guess. It seems pretty simple to me. That man hurt you." He reached out and touched my face. His blunt, calloused fingertips felt like balm on my bruised skin, like a warm breeze. While Duncan's touch had chilled me, Bill's warmed me. Where Duncan had felt wrong, Bill felt *right*. He started to take his hand away, but I grabbed it and held it to my face.

"You're right," I said. "It *is* simple. I want you, not Duncan Laird. Would you . . . ? Could you . . . ?"

Bill didn't wait for me to figure out the words for what I

wanted. He already knew. He pulled me into his arms and pressed me hard against his chest and bent my head back. He kissed the bruises on my face gently, then sank his mouth down to mine *not* so gently. He pressed me up against the door until I felt the hard length of him pushing between my legs. I moaned and went weak in the knees. He scooped me up and started for the stairs, but I wrapped my legs around his waist and bit his ear.

"No. Here."

He lowered me onto the polished oak floor of the foyer and crouched over me. Keeping my eyes on his face, I slid out of my skirt, half afraid that if I didn't keep my eyes on him he'd vanish. The rain lashing against the windows cast speckled shadows across the foyer, painting Bill's body with a dappled tattoo. When I reached for him, my own arms dipped into the rain shadows as though into a waterfall. For a moment we were caught in the same current and I thought, *Good, if he vanishes so will I,* and then he pressed the length of his body against mine and the strength of him anchored me. His skin against mine awoke a heat deep within—another coil of the wards that had bound me unwound as I pulled him inside me. As we moved together, our eyes locked on to each other's, I felt it coil around us, wrapping us in an endless spiral of desire.

"I could do this forever," I whispered in his ear.

"We have done this forever," he answered.

At some point, we made it up to the bedroom. We made love again and then slept. I awoke in the middle of the night to a room filled with moonlight. My head pillowed on Bill's chest, I saw the profile of his face etched against the silver light.

"It's stopped raining," I said.

"No," he said, turning to me, his eyes flashing silver. "It's witchlight. The woods are flooding. All the lost creatures are making their way back to the door before it closes."

"Bill, how do you know about all that?"

He smiled and traced his fingertip along my lips. "I don't. You're dreaming. You're also dreaming that I'm about to kiss you. Is that all right?"

"Yes," I said, my heart fluttering. "I suppose that would be . . ."

He pressed his mouth against mine, his lips spreading mine open. I felt the heat of him pouring into me, warming every last inch of me. I pressed against him and felt his heart thud against mine. My heart beat in answer to his. I heard an answering thud from deep in the woods. The door, linked to my heart, was opening wide, beating so loudly I could hear it . . .

I startled awake in the empty bed to the sound of pounding. Bill sat in a chair beside the bed, his face dark in the rain-shadowed room. I saw by his posture that he was alert.

"Bill? Was there moonlight a minute ago? And were you . . ."

"It's still raining," he said, getting to his feet, "and there's someone at the door. I'll go and tell them to leave. You shouldn't go out in this rain."

He left the room before I could stop him. I swung my legs over the side of the bed and sat on the edge for a moment, trying to reconstruct my dream. I went to the window. Through the rain, I saw the woods *were* filled with an eerie light: a white, glowing mist that rose off the wet ground and flowed along the forest floor like floodwater. It was full of shapes. Dream-Bill had been right. The woods were full of creatures heading toward the door. But how did Bill Carey know that?

TWENTY-EIGHT

$\mathcal{J}$ got dressed in jeans, a turtleneck, and heavy socks, and then took the Aelvestone out of the bag where I'd stashed it and stuffed it in my pocket, making sure it was carefully wrapped in flannel. I needed one other thing, which I got from my desk, then I crept down the backstairs with my waterproof hiking boots held in my hand, listening to the murmur of voices in the front hall. I could make out one excitable young man's voice and two lower, more mature male voices besides Bill's.

"I don't care how much you need her," Bill was saying as I walked through the library. "She's not well enough to go out in this weather."

"I'd like to see her myself and hear her say that. Who the hell are you, anyway?"

"This is Bill," I told Frank as I came into the foyer. "He's my . . . boyfriend." I felt silly using the word for a man I'd spent all of two nights with, but Bill's smile chased those scruples away. "At least I hope he is," I added.

"Well, that's sweet," Frank said, staring at Bill. I scowled at Frank and then at the other two men in the hallway. Mac

Stewart and his father, Angus, both in plaid rain jackets and plaid rain boots dripping water all over my parquet floor. I remembered that Liz said the Stewarts were some kind of protectors of the forest . . . but that shouldn't mean they couldn't remember to wipe their feet.

"I'll get a mop—and some hot tea for you, Callie," Bill said, following my glance and glaring at the Stewarts. When he was gone, I turned to Frank.

"What's going on?" I asked. "Why are the Stewarts here?"

Mac Stewart puffed up his chest proudly. I noticed he was wearing the owl feather he'd gotten from me the night we met in the woods. "Our family are the stewards of the woods! I didn't even know that until last night. We tracked that mean fish woman back to her hidey-hole and got her trapped there. See, I've got superpowers just like you . . ."

"Hush, boy," Angus said, not unkindly. "All she needs to know is that Lura's threatening to shoot anyone who steps onto her property."

"She says she won't let us take her mother away the way we took her fiancé—"

"That's enough, Mac," Angus cautioned, more sternly now. "We don't have to air all our business here."

"You do if you expect my help," I replied, dropping my boots and folding my arms over my chest.

Angus Stewart heaved an exasperated sigh. "Lura has it in her addled brain that the Stewarts did away with Quincy Morris."

"Why would she think that?" I asked.

"Because he was our cousin," Angus answered, "from the Morris clan over in Ulster County. He was supposed to be guarding the woods the summer he went courting Lura. Some of the elders didn't like it, on account of her having an undine mother. A few of them, my father included, spoke to Lura about it the night before the wedding—the night before Quincy disappeared. Lura thinks they scared him away or, worse, killed him so he couldn't marry her and disgrace the family. But my father swears they didn't do anything to Quincy. Told me Quincy wouldn't have been the first to find a bride in those woods. They spoke to Quincy that night and he was bound and determined to marry Lura, despite her being half-fish."

"So what happened to him?"

Angus shrugged. "We've never known. My father thinks he might have gotten cold feet after all, but it's not like a Morris to run away. Any road, we must convince Lura to let go of Lorelei. It's our job to protect the woods and Lorelei has proved herself dangerous."

"There's more danger in those woods than Lorelei," Frank said. "I don't believe those murdered fishermen were the victims of an undine—and I don't think an incubus did this to you," he said, touching my eye. "Explain exactly how it happened."

I told him about my attempt to unmask Duncan, embarrassed to be telling the story in front of the Stewarts. When I told him Duncan's story about the bat-winged imp, he snorted.

"What a load of bull hickey. This Duncan Laird is obviously not what he appears to be, but I don't believe he's your incubus. He only let you and Ann Chase believe that to deflect attention from what he *really* is."

"And what's that?" Angus Stewart asked.

"A Nephilim," Frank answered.

"Can't be!" Angus Stewart barked so loudly his son flinched. "The Stewarts fought those bastards back in the old country and killed every last one. They're extinct."

"That's what they wanted us to think," Frank replied.

"They went into hiding, marshaling their forces to gain allies among the witches . . ."

"Of course!" I exclaimed. "The Seraphim Club in London is a Nephilim organization."

"Exactly. I've long had my suspicions about them. The members might look like angels but there's nothing angelic about them. They've created a legend that they're fallen angels, but they're really elves who were thrown out of Faerie because of their treatment of human women. They persecuted witches who were friendly with the fey and recruited others with the promise of an endless supply of Aelvesgold. They're one of the few species of fey that can produce Aelvesgold outside of Faerie."

"So they've bribed the Grove into working with them," I said.

"And the board of IMP," Frank said. "I should have seen this coming."

"What do we do now?" I asked.

"There's an ancient spell for banishing Nephilim and one person in Fairwick who might know what it is." Frank exchanged a look with Angus, who nodded. "I'm going to go see her. In the meantime, you should go with the Stewarts to Lura's and see what you can do about getting Lorelei to go back to Faerie. Then go to the door and open it. The Grove won't try to close the door until everyone has gone through it and I'll be there before then. Once those Nephilim bastards have been banished, the Grove will realize they won't have any Aelvesgold if the door is closed. They won't dare close it then."

I started to tell Frank that they wouldn't be able to close it even if they wanted to because of the link I'd made with my heart, but before I could, I heard Bill's voice behind me.

"Let me help you."

He was standing in the doorway to the library with a mop in one hand and a cup of tea in the other. I was about to object—Bill had no idea what he would be getting himself into, but Frank was already extending his hand to shake Bill's. Bill leaned the mop against the wall, put the teacup down on the foyer table, and grasped Frank's hand in his. A secret understanding seemed to pass between the two men and I was damned if I knew what it was. For all I knew, they rooted for the same baseball team.

"Glad to have you on board, Bill," Frank said. "I could use your help."

There didn't seem to be anything I could say except a hurried good-bye to Bill. "There might be some things you'll want explained," I said.

"Let's leave the explanations for later," he said, kissing me hard on the lips. Then he was gone, leaving me to wonder what explanations he might have for me.

I went with the Stewarts to their truck—an enormous vehicle with jacked-up tires. Mac gave me a hand up into the high cab and then squeezed in beside me. The two Stewart men took up so much room I practically had to sit on Mac's lap, which made him grin until a scowl from his father wiped the smile from his face.

We drove down Elm Street and onto Main, which looked like it was under a foot or two of water. The only thing open was the Village Diner. As we passed, I saw a tired-looking Darla through the window filling sugar canisters. We passed Mama Esta's Pizzeria and Browne's Realty. Was Dory with Brock now? I wondered. I hoped so.

A bitter-tasting grief was rising in my throat as fast as the floodwater. "We can't let them get away with it," I said. "The town would never be the same."

"No, it wouldn't be," Angus agreed somberly. "The town's barely been hanging on with the economic downturn. This latest blow might destroy it totally."

We rode the rest of the way in grim silence, the rain and the slap of the windshield wipers the only sounds. We had to take a detour around the low-water crossing on Trask Road, onto Butt's Corners Road, which cut through the woods. As we came around a sharp turn, the headlights picked up dark shapes in the road. Angus slammed on the brakes just in time to avoid hitting the deer. The lead stag turned to regard us, his eyes glowing gold in the headlights. He stood facing us while the rest of the herd crossed the road in safety, his gold eyes seeming to look directly into mine. Even the enchanted deer were choosing to leave.

Back on Trask Road, we passed the Olsen farm. All the lights were on at the big house on the hill.

"They'll be keeping vigil over the woods," Angus said, "maintaining the wards until the door is closed. All this water disrupts the flow of energy. I imagine they're having a hard time of it."

"What about the Norns? Are they leaving?"

Angus shook his head. "The Norns are creatures outside this world and the world of Faerie. They say that when the first fey came to this world the Norns and certain other creatures were already here."

We drove on in silence for another few minutes, then I asked, "What *other* creatures?"

Before Angus could answer, Lura's house came into view.

"Holy cow!" Mac swore.

"Language, son," Angus admonished, but then muttered something in Gaelic which sounded far worse than what Mac had said.

Lura's house was bathed in flickering blue and green light. A multihued wall of light surrounded the house. A dozen men, all dressed in plaid shirts, stood in a circle around the house, their arms extended, their broad faces stolid in the pouring rain.

"What are they doing?" I asked.

"They're holding up the plaid," Angus said proudly. "That's what we Stewarts do. It's an ancient power handed down from our ancestors in Scotland. We can use the plaid to protect the innocent and banish the evil."

I saw now that the wall of light was indeed woven of glowing strands of red, gold, blue, and green—like a luminescent tartan. But I also noticed that water from the rising creek was seeping through it.

"The house looks like it's going to float away," I said. "Surely Lura and Lorelei will see they have to get out of there now."

"I don't know about that," Mac said, pointing to the porch.

A figure was sitting in a rocking chair. Waves of blue-green light reflected off the barrel of a shotgun laid across her lap. Lura was so still she might have been a statue of ash, but when the light caught her eyes, the hate in them was very much alive.

"You two stay here," I said. "I'll go talk to her."

I slid out of the truck into calf-deep water. I waded through it, my feet squelching in the mud. When I reached the tartan ward, two of the Stewart men parted it for me to pass. I kept my eyes on Lura the whole time, afraid she'd dart away or shoot me, but she remained perfectly still. When I got to the porch steps—the bottom two of which were underwater—I held out my hands to show her I didn't have a weapon.

"Can I come up?"

"Come aboard," she said. "I ain't gonna bite." She grinned, her white teeth shining ghoulishly in the watery light. They weren't as sharp as her mother's, but they weren't exactly human-looking either. I walked slowly up the steps, their wooden slats groaning under my weight. When I stepped onto the porch, the house swayed as though coming unmoored from its foundation. I glanced toward the stream and saw that even in the few minutes since I'd arrived, it had risen higher. Strange shapes bobbed on its swollen surface—branches, glass bottles, dead animals. There were live things, too. A whiskered nose poked out of the water and tried to climb onto the bank, but the current snatched it back into the water.

"Strange things have been moving through the woods all night," said Lura. "Creatures heading to the door." She scowled at me. "I guess you didn't have much luck convincing the Grove not to close it."

"No," I admitted. "But I've found a way to keep it open. Lorelei still needs to go back, though. She's a danger to folks here."

Lura's gaze moved toward the woods. "You know, I've sat here for close on eighty years watching these woods, hoping Quincy would walk out of them again. Then a few days ago my mother walks out instead. And now you want to take her away, too. This town won't be happy until it takes everything away from me."

"Lorelei's killed men."

"She tells me she hasn't." Lura looked up at me and raised the shotgun slightly. "And I believe her."

I sighed. I remembered the brief time I'd spent with my

mother in the labyrinth. For a moment, I'd been willing to stay with her there. Would I have listened to anyone who told me she was bad? Would I have let anyone take her away?

"Can I talk to Lorelei?" I asked.

Lura looked up at me, surprised. "You're either braver or stupider than I thought. She's not too fond of you. She might eat you."

"I know, but is she inside?" I looked worriedly at the water, which had risen to the top of the porch and was now lapping against the front door.

"She's upstairs in the bathtub," Lura said. "She's got to stay hydrated. Go on. I don't think she's modest, but if you hurt her . . ." The shotgun was still pointed at me. "I won't let you out of here alive. Understand?"

I nodded and walked to the front door. Flickering water reflections circled the doorknob. When I pushed open the door, water lapped over the threshold like a cat that had been waiting to get in. The glass and tin wind chimes floated in the wavy light like fish. The ceiling, too, was soaked through, water dripping from bulging blisters of plaster and streaming down the walls. It looked as if the creek was rising to take back this house. I just hoped it waited until I got out of here.

I climbed the narrow staircase, my feet sinking into spongy damp floral carpet. Old photographs hung framed on the walls: sepia-colored prints of stern, square-jawed men and women standing in stiff, formal rows in front of this house. A more lively picture was a group shot of men in fishing waders, each holding a huge fish up to the camera. I looked closer and noticed that some of the men wore the Stewart plaid and the Stewart family features. So the Trasks and the Stewarts had been friends once. At the top of the stairs was a picture of a seated woman with a baby on her lap, a man standing behind her. I looked closer at this cozy domestic scene. The woman wore a high-necked white blouse and her blond hair was gathered on her head in a puffy Gibson girl updo. One hand cradled the baby's head, the other grasped the man's hand resting on her shoulder. Her smile somehow seemed to be for both of them, her eyes full of love. I almost didn't recognize Lorelei, but that's who it was.

As I walked down the hall I saw more pictures of mother and child. I stopped at one of a slim woman holding a two-year-old toddler by the hand. Again I almost didn't recognize Lorelei. She was rail-thin, her hair dull and scraped back on her head in thin wisps, her face deeply lined with wrinkles, her shoulders stooped. I recalled that Duncan had said an undine was depleted of Aelvesgold after she laid her eggs. Lorelei had begun to fade fast after giving birth to Lura.

I lifted the picture off the wall, exposing a patch of wallpaper that still held the original bright, cheerful colors it had when Sullivan Trask decorated the house for his beloved bride and newborn daughter, and carried it down the hall toward the sound of splashing water.

The bathroom door was open. I saw the bathtub from the hall and heard splashing. "Can I come in?" I called.

"I suppose you will if I say yes or no," Lorelei answered.

Taking that as a yes, I entered the bathroom. At one time it had been papered in a lovely water lily pattern, but now blossoms of mold bloomed over the water lilies and the paper hung in long strips like seaweed. Brass shell-shaped wall sconces clung to the walls like barnacles, their lightbulbs long burned out but now filled with flickering votive candles. Even the taps on the sink were shaped like shells.

I turned to the bathtub. Lorelei was stretched out beneath a froth of bubbles that sparkled in the flickering light. Her hair was piled high on her head in the same style as in the old photograph. "You were wasting, weren't you?" I asked. "That's why you had to leave."

She shrugged. "I suppose. I did feel tired all the time," she said, blowing at the bubbles. "Taking care of a human baby is so much more work than laying eggs."

"So why'd you come back?"

"To mate. It doesn't work in Faerie. Even the humans who wander in are no good to us."

"Humans wander in?"

"Occasionally. Where do you think people go when they go missing? Sure, some of them are lying in a ditch with their throats slit or living new lives under assumed names in Mexico, but *some* wander into Faerie. It happens all the time in the woods when the door opens on the solstice."

I thought of the young men I'd seen with the undines in Faerie, of one in particular, a dark-haired man with sad eyes. "Did one happen to wander in about eighty years ago?"

Lorelei shrugged. "Time is different in Faerie. All I know is when it's time to mate . . . Now that you mention it there was a sulky boy who kept begging to go back, but it's not as easy to get back into this world as to get out of it."

Except maybe tonight.

"So, is that why you won't leave? Because you have to mate?"

Lorelei laughed and stretched one bare, foam-flecked leg up to the ceiling, daintily pointing her toe. "Oh, I've done *that* already. One of those pretty Stewart boys was quite accommodating. No, the reason I won't leave is this." She reached into the water and pulled out a dappled green oval. At first I thought it was bar of soap, but then I noticed it was glowing.

"Is that an egg? You've laid . . ." I peered into the tub, through a patch of foam near Lorelei's feet, and saw a pile of green-spotted eggs—and one gold one. An Aelvestone.

Lorelei shifted uneasily. "I should have laid them in the Undine, but those damned Stewarts warded the house. Poor things," she said, looking at the eggs. "They'll die if they don't get into flowing freshwater soon."

Lorelei was gazing at the egg cupped in her hand with the same expression on her face as she'd had in the photograph of her and baby Lura. She had loved Lura, but when she had begun to waste away she'd chosen to go back to Faerie. Perhaps that meant her love wasn't a very deep kind, but who was I—who hadn't been able to love Liam enough to make him human—to judge her? Frank didn't believe she was responsible for the murders of the fishermen—and now neither did I.

"I want to offer you a deal," I said.

She looked up, the flicker of interest in her moss green eyes making her look momentarily human.

TWENTY-NINE

*T*wenty minutes later, we came downstairs, Lorelei dressed in a green silk gown embroidered with seed pearls that I suspected had been Lura's wedding dress. I was carrying a canvas bag full of undine eggs. I called Lura in off the porch and told her what we planned to do. A fleeting look of sadness passed over her face when she realized her mother was planning to leave again, but she set her mouth and took the bag from me.

"I'll bring them to the headwaters," Lura said.

"That's near the door to Faerie," I said. "I'll walk that far with you."

"Won't the Stewarts want to accompany you, seeing as you're the doorkeeper?"

"I'll tell them to take Lorelei to the door."

Lura looked back at her house. The living room floor was under six inches of water. Bits of glass and tin bobbed on the surface. The house groaned and creaked, its timbers cracking under the strain of the water. It didn't look like it would last till morning, which—I noticed, glancing at the lightening sky in the east—was almost here.

"We have to hurry. I have to be at the door by sunrise."

Mac and Angus were waiting for us at the edge of the tartan ward. "Lorelei has agreed to go with you," I told them. "Lura and I are going to walk to the door ourselves."

"You shouldn't be alone in the woods right now. We've seen strange creatures about."

"We can take care of ourselves," Lura said, spitting on the ground.

Angus looked reluctant, but he finally agreed. The other Stewarts had formed a circle around Lorelei. Though a series of hand motions they wove a tartan shawl that they cast over her shoulders. Lorelei adjusted it as she might a mink stole and linked her arm through Angus's. "Let's go, boys," she said, tossing her hair back over her shoulder. She left without a backward glance for her daughter.

"I know," Lura said as the procession disappeared into the woods. "She's shallow and flighty, but she's my mother. I still remember her singing to me when I was small."

"I think she's doing the best that she can," I said. As we took our own path into the woods, I hoped the Stewarts could handle her.

Lura and I followed the Undine into the woods. At first neither of us talked, the rain and the rushing water making it difficult to hear anything we would have said anyway. Then the rain slackened to a drizzle. We walked in slushy silence a while longer, the sound of our boots sucking mud the only noise in the forest.

"Birds are quiet this morning," Lura commented. "They know something's wrong."

A little while later she picked berries from a bush, popped

one in her mouth and handed me one. "Bilberry. Good for night vision."

I put it in my mouth with some trepidation, but it was delicious—and familiar. I recalled the vision I'd shared with Raspberry of the taste of berries and wondered if Lura had fed them to her sister undines. A bit farther on she plucked a red flower from the ground, handed me the flower, and popped the leaves in her mouth. "Red clover leaves are good for my rheumatism, which'll be acting up after all this rain." She continued plucking plants from the trees and ground and telling me what they were and what they were good for.

"Where did you learn so much about plants?" I asked.

"My father spent a lot of time in these woods . . . His mother was a witch. Here, you'd better take this." She handed me a white-crowned flower and stuck one behind her ear. "Yarrow," she explained. "Provides magical protection."

Now that it was lighter I could see into the woods on either side of us. Creatures lurked within the white mist rising from the wet ground: cloven-footed satyrs, slim boys with antlers branching from their heads, small furry creatures with wide flat tails and long sharp teeth . . .

"Are those . . . ?"

"Zombie beavers," Lura said. "They're coming up with the floodwater. We'd better hurry. They'd like nothing better than to eat these eggs—and us."

We increased our pace but a hundred-year-old woman can go only so fast, even if she is part undine and part witch. The fat, bristly beavers scurried along the ground with surprising speed, gnashing their teeth and chattering back and forth to one another. Lura was chattering to herself as well. I was afraid she'd come unhinged, and who could blame her? The chattering noise itself was enough to drive one mad, let alone the sight of those sharp teeth and long claws. I was already terrified when a huge pine tree crashed to the ground inches in front of us.

"Go over it!" Lura screamed, grabbing my arm and scrambling over the huge tree. "They want us to run into the woods."

Or they wanted us to get tangled in the pine branches. The sleeve of my rain jacket snagged on a branch. I turned to free it and found myself nose to nose with one of the sharp-toothed predators. It snapped at me, its fangs missing my face by a centimeter as I pulled backward, peeling myself out of my jacket and landing on the ground. I scrambled to my feet and found myself next to Lura, trapped in a small square, hemmed in by downed trees. Teeth-gnashing beavers surrounded us.

Lura knelt and picked up two thick branches that had fallen off the trees and handed me one. She muttered a string of indecipherable words and the ends of both sticks burst into flames. She thrust the burning stick into the beavers' faces. They fell back, chittering. I swept my stick in a wide arc, singeing the whiskers off two of them. Lura muttered another series of strange words and a forked tongue of lightning split the sky and hit one of the beavers. When they saw their fallen comrade, the rest of the beavers scampered into the woods. Lura muttered a few more words and a sudden downpour extinguished our pine torches. "That should be the end of them for a while. They hate fire."

I helped Lura climb over a tree. She seemed suddenly frail and worn out, as if using magic had drained her. I offered to carry the bag of eggs, but she refused. "They're my sisters," she said.

We walked the rest of the way in silence. When I first met Lura, I'd thought she was a sad, pathetic recluse, but seeing her in these woods where she'd spent her entire life, I realized that she'd had a full life. She knew every inch of these woods and the creatures in it, whether they belonged to this world or Faerie. She'd watched over her sisters as they grew, protecting them against predators and bringing them treats to eat. She might have learned her first magic from her father, but she'd honed her craft in these woods. Looking at Lura and the way she regarded each tree and plant and creature, I saw that she loved the forest.

"Here," Lura said when we reached a fern-circled clearing. "This is the source of the Undine." I followed her through the ferns to a large granite boulder and knelt beside her. It was the spring that Soheila, Liz, and Diana had led me to almost a week ago.

Lura sat back on her heels and looked around the glade. "This is where I first met Quincy," she said, her eyes filling with tears.

She parted the ferns growing around the boulder and disclosed a heart carved into the rock with intertwined initials—Q and L—in the same design as the one carved into the bench at Lura's house. "We met here every day that summer. It's where he asked me to marry him."

"It's a beautiful spot," I said, admiring once again the spill of water from basin to basin, the wild irises fringing each pool, and the yellow water lilies floating on their surfaces. Weeping willow branches fell in a curtain over one of the pools. It looked like the spot in Faerie where I'd made love to Liam. My own eyes filled with tears at the memory and my heart with an unbearable sense of loss. Liam was really and truly gone. I was glad he hadn't come back as Duncan, but the fact remained he hadn't come back at all. It was time to let Liam go once and for all.

As I splashed cold water on my face to wash away the tears, I felt one more coil of the wards dissolve and the beat of my heart, slow and steady. I repeated the words of the spell that bound me to the door. *"Quam cor mea aperit, tam ianua aperit."* I could feel my heart beating up against the last cold link of the wards. They were almost all gone. I reached into the water again and met a pair of dark brown eyes. I froze, looking into a man's face. I sat back on my heels and looked over at Lura. She was also washing her face in the water. With each splash, her skin looked smoother and firmer. She trickled a handful of water over her head and her gray hair turned to gold.

I looked back at the face in the water. Quincy Morris was trapped below the surface studying me. But I wasn't who he was looking for. I reached into my pocket and found the stone I'd stuck in there earlier. The fairy stone, as my father had called it when he gave it to me. It was white with a hole in the middle. I slipped it over my ring finger and, holding my hand above the water, said, simply, *"Open."*

Nothing happened. The power inside me writhed, trying to break free, but it still was held in place by the last of the wards. Then I recalled the Aelvestone in my pocket. I took it out and held it over the water. Concentric circles appeared on the surface.

I dropped the stone in the water. The circles spun in a spiral, tunneling deep into the pool, opening up a funnel. Then a head broke the surface and a man rose up from the water. Hearing the disturbance of water, Lura looked up . . . and gasped.

"Quincy?" she said, all the years since she'd seen her lover falling away from her face like water rolling off a stone.

The dark-haired man—the same one I'd seen on the shores of Faerie—walked toward her, his face radiant. "Lura!" he cried, falling to his knees beside her and gathering her into his arms. "I came here on the morning of our wedding day to pick flowers for you and I fell into the pool. I woke up in a

strange place. I've been trying ever since to get back to you."
He held her at arms' length and looked into her face. "I was
afraid it would have been too long. I couldn't tell how much
time had passed, but it must not have been any time at all.
You look just the same."

Lura caught her breath and covered her mouth with her
hand, then she looked at me, eyes wide. The enchantment of
the spring water would end soon. I guessed that it wasn't van-
ity that made Lura fear the transformation, but the pain it
would cause Quincy to know how long he'd really been away.

"You can both go back to Faerie," I said. "The passage is
still open." I pointed to the still-swirling water.

Lura and Quincy looked at each other. "I probably
wouldn't know how to live in this world anymore," he said.
"Would you mind?"

"No," Lura said, "I wouldn't mind at all. There's nothing
to keep me here, only . . ." She touched the bag beside her and
looked at me.

"I'll put them in the water," I told her, "and watch after
them." I recalled that they wouldn't hatch for one hundred
years. "As long as I can, and then I'll find someone else to
watch them."

Lura gave me a beatific smile of gratitude. She had been
beautiful. She *was* beautiful. She stood and held her hand out
to Quincy. He took her hand and stood beside her. They
looked as they might have on their wedding day. There were
even flowers in Lura's hair. The yarrow she'd stuck behind
her ear had grown into a wreath. And he was wearing a tartan
mantle of the same plaid as the shirt he'd worn eighty years
ago—the same plaid that Lura had been wearing for eighty
years in his memory.

They each said "I love you," then stepped, hand in hand,
into the spiral circle and vanished into the water.

THIRTY

I placed the undine eggs into the pool below the spring, along with the Aelvestone that would nourish them as they grew in the shade of the willow beside a stand of wild irises. I didn't know what would happen to them in a hundred years if the door was closed, but I couldn't worry about that now. Every beat of my heart told me that I wasn't going to let the door close.

I walked toward the door. The sun was rising, the sky pink at the tips of the treetops, the sky above a deep lilac. It was almost dawn. The Grove would be working their spells, but I was confident now that I could stop them. I'd just sent two people to Faerie through a ring of water. As I repeated the words of the heart-binding spell, I felt my power thrumming through my body, from the soles of my feet to the crown of my head, cleansing me of the wards. Only one link remained—a rusty broken link snagged in my chest—a nagging ache that was the last lingering grief over losing Liam forever.

I followed the scent of honeysuckle to the dense overgrown thicket. From there, I followed the murmur of voices to a wide circular glade where I found a gathering of townspeople, college faculty, Grove members, and a motley assortment of other creatures. Standing on the edge of the thicket, I noticed that the glade seemed to have widened since I'd last been here. I listened to the creak of intertwined branches above me and had the uneasy feeling that the honeysuckle thicket had widened the glade to accommodate this morning's gathering—and that the thicket could just as easily tighten the noose again and squeeze us all to death in its grip. Nor was I the only one who seemed to feel that way. The nine members of the Grove stood on the far side of the glade, nervously looking up to the sky as if that might be their only exit. The crowd of townspeople and college faculty appeared, oddly, less anxious. They stood in small groups, talking softly among themselves, saying last good-byes. They were sad and resigned, or angry and indignant, but unafraid. I felt a stirring of pride in their bravery—and a renewed determination to make those farewells unnecessary. We would unmask the Nephilim and then I would open the door and keep it open using the heart-binding spell. But where were Frank and Bill? I looked around for them but didn't see either man. I caught Liz's eye and she hurried toward me. I stepped into the glade to greet her—hearing the branches and vines snick closed behind me.

"Callie, there you are! We'd begun to wonder if you were coming." A fleeting look of hope passed over her strained features.

"I had to see Lorelei," I said loudly and then, beneath my breath, added, "I have a spell to keep the door open and Frank has a plan to stop the Grove. He's with my friend Bill. Are they here yet?"

Liz shook her head. She looked around the glade, wringing her hands. "I can't believe it's come to this. Perhaps if I had been stricter in whom I let in . . . but each case was so compelling and I truly believed that diversity made us stronger.

Now look at us! What will the college and town do without all these good people?"

I looked around the glade at those we would lose. "We would be weak," I said, "a shadow of what we are. That's what the Grove and the creatures they've joined are counting on, but I'm not going to let it happen." I squeezed Liz's hand and leaned closer to tell her what Frank had told me about the Nephilim, but then there was a loud rustling in the trees above us. Even my grandmother and all the members of the Grove looked up nervously. All except the two blond twins who were striding through the glade, parting the crowd with the same preternatural force I'd witnessed before in Beckwith Hall, coming straight toward me. *Angelic-looking*, Frank had called the members of the Seraphim Club. These creatures had the features of angels, but there was a cold emanating from them that no one would ever call angelic.

Liz stumbled backward, pushed aside by a disturbance in the air that arrived with the blond twins. I felt it now, too—pulsing gusts that made the hair on the back of my neck stand on end. Then the blond twins turned to flank me and the disturbance was around us. There was a strange vacuum, as if the air had been sucked out of the glade. They each tried to grab one of my arms, but I shook them off and walked toward the rest of the Grove members, who moved aside to reveal an arched doorway in the thicket. The Grove members had been guarding the door—but why? It wasn't as if anyone here was anxious to get through the door to Faerie. Could they be worried about what might come *out* of the door?

"You're late," my grandmother said by way of greeting.

"I had some things to take care of," I replied, refusing to sound apologetic. "I see the Stewarts have brought Lorelei," I added, noticing now the plaid-clad group. The Stewart men stood around her protectively, fierce looks on their broad faces, more like an honor guard at her service than jailors now. She had managed to work her charms on them on the journey through the woods, but at least she hadn't made a break for it.

"I thought we'd start with her," Adelaide said. "What are you waiting for? You *can* open it, can't you?"

"Of course I can . . ." I began, but then hesitated. If the Grove was working their spells to close the door why did they need me to *open* it? "Can't you open the door?" I asked.

A look of annoyance crossed over Adelaide's face. "That's not the kind of magic we do, but if you like we'll destroy the door before you open it. Your friends will be trapped in this world forever without Aelvesgold—"

"That's not true," I said. She looked so startled to be interrupted that she didn't bother to deny it. I continued in a low voice only she could hear. "Your new friends at the Seraphim Club have all the Aelvesgold you'll ever need. That's why you want to close the door, so you'll have the only source of Aelvesgold in this world. Witches will have to come to you if they want to stay young, and the fey that remain in this world will become your slaves."

Her lips curled into a faint smile. "And why not? It's better than witches being the slaves of the fey, as they have been for thousands of years. Join us and you'll see how powerful you'll become with an endless supply of Aelvesgold to feed your magic."

"I don't need . . ." I began, but I suddenly thought of the Aelvestone I'd dropped into the spring. The power I'd absorbed from it was still thrumming through my body, but how long would it last if I couldn't keep the door open? Already I could feel a longing for more of the stuff. Of course I knew where the new Aelvestone lay, but Lorelei's eggs needed that one to grow. I'd never be desperate enough to take it from them, but would others find it and steal it?

Adelaide's smile widened. "Go ahead. Open the door and let the *good neighbors* of Fairwick go back where they belong. Once free of their influence, you'll see you've joined the right side. You owe them nothing. Even your incubus boyfriend has abandoned you."

The taunt nearly undid me, but, conversely, it steeled my resolve. Liam might not be here now, but he'd saved my life—and so had my friends in Fairwick. Frank was on his way now to destroy the Nephilim. I needed to stall for time.

"I'll open the door," I said, "but I won't let you close it." I drew the fairy stone from my pocket and saw Adelaide's eyes widen.

"I saw that in your father's hands once. I wondered what had become of it."

"He gave it to me, of course." I slipped the stone on my finger and turned to face the arched doorway. There was nothing beyond the arch but more thicket now, but I'd seen it opened onto a seaside cliff. With that image in mind, I passed my hand across the doorway.

Nothing happened.

My heart stuttered in my chest. Was the grief I felt over Liam keeping my heart closed, and so the door as well? Was *that* the caution I'd ignored in Wheelock? *Don't use this spell if you've recently had your heart broken.*

I felt Adelaide tense. All the eyes of those in the glade were upon me. Were they afraid I'd fail—or hoping I would?

I closed my eyes and pictured the time I was in Faerie with Liam beneath the willow tree. I felt the warmth that had spread between us, the way his face had been haloed by radiant light, his eyes full of love. If only we'd had more time together, I thought, if only he'd been able to tell me who he was when he became corporeal in this world, or if he hadn't changed when he took a new form . . .

I heard a gasp from the crowd behind me. I opened my eyes and found myself facing not the cliff and ocean but a green field that sloped down to the grassy bank beneath the willow tree: the place where Liam and I had made love.

"Good idea. Show them the prettier side of the place," Adelaide whispered. "They'll see the ugly side soon enough."

I wondered whether there really was an ugly side to Faerie or if Adelaide was just bound and determined to think so. I was glad, though, that I'd summoned this beautiful place. When I turned to the crowd behind me I saw the golden light reflected on their faces.

"I promise you that I will not let the Grove close the door. It will stand open on the solstices as it always has. If you wish to go now to visit Faerie, go ahead. I promise that you will be able to return as long as you pledge to do no harm in this world."

A murmur of voices rose from the crowd and I heard someone say, "We should go—at least we won't be trapped in this world."

Lorelei stepped forward of her own volition, looking calm and at peace. One Stewart walked on either side of her, each carrying a set of bagpipes. As they approached the door, they began to play.

The plaintive notes captured exactly the mood of the gathering. The two pipers separated and went to stand on either side of the door. Lorelei paused beside me.

I nodded at her and she understood that her children were safe.

The ghost of a smile lit her face, then she adjusted the plaid mantle around her shoulders and daintily stepped through the door. I watched her walk down the grassy hill toward the willow tree where Lura and Quincy stood waiting for her with a group of undines. Among them I could make out one undine with red-gold hair bouncing up and down on her toes and waving to me. Raspberry. I was glad to see her looking so happy.

When I turned back to the glade I saw Fiona Eldritch in a long green dress, her ash-white hair falling loose around her shoulders. As she stepped forward, bells chimed. I had never been fond of the Fairy Queen, but the sight of her preparing to leave this world forever squeezed something tight in my chest. The Stewarts piped a mournful dirge as she approached the door.

"This isn't the first time we have had to leave this world," said Fiona. "Always when humankind have thought they have no need of us they have soon enough seen the error of their ways and longed for us to come back. As long as one human longs for our return the door will not stay closed forever." She turned to me. "And I believe that this doorkeeper will make that happen."

Gathering her skirts and in a whirl of green and the chiming of bells, she stepped through the door. On the other side a man appeared, mounted on a white horse. His hair was the color of spun gold, the same gold that glittered on his horse's bridle and reins. He held in his hands the reins of another horse, white too, but with silver saddle, reins and bridle. Fiona's back tensed as she saw him, but then she bowed low, touching her forehead to the ground, her green skirts spreading in a pool around her. It was startling—and a little frightening—to see Fiona bow to anyone, but when she rose at his bidding I caught a glimpse of her face, radiant in the golden light of Faerie, and saw that she looked more triumphant than cowed. As she mounted his white horse at his bidding, I heard someone behind me say, "She's back in her domain."

I turned and found Casper Van der Aart and his boyfriend,

Oliver, standing beside me. "Do they fight often?" Oliver asked. "Because no one likes a bickering couple."

"We've probably got a few hundred years of happy reconciliation balls," Caspar said, and then, turning to me, he explained that Oliver wanted to come with him. "Although I keep telling him he doesn't have to."

"And I keep telling him I'm not doing it because I *have* to, I'm doing it because I *want* to. Besides, I'm dying to see this place. And no one is going to stop me." He glared at the blond twins who had taken up places beside the two pipers. Their lips curled in identical smirks but they made no move to stop Oliver from stepping through the door with Casper. As soon as they stepped through I saw a group of stocky white-haired men and women waving from the bank and Casper lifting a hand in greeting.

The denizens of Faerie were coming forward to greet their long-lost friends and relatives. As the Brownes passed through, they were greeted by a flock of diminutive creatures clad in leather pelts and peaked caps. Dory, the last of her family to reach the door, arrived hand in hand with Brock.

"We only just got you back," I said to Brock. "I promise I'll keep the door open so you can both come back."

"I know you'll do your best, Callie, but don't worry. If we have to stay, we'll be all right—and so will you. I hear you've found a good handyman."

I blushed, wondering what else he had heard about my new handyman, then I hugged Brock and Dory, trying not to cry. They stepped through the door still holding hands. Another group had gathered on the bank—tall blond men and women, a one-eyed man with a spear, a giant carrying a hammer, and a cavalry of women on horseback with winged helmets on their heads. As Brock and Dory walked toward them, the Valkyries saluted them. I turned away, my eyes overflowing with tears, and saw Diana Hart standing at the door, surrounded by a herd of deer, the golden-eyed stag in the lead. Liz stood beside her, holding her hand. Although it was summer, Liz wore her fur coat around her shoulders. Not just any fur coat—it was her familiar, Ursuline. Of course Liz wouldn't leave without her.

"Don't worry," I told Liz. "I won't let them close the door forever. I have a spell to stop them."

"I'm sure you'll do your best," Liz said, patting my arm. "But just in case I've asked Joan Ryan to step in as interim dean—and I'm hoping you'll help her. Goodness knows what will become of the college . . ." Her eyes filled with tears and I squeezed her hand.

"And take care of *this*." Diana draped something pink and scratchy around my neck. It was the scarf she had knitted to heal my spine, now a good six feet long and knitted in an intricate pattern that resembled the runes and spirals I'd seen on Skald's phone. "I knitted extra protection spells into it. It should keep you safe . . . and remind you of your friends."

I would need it, I thought. All my closest friends—human and fey—were leaving me. The one remaining chink of my wards grew heavier as I watched, with blurred vision now, the procession pass by me. I began to wonder if I really would be able to keep the Grove from closing the door. I had bound the door to my heart, but how reliable was that? And where was Frank? If he didn't come with a means of destroying the Nephilim, would I be able to stand against them?

The last person to approach the door was Soheila, accompanied by three women, all with Soheila's dark hair and flawless olive skin. Her sisters, I surmised, come to depart this world with her. Her sisters wore expensive designer clothes, as if they were going out to lunch instead of to Faerie, but Soheila was wearing a ceremonial caftan embroidered with a pattern of feathers. Her long dark hair was loose around her shoulders and seemed to move in a breeze of her own making. She smiled and I felt a warm, spicy breeze against my face that dried my tears and filled me with a sense of peace.

"Be well, Cailleach McFay," she said, letting her sisters go on ahead of her. "Don't forget us."

I was going to tell her that I could never forget her or any of the remarkable creatures I'd met this year, but a loud shout stopped me.

"Wait!"

Soheila and I turned to see three men enter the glade—Duncan Laird, flanked by Frank Delmarco and Bill Carey. Frank and Bill each had a hold of one of Duncan's arms.

As the three men approached, Adelaide stepped between them and the door.

"I've had enough of these histrionics, Dr. Delmarco. If you want to go to hell with your succubus girlfriend, go ahead. But do it now. The door will be closed soon."

"You're counting on this creature to close it, aren't you?"

"I don't know what you're talking about," she said, her eyes passing over Duncan as if he wasn't there and focusing instead on Bill. She frowned, looking puzzled. "What *are* you?" she asked.

"The question is what is *this* creature?" Frank said, pushing Duncan forward. Adelaide recoiled, as if afraid to come into contact with Duncan. There wasn't much Adelaide was afraid of.

Frank dug his hand into his pocket and pulled out a handful of powder that he threw in Duncan's face. I smelled clary sage and bluebells, the same herbs I'd used in the unmasking spell, and another herb I couldn't identify. Frank uttered a few words in what sounded like Gaelic. Duncan growled and wrenched his arms free of Frank and Bill. Both men fell back, thrown by a force I felt from several feet away. A great whirling maelstrom was pouring out of Duncan's arms as he stretched them out to either side. A blazing gold light burst from him, blinding me. I closed my eyes against it. When I forced them open again, Duncan stood before me, but it was no longer Duncan. Giant wings had sprung from his back and were beating the air into a froth. His skin beneath the tattered scraps of his torn shirt was golden, his eyes colorless ciphers. His hands had grown long, sharp claws. He raised one of the claws and I stepped back. He stepped with me and laid one claw beneath my jawbone.

"Is this what you wanted to see, Cailleach?" His voice had turned into something strangely musical, like harp strings plucked by steel claws.

"Stay away from her," Frank and Bill shouted at the same time. They moved to stand on either side of Duncan and me. Out of the corner of my eye, I saw the blond twins—also now transformed into winged monsters—moving toward us, but the Stewarts stepped in front of them and raised their shields.

"Ye wee bastards!" growled Angus Stewart in a surprising reversion to a Scottish burr. "How dare ye show your faces in my town?"

"These are the creatures who are behind the Grove's attempt to close the door," Frank said in a loud voice so that those remaining in the glade could hear. "They are the ones who attacked the fishermen in the woods and made it look as if it was the work of an undine. Look at the scars on this one's back." Frank pointed to the marks that Duncan claimed had come from the bat-winged imp. "Those were made by Nephilim claws. They're liars and fiends who are able to get inside your dreams . . ." Frank looked at me, and I recalled how Duncan had claimed it had been Lorelei who had tried to drown me in my dream. It had been Duncan all along.

". . . and would enslave you all." Frank began to recite a string of Gaelic words. Duncan flinched with pain. The spell was working, but then he recovered, flexed one wing and knocked Frank backward as lightly as if he were swatting a fly.

Duncan turned to me, smiling. "Yes, we are Nephilim, the sons of angels . . ."

"The sons of bastard elves," Frank muttered from where he lay on the ground.

"No," Adelaide said, stepping forward. For a moment I thought she was going to defend me and my heart warmed. I realized that I'd never entirely given up on the idea of my grandmother loving me. But then she crushed that hope. "That's a false story. The Nephilim are the sons of angels, not elves. They're the only creatures who don't need to go back to Faerie for Aelvesgold. They create it themselves. Look." Adelaide stepped closer to Duncan, bowing her head reverentially, the first time I'd ever seen her do such a thing. She whispered something in a language I didn't know. His upper lip twitched into a sneer that I could see, but Adelaide, on his other side, could not. Then he bowed his head and plucked one of his own feathers out of his wing and handed it to Adelaide. She brushed the feather against her face and the lines of age fell away, her hair turned from silver to gold, and her skin glowed with youth . . . and Aelvesgold. "Who but an angel could do that?" Adelaide said, practically purring with pleasure. "This is why the fey were jealous of them."

"The fey recognized how dangerous they were," Soheila said. "They were mating with humans, creating a race of heartless monsters. They would have destroyed the human race."

"Which would have been very inconvenient for those of you who feed on humans," Duncan snarled. "That is why the fey imprisoned us. But now we are free, and once the door closes there will be no one to stop us."

"I won't let you close it," I said, and then repeated the words of the heart-binding spell.

Duncan's lips curved into a slow, sensual smile. He ran the tip of his claw down my throat and between my breasts. I took another step back from him, still repeating the words of the spell, appalled that I'd ever let this creature touch me. Out of the corner of my eye, I saw Bill step toward us.

"Are you sure, Cailleach? I'd rather keep you alive. I've enjoyed our time together, despite your reserve. I'm sure we could break through that in time."

A growl came from Bill that wasn't entirely human.

"I'd rather die," I snarled, and then repeated the spell, louder now. *"QUAM COR MEA APERIT, TAM IANUA APERIT!"*

"Ah," Duncan said, "A heart-binding spell. How clever of you. But surely you read the caution in Wheelock? The best way to disarm a heart-binding spell . . ." He lifted his hand, one claw poised in the air as if he were making a point. ". . . is to stop the heart of the doorkeeper."

I felt the disturbance of air as his claw descended in a violent swoop toward my throat. I raised my hand to ward off the blow and his claw sliced through my flesh. His hand raised again and I saw the flash of gold-tipped claws coming toward me, but then something moved between us. It was Bill, riding a stream of moonlight that moved fast as quicksilver. He pushed me aside and took the blow meant for me. He fell to his knees, his hand to his neck. I dropped down beside him, my hand meeting his over the gaping wound in his throat.

"Bill!"

Hot blood poured over our joined hands. He looked down at it, surprise widening his eyes. "Callie, look! I'm human.

That must mean you . . ." He slumped in my arms and fell across the threshold of the door, his blood spilling on the wet ground with the last beats of his now human heart.

"Bill!" I cried, cradling his face in my hands. For a moment I saw Liam's face superimposed over Bill's, then the face of the incubus I'd seen in Faerie, and then just plain Bill. The man who had fixed my roof, removed a splinter from my hand telling me he was sorry he'd hurt me, and who had made love to me the last two nights. The man I finally understood I loved—a moment too late.

I looked up at the winged creature above us and something broke inside me. The last ward shattered in a million pieces. Maybe it was finally understanding that I loved Bill—or maybe it was the clarity of hating Duncan—that burned it away. I felt the last coil unwind around my heart and my full power surge in its wake. I stood and held up my arms. A great wind roared through the glade, knocking all the humans in the glade to the ground. Even Duncan stumbled backward a few feet, but he held his ground and started to laugh.

"Ah, so you've discovered your power, little witch. It won't be long until you join us. I'm glad I won't have to kill you after all. It looks like a drop of your blood mingled with the blood of one who loved you is all the blood sacrifice needed to close the door."

I turned and saw Bill's body dissolving into light. When he was gone, the door filled with a red-gold glow and then exploded into a fireball. The force of the explosion rocked the earth and knocked me off my feet. I felt myself hurtling backward through space—and then nothing at all.

THIRTY-ONE

When I came to, Mac Stewart and Frank were kneeling beside me.

"Thank goodness, she's alive," Mac cried.

"Of course she's alive," said Frank. "It takes more than a firebomb to take this girl out. Right, McFay? And you didn't really need those eyebrows."

My hands flew to my face. My skin felt hot to the touch and suspiciously smooth above my eyes. I sat up and looked around the grove. The ground was scorched black, the honeysuckle trees gray skeletons against a smoky sky. A wraithlike creature in a long tattered dress appeared out of the smoke and hurried toward us. I thought it was the angel of death until she got closer and I saw it was Soheila, her face covered with soot. She held a dripping piece of cloth in her hands. "From the Undine spring," she said, pressing the cold wet cloth to my face. "It will heal you."

"What happened to everyone?" I asked. I shuddered, recalling the claws that had ripped through Bill's throat. I didn't ask where Bill was. I had seen him vanish before the door closed. I would never see him again.

"The Stewarts helped anyone who was injured to the hospital," Frank told me. "The two pipers who were by the door were badly hurt. The Grove has beat a tactical retreat, along with the Nephilim . . ." Frank hung his head. "I'm sorry, Callie. I thought the spell would be enough to destroy them."

"You couldn't have known how powerful they've become," Soheila said. "They said they'd be back in the morning to discuss the 'new administration.' I think they plan to take over the college."

"We'll fight them," I said, pushing the wet cloth away and struggling to my feet. Frank and Soheila each grabbed an arm as I started to sway.

"I'm afraid we're not strong enough. All our people have been sent away." Soheila looked longingly toward the charred remains of the doorway.

"Nonsense," Frank said. "Did you see McFay knock that Nephilim bastard back on his ass?"

"I think I budged him a couple of inches," I said. "I finally got rid of the wards on my power. If you two will work with me, maybe I can learn to use that power."

"What do you mean two?" Mac said, hurt in his voice. "I can help. And my family, too. The Nephilim are the ancient enemy of the Stewarts. We were able to hold back two of them and it was my nan who gave Mr. Delmarco the spell, wasn't it, Mr. Delmarco?"

"Yes, Mac, it was. Your grandmother once told me your family had encountered the Nephilim before. We'll welcome the Stewarts' help. We'll have to rally everyone who's left—the witches, the vampires . . ."

"There were some creatures who went underground," Soheila said. "Who chose to exist without Aelvesgold rather than leave this world." She looked toward the door as if realizing for the first time that she was in the same predicament.

Without Aelvesgold, she would begin to fade—unless she went to the Nephilim to get it. I didn't think Soheila would, but I wondered how many of the fey left behind would be tempted to do just that in the coming years. Frank glanced from Soheila to me, perhaps thinking the same thing.

"Do you think you'll be able to open the door?" he asked.

I stepped toward the smoking ruin where the door had been and knelt down, placing my hands on the charred ground where Bill's blood, mingled with mine, had been spilled. I tried to feel a remnant of his spirit, but felt nothing. I tried to feel some connection to that other world, but even the memory of Faerie seemed to be draining away from my mind as swiftly as Bill's blood had soaked into the ground. I had bound my heart to the door and when I finally realized that I loved Bill and watched him die for me, my heart had shattered—and so had the door.

"No," I said. "There's no door here anymore. It's gone."

We walked back through the woods, making our way slowly over the charred, smoking ruins of the honeysuckle thicket. Frank and Soheila walked on either side of me, supporting me. The blast had scorched the whole forest. There wasn't a trace of Faerie left in the woods. I was weaker than I first realized, drained by that explosion of power inside me. Frank and Soheila discussed what they each knew about the Nephilim.

"We'll have to find out all we can about them to defeat them," Frank said, exchanging a look with Soheila that made me want to disappear and leave them alone. They had a lot to talk about. When we reached Honeysuckle House they both offered to come in with me, but I assured them I was all right and sent them away.

The first thing I noticed when I opened the front door was

the cup of tea Bill had made for me sitting on the foyer table. Holding it up to my nose, I smelled Earl Grey with honey, just the way Liam had always made it for me. How could I have not known Bill was the incubus?

I leaned against the door and cried until the foyer grew dark around me. Eventually Ralph came downstairs, curled up in my lap, and nudged my hand. When I looked down I saw that he was carrying a torn, crumpled piece of paper in his mouth. I uncrumpled the paper and saw that it was an illustration of a Nephilim torn out of one of my books.

"That's why you kept pushing books off the shelves. You were trying to figure out what Duncan was."

Ralph squeaked an assent.

"Well, you got it right, pal, only a little bit too late. Sorry," I added, seeing his bright eyes looking up at me beseechingly. "We were all too late. Bill is gone . . ."

Ralph squeaked and jumped out of my lap, ran a few feet, and then looked over his shoulder at me.

"Okay, Lassie," I said managing a weak smile, "Take me to Timmy."

I got up and followed Ralph. As we climbed the stairs we came to muddy footprints. Ralph paused at them and looked back at me. "Men," I said. "They never remember to wipe their feet."

Ralph squeaked and followed the footprints upstairs where a trail of them led to the front bedroom. To Liam's old study. I walked slowly down the hall, willing myself not to break into a run, my heart beating wildly, afraid of the hope that was whispering in my ear. *He's come back! Somehow he survived and came back!* I turned the knob with a shaking hand and opened the door . . .

Onto an empty room. I almost sank onto the floor again, but I watched as Ralph scurried across the room and up onto

the windowsill, where one of the gray river stones was bal-
anced on the ledge of the open window weighing down a
folded sheet of paper that fluttered in the breeze.

Bill had left me a note!

I crossed the room and lifted the stone, its cool weight like
a balm in my blistered palm.

Bill had left me a love note!

But when I opened the note I saw he'd left me something
much better. There was a single line on the page. It read:

There's another door.

Read on for an exciting preview of Juliet Dark's

next novel in this series

ONE

"*D*o *you* believe in fairy tales, Professor McFay?"

I turned to the young man who had asked the question, searching his bland and innocent face for traces of sarcasm or derision. I'd just finished going over the syllabus for my Introduction to Fairy Tales class and had asked the class to write a short essay on their favorite childhood fairy tale. When I asked if there were any questions, I'd gotten the usual: "How long does it have to be?" "Can I use the personal pronoun?" (Who, I always wondered, had ever told them not to?), and "Can I borrow a pen?" I wasn't expecting an inquiry on my personal beliefs on the existence of fairies. The young man, however, looked harmless enough. Like so many of the new freshman class he was tall, blond, and athletically fit in his snug Alpha Delta Chi T-shirt. He had the face of an angel—but that, I had learned recently, wasn't necessarily a good sign. I decided to do what all good academics do. Dither.

"That depends on what you mean by 'believe,' 'fairy,' and 'tales,' Mr. . . . ." I looked down at my roster to remind myself of the student's name. "Mr. Sinclair. I think that fairy tales are culturally important, that they provide an essential outlet for a child's imagination, and that by studying them we gain a critical understanding of Western literature. I believe in the value of fairy tales."

"But do you believe that the things that happen in fairy tales really happen?" he persisted. "That pumpkins turn into carriages and frogs turn into princes? Do you believe in fairies?"

He was definitely a plant. What eighteen-year-old would ask that question with a straight face. Of course, it would be easiest just to say that I didn't believe in fairies. But somehow I couldn't do that. I felt like I'd be killing Tinker Bell.

"I believe, Mr. Sinclair, that if I spend any more time on your question I'll be shortchanging the class of the thirty-five minutes allotted by the English department to complete the diagnostic essay," I said. "Why don't we put your question off to another day?"

Adam Sinclair smiled and shrugged, then picked up his pen and began writing, as did the twenty-three other young people in the class. I breathed a sigh of relief and picked up the extra copies of the syllabus I'd handed out. As I shuffled the papers together I noticed that my hands were shaking. Sinclair's question had disturbed me more than I'd realized. Maybe it had been a mistake to teach this class. I'd thought at first it was a tamer choice than my usual Sex Lives of Demon Lovers or Kick-Ass Vampire Slayers classes, but I was beginning to wonder if teaching a class on fairy tales at the *new* Fairwick College wasn't akin to running up a red flag.

I retreated behind the podium and made myself look busy. Usually I wrote along with my students to model the assignment, but when I picked up my pen and asked myself what my favorite fairy tale was I nearly laughed out loud. Then I started scribbling furiously.

There once was a girl who came to a town where fairies and witches lived together. She moved into an old house cov-

ered with honeysuckle vines. The house was inhabited by a prince who had been turned into a demon by the Fairy Queen, cursed to be a demon until someone loved him. The girl almost fell in love with him, but when she realized he was a demon, she sent him away. He came back a second time, and although she didn't recognize him (she was a very stupid girl), she fell in love with him at the exact same moment as he was killed by an evil monster.

A drop splatted on my paper smearing the ink. I wiped the tear away quickly and looked up, hoping no one had noticed it. Most of my students were hard at work, their heads bent over their blue books—all except Nicky Ballard, who was looking at me with concern. I smiled at Nicky and mouthed "allergies."

I looked back down at my paper and reread what I had written. What a lame fairy tale, I thought. The heroine fails twice . . . shouldn't she get a third chance? But there wasn't going to be a third chance. I crumpled the paper up and tossed it in the garbage can.

"Time's up," I said, then glanced at the clock and saw there were ten minutes left to the class. *Crap*. The last thing I felt like doing was leading a discussion, and if I asked if there were any questions Sinclair might start in again asking if I believed in fairies. "Would anyone like to read their essay aloud?" I asked without much hope of getting a volunteer. But then Nicky Ballard—bless her—raised her hand.

I called on her and she began to read.

"The story I loved when I was little was called Tam Lin. . . ." I almost stopped her. Although it had been my favorite fairy tale when I was little, it was the last story I wanted to hear. My parents had told it to me, and then after they had died, I had imagined a fairy-tale prince had come to tell me the story. Only it had turned out he wasn't really imaginary.

"I always loved Tam Lin," Nicky continued, "because the heroine, Jennet Carter, doesn't listen to what people tell her. They all tell her not to go to Carterhaugh because there are boggles and haunts there, but she goes because Carterhaugh belonged to her family once and she's determined to get it back."

Ah, I thought, no wonder Nicky liked this story. The Ballards had once been rich and powerful but had fallen on hard times. In fact, they had been cursed. Generations of Ballard women had squandered their beauty and intelligence on alcohol, drugs, and teenage pregnancies. Nicky would have gone down the same road, but I'd discovered last spring that it had been my family who had cursed hers. I was able to lift the curse, but Nicky still lived in a decaying mansion with her ailing grandmother and alcoholic mother. Maybe she dreamed of reclaiming her family's honor like Jennet Carter.

"So she goes to Carterhaugh and meets Tam Lin, a handsome young man, who tells her he was kidnapped by the Fairy Queen seven years ago and tonight, on Halloween, the fairies are going to pay their tithe to hell by sacrificing him. Then he tells her how she can save him."

At least Jennet got clear instructions, I thought enviously. But then Jennet doesn't waste time worrying about whether she really loves Tam Lin or not. Not like some people I knew. . . .

"She goes to the crossroads at midnight and waits for the fairy host. They ride by on horses decked out in gold and silver, with goblins and bogies leering and shrieking, but Jennet doesn't run. She stands fast until she sees Tam Lin, wearing only one glove . . ."

"Like Michael Jackson," someone sniggered. Nicky glared at the interruption but kept on going. *Good girl*, I thought, she'd grown up a lot during her summer abroad.

". . . and one hand bare, the sign he'd told Jennet to know him by. She pulled him down from his horse, and immediately he turned into a fierce lion, but Jennet held onto him because he'd told her that the Fairy Queen would make him change shape. Next he turned into a writhing snake . . ."

"Oooh . . ." a girl began, but Nicky and I both glared her into silence.

"But still she held fast to her Tam Lin. Next he because a burning brand, but Jennet didn't let go. When he was Tam Lin again, she wrapped him in her green mantle. The Fairy Queen was really pissed."

A few students laughed, but I didn't check them. They were with Nicky now. Even though it was time to go they weren't collecting their books or texting on their phones. The story had caught their attention.

" 'If I had known you would leave me for a human girl,' the Fairy Queen said, 'I would have plucked out your eyes and heart and replaced them with eyes and heart of wood.' But Jennet held onto Tam Lin, and there was nothing the Fairy Queen could do. She rode away to Fairy-Land, and Jennet and Tam Lin married and lived in Carterhaugh. I like this story because it's the girl who saves the boy and also . . ." Nicky paused, swallowed, and looked up at me. "Because it shows that sometimes you have to believe in people even though they look like monsters. Because people can change."

There was a murmur of assent from a couple of upperclassmen and one girl, Flonia Rugova, who had roomed with Nicky last year, reached over and squeezed Nicky's hand. I imagined she knew, as I did, that Nicky's mother, Jaycee Ballard, had joined AA and was trying to clean up her act. "Absolutely," Flonia said. "People can change."

"That was lovely, Nicky," I said. "I think Nicky has answered Adam's question for me. That's the kind of fairy tale I believe in, Mr. Sinclair. The kind that gives us the courage to persevere through hardship and fight for what we believe in. Think about Nicky's story while you're reading the Bettelheim chapter for next class."

With only ten minutes to make it to their next class—and a new Zero Tardiness Tolerance in place—most of the students took off in a panicked stampede. But Nicky lingered behind and fell into step beside me as I left Fraser Hall.

"I don't want you to be late for your next class, Nicky. You know the new administration is cracking down on lateness."

"I'm free next period," Nicky said. "What's up with all the new rules, anyway? The college is totally changed."

I sighed. "I know. It's the new administration. They have a rather different . . . um . . . pedagogical philosophy."

"No kidding! We've got curfews! And mandatory dorm meetings. I get, like, twenty emails a day from campus security . . . and those new security guards are creepy." Nicky lowered her voice as we passed one of the new guards, a short, broad-shouldered man in a green jumpsuit. He leered at Nicky in a distinctly unsavory way. "I don't want to be mean, but they look like *trolls*."

Now that Nicky mentioned it, they *did* look like trolls. I wondered . . . "Stay away from them," I told her. "If you have a problem, call me or Professor Delmarco or Professor Lilly."

"Thank God you guys are still here, but so many of my favorite teachers are gone. I was going to take Stones for Poets with Professor Van der Aart, but he's gone on a sabbatical. Now I have to take two required science classes *and* a class on Milton."

I let out an involuntary groan. I'd barely been able to get through *Paradise Lost* in grad school; requiring the entire college to read it seemed crazy. "I know the new requirements are onerous. Some of the faculty are trying to . . . er . . . *persuade* the administration to change their policies. We're meeting this evening to go over our . . . er . . . strategies."

"I'm sure you're doing everything you can, Professor McFay. I don't mean to complain. It's just that everything is so different—even the students. Like that Adam Sinclair and his frat brothers. I mean, one of the things I liked about Fairwick was that it didn't have a big Greek life like the state schools. But this new fraternity . . . well, look at this flyer I got in my mailbox this morning."

Nicky took out a piece of bright magenta paper and unfolded it. Beneath three large Greek letters—alpha, delta, chi—was a crude drawing of a muscular man in a toga. "Hey, ladies!" the speech bubble by his head announced. "It's never too early to try out your Halloween costumes. Whether you're going this year as a slutty vampire, a slutty cat, or just a total slut we invite you . . ."

"Ew," I said, taking the virulent page from her, "that's gross . . . and completely inappropriate. I'm on my way to the dean's office right now with a list of complaints. I'll add this invitation to them."

Nicky shrugged. "Don't get yourself in trouble over it. No one I know is going. It's just that those Alphas act like they own the campus. . . ."

Nicky's next words were drowned out by the pealing of bells. Loud obnoxious bells ringing the quarter hour. "And that's another thing," she yelled over the clanging. "Those bells! They wake us up at the crack of dawn!"

"It's on my list," I told Nicky, giving her a wan smile. We'd reached Main Hall. The gothic gray stone exterior had always given me a sense of calm and stability, but now that it housed the new dean, it felt like a brooding, unassailable castle out of *Dracula*.

"I feel better knowing you're doing something," Nicky said. "But I didn't just follow you to complain. I wanted to talk to you about my research paper."

"Let me guess, you want to do it on Tam Lin."

"Well, not exactly. You see the thing is I'm actually feeling a little . . . well, *disenchanted* with fairy tales these days."

"Oh," I said, unable to hide my disappointment. "You're not dropping the class, are you?"

"Oh no! You're my favorite teacher, Professor! It's just . . . well, when I was in Scotland this summer I came across this collection of fairy tales and ballads that were collected in the Border Country by a woman folklorist named Mary MacGregor White. There's a ballad in it that's a sort of variation on Tam Lin. I wrote about it in my essay, only I didn't read that part in class. Anyway, I thought it was interesting that the stories were collected by a woman folklorist, and I'd like to find out more about her . . . like what made her interested in folk tales and how she came to write about them. I thought it would be interesting to write about a real person instead of just writing about fairy tales."

"Hm . . . I've never heard of her . . . or about any female folklorists of that time period. It sounds like a fascinating topic, Nicky. Of course you can write about that. I look forward to seeing what you dig up."

"Thanks, Professor. And I hope you don't mind what I said about fairy tales. I know they're your thing."

"It's perfectly all right, Nicky," I told her as I turned to go into Main Hall. "There are days lately when I wish I had specialized in something a little more practical myself."

TWO

I paused for a moment outside the door to the dean's office to collect myself. My conversation with Nicky had unnerved me. It was one thing to watch my college be taken over by evil forces and another to see the effects of that takeover on the students I cared about. The students had no way of knowing why the college was so different. They didn't know that the Grove—a club for ultra-conservative witches to which my grandmother happened to belong—had conspired to close the door to Faerie with a mysterious all-male British club that turned out to be run by nephilim. I hadn't even known about nephilim a couple of months ago. My specialty was fairy tales, not Bible studies. Truthfully, I'd never had much interest in angels, fallen or not. They always seemed much blander than fairies, pixies, elves, and goblins.

But the nephilim weren't bland at all—and they weren't even fallen angels, as much as they liked to think they were. According to Soheila, they were elves who had been kicked out of Faerie because they couldn't keep their hands off human women. For hundreds of years they had nursed their resentment of the fey—and the human witches who aligned themselves with the fey—and conspired with the Grove to close the door to Faerie. Once the fairies were all gone—and a number of humans, including Dean Elizabeth Book who had gone to Faerie with her partner, Diana Hart—they had free reign to take over Fairwick. Duncan Laird, the leader of the nephilim, had taken over as dean. I wondered if Liz would have left if she had known what would happen to her beloved college. She would be furious to see the changes the nephilim had made.

"Are you going to come in, Professor McFay?" A voice came from behind the door. "Or stand out there in the hall all day?"

I'd forgotten what good ears the nephilim had . . .

I opened the door.

. . . or what big teeth.

Duncan Laird, DMA (Doctor of Magical Arts), Oxford, Wizard of the 9th Order, and nephilim, sat behind a large desk, grinning. Even from across the room those teeth looked too white and shiny, reminding me of the long, sharp fangs he'd revealed when he'd finally been unmasked and taken his true shape. I glanced at his hands, folded over a thick folder on top of the desk. They were smooth and manicured, giving no hint of the claws that he'd nearly slashed my throat with—nor was there any sign of the wings that he could extend at will. As I crossed the room, though, I could sense a disturbance in the air, a fluttering. . . . I studied the wall behind Duncan, but all I saw was an array of framed diplomas. Perhaps the sound was only my own heart pounding with fear.

"Have a seat, Professor McFay. I won't bite."

"You tried to rip my throat out," I reminded him as I sat on the edge of a leather chair in front of the desk.

Laird pursed his lips and made a tutting sound, as if recalling some small social faux pas. "Oh, Callie," he said, leaning forward, "if I had *tried* to rip your throat out you wouldn't be here right now. I only needed a drop of your blood mixed with the blood of your beloved incubus to close the door. I never intended to harm you."

"You killed Bill," I said.

"An incubus who had been preying on you!" he exclaimed, spreading his hands out in a gesture of appeasement. The motion had the fluid grace of wings opening, and once again I had the impression of invisible wings beating the air. Was that part of the nephilim's power? I wondered. Did they use their wings to move and effect the air around them? "Do you really believe you had a future together?"

"I loved him," I answered. "He had just become human."

Duncan shook his head. He looked down, noticed the folder on the desk—which I saw now was actually a thick envelope with many foreign stamps affixed to it——and turned to put it in the file cabinet behind his desk. "Ah, that was unfortunate timing then. I had no idea you felt that way about Handyman Bill. . . ."

"That was just the incarnation he took," I said defensively. Then, realizing I'd sounded snobbish, added, "Not that I wouldn't love a handyman if he was as kind and good-hearted as Bill Carey. He became what I needed most." I blinked back tears, determined not to show weakness in front of Duncan Laird. I'd worked out why my incubus lover who'd incarnated once as a hunky poetry teacher had chosen to come to me the second time as a taciturn handyman. He'd inadvertently knocked my own handyman, Brock, from the roof when he arrived from Faerie, so he'd taken the shape I needed most. It had also given him the opportunity to fix some things he'd broken during his incubus rages. In the two months since Bill had died, I'd had ample time to notice all the little things he'd fixed in the house and to appreciate a man who fixed things rather than broke them.

Duncan Laird canted his head to one side and studied me with sharp blue eyes. I felt a fizzle of electricity at his gaze, a sensation

I'd almost mistaken for attraction when I first met him, but now, although I could recognize in the abstract that he was handsome, I knew the sparks between us were warning signs. Still, when he purred, "Is that what you *really* need most, dear Callie?" I felt a flash of heat course through my body. The nephilim, I'd learned through intensive research these last two months, produced their own Aelvesgold—the magical elixir of Faerie—and could transmit it through the air as an aphrodisiac. Over the millennia they had used their powers to seduce human women—or worse. I suspected that some of our new freshman class might be the offspring of such unions. Which reminded me . . .

"What I *really* need right now," I said, slapping the magenta flyer on the desk, "is a campus where women aren't denigrated and exploited. This flyer is lewd and insulting to women. I can just imagine what will happen to any hapless girl who is fool enough to go to this thing. What are you going to do about it?" I demanded, glad to have a channel for the heat in my body.

Duncan Laird picked up the flyer and examined it, his face grave. If his lip had so much as twitched I would have accused him of sanctioning the fraternity's misogynistic language, but his face remained suitably grave. When he looked up at me his gaze was serious. A little crease had appeared between his eyebrows.

"You're absolutely right. This is unacceptable. I'll talk to the president of Alpha Delta Chi immediately and demand he issue an apology to the female student body."

"Okay . . ." I said tentatively, thrown off guard by his compliance. "And what about the party?"

"I'll send security to monitor it," he said. "I don't want anything going wrong there anymore than you do, Callie. Especially when it's so close to your house."

"That has nothing to do with it," I snapped, although of course it did. It had broken my heart to see frat boys move into the Hart Brake Inn, not just because it was across the street from my house but because it had profaned the memory of my friend Diana Hart. "Why not cancel the party as a consequence of this offensive flyer?"

"I think that would be an overreaction and initiate a chain of bad feeling throughout the campus. Better that the new class learn to play by the rules and assimilate into the campus culture."

"If anything does go wrong . . ."

"You have my assurance that nothing will." He learned forward again and smiled. I heard that rustling again and felt a sizzle in my veins. I summoned all my power to resist the pull of Duncan Laird's charisma. "I would like us to be friends, Callie. . . ."

I snorted.

". . . But if that's not possible, can we not be congenial colleagues? I welcome your input and suggestions and will be happy to work with you for the good of the college. Isn't that what we both want?"

The warm sizzle in my veins chilled as I realized what Laird was proposing. I could prevent harm to the students if I collaborated with the administration. And in truth, wasn't that why I had stayed at Fairwick? After the door to Faerie had closed with most of my friends trapped behind it, I had considered leaving. The academic job market wasn't in great shape, but I could have gone back to the city, kicked out my subletter, and taken adjunct jobs until I got something better. I could have turned my back on Fairwick and the world of fairies and witches and gone back to the life I'd left only a year ago. But then there was Bill's last note to me.

There's another door.

If there was another door to Faerie and there was any chance of freeing my friends—and any chance that Bill was still alive there—I had to stay here in Fairwick and look for it.

So why not go along with Duncan Laird's proposal and wield what influence I could on the new administration to keep my students safe?

Because I'd never be able to live with myself.

"We don't want the same things at all," I said. "I want you out of here and my college back."

Duncan smiled—or maybe he was just baring his teeth. "Fair enough, Professor McFay. I appreciate your honesty. Now, if you'd give me the diagnostic essays your class did this morning . . ."

"No," I replied.

"No?"

"No. I'll read them and respond to them."

"Didn't you get the memo specifying that all English faculty were to hand in their students' essays for review by the administration?"

"Yes, I got that memo and the ninety-six other memos your office has issued in the last week, but I have no intention of handing over my students' papers. If you persist in the request, I'll go to the MLA and complain. Fairwick College won't be as useful to you if you lose your accreditation."

Duncan's smile vanished. His jaw tightened. I thought I could hear teeth grinding and invisible wings beating. "You might be surprised at how the MLA would respond to your complaints. We have friends there. I think you'll find we have friends . . ." He smiled again, but without showing his teeth. "Everywhere." He splayed his hands out in the air again. "But I believe in picking my battles. Keep your papers. I'm sure I'll have ample opportunity to get to know each and every one of your students."

He held his hands higher. The gesture would have seemed conciliatory but for the shadow they threw on the wall. They looked like giant wings overshadowing everything.

JULIET DARK is the pseudonym of bestselling author Carol Goodman, whose novels include *The Lake of Dead Languages*, *The Seduction of Water*, and *Arcadia Falls*. Her novels have won the Hammett Prize and have been nominated for the Dublin/IMPAC Award and the Mary Higgins Clark Award. Her fiction has been translated into thirteen languages. She lives in New York's Hudson Valley with her family.